VOLCANO WATCH

VOLCANO WATCH

THE FORENSIC GEOLOGY SERIES
BOOK 3

TONI DWIGGINS

TD

All characters and events portrayed in this work are fictitious. Certain geographical features have been slightly altered.

Cover design: Wicked Good Book Covers

— To be notified of new releases, sign up for my mailing list:

https://eepurl.com/GtdZn

— Contact me at:

Website: tonidwiggins.com

Facebook: facebook.com/ToniDwigginsBooks

"Many visitors hike, ski, mountain bike, and fish in the area without realizing they are inside, on, or next to a volcano."

— United States Geological Survey

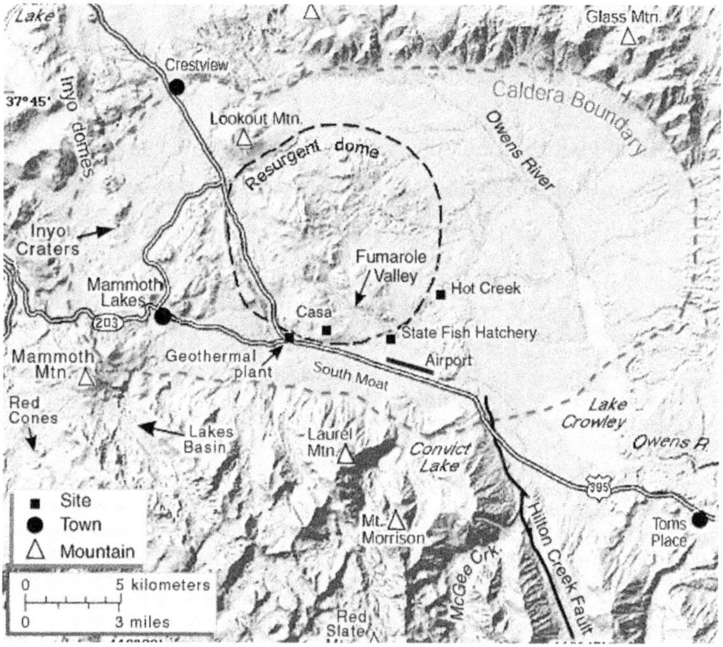

Long Valley Caldera and Environs

caldera boundary shown by dotted line

USGS

PROLOGUE

TOWN OF MAMMOTH LAKES
MONO COUNTY, CALIFORNIA
SIERRA NEVADA RANGE, the land of fire and ice

TWICE, the mayor of my hometown gave me advice.

The first time was when she joined my third-grade class on a snowshoeing trip to chop a Christmas tree. She was nobody's mom—just the town's busybody mayor who volunteered for everything. Her name was Georgette Simonies. *Call me Georgia* she'd boom to any kid who addressed her otherwise, and since she was barely five feet tall, kid-size, we could do that. Out in the wilderness that day, I got myself lost. Trees suddenly thick, shrouded. That snow-blanket silence. Georgia was the one who found me. *Next time wear a bell*, she boomed.

The second time Georgia Simonies advised me, I was eleven. My little brother Henry had recently died. He had hemophilia, wherein the blood refuses to clot. He'd gotten sicker that year, bleeding out again and again, and my parents stockpiled pressure bandages and I fed him pureed broccoli to replace the lost iron, but his luck ran out when he bumped his head and bled into his brain.

I had night terrors for weeks until my parents, cartoonists, did the only thing they really knew how to do. My mother drew me a cartoon-brother snugly dead in his box. My father wrote the caption: death by God.

My older brother added a comma: death, by God.

I knew better.

A week later Georgia dropped by our house and studied the cartoon and then took me aside. She asked, "You feeling guilty?"

I nodded.

"You couldn't watch him every minute."

"But I was in charge."

She put a gentle hand on my shoulder. "Nobody blames you."

"Nobody lets me say I'm sorry."

She picked up the cartoon and put it on the table in front of me. Gave me a pencil. "Say it that way."

It took me over a week, and an hour with a thesaurus, but I finally added my own caption: death by inattention.

When I turned thirty, it was halfway through Georgia's fifth mayoral term. She'd been in and out of office for twenty-five years, mostly in.

She's been missing almost five weeks.

I've been catching the talk around town. People grumble that she can't disappear on us now, when it's a question of the town's survival. A couple of jerks have made bets: accident, or foul play? A couple of wits say she'll be back, she wants a sixth term.

As for me, I'm paying relentless attention.

1

IT WAS AN ICY DAWN.

The four of us huddled, shivering, at the Red's Meadow trail head, nursing coffee, inhaling steam, hands stealing warmth from the mugs. Seemed like we'd continue nursing that brew until hell froze over, which appeared imminent. I drained my mug, slushed it out with snow, and gave the three men a look. They cleaned their mugs. I collected the mugs and stowed them in my pack, along with the thermos. Always the female who brings the coffee.

And then there was nothing for it but to snap boots into bindings and get going.

There's a body on the mountain. From the report made by the ice climber who'd found it, the body had been there awhile. Until proven otherwise, the police had to treat it as a suspicious death. This recovery mission had already been delayed three days because of bad weather, and another storm was forecast for tomorrow.

The corpse, according to the ice climber, was female.

Could be Georgia.

Nobody wanted to postpone.

The climb was too steep for snowmobiles and the weather too iffy for choppers. We had to ski it.

The four of us strung out on the trail, packing yesterday's snow. We were a silent group but I chalked that up to the weather, to the stress we've been under with a missing mayor and our hometown existence touch and go. No need for talk, though, because I knew this team down to the ground. Detective Eric Catlin took the lead, cutting trail the way he worked a crime scene, muscular and precise. Recovery team volunteer Stobie Winder followed, ski patrolman in winter and horse wrangler in summer, thickly muscled as one of his pack horses—and that's why he was hitched to the sled we'd use as a litter. I followed the sled: Cassie Oldfield, meeting although not beating the local athletic standards, gloomy for a time in adolescence and now only in her dreams, good with rocks like Stobie's good with horses, precise as Eric in her work, once-student and now associate forensic geologist to the persnickety man following her: Walter Shaws, mentor, father-figure, the backbone of her life.

Eric set a climbing pace but I set mine by the rasp of Walter's skis. I had to slow, and slow again, to pace his fitful stride. A gap opened between us and the others and within an hour Eric and Stobie had left Walter and me behind.

Georgia would have been slower, had she come this way.

It was a wicked climb. Back when the old sea floor lifted to become the Sierra Nevada range, it tilted sharply westward, so this eastern flank rises without mercy. We live on a plateau of eight thousand feet at the base of an eleven-thousand-foot peak, and we consider a pass of nine thou low. But this climb goes up to twelve. There are those of us who'd hike it or ski it just for the thrill of it, but Georgia tackled the outdoors only by necessity—to take a school group snowshoeing, to ski to the market when the roads weren't plowed. She fought off her extra pounds on a treadmill, not on a mountain. It took three million Pliocene years to raise this range and it would take three mill more to convince Georgia Simonies to climb up here for fun.

Which could argue that it wasn't Georgia up the mountain.

Walter and I turned up the next switchback, a pleat of a trail that would lift us another hundred or so feet.

I glanced up. Eric was positioned on the cliff edge above, watching our progress.

We topped the switchback and found Stobie with folded arms, poles dangling from his wrists.

Eric edged down from the cliff. "Listen up folks, I phoned for a weather update and that storm's moving in faster. We've got to make time. Stobie and I talked about it and we can handle this. Cassie, Walter, why don't you two head back down."

Walter stiff-armed his poles for support, recovering his breath, eyeing Eric.

When my own breathing had steadied, I said, "What the hell?"

"Hey Kiddo," Stobie chimed in, "getting snowed-in up there's no joke. Eric and I can boogie-woogie it a whole lot faster." He shook his rump, waggling the sled.

I regarded Stobie, who's called me *Kiddo* since we were kids, me being two years younger than Stobie and Eric, the two of them part of my older brother's group. Stobie's always quick with a smile, kidding around, more a big brother than my own flaky brother. Now, he smiled but without any warmth. Perhaps it was the cold. I turned to Eric. Eric's always slow to make a joke, although easily amused. He has inky blue eyes, the left one glass. There's a delicate network of scars beneath that eye and when he's amused the skin there crinkles like crystallized ice. The skin stayed taut.

No, I thought, nobody's kidding.

"I'll bag your evidence for you," Eric said, evenly. "Don't be territorial."

"But we are," I said. "And you've worked enough scenes with us to know that."

There was a thick silence, all of us looking past each other and the air heavy with retained snow.

And then Walter smiled. He has a beautiful smile, in a rough seamed aging face. Walter himself calls it a geologist's face: it looks igneous. "Eric," Walter said, "I will get there when I get there, which I can assure you will be no later than twenty minutes after you get there, during which time you can busy yourself with your own duties, and perhaps you, Stobie, can busy yourself photographing the scene, and as long as neither of you disturbs the geology before Cassie and I can put our eyes upon it, all will be well."

Eric exhaled a long breath. "Your call." He did a kick turn and took off up the trail.

Stobie pulled a rueful face, and fell in.

And then Walter and I were left stony-faced, looking at each other wondering what just happened here, why had half the team acted like the other half was downright unwelcome on this trip?

But the first half of the team was already leaving us behind and so we fell in as well. Walter set himself an ambitious pace. I followed, taking note of the ease of his stride. A couple of years ago Walter had suffered a series of tiny strokes; according to his doctor he was now fully recovered. Nevertheless, I kept on keeping watch—and keeping it to myself.

It took me some time to find my own pace. There's a rhythm to be had on skis, even uphill, a rhythm that takes over the body and relaxes the mind, and I aimed for that.

A couple hours later we gained the last switchback and the land leveled into summit country. A wide snowfield lapped up to the jagged tips of the mountain range. The sole representative of the living was a whitebark pine, branches clawing the ground, battered into submission by ages of steady wind.

One by one, we stopped to add layers of clothing.

Eric started off again, leading the way across the snowfield.

We followed our own trails and our own thoughts.

In the distance, Eric stopped and faced up to the headwall of the range. As I neared, I saw what he was examining: a glacier cupped by a steep rock outcrop. This range was littered with remnants of the Little Ice Age, and this glacier was a larger one. Waves showed its progress, the spacing between the crests marking the amount of ice flow in a year. In places, the down-flowing glacier had run over ridges and cracked open into crevasses.

The others drifted in. Walter was winded, but hanging on. I thought of the whitebark pine.

After a rest and power-bar snack, we advanced up the glacier. I anchored for a moment near a crevasse, peering at the bluish ice within, thinking what the world had been like when that old ice was water. Thinking how one could dive right down into oblivion.

"Here!" Walter called. He squatted at the head of the glacier.

We converged and looked down.

This was the bergschrund, where the downflowing ice separated from the rock headwall and opened a cleft. It looked to be fifteen or twenty feet deep. Down there on the floor of the schrund was a sprawled form, sheathed in ice but recognizable nevertheless as a woman. She was face-down, arms and legs askew, and a woman's generous hips humped up. Someone—I assumed the ice climber who found her—had scraped her clean of loose snow.

Stobie dug a spotlight from his pack and planted it on the

edge of the schrund, illuminating the scene down below, highlighting the details.

She wore hiking boots. She wore pants, parka, and gloves, matted with mud and ice. She wore a wool cap, beneath which darkish hair hung out. She could be a perfect stranger. She could be Georgia. Georgia had bottle-brown hair. Georgia had disappeared five weeks ago, in early December. It would have been cold. Not a lot of snow then; the big Thanksgiving ski weekend had been a bust. Georgia had complained to God but it wasn't until mid-December, after she'd disappeared, that the storms came.

"Hiking accident," Stobie said.

"We'll know," Walter said, "when we establish the career of the body."

Eric's eyes ticked to Stobie, the glass eye a tick out of sync. "He means what happened to her, Stobe. How she got here."

The career of the body would be written in the soils she picked up. I glanced around. Certainly, the basin rock would feed minerals into the glacier, but down here on the schrund floor those soils were locked in ice. She could have picked up basin soil up top, around the glacier—walking, sitting, falling?—before she went into the schrund. Assuming the soil was bared then. There could have been bare patches in early December, before the storms hit. I realized I was already identifying her as Georgia. I stared down at her, my eyes aching with cold, as if she could be somebody else. Whenever, however, she got here, she'd come to the end of her career. The career of the body stank.

"Odd," Walter said. "The climber noticing the body down there."

"Nah," Stobie said. "Ice climber wants to get to that rock wall, he'd be checking out the schrund before he crossed."

Eric opened his pack. "Let's get on with it."

Walter and I began sampling the soil in the glacier basin, digging where it was thinnest beneath rock overhangs.

Eric and Stobie rigged a rope ladder and climbed down to the bergschrund floor and then set to work with ice axes. By the time the sky had hardened into a gray roof, enough ice was quarried to loosen the body.

Walter and I clambered down to join them.

And now that I was down there, I took note that the body was that of a short woman. Just how short was hard to tell, the way she sprawled. The face was obscured, planted nose down into the ice, hair fanned like a frozen drape. I had the urge to sweep the hair back, get a look. Bad scene protocol. I kept my hands to myself.

Eric moved in first, to collect evidence that might jar loose when we move her. He exchanged his ski gloves for latex. He plucked out a thick fiber caught in the waistband, and bagged it. Looked like rag wool—heavy-duty winter wear. Could have transferred from her hat or her gloves. Or could have come from somebody else's. It looked like the rag wool of my own hat. Or Stobie's gloves. Or Walter's socks. Eric moved to the right boot and plucked out something caught at the collar. He studied it. He took his time.

Walter said, "What is it?"

Eric said, finally, "Maybe a horse hair."

I glanced at Stobie, as if the horse wrangler might have an opinion on the matter.

Stobie was silent. And then, almost in afterthought he whinnied.

That was for my benefit, I thought. Showing me the old Stobie, kidding around when things got dicey. Somehow, it did not ease my mind. I said, "Could she have ridden a *horse* up here? That makes no sense."

"Her car was left at her office," Walter said. "However she got here, she didn't drive to the trailhead."

"Maybe she caught a ride," I said, "with somebody else."

Eric finished his collection and moved back from the body.

Now it became Walter's and my show. We gloved up. Walter examined her clothing, her hair. I took the boots. I was numb with cold, too cold to speculate whose feet were in those boots. I grasped the left heel, toe still locked to the ice. There was a generous layer of soil preserved in the waffle sole. With the small spatula I pried loose plugs, then with tweezers transferred the plugs to a sectioned culture dish. I shivered.

Walter cast me a sidelong glance. "Something?"

"Not a good match," I said, "just eyeballing it." It was a quick and dirty field guess, but the boot soil did not look much like the basin soil we'd collected. Which argued that she didn't walk here, that she walked somewhere else and picked up soil in her boots and then was dumped here.

I was talking murder, but yet not out loud.

I heard the ratcheting of Stobie's Nikon and glanced up. He was shooting a roll of the body. He aimed the Nikon at me, and snapped. "Beautiful."

On my best day—auburn hair clean and shining, gray eyes framed with liner—I'm not beautiful. Been called pretty. And now...nose red, skin bleached cold, eyes squinting, hair roping out from beneath my wool hat. Knot in my chest, although that wouldn't show in the photo.

I looked away, at the ribbon-like bands of blue ice on the schrund wall, shimmering in the glow cast by Stobie's spotlight. Beautiful. And then the wall seemed to lean in and all I wanted to do was escape.

But she was still bound here.

When Walter and I finished our collection, we all worked together to chip away the last bonds of ice. Then we eased our arms beneath the body. It was like lifting some valuable piece of furniture you dare not drop. And now that we held her I could not deny who she was. We eased her onto her back.

There lay our mayor.

My heart plunged.

Arms and legs askew, she looked as if she were trying to run. She was iced all over, smooth in some places and rough where chunks of her glacial bed still clung. Her face was abraded and there was damage to the forehead. The ice on the right side of her face was sheet thin and the texture of the skin there was apparent. White and waxy, like boiled fat.

Walter bowed his head.

Eric pulled out a notebook. His face was pale as hers. "Overt marks of trauma to the head," he said, voice not his own. "No apparent lividity in the visible skin of the face and neck. Suggesting she didn't die in the position she was found, face down." He grimaced, and wrote it down.

I said, fury rising, "Suggesting someone put her there, after she died."

"Aw shit," Stobie said. "Shit."

"Dear God," Walter said.

None of us took it particularly well.

We had made our collections on her anterior side—more wool fibers, another horse hair, a few more mineral grains—and we were easing her into the body bag when Walter noticed a bulge in her parka pocket. Eric unzipped the pocket, fishing out a small clutch bag. Shiny vinyl, wild tropical print, pure Georgia. I recognized it. She carried it in place of her big purse, when convenient. Eric unzipped the clutch, dumping the contents onto the ice. Keys, cell phone, comb, lipstick, micro-wallet, pen, small notebook.

Walter said, "What's the notebook?"

I looked. "Weight Watchers—her pocket guide. Calories and all that."

Walter indicated the pen. "She wrote in it?"

Eric picked up the notebook and flipped through it. "Yeah. What she ate, some kind of point system."

I asked, "When's the last entry?" thinking that might pinpoint the day she died because I knew Georgia damn well wouldn't have skipped a meal or skipped holding herself accountable, and I waited while Eric flipped to the last written entry and read it, while his face closed up tight. "What?" I said. "*What*?"

Eric passed it to me. Walter and Stobie crowded in. I read the inked notes, then read them again. It looked like she'd been trying different ways to word something. Mostly cross-outs. Nearly blotted-out, the way you'd slash your pen angrily because you can't get the words right. I could decipher *just found out* and then, at the end of the slashed-out section that nearly tore the page, she'd found the words she wanted.

No way out.

2

ON THE WAY down the mountain Stobie took the lead and Eric roped the sled from behind, holding it in tension. Walter followed and I stayed close on his heels.

At the last ridge before the final descent, a sled strap came undone and we had to stop. While Stobie fussed with the litter, I went to look at the view eastward, way out in the distance.

I found what I was looking for: the mountain ranges and ridges that join to make a giant loop around the high desert floor. The loop closes against the abrupt wall of the Sierra, embracing Mammoth Mountain and enclosing our hometown of Mammoth Lakes.

What it is, in fact, is a cleverly camouflaged volcano.

Seven hundred thousand years ago it blew the hell up, blowing so ferociously that it sank a fifteen-by-twenty mile block of the earth's crust a mile and a quarter deep. The eruption left a hole so vast that people passing through today see desert and mountains and don't recognize it as the bowl and rim of a volcanic caldera. Beneath the bowl, the magma chamber has been refilling. Six months ago, within the span of a day, four big quakes hit this area. With these abrupt shivers, the volcano awoke.

That was five months before Georgia disappeared. Her last five months were her best. She rose to the occasion. She'd downplayed the volcano through four mayoral terms, as it sporadically stirred. Don't spook the tourists. She simply told us what we wanted to hear—which was that things would quiet down—and she was always right. But this time was different. This time, seismographs and tiltmeters said *time to worry*. To our utter amazement, Georgia promptly called in the feds. If an eruption was coming, she was going to get us ready.

Stobie called "fixed" and I abandoned the view and rejoined the team.

I said, "About Georgia's notes..."

"We keep that quiet," Eric said.

I shrugged. That was a given; we don't discuss case details with anyone not authorized. I glanced at Stobie, the only one of us not involved in criminalistics, but he was official Search, Rescue, and Recovery and I assumed they followed the same code.

Stobie held my look. "We don't know jack about what she meant. Who says it has anything to do with anything?"

"This is what needs to be established," Walter said.

"In the meantime," Eric said, "we don't need the whole town speculating."

We resumed our descent.

Two switchbacks down, it began to snow. Snow like white cement stuck to the body bag until it looked like we were transporting a snowman. Snow woman. The wind picked up and drove wet slugs into my face. If I cried now, snow would hide the tears. I had no tears. Just cold misery and a hot poker in my gut.

I stared at the shape on the sled. What did you find, Georgia?

You mind me talking to you? I talked to my little brother

Henry for years after he died. Nothing woo-woo, I don't believe in ghosts, just in talk therapy. So explain yourself, will you? What did you *just find out*? And what in the name of all that is logical does *no way out* mean? Does it mean you couldn't dodge the volcano issue this time? Couldn't pat us on the head and say 'there, there'? You just found out how serious the unrest is? You couldn't see any way out of that predicament?

I can almost raise your voice Georgia, but, sad to say, I can't put answers in your mouth. All I can do is read the message you left behind. I'm not talking about the notes, now. I'm talking about the bits of the earth embedded in your boot soles. I'll track that soil and find out where you died, how you died. And why you wrote *no way out*.

So long, Georgia. I swear we'll find whoever did this to you.

3

A SMALL CROWD watched through curtains of snow as we dragged into Red's Meadow. Eric had radioed ahead and it looked like the entire police department had mobilized—and a few town officials, to boot.

Afternoon was fading but the scene was lit with huge police department lanterns.

We halted and I knelt to unfasten my iced bindings, fumbling with cold gloved hands. There was such a din that I jumped when someone touched my shoulder. I turned. A man stood over me, so close I had to crane my neck. I couldn't make out his face, which was recessed in the depths of a parka hood. I must have shown my shock, for he dropped to a crouch like a large animal making itself smaller so as not to cause alarm.

"Hell," he said, "it's me, Adrian Krom." He threw back his hood and showed his face. "I don't bite."

"You just startled me."

"Cassie, right? You work with Walter."

"Right." I'd seen Adrian Krom in meetings—the emergency-ops guy sent by the feds—and a few times in the Ski Tip cafe, where everybody in town gathers at one time or another. I'd never actually spoken with him. I said, "Hello Adrian."

"Adrian, good. Some people call me Mr. Krom. I hate the formalities." He folded his arms, still in a crouch. "I prefer to be chums."

It struck me that he was like Georgia, insisting on first name only. Maybe it was a politics thing.

"Cassie, tell me if that's Georgia. Have we lost our mayor?"

Ours? Adrian Krom has been in town only two months. We looked in unison at the snow-packed body bag, and I nodded.

"Hell," he said, voice thickening. He bowed his head.

All I could see was his brown pelt of hair. I hesitated, then patted his shoulder. He reached up and grasped my hand. After a decent interval, I slipped my hand free. He came out of his crouch and stood, looking down at me. "You know what Georgia would say right now?"

I thought, this guy likes his drama. I got to my feet. "What?"

"We're all in this together."

4

I HAD to park in the Community Center lot and walk four blocks up Minaret Road threading my way through the crowd on the way to work. Feeling I should say something to these people. Some kind of cautionary thing.

Always park your car facing downhill for a quick getaway.

They acted like nothing was wrong, like this was a normal Saturday in January after a good snowfall. The town of Mammoth Lakes in boomtown gear. Every other car carried skis or snowboards and now, before the lifts opened, there wasn't a parking spot to be had. The road pooled with slush and the snow was embedded with grit and mashed pine cones and shards of Styrofoam cups and it rasped underfoot but that didn't slow the jostling snow crowd.

No, I amended, they acted like they knew something was wrong and that's why they came. Ever since the volcano stirred, the snow crowd has swelled along with the ground. That's what got to me. We could get hit, so we're edgy. Extreme sports. We've never been edgy before—we've just been slopes and condos and cafes and kitschy shops a half-day's drive from Los Angeles. Now we're hot.

And the hometown crowd has been riding the boom. People up and down Minaret Road cleared snow from the paths in front of their businesses. Motels flashed No Vacancy and condos were renting by the week. However, for anyone who cared to see, the signs said otherwise. Sierra Properties windows were plastered with HOMES4SALE. Mountain Hardware screamed CLEARANCE! And new signs were welded to the traffic light poles: orange evacuation arrows that pointed the way out.

Nobody cared to see.

I passed Uphill Sports where guys were unloading snowmobiles from a flatbed truck and I asked how's it going and one of the guys cupped his palms and intoned "biiig bucks."

I came to the Ski Tip Cafe and there was a crowd out the door, eager to grab breakfast before heading up to the slopes. Once they'd filled their bellies and bolted, the locals would drift in. The Tip's owner Bill Bone appeared in the doorway, juggling a clipboard, all elbows and knees, looking like a gawky middle-aged busboy. He called a name and a group cheered and elbowed forward and Bill shot me a gloomy nod. Worrying about running out of eggs, no doubt. I felt a pang of affection for Bill and the Tip, even for its hokey chalet decor. I'd had my first milkshake there, my first legal beer.

I studied the place, with a sudden need to burn it into my memory.

And then I crossed the street to the lab—Sierra Geoforensics big and bold and authoritative on the door—and like everyone else I acted like this was a normal Saturday. Through the lab's big street-side window I saw Walter inside at his workbench. Entirely normal for us to work on a Saturday on a big case.

This case qualified. Oh yes.

Walter threw me a thin "good morning" as I walked in.

We'd returned yesterday from the glacier too spent to do

more than sort our samples. I'd slept badly, dreaming of Georgia. Georgia, I saw, was wearing on Walter as well.

I grabbed a cup of coffee and set to work. On my workbench was the culture dish I'd prepared last night—soil plugs from the left boot. I put the first plug on the stage and bent to the scope. I imagined Georgia at my shoulder, angling for a look. Busybody was her middle name. I took the scalpel and teased apart the clumps of soil. Weathered red cinders and fluffy bits of pumice —volcanic. Yellow sulfur crystals, which could come from fertilizer or pesticides or, more likely, volcanism.

At my shoulder, Georgia cackled. Sulfur was known, in Biblical quarters, as brimstone. Georgia would run with that, I thought: fire and brimstone awaiting the perp.

It didn't do much for me. Georgia had picked up volcanic soil but that was the norm around here.

I poked further and saw shiny mica, black chips of hornblende, milky quartz, pink feldspar—the stuff of granite. Well, the Sierra is granite country. And now I found grainy white stuff with a rhombic cleavage—calcite. Calcite's common as furniture.

I told Walter what I'd found. He grunted.

Cinders, pumice, sulfur, granite, calcite: not a telling mix. And not necessarily acquired at the same place, or the same time. Collect a bit of pumice here, a pinch of calcite there.

Still, it was the same mineral suite as the grains Walter had plucked from her clothing, on the ice. Hat, gloves, jeans, parka, front and back. I thought that over. She not only walked in the stuff, she appeared to have rolled around in it.

I turned the scalpel to a nut of compacted soil. It cracked open. Here was something—a wink of silver. It was a disk, concave, with parallel striae. Unmistakable. I let out a soundless whistle. "Walter," I said, "I've got gunpowder."

Most gunpowder that comes out of a firearm comes out

burned and it takes a scanning electron microscope to find that residue, but a few particles usually emerge unburned and those are large enough to be easily seen.

"How many?" he asked at last.

"Just one."

"Don't fall in love."

"Well I haven't." A single disk was not significant. Soil is a collector; it likes to latch onto foreign elements. A particle of gunpowder could have blown in on the wind or been ferried on an animal's fur. Georgia could have picked it up miles from where she died and ferried it herself. It didn't necessarily say that she last walked in the vicinity of firearms. But, then, maybe she did.

I said, "You finding anything of note?"

He looked up from the glacier basin soil he'd been examining. "Noteworthy, so far, in that it doesn't match the soils from the clothing or the boots."

"So she didn't walk at the glacier. The final place she walked was ... elsewhere."

"Preliminary, but so it appears."

I said, "What do you think made her write *no way out*? That's strong stuff."

"That it is."

"You know," I said, "that could mean something personal."

"As opposed to something involving us all?"

I said, tight, "Meaning the volcano, you're saying?"

"Meaning the volcano," he said.

I said, tighter, "What could Georgia have possibly found out about the volcano?"

"I've wondered that, myself." Walter glanced out the window. "That's why I've asked our volcanologist to drop by."

Not a bad idea, I thought. Although the need of it sent a chill down my spine.

Ten minutes later the door opened and Lindsay Nash, our volcanologist, swept in.

"Let me have your coat," Walter said, ushering her inside, "and you'll want coffee?"

"It's not a coat and I'm still chilly." She wore a gray and black wool poncho that set off her hair, which was gray with flecks of black like biotite mica in granite. She produced a bag from beneath the poncho. "Use this. It's fresh. Garuda."

Walter said, "We have fresh Kona."

I've known them to spend an hour spatting about who should have made dinner reservations, or whose work was more crucial. They've danced this dance for over twenty years, spatting like an old married couple although they never got around to marrying. They'd give each other anything—their lives if necessary—but they wouldn't give an inch without making a point.

I relaxed an inch, at the sheer normality of it.

Walter took the bag and went to the workbench we used as a kitchen. We have, on Fridays, a supply of donuts, which Lindsay doesn't touch and I try mightily to avoid. Since Walter and I were on the mountain yesterday, we have Friday's leftovers today. We always have coffee. Walter dumped out the Kona in the carafe—a good two cups worth—and ground Lindsay's beans.

Lindsay came to me. "Working hard?"

I went for the light tone. "Always something."

"If you'd gone into volcanology, it would be something finer."

She gave me a hug and I smelled perfume in the fine merino wool of her poncho. She'd given me a sweeter version of that scent for my twelfth birthday. That, and a gas mask for a tour of her volcano sampling fumarole emissions. And so it began, Lindsay grooming me as an acolyte. I'd met her via Walter. I'd met Walter the previous year, taking refuge in his lab when my brother Henry stubbed his toe on a rock and was rushed to the hospital. I came back to the lab again and again. Walter taught me how rocks could be used to solve crimes and offered me an after-school job doing scutwork, and that was that. I acquired a new, and mixed vocabulary: fumarole, lightscope, tiltmeter, exemplar. I showed off at home. My father joked that I'd acquired a smarter set of parents. He missed the mark. Even before Henry's death, my cartoonist parents drew themselves into a closed circle. Walter's and Lindsay's lives also revolved around their work, but the difference was that they drew me in.

Lindsay pulled up a stool, blew a patch of my workbench clean, and rested her arm. "Walter says you two need a consult about Georgia."

I shifted back to uneasy. Lindsay had detested Georgia. I said, "Yeah."

"This note of hers.... No way out. Very dramatic."

I took a moment. So Walter had told Lindsay about the note. We'd all agreed on the ice to keep it quiet. But, then, since he'd asked for a consult, I supposed it made sense to tell her everything.

"And *why*," Lindsay asked, "do you think this note involves my volcano?"

"Because she said she *found* something. Because she'd picked up volcanic soil, likely where she died. Because your volcano is a hot topic."

Lindsay shrugged, acknowledging the truth of that. "Very well, where did she pick up this soil?"

"We don't yet know."

"Then give me one of your wild-ass guesses."

I preferred to call them onageristic estimates; an onager is a wild ass. I said, "Wouldn't be useful." At this point.

Walter set a mug of coffee on the workbench in front of Lindsay. He'd siphoned off the first of the brew for her.

"Thank you, honey." She waited until he'd scooted his stool over to my bench, to join us. She said, "If you don't know where Georgia died, I don't see how I can tell you anything about what she may or may not have found."

"What might *you* find," Walter asked, "that would be a new threat?"

"Good heavens, I've been trying to teach you two volcanology for decades, and *now* you want to listen to me?" She sampled her coffee. "I *can* tell you this. I keep a close eye on my volcano. Anything Georgia might think she found would be as useless as tits on a boar."

Walter's eyebrows lifted.

I smiled. "Just give us a wild-ass guess."

"That wouldn't be useful." She raised her mug to me. "But touche."

"Here's the thing, Lindsay," I said. "Georgia found out something that spooked her so much she damn near ruined a page of her Weight Watcher's notebook writing it down. And yeah, it could have been some personal trouble, but..."

"But?" Lindsay has a fine aristocratic face and it always shows composure.

"But what if it was something bigger? What if somebody killed her to keep it quiet?"

"How did she die?"

Walter answered. "A blow to the head is the probable cause."

"That's not how I would kill her." Lindsay drummed her fingers on the workbench, her rings popping up like knuckles. "I'd use a gun."

"*Lindsay.*"

"I'm thinking 'means' Walter. Is this not the way you two talk about a case? This is your territory, not mine."

I cut in. "We usually say 'weapon,' until we know otherwise. We usually say 'perp.' As in, maybe the perp came upon her and...saw whatever she found, learned whatever she knew...and the perp was surprised, and used what was at hand. An as-yet unidentified weapon. Or maybe there was a fight."

"Weapon. Perp." Lindsay bowed her head, appearing to gauge the depths of her coffee. "Yes, I see that's preferable."

I thought, this really is too weird, Lindsay consulting on Georgia's death. The two of them had dueled for years, the volcanologist issuing warnings and the mayor playing down the threat. And then, when the volcano got truly serious and Georgia called in the feds, FEMA sent us Adrian Krom. That set off Lindsay. She had a history with Krom and argued against his appointment, to no avail. So, weirdly, Lindsay's new allies in volcano response were her longtime enemies. They made an odd team, if team was the right word. In any case, Adrian Krom and Georgia Simonies and Lindsay Nash were the three people in charge of keeping us all safe. One of them was dead now. I thought of Adrian Krom in Red's Meadow yesterday, bowing his head upon learning it was Georgia we'd recovered from the ice. And so now there were two people left alive in charge of keeping us safe. Two people who detested each other.

Walter said, mildly, "If you'll speculate on the means of death, Lindsay, might you not speculate on what Georgia could have found?"

"I'm sorry I can't be of help." Lindsay abruptly produced her purse, took two twenty-dollar bills, and placed them on my workbench. "On the other hand, I'd be happy to contribute to the cause."

I stared.

"Bill Bone's birthday." She glanced out the window at the Ski Tip Cafe across the street. Then back at me. "You *are* the one collecting?"

I nodded.

"I'm thinking," she said, "a jacket. Raw silk. Cream, or tan, yellow undertone. Depending on how much you've collected, we can accessorize from there."

Walter snorted. "Let him put the money toward that remodel he talks about."

My stomach tightened. That implied we'd all be here long enough for Bill to remodel the Ski Tip.

Lindsay stood. "My dears, if there's nothing further?" She took her coffee mug to the sink, running the water until it steamed.

Walter frowned. "You're going?"

I watched her. Washing her mug just like she always does because she hates to have anyone clean up after her. As if this visit had gone just like always. But it hadn't. Lindsay thinks geology *is* volcanology and here she was talking forensics with us. Or not talking. Talking birthdays. She'd been evasive. Evasive as, I suddenly thought, Eric and Stobie had been on the mountain. I fiercely wanted this Saturday in the lab to turn normal. I wanted Lindsay to pour a second cup and stay. Send out for pizza for lunch. Pat Walter's butt when she thinks I'm not looking. Normalize the situation.

She caught me staring. She winked. "Got to run—the soaps are on." This was her running joke, whenever the volcano acted up, whenever the news played it as soap-opera drama.

I fell in. "Take care of it, will you?" This was my running joke, that the volcano responded to Lindsay like a dog to its mistress.

"Don't forget tomorrow night," Walter said. "We'll pick you up at six *sharp*."

Tomorrow night was a meeting about the volcano. Adrian Krom called it.

Lindsay moved to the door, blowing us a kiss in lieu of an answer, and she was gone.

She left behind a vacuum, in which Walter clattered his tools and I stared at the dirt from Georgia's boots. Feeling a tension that tightened my neck. I hitched my stool up to the workbench. Okay, you want to know what Georgia found, then find out where she walked.

Just do the geology.

I selected the next soil plug and found myself a prize. By color, there were two distinct soil horizons and, even better, a piece of leaf was caught in between. Normally, when someone walks, new soil is forced into the crevices of the shoe and with each footstep gets mixed with the soil already clinging there. Once in a while the walker takes a lucky step—lucky for us—and picks up something like this leaf which protects the purity of the layers. I pried apart the strata and plucked out the leaf. Long and narrow, going brittle. Mountain willow, I hazarded. It grows at a variety of elevations. Could be a marker or could have been ferried to the site. More important, the leaf isolated the top layer of soil, the final piece of earth that Georgia stepped upon. Gently, I broke the layer into clumps. Cinders, pumice, sulfur, granite, calcite. Not unlike the other plugs.

I sliced into the largest clump and it broke apart like a dried seed pod and the seeds inside were silver.

I breathed out softly, so as not to disturb the display. This was good stuff. "Walter, I've got gunpowder again." I coaxed the disks apart. "Two identical to the first, and six that look to be different makes."

"Let's have a look." Walter came and adjusted my scope. When he finished, he was nodding.

The resistance in my neck eased. I was gaining confidence in the gunpowder. There's a point in an investigation when I gain traction, go on the lookout—for a unique mineral, for a particular consistency of the soil, for an inclusion like gunpowder that could place the evidence in a known plot of the earth. Give it an address.

Walter said, "Well, the Casa Diablo shooting range comes to mind."

Along with the backyards of half the town. But I was already picturing the soil out at Casa and nodding. Casa Diablo is down in the high desert, near the intersection of the major highway and the road up to town. Site of our geothermal plant, along with the shooting range. There would surely be gunpowder there.

Walter scratched his ear. "Here's what I propose. Finish your batch, and then let's send what you find to a gunpowder lab for ID. You might run the powder over to the cop house, see what lab John's using—he has a courier account. While we await the report, you might take a turn out to Casa Diablo and collect exemplars."

"Careful," I said. "You're falling in love."

"A mild attraction."

I got a cup of coffee and a donut and went to the window. It had started to snow, light. Dry snow falls so slowly you can pick out a flake and follow it to the ground, see one crystal pile on top of another, like toast crumbs.

Geologists hate snow. It hides everything. To hit soil I'd have to dig.

Through the window I watched a woman scrape her boot on the curb, removing a stratum of acquired crud. I wondered if Georgia had acquired her crud at the shooting range.

And if so, why.

5

Before I could return to my workbench, the medical examiner called.

Georgia lay on the metal tray with her mouth pried open.

"Just getting started," Randy Burrard said. "Afraid I've been out with the flu."

I focused on Randy, who's way too sweet-faced for this job. Actually, he did look a little green. As far as I'm concerned, anybody who dissects the deceased has a right to look green. I said, "Feel better," meaning it.

"Thanks." Randy gestured at Georgia. "Surprised the heck out of me when I looked in her mouth. Thought you'd want to get this out yourself."

Yeah.

I went over to the table. Randy had covered her with a sheet but it barely rose over her breasts. I tugged it to her chin. I wanted to say something to her. I could think of nothing.

But it wasn't Georgia, it was her husk, and so in the end I just bent and looked at the soil in her mouth.

"Livor mortis discoloration on her lower back and buttocks," Randy said. "Livor starts soon after death and is fixed within four to five hours. So she died lying face up, or was quickly rolled onto her back."

I nodded. That's what we'd assumed on the ice. We'd found her face down but there was no livor purpling on her face. She'd lain on her back long enough for blood to pool and livor to fix. But if she'd died on her back, how had the soil gotten into her mouth? Maybe a struggle, and her face was forced into the dirt, and then she was rolled over. Maybe. I gently probed between her teeth and gums. Nothing there. In fact, the grains primarily coated her tongue, the roof of her mouth, the insides of her teeth. However the soil got there, she must have lost consciousness or died right then; otherwise she would have spat the stuff out. My own tongue quilted; I wanted to spit. Instead, I tweezered the stuff out of her mouth, collecting half a thimbleful, and examined it under the brutal autopsy lights. Pumice, and bits of tree bark.

I thought about that. If there was enough bark in the soil to show up in this thimbleful, why wasn't there bark in the samples from her boots and clothing?

Randy said, "You notice that bruising around her mouth?"

I placed my hands above the marks, spreading thumb and fingers apart. My thumb fit just beneath her lower lip, and my fingers rested along the cheek and chin opposite. Someone had forced her mouth open. Held it open.

"Nothing down her throat," Randy said, "although I'll get a better look when I..."

I said, "I understand."

But I didn't. Someone had opened her mouth and dumped in pumice and tree bark? Maybe during the death struggle—he's trying to suffocate her? With half a thimbleful of soil? That was hardly enough to choke on. In any case, Randy's initial assessment, on the phone, was that she'd died from a subdural hematoma. So, blow to the head and she's dead, or nearly so.

Then why the soil in the mouth? Some creepy arcane message?

I brought up the image of Georgia's face, after we had set her on her back on the ice. Her mouth had been closed. Had she shut it herself, before dying?

Or had the killer done it, unable to look at her lying there dead, open-mouthed.

What species of killer closes her mouth to end her silent scream?

6

I HEADED for the cop house carrying samples of gunpowder.

I'd returned from the Medical Examiner yesterday and dived back into the boot soil and it was like hitting the jackpot again and again, cracking open plug after plug and finding the silver prizes. Gunpowder. Seven distinct makes. Georgia had walked in soil rich in gunpowder. Walter and I worked late last night and came in early this morning. As of ten A.M., Walter had finished the glacier basin samples and not found a single grain of powder. It was no longer preliminary—we could say with certainty that Georgia had not taken her last steps at the glacier.

Wherever she'd walked, someone had done a lot of shooting.

I had recovered several grains of each type of powder and tubed one of each to send to a gunpowder lab. We needed these grains ID'd.

I turned off Minaret Road onto the side street where the red-brick cop house squats.

Jasper Rinehart was at the front desk, watching a hockey game on his laptop. He waved me through with a sudden curse, which I realized was directed at the goalie and not me.

I headed through the bullpen for chief John Amsterdam's

office, and ran into Eric.

He smiled. "Morning, Oldfield."

"Morning, Catlin." I smiled. "John in?"

"On a conference call."

"I'll wait."

Eric cocked his head. A thick silence fell—Eric clearly wondering what I wanted with the chief of police, why the detective wouldn't suffice, and me wondering the same thing. It was as awkward as our exchange on the ski up the mountain, when Eric tried to send me and Walter back.

Eric recovered first. He offered me a comb-back chair in his cubicle and pulled in a matching chair from the cubicle next door. We sat, knees bumping. He reversed his chair and straddled it. "Coffee?"

"No thanks. I'm fully caffeinated."

We smiled. Stiff smiles.

I looked away, as if the tumbledown cop-house decor was what I'd come to see. Normally, Eric and I dodged our interpersonal awkwardness by shooting the shit about work, or bitching about how redevelopment's ruining Mammoth. But now the town was more concerned with survival than with redevelopment; neither of us cared to bitch about survival. And work currently meant the Georgia case; difficult to shoot the shit about that when we were both holding back.

So I plunged ahead. "Anything yet on the rag-wool fibers?"

"Too soon to hear from hair-and-fiber." He shrugged. "But we sent the techs everything from her closet that could be a match."

"What about the hair? Is it horse?"

"Too soon."

"Anything else?" I asked. "What about her cell phone?"

"Last call she made was the night before she disappeared—which we already knew from her phone records."

"Who'd she call?"

"Ski Tip. Asked Bill to get a take-out order ready."

"What about the rest of the contents of her little bag?"

"Her prints, on everything. Bag too." He held my look. "And the Weight Watchers notebook. Her prints. The notes looked to be in her handwriting, but we're having a documents tech check it all out."

I nodded. "I, um, know we agreed to keep quiet about the notes but Walter and I had to tell Lindsay."

"Why?"

"Georgia said she *found* something. What if she found something about the volcano?"

"What did Lindsay say?"

"Lindsay wasn't real interested." I shrugged. "Anyway, Georgia might have meant something personal. And we should consider that. We don't know when she wrote the notes. Maybe she had financial troubles. Or man troubles. *No way out*. That could fit."

"We could come up with a dozen theories that fit."

"At best, half a dozen."

He shrugged. "How about your dirt?"

"Stuff's mostly a volcanic mix."

"*Stuff*, Oldfield?" The scar tissue below his left eye quilted. "Love your scientific precision."

I relaxed an inch. This was more like it. I said, "Trachybasaltic cinders, calcite with a nice rhombic cleavage..."

He put up his hands. "Stuff'll do."

"At this point, stuff says Georgia didn't walk at the glacier."

"Oh?"

I could have stopped there. But I didn't. "You know what I'm saying?"

"Help me out."

Why's he need help? He's a crackerjack crime-scene tech. I

said, evenly, “Murder.”

“Murder’s a workable theory. Especially considering the fact that we found her face down, and livor says she died face up.”

“And what about rigor? What does that say?”

“Rigor mortis sets in within two or three hours. Lasts about twenty to thirty hours. Not sure what else it says.”

I said, “How about that it’s hard to move a body in the stiffness of rigor on a horse. So wherever she died, she lay there long enough for livor to fix and rigor to come and go. That makes it over a day. And then she was moved.”

“That’s a workable theory.”

I nodded. And then I told him about the stuff in her mouth, the bizarre pumice-bark mix.

He said, “Got a theory about that?”

“Nothing I’d care to offer.” Just wild-ass guesses.

His look skated to his wall clock, to John’s office, and then he looked back at me with that damned awkward smile.

I said, “And I don’t have a theory for why you were such a jerk on the retrieval. Trying to send Walter and me back.”

He took a long moment, then said, “You got me.”

“I do?”

“I was a jerk. I expected the body to be Georgia and I didn’t know how you’d take it.”

“Why me? Why not worry about Walter and Stobie?”

“Because I don’t like seeing you upset.”

I went cinder red. Was this some big-brother thing? That’s the way we’d begun, way back when we were kids. There was six-year-old me tagging along after Eric and my brother Jimbo, perfecting the art of annoyance. And then there was nine-year-old awakening me writing Eric mash notes and burying them in the box with my dead turtle. And then, after the summer day that changed everything, there was the both of us waiting for one another to get past pride and hurt. And here we are now, adults who've perfected the art of surficial interaction. Shooting the shit, needling one another over the merits of chick flicks versus action movies. If I were to do a forensic dig on our relationship, I would uncover layer after sedimentary layer—eroded events and words deposited over the years and compressed and hardened into rock. As long as we didn't let that summer day fissure up through the sediments, we'd be fine. That day, along with my love notes, could sleep with the turtle.

I said, finally, "I should get back to work." I opened my purse and took out the bubble-pack envelope. "I need to get this to a gunpowder lab. Sacramento or Bakersfield, whichever John's using."

Eric drew back, the way he shies when something comes abruptly into his field of view from the blind side. He said, lightly, "Powder in the evidence?"

"Surprised me too."

He put out his hand. "I'll take care of it."

I hesitated. Again. And then my eye caught on the shredded target pinned to his cubicle wall. All bullseyes. I'd seen it dozens of times but for the first time I wondered where he'd gone target-shooting.

And then the obvious hit me.

The biathlon range.

I looked to the hook where his ball cap hung. I'd seen it hundreds of times but now I saw it anew. The US biathlon team logo is stitched over the bill: stick-figure skier in a lunging stride, rifle strapped to its back. World Cup races start next week. Eric's racing, along with my brother Jimbo, and Stobie is the team armorer. I remembered the guys, as kids, trekking up to the Lake Mary biathlon course nearly every winter day after school to ski and shoot. Year in, year out, rifles firing, unburned powder falling into the snow and sinking with snowmelt into the soil.

My stomach tightened.

I remembered Lindsay driving me to the course to cheer my brother when the boys started holding races. She got interested. She got them organized and into the U.S. Biathlon Association. And that's how Georgia was drawn in. The mayor saw the biathlon as a fine place to divert boys who were into civic mischief. So Georgia and Lindsay—already at odds over the volcano—became uneasy co-den mothers.

Mothers without children of their own.

Mothers with a loving blind spot. They had lobbied this year's World Cup races to Mammoth. And then the volcano stirred again and they joined forces to prepare the town. But they could not bear to cancel the Cup. Oh, they got Squaw Valley as a backup but unless there is lava flowing here day after tomorrow, the races will proceed here as scheduled. Georgia would kill to watch her boys compete in the Cup on their home turf. Would have killed. Lindsay would...what? Sacrifice her good judgment to cheer on her boys, I thought sourly. While keeping a damn close eye on ground deformation and quake patterns, I hoped.

I fingered the bubble-pack envelope, wondering if my unidentified gunpowder originated at the biathlon range. Thinking, the mayor's dead, the volcanologist is weirdly interested in how she died, the FEMA guy is oddly devastated, and the cop I most trust in the world tried to get a jump on the crime scene. Thinking, these are the people whose job it is—or was—to keep us safe.

Eric had been looking where I looked—the target, the ball cap—and now he came back to the envelope I was mangling. "Never mind." He laced his hands behind his head. "It all works out. I'm a jerk on the retrieval, you're anal retentive with your powder. Save it for John."

"No need." I passed the envelope to Eric. "We're on the same team."

7

"WE DON'T WANT to be late," Walter said. He pried me from my scope, sent me home to change, collected me within the half-hour, collected Lindsay at six sharp, and in his fire-engine red Explorer he ferried us up the mountain toward the lights.

I had to wonder about this meeting. Why did Adrian Krom call it on the mountain, up at the Inn? Why not call it at the Community Center? Why call this meeting with just one day's notice? Why call it at all, since we had a meeting a week ago and covered everything conceivable. I reached over the seat and tapped Lindsay. "Are you talking about raising the alert level?"

"No," she said, "we're still at ADVISORY."

I sat back. The Geological Survey issues four-tiered volcano alerts, starting at NORMAL, meaning typical background activity, all the way through WARNING, meaning get the hell out. We've been at ADVISORY, meaning elevated unrest, for the past six months. I said, "If nothing's changed, why'd he call this meeting?"

"Ask Walter," Lindsay said. "He's become such great pals with Adrian."

Walter said, mildly, "Adrian's doing his job."

I had to agree, although I did not care to say so in Lindsay's presence. Walter had put his faith in Adrian Krom—just as I had —because Walter believes in authority. Just as I do. Adrian Krom certainly has the authority, and the resources, to prepare us for what looks like is coming. But Krom had gone beyond the mandate from FEMA. What Walter saw in Adrian Krom was a man who came to town and leased a condo and settled in and linked his fate to ours. And that, to Walter, was loyalty.

Lindsay said, "You think he's a prince, Walter. He's not a prince."

Walter took the curves a little fast, throwing us all into silence.

Two curves later Walter's headlights caught the silhouettes of stripped conifers, and I looked hard. Was this patch of dead trees bigger than last time I came this way? Tree-kills around Mammoth were old news—quakes breached a fault and gas has been leaking up from an old magma chamber, asphyxiating trees, along with a few people. What we do is tread carefully. Don't camp near tree-kills. Don't ski roped-off areas and if you do be sure not to do a face plant.

This tree-kill looked no larger. Okay, then. Steady at ADVISORY.

We topped the road and parked at the shuttlebus plaza, getting out near the statue of the woolly mammoth. Once, the real thing roamed here and now its iced effigy rears in bronze, town mascot. Our nod to the Pleistocene.

We were on the broad shoulder of Mammoth Mountain, two thousand feet below its summit. I glanced up. Impossible not to. The mountain's great bulk showed by starlight—a hotshot's mountain with headwall chutes and plenty of vertical drop. I once took a header down the chute known as Grizzly, which in my opinion should be skied only by paramedics. Down here on the shoulder, backing into the mountain, were the lodge and lift stations, where I used to earn my paychecks. Across the shuttle roundabout was Mammoth Mountain Inn, alpine fancy, where I endured my senior prom. Light spilled from the Inn and mixed with the inky night to grease the snow with a butternut glow.

We trudged toward the Inn, snow coating our boots like spats.

Mike Kittleman was on the porch, sweeping loose snow. Walter and Lindsay went inside but I paused to watch Mike.

Only Mike would wear a jacket and tie to sweep the steps. He's a lean wiry guy with easily sunburned skin and wild blond frizz taming himself to fit into any look he thinks will impress. Or maybe that's just through my eyes. Mike is another of the guys in my brother's circle. I've known him since we were kids, but it wasn't until we were in our teens that our lives intersected. I glanced across the roundabout to the gondola station where we worked together one summer loading mountain bikes and learned to loathe each other.

Long time ago.

I looked at Mike now. He's the soul of the work ethic. He's worked his butt off at every job he ever held and accepted overtime like it was a certificate of honor. These days, he's been working road construction on the evacuation route, along with my brother and a dozen others who finds it pays better than selling lift tickets or ski patrol.

And yet here he was sweeping snow.

I knew he saw me. "Hi Mike. Thanks for clearing the steps."

He glanced up. "It's for old people. It's so old people won't slip."

"And the rest of us?" I smiled, making the effort. "So, you working for the Inn now?"

He reburied his attention in the broom. "For Mr. *Krom*."

Ah, that explained the tie. I'd seen him moonlighting for Adrian Krom—delivering the bulletins Krom generated, taking notes at meetings—and he always dressed the part. But still. "Is this some kind of memorial? For Georgia?" I sure wasn't dressed for it.

The cloth of his jacket pulled tight across his back and for a moment I thought he was hunching into a sprinter's crouch. Anything to get away from me. But he stayed put, frozen as the bronze mammoth. He tunneled me a dark look. "What do you mean?"

"I mean is this a memorial? Mr. Krom...Adrian...seemed upset about her death."

"Just go in."

"Okay." Why'd I bring up Georgia? I thought again of the biathlon team, back when Lindsay and Georgia had organized the boys into a team. Mike had been one of those teenage biathletes, but he had a temper and he took offense quickly at the needling that was part of team camaraderie. He threw a punch almost as well as he shot his rifle. Finally Georgia got fed up with his fighting and kicked him off the team, kindling Mike's hatred. I thought, now, Mike was fully capable of holding the old biathlon grudge against Georgia beyond the grave. In fact, he was capable of carrying it to his own grave. And he was clearly working his way into the new power structure in town, with Krom. If Krom was holding a memorial for Georgia, I guessed that wouldn't sit too well with Mike.

I headed for the door.

Mike pulled himself erect, the consummate doorman, but for his right thumb which began digging mercilessly at the knot of his tie.

8

THERE WAS a huge map pinned to foam board on an easel by the fireplace.

There was a coffee urn and Styrofoam cups, but no flowers. The DeMartini twins were here but without harp and guitar, meaning no Pachelbel Canon, no memorial service. People were dressed pretty much as I was, mountain spiffy, meaning nice shirts with jeans, and the good boots. The only tie, other than Mike's, was Walter's, with his chamois shirt. Lindsay would normally wear her silk pantsuit to a place like the Inn but she hadn't bothered to change from her field clothes. That had won a frown from Walter.

The Inn's great room was packed to the walls. The room is styled on the lofty old national park hotels, with colonnades of sugar pine and Paiute-weave carpets and a boulder-framed fireplace large enough to roast a bear.

If Adrian Krom called the meeting here to pull in a crowd, it worked.

I buffeted my way forward and ran into Stobie. I hadn't seen him since he pulled Georgia's sled down from the glacier. "Hey Kiddo!" he boomed, the easygoing Stobie I'd always known, not the tense guy on the recovery mission. He caught me around the waist, dipped me, and whispered, "Beer."

I whispered back, "I think there's coffee."

"Bill's birthday. Beer. Designer. Club. Monthly." Stobie righted me, then bellied through the crowd toward his buddies —Eric and my brother Jimbo. The three biathletes, lifelong friends, lounged against a colonnade, shooting the shit, hanging out.

As if all was normal.

And then I caught sight of Bill Bone himself, over at the snack table restacking the sugar packets. Beer? I thought. Well, Stobie used to bus dishes for Bill at the Ski Tip, so Stobie would know. I suddenly was desperate to get Bill's birthday gift right. I knew he wouldn't care—he'll be monumentally touched no matter what we get him—but it mattered to me. *We're a community*, Georgia always preached, we're more than L.A.'s playground. And no matter how windy Georgia got I'd always find myself grateful to be included. And now we were a community without our longtime mayor, a community without an insurable future, and if we intended to keep acting like a community then we should goddamn know what the proprietor of the Ski Tip Cafe wanted for his birthday.

I checked my parka and then scanned the room for the man who'd called this meeting. I spotted him finally, the burly man light-footing his way through the crowd, turning anxious heads. A touch more formal than his guests. Brown sweater, brown cords, brown hair, deep tan. Every time I've seen him he's wearing brown. Actually, I hadn't seen him since Red's Meadow, four days ago. What stayed with me was my hand in his. I'd had the impulse to keep holding on, because Adrian Krom's the closest to a safety net we'll get.

Mike Kittleman came inside and flattened himself against the far wall. He stood alone.

I spotted Lindsay and Walter, who were chatting with Jefferson Liu. Jefferson stepped up from his position as head of the town Council to become acting mayor, after Georgia disappeared. And Adrian Krom held his position as Emergency Operations Chief at the pleasure of the Council, and the acting mayor. I guessed silver-goateed Jefferson qualified as one of Mike's 'old people' and I could see why Krom would not want him to slip and fall.

I came up beside Lindsay, and nudged her. "Anybody else here from the Council?"

She said, tight, "All of them."

Then it's big.

There was a shifting in the room toward the fireplace, where Krom leaned against a table. He could not have chosen a better frame: the hearty fire at his back, the table a huge chunk of red fir polished to a cinnamon gleam. Krom held up a hand and the nervous chatter ceased. He said, "It's been, what? Couple of months. You all know me. Right?" He paused. The room was still. "No, you don't. Let me reintroduce myself. I'm Adrian Krom. I'm your worst nightmare."

In the strained silence, somebody giggled.

"You say no? I say yes. I've been your best friend. It's not working, chums."

I began to grow worried.

He moved to the easel. The map showed the geography of the town and the greater environs. "Look hard. You know the geography. What the hell were you thinking? *I've* walked it. Have you? Scared the bejesus out of me. It's time to scare the bejesus out of you. If you're not scared, if you're not prepared to see me and this map in your dreams, then go home and watch TV."

Nobody moved.

"Then let's get serious." Krom flipped an overlay, superimposing it on the map. It looked like a child's drawing, a crooked line and two circles alongside. “This,” he dragged a finger along the line, “is the Bypass.”

I glanced at Lindsay, who’d gone on alert. Was Krom trying to start a war? The Bypass is hers—an escape route, currently only half-done. She’s the one who walked the geography and conceived the Bypass, she’s the one who pushed the Council to fund it, and she’s the one who named it. A mile was already bulldozed when Krom first came to town.

But until the Bypass is finished, there’s only one road out of town: Highway 203, which leads to the major through-road in the eastern Sierra, Highway 395. That highway runs all the way south to Los Angeles and north to Nevada, following the Sierra scarp like a fault. You can’t go anywhere north or south without taking 395.

Highway 395 runs through the caldera, the gigantic crater that encircles Long Valley and Mammoth Mountain and our hometown. You can’t escape to *anywhere* without taking 395.

That’s why *any* road out of town must connect to 395. Problem is, 203 connects with 395 in a very dangerous place in the caldera—near the heart of the awakening volcano, where the magma has been rising.

That’s why, when the volcano got serious, Lindsay said we needed a second way out, a way to connect with 395 at a less dangerous place. She’d been saying this for decades, but this time she said *now*.

Lindsay was glaring at Krom’s map. He’d drawn a line, extending the half-built Bypass to show the finished route. When finished, it will connect with 395 well north of the caldera’s growing magma chamber.

We all stared at the Bypass on the map, our lifeline. There was a camera flash and then the *Mammoth Times* editor Hal Orenstein slipped to the front of the crowd, his stringbean form hunched to angle a shot for the local paper.

Now Krom studied the drawing anew, as if the flash had illuminated something revealing. He let the moment run, then turned to us. "Why are you building this? Isn't the point to evacuate and live to tell the tale?"

I reached for Lindsay but it was too late. She was on her way.

"I know your attention is on the caldera," Krom was saying, "and rightly so—but what exactly is the point in running your new escape route smack dab through *this*?" He fingered the circles. "Volcanoes, chums."

I saw what he was doing. It wasn't fair. He was diverting attention from the active caldera to the Inyo System, which is another volcanic system entirely. Inyo's volcanoes have been dormant for hundreds of years. They're dormant now. Otherwise, Lindsay wouldn't have championed a road that ran right past them.

She strode up to the easel and peered at Krom's drawing. She shook her head, as though she couldn't believe the line he had drawn was the Bypass and the crude circles he had drawn alongside were meant to represent the old Inyo explosion craters. She said, "Are you a volcanologist, Adrian?"

"I'm trying to run a meeting, Lindsay."

"Are you a volcanologist?"

He folded his arms.

"*Are* you a volcanologist?"

"For anyone here who doesn't know, I've worked around volcanoes for over a decade."

"Not Inyo, you haven't." She drummed her fingers on the drawing. "I monitor the Inyo system every day and I assure you it's quiet."

"Can you assure us it will be quiet tomorrow?"

She smiled, almost in pity. She took the marker from the easel tray and went to work on Krom's overlay and when she'd finished, the map was marked with circles and stars and crosshatches, crude as his. "Vents," she said, "and domes and fumaroles and seismic hot spots. The *whole system* is capable of mischief. We live in active country. There's no way around it. You have to go through it. You can't build a road that does *not* go through it."

A chill ran through me. I thought, suddenly, *no way out.*

"You understand now, Adrian?" She tossed the pen to Krom.

He caught it. "Do you work for FEMA, Lindsay?"

She eyed him. She saw the tables turn.

Say something, I thought.

"Lindsay?" he said, gauging the attention of the room, "are you on staff with the Federal Emergency Management Agency?"

She said, icy, "I consult."

He smiled. "FEMA worked hard to overcome its past troubles. I'm certain they welcome your expertise."

"Yes Adrian. They do."

"Delightful. And so you know how to work the channels to get the resources?"

"We're building the road."

"Who calculated capacities? Who ran the numbers on visitor population fluctuations? What's the peak vehicle load, adjusted for weather and disrupted communications?"

"There is nowhere else—adjusted or not—to build an escape route."

"How many emerg-ops have you run?"

She said, "You mean like Rainier?"

That sent a puzzled buzz through the room. But I sucked in a breath, as did Walter and acting-mayor Jefferson Liu, beside me. I thought, now *she's* the one being unfair. Rainier was Adrian Krom's worst nightmare, the volcano that nearly ended his career. But he's been working his way back. The last thing he needed here was to have to defend himself for a mistake he'd long ago corrected. The last thing *we* needed, I thought, was to question the capability of our emerg-ops guy.

Krom said, icy, "Who ran the numbers, Lindsay? The numbers *here*. Let's stick to the point. Nobody from FEMA ran them *here* because you started before I *got* here."

Jefferson Liu cleared his throat. "Winter was coming, Adrian."

"Winter's here," Krom said. He turned to the easel and drew a new line connecting town to Highway 395.

I strained forward, along with everybody else. Hal's flash lit it up. This new line connected with 395 well south of the active magma chamber—and it did *not* run near the Inyo system, like Lindsay's Bypass. I thought, stunned, Adrian Krom had come up with an alternate escape route.

Lindsay lifted the overlay and squinted at the map. "Pika Canyon?" She let the overlay drop. "That's what you came up with? It's a bobsled run."

"No," Krom said, "it's a forest service road."

"*It's a one-lane dirt road through a narrow canyon.*"

"And," he said, "it can be extended a couple of miles to link up with 395."

"It would take three times as long to evacuate on that as it would on the Bypass."

"You're the volcanologist," he said, "you tell me. Is there any one of your babies that will take out that road?"

Her fine features hardened.

Krom scanned the crowd. "Jimmy! Can you build that?"

Jimmy Gutierrez, cornered, came forward. Jimmy's chief engineer on the Bypass. He's a perpetually sunburned man with a mass of white hair and the gangly mien of a hound, and he paused beside Lindsay. Chief engineer of *her* escape route. "See Lindsay," he said, nervous, "Adrian *did* have me look at a few alternates—just rough estimates."

She lifted her chin.

Walter whispered, "Let's get her out of here."

"Wait," I said, heart slamming. I wanted to hear what Jimmy had to say.

Jimmy began shredding his Styrofoam coffee cup, and turned to Krom. "It's like I told you before, Adrian. Pika's not plowed and it's gonna be hard getting the big cats and dozers up in there and at the other end you gotta go from scratch. You'd have to divert everything we got going now on the Bypass to this here if you was serious about doing it." He stored bits of foam inside the diminishing cup. "Can't do both. It's a question of time and resources."

"No," Krom said, "it's a question of safety."

Lindsay looked like she'd been slapped.

I had the urge to step between Lindsay and Krom but I didn't know what I would say if I did. I didn't know why it had to be a question of safety, anyway, because between the two of them, they should know. Why couldn't the volcanologist and the emergency-ops czar work it out?

"Jeff!" Lindsay looked to the acting mayor. "You saw no reason to doubt the safety of the Bypass back in November when you voted to build it."

Jefferson massaged his goatee. "I didn't know we had an alternative."

People milled on the porch outside, zipping jackets, plunging hands into gloves, broaching the cold of the night.

Walter jostled me. "Do you see her?" In the crush of the meeting's adjournment, we'd lost Lindsay. We made our way forward and went safely down Mike's swept stairs and came upon Krom. He stood shivering in his sweater.

Walter said, "You'll catch your death out here, Adrian."

"Seeing the guests off. Couldn't get near the coat-check."

I said, "What about the road?" and Walter sent me a look, and I said, "I'm sorry, I'm cold, so I'm just cutting to the chase."

Krom laughed. "So you are. Don't worry, I'll convene the Council and we'll discuss the options. Lindsay will join us." His attention shifted. "And here she comes, as we speak."

In her field clothes, Lindsay looked like she looks when she's tramping happily around the caldera looking for trouble. She waved. She had a cell phone in her hand.

"*There* you are," she said to me and Walter. "I just got off the phone with Len. That's Len Carow, Cassie—he's Adrian's boss at FEMA. We all met on Adrian's first volcano. A fellow named Rainier."

I thought, oh shit here we go.

She turned to Krom. "Be good to see Len again. Tomorrow, nine A.M. shuttle from LA—assuming his DC flight gets into LA on time. Must say, I'm miffed he's waited so long, since I've been asking ever since you got here that he send someone to replace you." She gave a graceful shrug. "Bureaucracy. You hear nothing and then the big man himself decides to come." She pocketed the phone. "Fait accompli."

Krom was silent, like he was trying to figure how many ways that phrase could be translated.

"Len simply couldn't understand, Adrian, why you wanted to throw months of roadwork and our hard-earned funds by the wayside. He wants to see for himself."

Krom spoke then. "Be careful what you ask for, Lindsay."

She smiled her cat's smile.

9

I TOOK Highway 203 out of town, counting cars.

This has been the road out of town since the town was built. The Bypass, or any other emergency evacuation route that gets built, will be a secondary way out. Right now, this is the only way out. Highway 203 runs five miles from town down into the high desert, intersecting Highway 395.

I'd never given much thought to traffic on 203, unless I was stuck in it, but I sure did now.

Within a mile, thirty-one cars—twenty with skis and eleven with snowboards—passed in the westbound lane heading into town. I saw three cars in my eastbound lane and a bus in the rearview. Of course it was morning; most people were coming *into* town now to get to the slopes, not trying to get out. On a big ski weekend we probably get twenty thousand people. I increased the traffic on 203 to bumper-to-bumper, peak vehicle load. If the day was clear like this morning—and no flat tires, no disrupted communications—we should all keep crawling along. I adjusted for weather. Fog, snowstorm, black ice—well that would make it stop-and-go.

And to top it all off we'd be evacuating, for awhile anyway, straight into trouble. For it's out here in the caldera where our attention, rightly so, has been fixed.

Out here the rising magma is stretching—and breaking—the earth's crust.

Lindsay likes to tell the Paiute story about Coyote, who is walking along a path and suddenly finds himself in darkness. He meets an old woman who warns that he has entered the mouth of a giant and is now inside the giant's belly. The giant is so huge that his belly fills a valley, so huge that Coyote cannot see all of him, so huge that Coyote had not even realized where he was walking and what lay ahead.

This, then, is the caldera: a volcano so huge you cannot see it for what it is, even as you go about your business within its perimeter. The giant's head, I'd say, is Mammoth Mountain and his mouth is my hometown, and Highway 203 slides down into his belly. The Bypass sidles along the giant's left shoulder and when completed will hit Highway 395 at his northern flank. Krom's road would take the giant's right shoulder to 395 on the southern flank. Deal is, Krom's road doesn't skirt the Inyo craters, and it escapes the giant a whole lot sooner.

I wondered what Georgia would think. I wished she were here to say.

I took 203 across 395 into the desert, parking near the steam vents at the Casa Diablo geothermal plant. Steam vents that, interestingly, deposited sulfur into the soil.

Fire and brimstone.

Indeed, this area is the heart of the growing quake swarms. Had that drawn Georgia out here? The mayor on a learning tour? And who drives her here, and leaves her behind? Somebody who doesn't like her crusade, some realtor pissed about falling prices?

I got my gear and started up the path.

It was a fine field day, crisp and clear. Here and there, a shoot of bitterbrush poked through the snowpack. The grayish squat pinyon pines had yet to produce nuts.

But I was on the lookout for different flora. The telling leaf in Georgia's boot soil was indeed mountain willow. None in sight here but they grow along the banks of nearby Mammoth Creek. A leaf could surely blow here on the wind. And the other flora in the evidence—the tree bark from her mouth—I'd identified as Jeffrey pine. Just north of here, Highway 395 enters a huge forest of Jeffrey. Flora-wise, Casa Diablo held my interest.

I turned my attention to the shooting range.

Someone could kill someone here, I took note, and not be seen from the road.

The range, in the shadow of a long cliff, was entombed in snow and the targets were still down. I chose a spot near the target site. Generally, unburned particles of gunpowder are blown downrange. I kicked through the soft stuff until my heel struck hard-packed snow, then got a trowel from my pack and knelt to dig.

I sank the blade into the snowpack and it was the work, finally, that settled my nerves. Excavating a dig is the most mindless portion of the job but I find it satisfying because every ounce of effort produces a measurable result.

"Hello the camp!" a voice called.

My trowel skipped.

Adrian Krom was striding up the path from the parking lot, scattering loose snow like sand. He drew up to my dig and gave it the once-over. With my gear lying about, it did look as though I was setting up camp.

I got to my feet. "Good morning."

"You worried about last night?"

I found a smile. "Cut to the chase, hey?"

"It's what you said you like. You're like me, in that."

I felt, acutely, aware of myself. He was frankly looking me

over. Was he coming on to me? I kept my eyes steady on him. He wore the big tan parka he'd worn at Red's Meadow. His Ray-bans hung by a brown strap around his neck. His thick brown hair was neatly combed. I had the sudden urge to reach up and tousle it. Crazy. I wasn't attracted to him, and if I had been I certainly wouldn't have jumped him. I could see, though, how women would be attracted. He wasn't handsome but his eyes were arresting—heavy-lidded, polished brown eyes like stones. Strong nose, full mouth. Animal magnetism, you'd call it.

I said, "Yeah, I'm a little worried."

"Don't be. The Council's meeting in a couple of days to consider the options. Be assured, Lindsay and I will cooperate."

"That's what you said last night." It came out harsher than I meant. "Which is good. So listen to her, she knows what she's doing."

"Do you listen to her, about the Bypass?"

I felt, actually, irked with her. I couldn't even *consider* another road without feeling disloyal. I said, "She always orders the grande mocha, but that doesn't mean I won't go for the latte." I shrugged. "Doesn't mean I will, either."

He seemed to be trying to fathom this.

I glanced at my dig. "I should get back to work."

He followed my look. "Find anything?"

"A lot of snow." I shrugged. "What else can I do for you?"

"Get serious."

I went cold. "I'm dead serious."

"Then we're as one."

"I don't think so."

"Georgia was a colleague, Cassie. I want to know what you find. If you require persuading, talk to your chief of police."

"John Amsterdam sent you?"

"John sent me to Walter. Walter told me you would explain what it is you do."

Thank you, Walter. I knelt and took up my trowel. "First, you dig."

Krom got down to his knees beside me, as he had at Red's Meadow.

I said, "Ever take a cake out of a pan?"

"No."

"Finesse it." I pried out a neat wedge of snow.

"I don't have time for coy. What are you digging for?"

I said, evenly, "Okay, here's what it is I do. I take a look at the land. We're in the rain shadow of the mountains, which means low rainfall. Land's mostly flat so there's not much cloud building. All that sunshine evaporates moisture, so there's not a lot of water percolating through the soil leaching out salts. So I expect to find a good distribution of calcites."

"You're digging for calcites."

"Calcite is real common, Adrian."

His eyes shone. "But that's what brought you out here. So calcite must be in your evidence."

"You're not asking how it's done. You're asking what we've found."

"Yes."

"Walter say I'd tell you that?"

"Is Walter your boss?"

"Partner."

"Well then, partner, answer what you will. Is there calcite in the evidence?"

I shrugged. What brought me out here was gunpowder, but that wouldn't be apparent with the targets down.

"Let me speculate," Krom said. "You're a geologist so the evidence must be some kind of earth material. Something you found on the body? Dirt? On her clothes." He snapped his fingers, sound like a gunshot. "And what about the *shoes*? People walk in dirt. My lord, can you follow somebody's tracks after they're dead?"

I said, cautious, "To an extent."

"Then you do amazing work."

I was very nearly flattered. I buried my face in the dig. I struck rock-hard ice and abandoned the trowel. I got matches and a chunk of Presto log from my pack and built a small fire in the hole. Krom watched, rapt. Interested, after all, in how it's done. "Trade secret," I said, "thaw it out."

"Very smart."

Whoa, I'm easily bought. Give me an appreciative audience and I show off. I silently chose a second site and wormed my boot into the snow.

He followed along. "What if the dirt doesn't match? What do you do next?"

"Go somewhere else."

"I hope to hell you find it soon."

"It?"

"The place your evidence came from. That *is* what you're looking for?"

I nodded. Obvious enough. I wasn't out here digging for gold. I knelt and sunk my trowel into the snow. "Did you work closely with Georgia?"

"Very." He began to pace, in front of the dig. "She was invaluable. I want to know what happened to her."

"We all do."

"And I *need* to find out what she found. What she was referring to in her note."

I froze. Hand on my trowel, trowel in the frozen ground. I looked up at him. "You know about that?"

He halted. He came into a crouch, that balancing act of his. He held my look. "You think I came out here for a stroll, Cassie? Of course I know. John told me. *We're* colleagues. The chief of police and the emerg-ops chief have a common goal. Keep this town safe. We shared that goal with our mayor, but now our mayor is dead. Our mayor found something. Something that caused her to write an alarming note. *No way out*. Does that not interest you, Cassie? It interests John. It interests me."

I said, "She wrote 'just found *out*'. Could mean she learned something upsetting, something personal."

"Could be." His eyes warmed to copper. "Could be she found something we need to know about. Considering that Georgia was a conscientious mayor, I would like to know what the hell it was. How about you?"

Yes. Oh *yes*. I said, lightly, "Any guesses?"

"I don't guess. I want to know."

I didn't mind guessing. The wildest-ass of guesses. Something that got her killed. Something someone didn't want her to find. I glanced around. Was it something out here—the geothermal plant? She found evidence of some planned sabotage or something? If the plant got bombed, say, that would sure impact the intersection of highways 395 and 203. That would qualify as no way out. That is, until an escape route is finished.

Krom stood. He checked his watch, a rugged sportsman's model with a brown leather band. "I have to be at Hot Creek in half an hour. I'd like you to come."

"Hot Creek?" It's not far from here, but what the hell? "What's happening at Hot Creek?"

"I think you should come and see for yourself."

10

I LEFT the fires to burn through the ice in my digs and went along with Krom to find out what was up with Hot Creek.

Krom drove, a blue Blazer four-wheel drive. Good vehicle for an evac.

We headed south on Highway 395. If the evac is southward, we'd continue this way the forty miles to the next town, Bishop. If Bishop can't absorb us all, we keep going to Big Pine, and then on to the next town. Sierra towns are strung along the highway, leagues apart, their backsides dug into the mountains. If the evac comes on a big ski weekend, the twenty thousand visitors can head back where they came from, all the way to L.A. I used to make the drive when I was doing grad work at UCLA. I tried to imagine it with an eruption in the rearview.

We stayed on 395 only minutes, then turned onto the narrow Hot Creek road. There are few roads that breach the caldera; they don't go far and they're intermittently plowed.

Krom took another turn, toward our little airport.

I looked at him.

"Len Carow's due in," he said, pulling into the parking lot, "and no, I didn't forget to mention it back there, I chose to sandbag you here." He stopped the Blazer and shut off the engine. "Len's my immediate superior at FEMA HQ. Len's my boss. There are some dirty politics being played. I didn't think I had a chance in hell of getting you to come if I told you that back at Casa Diablo."

I sat stiff. He got that right. "I don't like being sandbagged."

"Then let me make it worth your while. Decisions are being made that affect you. I'm making some of them. Len's aiming to stop me—courtesy of Lindsay. It's that simple."

"You're saying he's going to fire you?"

"He can't without cause, and I'll give him no cause. As long as I have the support of your Council, I'll do my job. They invited me, and they can ask me to leave, but I won't give them cause."

"The escape clause."

He gave a half-smile. "Is that what you call it?"

"It's what Lindsay calls it," I said, then softened. "Look, I just want somebody who knows what he's doing and if you're it, then outstanding."

"I am it. But Len's not interested in my qualifications."

"Why?"

"Goes back to Mount Rainier. Up in Washington state. Lindsay told you about Rainier?"

"She did. But tell me your side."

He stared straight ahead, at the runway. "It was my first posting. I wanted to do my best. I wrote my own eruption-sim software and ran the numbers, of course, but I didn't stop there. I got to know the towns in the volcano's flow path. I drove the roads, I walked the land. I knew by how much the population of Puyallup was swelled by its annual fair. I went with the Tacoma mayor to his favorite brewery, and I went back again to meet the locals. I needed to understand their fears, and I needed them to trust me when I made the hard calls." He craned his neck and peered at the sky, where a slip of silver separated itself from the blue. "Len and Lindsay were at Rainier, too. Len was senior to me and he thought he should be in my job. She thought so too. Len and Lindsay. You didn't find them at the breweries, they kept to their own."

I said, "She's a wine drinker" and then I said, "never mind."

"Rainier got serious but the volcanologists kept dithering. I had a call to make—and it's a hell of a call to order the evacuation of entire towns—and the officials, my *friends* at this point, were on the spot too. But my obligation was damn clear. It was to the locals. The everyday people who were sitting in the way of disaster. I made the call. We emptied the towns. It was a month before it became clear Rainier was not going all the way." His head turned, as he followed the jet down onto the runway. "Cost the towns a lot of money. Lost business. Disruption. I felt like hell about that. But Lindsay..." He unbuckled his seat belt. "She crucified me. She told the press I was out of my depth."

His voice held so much bitterness I thought he might stop.

He went on. "I accepted a demotion. And I'm still trying to rebuild my reputation. At the start, I did it on my own time. When a volcano acted up—anywhere—I flew there on my own nickel. I listened and I learned. FEMA was still rebuilding its own reputation and they had to be convinced to give me another shot. I convinced them. I've been proving my worth. Again, and again." He angled in the seat to face me. "I made a mistake at Rainier, I won't dodge it, but it was a mistake in timing, not priorities. I wanted to save lives. That's what I aim to do here. I want you to know you can count on me to be single-minded in the pursuit of my job. I'd like to show you. If you'll come to Hot Creek, there's a slight chance in hell Len Carow will agree to come too. You're one of the lives I'm here for, and he can't ignore that. I'm going to show him I'm on the job. He'll have to put it into the record."

I believed Lindsay had crucified him, all right. I knew she didn't suffer fools lightly, not when it came to her job. But I wasn't convinced Krom had been a fool, at Rainier. I had to give him credit, now, for owning up to his mistake. And I couldn't argue with his priorities. But if Lindsay was trying to crucify him again, now, she'd have a reason. She would never let her animosity interfere with her volcano.

"I'll come," I said. "But just so you know—Lindsay taught me everything I know about this volcano."

Len Carow clearly did not like being sandbagged, either.

He stood by Krom's Blazer, suitcase in hand, frowning. "Fuck d'y think yr'doin, Adrian?" He waved an unlit cigarette at me. "Sorry—Oldfield?—language."

He reminded me of one of those financial types Walter watches on TV: thin-faced, thin-haired, glasses, cranky. I said, "No problem."

"S'posed to call Lindsay when I get in, Adrian. Go see her road."

"Did she inform you of the upcoming Council meeting on the subject? Nothing's set in stone."

Carow gave a brusque nod.

"So, can you spare us an hour right now, Len?" Krom skated a glance at me.

Carow toyed with his cigarette, sliding his fingers along its length, upending it, reversing it.

I said, "Hot Creek's just up the road."

11

We bumped along in silence the two plowed miles to the creek.

There were several cars in the clifftop parking lot. "Tourists," Krom said. "Hot Creek's on the sightseeing maps."

Len Carow grunted.

As we got out of the Blazer, Krom took a pack and hitched himself into it. He caught my look, and put a finger to his lips.

We went to the rim. We both watched Carow look down.

Hot Creek is a meandering watercourse that has dug a deep gash into an old rhyolite volcanic flow. For the most part the creek is placid but in places, like down below, it churns where channels of cold snowmelt meet magma-heated water so hot it will take off your skin. I used to know how to find the warm currents where the waters mix, and I used to come out here to soak under the Milky Way. I used to worry about the boys catching me in the raw, not about what put hot water into a cold river.

Krom set off and Carow and I followed, making our way down the switchbacks into the gorge. Carow paused to read the Forest Service sign warning that swimming is inadvisable: arsenic in the water, sporadic geyser eruptions, abrupt changes in temperature. Lindsay had the sign put up several years ago, last time the volcano stirred. The message got through. No one dips in Hot Creek any more.

There were a few people down here, picnicking on snow-cleared rocks, kids poking around. Krom threw Carow a look, then hiked a thumb downstream.

We set off downriver. This part of the creek is deceptively bucolic. Long-stemmed reeds haired the snowy banks and ouzels skimmed the water in search of insects. The waters churned, and steamed, but it looked inviting as a hot tub. We hiked in silence, Krom growing noticeably tense, then we rounded a bend and Carow stopped to read the second Forest Service sign, which warned that continuing beyond this point was inadvisable. Nevertheless, the trail continued beyond this point, and within a few yards it slipped into a steamy haze and then disappeared around a bend.

Carow indicated the sign. "Yours, Adrian?"

I spoke. "Lindsay's. It gets dicey further downstream."

"Fine," Carow said, turning, "end'a the line."

"No," Krom said, "we keep to the path and we'll be safe."

"We go back'n we'll be safe."

Krom said, "It's part of the job, Len, seeing it. Looking at it on a map doesn't put you in the shoes of the people we came here for."

Carow glanced at me. "Adrian likes't play hero." His look shifted to the steamy landscape downstream. "Fuck heroes. Not what we do."

Krom said, "Cassie?"

He didn't have to worry. I was hooked. I wanted to know what had changed downstream. I wanted to know what was in Krom's pack. Mostly, though, I felt Krom had made an exceedingly good point. FEMA should get out in the field. I said, "Yup, I'm coming."

Krom threw me a smile. Best friends.

Carow, with a sour look, stalked past the sign.

We set off downriver, meeting the leading edges of drifting steam. We rounded the bend and surprised a damp-faced man with a camera peering like a kid from his jacket, and then we passed him and continued on.

It was like passing from winter to a peculiar kind of summer, for the air grew warmer and the thinning snow receded until we entered a landscape licked nearly clean by steam and heat. The steam-pocked rocks were the colors of summer, pink and orange, and the walls of the gorge had been stained a daisy sulfur yellow. The bubbling hot pools and sucking mud pots and hissing vents filled the air with the industrious thrum of activity. A frog lent his croak to the music. At creek-side a seam had ripped open along the bank, spitting mud and pebbles like grease from a frying pan. Everywhere there was steam, billowing from fumaroles, clinging to us as we skirted the vents, lending a brassy tinge to the sky.

Carow had to remove his glasses.

I hadn't been here for two years but I'd prepared myself for the intensity of activity. Lindsay monitored it, Lindsay kept me posted. Still, a vague unease settled over me, as if I'd returned to a familiar street after a long absence and the houses and trees were there, yet something had changed. I couldn't put my finger on it. It wasn't the increased vigor. I was, simply, disoriented and I didn't know why.

Carow paused to look at a gem-like hot pool.

Krom moved to stand beside him.

The pool was large. Its milky blue water steamed. Bubbles skated across the surface. Minerals dissolved by the water had built a thin white lip around the edge. I knew this pool. I glanced around. No, maybe not. Hot pools change. I turned back.

The water domed, as if the pool were drawing a breath. I said, "Back off. *Now.*"

Krom threw an arm across Carow's chest and we all leapt back as a geyser jetted into the air, sizzling steam.

Carow muttered "fuckin hero" and fumbled in his pocket for a cigarette.

I turned to scan the creek and found a bulge jutting off the cliff like a rooster's breast. I looked downriver to the spot where the creek takes a hard right hook. I came back to the pool—and now knew where I was. I *did* know this pool. Hydrothermal phenomena come and go, but this was not a question of coming and going. This pool used to sit out here all by itself and there was *nothing* within a couple hundred meters. Now, it's spitting close to the mud pots and fumaroles we'd just passed. The old neighborhood used to be one block long. Now, it's two.

Did Lindsay know? She must.

Krom had moved over to inspect a shelf of rock. He unslung his pack and removed an oblong box. So that's the big surprise, I thought. It looked to be some kind of monitoring device. I moved in closer, and my eyes stung. Krom turned. His eyes were reddened.

"*Gas,*" I said, "move away. Hydrochloric, I'm not sure, some sort of acid."

"I'll let you know." He fiddled with the box, coughing, then retreated.

"Whose *is* that?"

"Mine." He wiped his eyes. "Work around enough volcanoes and you learn how to take their temperature. When it's your call, you get interested. I don't depend on the scientists. They're clubby. I got hold of one of their devices and improved it. Mine has a camera, and the data can be telemetered. I always offer one of mine for their use but they don't like innovations from outside the field." He shrugged. "So they watch him their way and I watch him mine."

This was for the record, I thought, showing Carow that Krom's on top of things.

Carow was mashing out his cigarette, which he'd tossed at the word *gas*.

"You have to keep watch on him," Krom was saying. "There's one thing you should never forget—he's an unpredictable chum. But it's not personal. He doesn't care who gets hurt. Which makes him all the more dangerous, don't you think?"

It sure sounded personal to me. Maybe that's what he'd learned during his exile after Rainier. Take it personally.

Krom turned abruptly and went to the creek bank. He dropped to a crouch, examining something.

I tensed. More gas?

He stayed poised on the bank for what seemed like minutes, then he lunged and stood, all in one movement. He held something cupped in his hands. He walked past us and approached the hot pool, testing the ground with each step. He was within a stone's throw of the water.

Carow turned to watch. "*What* the...?"

I said, "You're too close, Adrian."

Krom crouched, holding his cupped hands outstretched. Then he brought his hands to his chest—like getting ready to pitch—and he did pitch, a soft one, and his ball landed just at the edge of the pool and I wondered if he'd missed, if he'd meant to throw it in.

It was a small frog. Yellow-legged mountain frog. It sat frozen, but for the eyes, which swiveled wildly. Then its legs flexed and it launched and landed and hopped again, unhappy with each landing because the ground was rough with pumice. It hopped once more—this time toward the pool, the bubbling sound of water—but it did not land as it must have expected in wet creek-side mud. It lit on the thin lip of the pool. The delicate crust cracked and gave way beneath the minuscule weight of the frog, and crust and frog dropped into the scalding blue water.

I clenched in expectation of a scream, even the smallest scream, but there was nothing.

Carow was looking at Krom with open disgust.

"Picture the guy with the camera going in for a closeup of that pool," Krom said. "Picture kids running loose." He folded his arms. "If Lindsay'd agreed to close this area—and I mean barricade the road, shut off access to the whole place—we wouldn't be here having this talk and that little creature would die of old age."

Carow stared. "Why didn't she close it?"

I didn't know that Krom had asked her. "If she said no, *listen*."

Krom flipped a hand. "She says jump, you all jump. She says wait, you all wait. I say barricade, she says it's too soon."

I said, "She puts up a barricade too soon and she's crying wolf."

"Define *too soon*."

I couldn't.

He smiled. "You've all been too close too long. The cult of Lindsay Nash."

I said, tight, "She knows this place like you'll never know it."

"Then she should know better." Krom strode over to pick up his pack. "This place warrants closing."

Carow worked another cig from his pocket, and the white stick steadied his hand. "Fuckin good idea."

I felt the heat rise. I'm a fool. You fool, I thought, you clueless little sandbagged frog, you sure played your part. Getting Carow out here so Krom could turn Hot Creek into a battleground. And Lindsay's not here to defend herself.

I walked away.

Krom called after me, “Cassie, this isn’t a question of loyalties.”

I kept going. I knew Lindsay wasn’t against a barricade just because Krom was for it. She had a reason. Don’t cry wolf. A fumarole hissed as I passed. I knew if it got to the point that the whole area needed closing, she’d say so. She’d come out and build the damn barricade herself.

My eyes stung and my throat was on fire.

I thought of Coyote. Coyote, in the end, did escape the giant’s belly: he came upon a swelling volcano and recognized it as the heart of the giant. He could not resist. He pulled out his hunting knife and hacked at the heart. Lava spurted, and the belly trembled, and the giant opened his mouth in a roar of pain and Coyote ran out with the terrible fire scorching his heels.

12

"So you coming out for the race tomorrow?" my brother asked.

Jimbo and I were shoulder to shoulder at the kitchen counter, shredding lemon peel and grating nutmegs. Hot spiced cider in our house has always been a beverage of balm—bad day, fall on the slopes, D on a test, didn't get the job, out comes the cider pot. My day today, watching Krom cook a frog, had been less than perfect. Jimbo's day, training up at Lake Mary, had been foul as well. He'd missed a shot and taken two falls, and in the biathlon 20K race that's all she wrote.

As if losing a race was the worst thing that could happen tomorrow at Lake Mary.

I focused on the lemon peel. Not my job to make a fuss about race scheduling. I said, lightly, "Tomorrow? I really should wash my hair."

Jimbo fired a nutmeg at me.

I caught it. "Shoot like that tomorrow and you'll win."

"Wash your hair tomorrow and I'll shoot you."

I said, "You are seriously sick," and he nodded. The old black humor. I'd finally adopted it myself, the family black-humor gene expressing. The humor got darker as we grew from kids into teenagers, from teenagers into adults, as time took us farther from our brother Henry's death, by God. Jimbo and I are living together now because we both got the jumps after a big quake swarm hit a couple weeks ago. My crummy condo is a couple blocks away and I've been gradually ferrying my stuff here. Jimbo's scummy house, rented with four other guys, is on the other side of town and Jimbo goes back mainly to play beer pong. It's weird, but good, living again at home.

Technically, we're house-sitting while Mom and Dad are in Scotland settling property Dad inherited. Jimbo has his old room upstairs and since my old room is now my parents' workroom, I have the cottage out back. And we seem to feel better having the jumps together, here. Tonight, the old black humor fit like a skin. Would you rather be buried in lava, Jimbo asked after the latest quake, or smothered in ash? It's good to be back home.

I tossed the nutmeg back to him. "Trade you for a biathlon cartridge."

He missed. "Say what?"

"Cartridge. You shoot them instead of nutmegs."

After Hot Creek, I'd finished my dig at Casa Diablo and then returned to the lab. I'd spent several hours oven-drying my samples and catching up on paperwork. I'd nuked a burrito for dinner. I'd come home beat and taken a marathon hot shower. In an hour or so—after my cider nightcap—I plan to haul my rejuvenated carcass back to the lab and find out what I'd got at Casa. And if the gods are with me, and the soil and the gunpowder match the evidence, I'll know where Georgia last walked.

And if the gods are indifferent, and there is no match, I'll know where I have to go next: the biathlon range. Which is okay. If she last walked there, it did not mean anything other than she took a stroll at Lake Mary. And so I convinced myself that my dread of a dig at the biathlon range was nothing more than dread of digging through a shitload of snow. And then, as I'd been showering, I'd had the brainstorm of getting a cartridge from Jimbo. I know this about biathlon: the ammo is specifically designed to work in the cold. Few other than biathletes use the stuff and they use it in limited circumstances. If I could rule out biathlon powder, I'd save myself a dig.

I said, "Georgia picked up some gunpowder and I'm trying to trace it. If it's biathlon, that'll narrow the field." And if it's not, that'll make my day.

Jimbo gave me a sidelong look, then swept up a handful of nutmeg and lemon peel and carried it to the pot of cider on the stove.

Our kitchen is huge—our house is huge, like a rambling old train station—and the counter is a long way from the stove. My brother remained across the room, needlessly stirring the cider. Jimbo is slender and wiry and almost always in motion. He has wing-cut blond hair that sails with every move. Even indoors, just hanging out, he moves—stretching, bobbing on the balls of his feet like he's going to launch into a sprint, coming around you to knead your shoulders. Now he stood quietly, hand on the spoon.

"It's a quick test," I said, "compare the evidence to known powder."

"Mine."

"Anybody's would do. You and I just happen to be living in the same house."

"You saying Georgia got whacked on the biathlon course?" He gave a weak grin.

I did not return it. "I'm saying she might have walked where you shoot. Nothing more." I waited. "*So*, my brother, do I get a cartridge?"

"No can do. My gear's not here."

Where, then? I knew his skis were in the ski locker on the front porch, with mine. Where else would his shooting gear be but safely stowed in his room? I said, "Then help me with this. Obviously, you guys shoot up at Lake Mary on the range. Anywhere else?"

He popped his thumb on the spoon handle. "What makes you think you got biathlon powder?"

What makes you so touchy about it? I said, slowly, "It's one option."

"There's a shitload of other options. Why don't you go scope out Casa?"

"I have."

He gave the spoon a shove and headed out of the kitchen. "So good luck."

"Wait a minute."

He started to hum—the *Looney Tunes* theme—then flattened himself against the doorjamb. "Look, I can't get into this. I don't have space for it. I just got space for my skis and my rifle and my body and my mind. *Race*, remember? I gotta keep it in control for the Cup." He jerked upright and moved into the hallway.

I was absurdly relieved. It's just Jimbo being Jimbo. This is the way my brother always plays it. Put in an appearance and then get called away by a pressing need to do whatever he wants to do. Clear his plate from the table and leave me to do the dishes. This is what Jimbo does best—enlist your sympathy for whatever is bedeviling him, then bug out. So now he's bedeviled by his lousy performance at practice today, and he doesn't want to carry an image of Georgia tomorrow at Lake Mary.

I didn't blame him. And I didn't want to dig for biathlon powder unless I had to. I went after him and blocked him in the hallway. "Answer me, Jimbo, is there anywhere else you shoot?"

"I go out in back and plink at rats in the woodpile."

"*Biathlon*. I'm going to sample the range at Lake Mary. Should I be looking anywhere else? It's a simple question."

"Just Casa, like I said."

"*Biathlon*, Jimbo

"*Yes*, Catherine." He raised his hands like I'd put a gun in his back. "That's a ten-four, ma'am. We did, in the line of duty, shoot biathlon ammo at the targets at Casa Diablo."

"Come on," I said.

He swiveled, grinning, hands still high. "It's this way, ma'am. We like to practice with the same ammo we use in a race. Can't practice at Lake Mary in the summer. Not allowed to shoot the campers. Summer we shoot at Casa. Ma'am." He sidestepped around me.

"*I'm trying to find out where Georgia died.*"

Silence in the hallway. Whine of warp speed from the TV in the living room—into the unknown. He said, finally, "Get's weird, you know, having a forensics chick for a sister."

"Gets weird having a brother who ducks the question."

"I *answered*—Casa and Mary." He gave me a light punch in the shoulder. "Hey, here's another answer for you—got an idea for Bill's birthday. Vegas. Hotel, meals, shows, and then he can roll the dice with the leftovers. Win maybe, blow his mind." Jimbo sauntered toward the living room.

This is what Jimbo does second best—switch the subject. I called after him, "I still need a cartridge."

His voice came, above the threshold of hyperspace, "I'll get one to you."

I knew my brother. I knew he'd just bagged me. I dearly hoped it was just Jimbo being Jimbo. I took the stairs to the second-floor hall.

The lights were off. You a shareholder in the power company? my father asks anyone who leaves the lights on. I flipped the switch; Scotland's halfway across the world. I passed my old room and then the laundry room—which had been, once, Henry's room, where I was babysitting him, bored out of my mind, watching out the window as my older brother and his friends set off bottle rockets, yearning to join them, paying no attention to Henry jumping on his bed. Falling and striking his skull.

And then I came to Jimbo's room and went inside and shut the door and turned on the light.

My brother's room was neat, uncluttered. His childhood stuff, whatever he'd kept, was stored like mine in the attic.

I passed his dresser; drawers were too short to accommodate a .22 rifle. I yanked open the closet door. Clothes, shoes, a damp wool sock. I cursed it. Angry at having to search, angry for letting myself search. My hand brushed heavy nylon. I shoved deeper into the closet and pulled out a long bag.

It was his gun sack. He had lied. His gear was here.

I went very cold, and then I told myself you don't know anything yet.

I worked the zipper, removed the rifle, and felt around the bottom of the sack. Nothing. Where was the ammo? I'd seen his gear often enough, spread on the living room floor. There should be a cleaning kit and a metal ammo box.

Okay, I thought, there's another way. The rifle stock, where I gripped it, had an ammo clip attached. I had once pestered Jimbo into showing me how his rifle worked; I'd missed the target several times and lost interest. My fingers played along the edge of the clip, found a catch, and it popped out. It was so small that I wondered if Jimbo ever fumbled it in the rush to snap it into place for firing. Seconds count like dollars in a race, he'd told me. At the open end of the clip was a cartridge. I rolled my thumb across the bullet tip, wiggling it, but it didn't want to come free. Jimbo never showed me how you got the cartridge in and out of the clip.

I expelled a breath. Toughest thing in a race, Jimbo says, is that you're skiing so hard your pulse hits 180 and then you dead stop and try to get your breathing under control so you can shoot straight.

I knew how to get a cartridge. I snapped the clip into firing position, the way Jimbo taught me. I found the bolt, palmed it up, drew it back, slid it forward, pressed it down. Should be a round in the chamber now. I fumbled with the clip, seconds adding up like dollars, and extracted it. Okay, four rounds in the clip, one in the rifle. This was like my first days in the lab, keeping meticulous track of everything I touched.

I had a loaded rifle. If it went off, it was going to shoot a hole in my brother's ceiling and bring him stampeding upstairs.

Avoiding the trigger like the plague, I pulled the bolt upward, and back. There was a pop as the bolt-action ejected the cartridge. I stashed the slick metal plug in my pocket. Breathe. I replaced the clip, jockeyed the rifle into its sack, and returned it to the closet. I was at the door when I realized what I'd done wrong. There are five targets on the range and the athlete carries five rounds in the clip, one per target. I'd left Jimbo with four. Of course he'd check before racing, and reload, but he'd know a cartridge was missing.

And maybe by that time I'd know why he lied, why he hadn't wanted me to compare his powder to my evidence. My brother has contributed his share to less-than-perfect days but he's never before told me a bald-assed lie.

My mind jumped to Eric on the retrieval, trying to send Walter and me back. Explaining, at the cop house, how he hadn't wanted to see me upset. I didn't know what his real reason was but I did know it was a real bad call.

I thought of Stobie on the retrieval, chiming in with Eric, giving me that bizarre cold smile.

My pulse was heading back up.

Eric and Stobie, two bad calls. Jimbo, one lame lie. Three biathletes trying to keep me from doing my job, or so it seemed to me. There had to be a reason but it was beyond belief that any of them contributed to Georgia's death. They'd never had trouble with Georgia.

The same could not be said about Lindsay, who'd clashed with Georgia as long as I could remember. Or Mike Kittleman, kicked off the biathlon team by Georgia.

I fled my brother's room.

The hallway light was dazzling, painful. I found the switch and flipped it off, saving my father a penny or two, then took the two flights of stairs down to the garage.

13

I WAS on my way to the lab, at the intersection of Canyon and Minaret, when a blue Blazer passed heading east.

Other than my Subaru and the Blazer, the roads were deserted. It was nearly midnight. A gibbous moon irradiated the night, and if Adrian Krom had looked my way he could have recognized me and my car.

I waited until the tail lights disappeared, as the Blazer followed Minaret's bend. The slug in my pocket pressed into my thigh, which argued for a left turn toward the lab. Instead, I turned right and headed east on Minaret.

It's the unexpected that shakes faith. A lame lie. A frog sacrifice.

For all my worry, I couldn't figure the frog. Everything was working for Krom—I got Carow out to the creek, Krom got his monitor on the record. The place was clearly dangerous. He could have just gone with that, playing the hero and making Lindsay the fool. Maybe he thought he needed the frog for dramatic effect. Maybe, but it gave me the creeps.

We wound along Minaret Road, me keeping my distance, pacing him.

I followed Adrian Krom, I guess, because he was beyond my reckoning and I wanted to know where was going at midnight in January.

Minaret intersected Highway 203 and Krom turned left and then I knew we were heading out of town.

And then, partway down 203, he stopped. I hit my own brakes. Looked like he'd stopped right about where the road arches over a stream bed. Road humps there, bridging the culvert, and I thought maybe it's that little rise in elevation that gave him a new angle in his rearview, gave him a new line of sight that revealed my identity.

I didn't know what to do. Turn around and go back? Drive on and say hi, where you going? And then he asks, where are *you* going all alone at midnight on a Saturday night?

He started up again and I followed suit.

He took 203 to the intersection with 395 and turned south, as did I. We accelerated to sixty. We had the highway to ourselves. We slowed as we approached the Hot Creek turnoff, and he took it.

I didn't have the guts to follow him there.

I continued on 395 the five miles or so to the McGee Canyon exit and doubled back, thinking I was going to head straight to town and the lab. But then as I approached the Hot Creek turnoff and peered along that road and didn't spot any tail lights I thought, I can do this without being seen.

I knew what I used to do at Hot Creek at midnight, but he didn't have a date.

I took the turnoff.

No barricade. No skull and crossbones. I stopped dead in the road. No tail lights ahead. I checked the rearview. Nobody coming up from some hiding place to say boo, either.

I nudged the gas. Warp speed, into the unknown. The Subaru did about five miles per hour, undulating over the snowplowed bumps. A few yards short of the Hot Creek parking lot, I did a U-turn and parked by the snowbank. I grabbed my parka, got out, locked the car, and started to walk.

I went back and got a lug wrench from my tool kit, then started off again.

The Blazer was alone in the parking lot. About twelve hours ago, Krom had driven Carow and me here. Now, Krom's Blazer was empty. He must have gone down.

I wondered why.

The trail down the gorge switchbacks several times and it is possible, by hugging the cliff wall, to avoid looking down. Which means anyone down there looking up doesn't have the line of sight to see me. At least most of the way. I inched down, my boots making the faintest squeak on the packed snow. I hoped that the creek would be making enough noise below to mask my approach.

At the bottom, there was no immediate cover. I came the final steps in a crouch, gripping the wrench.

It was a beautiful night, moonlight bleaching the snow whiter, moonlight silvering the water. Cold enough to shiver when you stop, which made the heat emanating from the creek all the more inviting. I've soaked out here under just such a moon as this, with a beer banked in the snow for when I'd cooked enough.

I listened. Rush of creek water. Hiss of hot water hitting a cold pocket.

I scanned the creek and banks and saw nothing I hadn't seen here before. I sprinted to a tall boulder and crouched there.

He must have gone downstream.

There came another sound, from the creek. I've heard this sound before—I've made it. It's when you accidentally hit a cold spot and the shock of it pulls a *hnnnh* from you and you madly paddle away. I sat still, still as Coyote when he first learns he has entered the giant's belly.

And now came a cry—part coyote, part exhilaration.

I've made that sound too but only when I was out here alone.

I peeked around the boulder just enough to gain a line of sight on the creek, and now I saw him.

He was bronzed by the moonlight.

Nude as a Greek god. I could see him down to the thighs. He stood thigh-deep in the middle of the creek. He had to be standing on one of those sandbars that abruptly change the water's depth. His body was better than I'd thought. I'd thought that under his loose-fitting clothes some of his bulk was fat, but he was solid.

He crouched, then, cupping his hands to dip water and I thought, I've done that, dousing my face with the water to cool off, but he didn't splash his face, he drank. *God.* Hadn't he read Lindsay's sign? This water's not fit to drink. Even when I was a kid out here we didn't *drink* it. Sure, we'd get some in our mouths inadvertently, and we'd spit it out. The taste is bitter. We'd accuse each other of peeing in the creek. My brother would needle me—Cassie drinks water fish screw in, ha ha ha—and I'd swear up and down I didn't drink any such thing. But Krom drank.

He straightened.

No one swims in Hot Creek anymore. Except Krom.

He raised his arms, showing muscle, and gave a long stretch. The move turned his inner arms outward, my way. The skin there was a shade lighter. There was something on his inside right arm, covering half the forearm. Dark, mottled, with a whitish background. If I had to guess I'd say it was a tattoo.

I realized I'd never seen him with his shirt sleeves rolled up.

He dove into the water and went under and I held my breath along with him and nearly burst before he came up, farther downstream. Now just his head was visible, wet and brown and slick. He had surfaced a few feet, at most, from where the steam gathers above the water.

That was risky.

The knees of my jeans were wet from the snow. I shivered, planning. Get out before he does. If he goes first he'll pass the Subaru and he'll know—assuming he didn't already know. And that's assuming he doesn't see me pressed against the boulder on his way to the trail. Where were his clothes? I'd have put mine on the boulder so they'd stay dry. Maybe he'd gone in the water downstream. Maybe he was heading back that way to get dressed.

I was right.

He came out of the water downstream, rising so smooth and fast that the water sheeted off him. He stopped at the bank, feet still in water. One more step and he's walking barefoot in snow.

There came a sound. I've made that sound here, more than once. Laughter.

But it scared the bejesus out of me.

His laugh was rich. He was having a good full-throated laugh at something. He threw his head back, baring his throat like he was going into that coyote exhilaration cry again but he just went silent and stared up into the night.

I was wrong. He wasn't getting dressed. I started to rise.

His head snapped down and he looked right at me.

I froze.

He was not looking at me. He was scanning the creek bank, the water, the gorge wall, the clifftop, then back again to fix on the creek. He was staring at the spot where the steam boils off, where the water gets just too hot. And then with his surprising grace he bent at the waist, right arm outstretched, palm up, tattoo showing again in the moonlight. He was bowing. He was bowing to the steamy creek.

He straightened, right arm still outstretched, and extended his middle finger.

I sank back down into the snow, hugging the boulder.

What had we gotten ourselves into?

I got so cold I had to move, and when I looked again he was gone. Underwater, downstream, or maybe the earth had swallowed him up. I didn't know and I didn't wait to find out. I took my chance, skittering across the snow to the trail. Up the switchbacks, boots thudding, heartbeats not far behind. I hugged the wall and never once looked down or back and so I didn't know if he resurfaced and watched me hightail it out of there.

As I passed his blue Blazer I glanced inside and solved one mystery, at least. His clothing was piled neatly on the passenger seat, and his boots sat patient as dogs on the floor. Whoa. He'd walked buck naked down into the gorge. He'd walked stone cold barefoot in the snow. That's what he does at midnight on a Saturday night in the middle of January.

I took off in a fast lope and as my hands swung free I realized I'd left the wrench in the snow.

I loped to the Subaru, fumbled the key, scratched the paint around the lock, got the door open, and congratulated myself on parking the car so that it faced the way out.

Speeding north on 395, I kept watch in the rearview for my unpredictable chum.

14

WERE it not for Jimbo's cartridge burning a hole in my pocket, I would have gone straight home for reheated cider and a hot bath.

Instead, I cranked the lab thermostat up to seventy and nuked this morning's coffee. I got the tube of gunpowder from the secure evidence vault, hitched my stool up to the comparison scope, yanked the nose off Jimbo's cartridge, and spilled half the powder onto the floor. *Slow down*. I slowed, pouring the remaining powder into a culture dish.

I got up and locked the lab door and pulled down the blinds.

Now focus. I focused.

Gunpowder, Walter likes to say, has a fingerprint. During manufacture it is cut into tiny grains, and the cutting leaves tool marks. These show not only who manufactured the powder but also what batch it came from. The tool marks are like the whorls on fingertips.

I put a grain of Jimbo's powder on one slide and an evidence grain on a second slide. There had been a wealth of gunpowder in the soil from Georgia's boots—seven distinct makes. I'd put one of each make into the envelope that was couriered to the gunpowder lab, and kept the rest. I had eighteen grains to compare against Jimbo's powder.

I snapped the slides in place. Two fields of view came through the prisms of the comparison bridge, putting the grains into lineup. Jimbo's biathlon grain was dimpled, like clay indented with pencil points. The first evidence grain was cross-hatched. No match. I did the next. No match. And no match a third, and a fourth time.

I paused, thinking I heard steps outside. Nothing. Nerves. I refocused.

Evidence grain five, shiny as a new dime, was dimpled.

Evidence grain five—which Georgia had picked up in one of her last steps on earth—was a dead-on match to the grain from Jimbo's cartridge, the ammo he had lied about. I felt a little sick.

Same dimples showed up six more times. That made eight total that matched, out of eighteen grains. Nearly half the powder from Georgia's boots was biathlon powder.

Biathlon powder, I had to remind myself—not, exclusively, Jimbo's powder. Any biathlete's powder would presumably have matched.

Okay. Move on to the samples I'd collected at Casa Diablo.

I first went to the window and scissored apart two vanes of the blinds but all I could see was the reflection of my own eye in the glass. I closed my eyes and saw Krom at the creek, only in my fatigued imagination he bowed and extended his middle finger to me. I let the blinds snap shut.

Death from being a dumbshit.

I went back to work.

From lockup I got the Casa Diablo soil samples and combed through them, separating out the gunpowder. I lined up the Casa grains, one by one, against the evidence grains. The only make that matched was dimples. Like Jimbo said, they practiced at Casa with the powder they use in a race.

But I still had six makes of gunpowder from the evidence soil that did not match any of the Casa grains, which argued that Georgia's boot soil did not originate there.

Dimples was my only ID. Dimples, in quantity. Dimples said, you lose. You're going to have to dig through a shitload of snow at the biathlon range.

Tomorrow. Right after the races.

I was cleaning up when I heard a noise outside. I grabbed the nearest thing to hand—the heavy marble pestle from the bowl of the mortar, our mineral-crusher—and went to the door and listened. Silence, then a shuffling like snow sloughing off a tree limb. Then silence again. I could stand no more. I opened the door and came out.

Krom was at the window, forefinger raised. He said, "Saw your lights. Didn't want to disturb you. Didn't want to just walk on by like we're strangers." He touched his finger to the window then wiped his hand on his pants. "Your window is dirty."

I came all the way out and looked. The glow from inside the lab seeped through the blinds enough to illuminate the dusty glass and show the circle and dots and curved line. It made me think of the circles and lines he'd drawn on the map overlay at the Inn, only that drawing was of the Inyo craters and evac routes and this, which he'd put on my window, was a smiley face.

Show Len Carow, I thought. And tell him about the creek.

Show him a smile and tell him about a swim?

I said, "What are you doing here this time of night?"

"I'm a night owl, like you. I like to keep an eye on things when everybody else is sleeping. No distractions. Some nights I stroll through town for hours. Gives me the feeling I own the place." He pulled a wrench from his big parka pocket and held it out, making me a little bow. "Yours, I believe."

I had no choice but to accept it. Subaru lug wrench in one hand, lab pestle in the other, I stood speechless, armed to the teeth.

He smiled and bid me good night.

15

TWO MILES SOUTHWEST OF TOWN, one thousand feet higher, the Lakes Basin is more wintry than town. Trees are weighted with snow, ground-feeding birds have gone, lakes are frozen.

This is nirvana for the biathlon. The race course begins on the white bank of Lake Mary, climbs and drops through forests of white fir and mountain hemlock and loops the skiers back to Mary to shoot the targets. They'll make the circuit five times in the 20K and nearly die before they reach the finish.

The Cup races were scheduled here a year ago, and when the rumbling started and US biathlon officials made noises about moving this Cup, Georgia and Lindsay went to bat and kept it here. I envisioned a USBA official in stripes like an umpire sandbagging Georgia—near the stocky Jeffrey pines on the lake's south side. Our volcano has scared the bejesus out of him and he and Georgia come to blows.

Absurd, but I wished for a scenario like this.

I saw Lindsay pacing the officials area like a mother bear.

She damn well better have taken the temperature of the volcano before she came up here this morning.

The athletes were tense: stretching, tying on bibs, rewaxing skis, zeroing rifles on the range to ensure that the sights are true. The crowd was loose, shooting the shit about who's off and who's on today. It was mostly locals with a mix of foreign boosters who follow the circuit. Nearly all the foreigners spoke English, and the predominant accents were Scandinavian and Russian because these are the demigods in biathlon. There was the smell of damp wool and beer and chocolate, and the sound of rifle fire from the range, like corn popping. At the far end of the spectator area a snowshoe volleyball game was in progress.

Walter was talking to me about the biathlon powder I had identified, and he was almost as eager to dig here for gunpowder as he was to watch the race. Almost.

I saw Jimbo on the range, zeroing—which meant he'd already checked his clip and reloaded. I'd wait and see what the dig turned up before raising the issue of the cartridge with him.

The loudspeaker screeched. Walter and I flowed with the crowd and grabbed a spot at the fence that separated the spectator area from the course.

Whistles and cheers as racers approached the start gate.

I saw Stobie in the start area, the armorer keeping track of the shooters' artillery. Stobie's workmanlike skiing was suited for search missions, not races, and his shooting skills were iffy, but his closest buddies were biathletes and so he'd taken on the job nobody wanted, just to be on the team.

I shifted attention to the officials area and saw Lindsay ushering Len Carow to a folding chair. That surprised me—the FEMA honcho turning out for the race. My vision jumped, to Krom crucifying Lindsay at Hot Creek and Carow with his pinched shocked face seeing it Krom's way. So what was Carow seeing here today? Business as usual, don't cry wolf—because here he was schmoozing with Lindsay. I wondered if she'd had the chance to show him the Bypass. I wondered what he'd said. It struck me that Lindsay was onto Krom's turf with the evac route and he was onto hers with his monitor at Hot Creek. And I couldn't help myself, all I could think was it's my future they're battling over.

There was an intoxicated clanging of cowbells as somebody's favorite came out the start gate. I forced my attention to the race. Skiers start in intervals, and the fifth racer to start wore the red-white-blue racing suit and he elicited a deafening roar. I saw a tall figure with a telephoto lean over the fence for a clear shot—Hal Orenstein, always here for a race, always runs it front page in the *Mammoth Times*. I saw Bill Bone, puffed up in a parka with the Ski Tip Cafe logo, waving his hands like they were on fire to help the American along. My pulse quickened. The sentiments came. Go for it. *Whip 'em.*

The Americans are often the laughingstocks of the biathlon circuit. Officials joke they should start the Americans ahead of everyone else so the Americans can finish before the time-keepers have to leave for dinner.

"Go for it!" I yelled.

Jimbo tore past us in a furious stride and I watched him disappear into the woods, and by the time he'd skied his first four kilometers and come back down the track I knew he had a good time. When he hit the flats I screamed "go go go go go" and got out my camera. In my viewfinder he's skating for speed and the rifle on his back looks like it grows out of his spine. He's grimacing at the pain of it.

He came onto the range, unslung his rifle, and dropped to prone, his skis spread-eagled beneath him.

My mind jumped and I pictured the soil beneath him, beneath the snow, mostly glacial till but there could be volcanics intermixed, and of course gunpowder, unburned biathlon grains tracked about this entire area. I pictured Georgia lying prone in the snow, a halo of red spreading from her head. And who stands above her with bloody hands?

Jimbo inserted a clip into the rifle, dug an elbow into the snow, and brought the rifle to his cheek.

Five rounds in the clip. Unless he hadn't checked.

My brother trued his aim. The target was fifty meters uprange, five black circles on a white plate. Five targets for five rounds. Orange wind flags hung limp. Easy shooting. I raised the camera and through the viewfinder saw a shudder run along his body. He was going to have to kick that pulse down, get into a cadence if he wanted to hold his firing position. I saw him inhale and pull the trigger, so slowly it seemed the pin would never fire, and then he exhaled and the shot finally came like a surprise at the end of the exhalation. One eye winked out on the target.

"*Well*," Walter said, voice honeyed in satisfaction.

I gazed upward and made a little prayer. Rifle fire popped. I looked to find Jimbo already up, hunching into his rifle sling. There was a swagger to the way he kicked his skis into motion, which told me what I wanted to know before I checked the targets. He'd aced all five. I punched Walter's arm.

"Here's Eric!" Walter yelled in my ear.

I followed Eric as he came in a tuck down the track, skated the flats, and hauled onto the range. He just powered those skis. Every muscle popping. He was beautiful. I watched him shuck out of his rifle sling and drop to prone. He shuddered. My heart was in my ribs. I tried to get my breathing down. I watched him raise his rifle, pausing to calculate. He approaches the biathlon like it's a case. He figures every angle, he has to compensate for that lost eye. I watched him on his belly, measured breathing. I thought, just shoot. Hurry up. He shot, and took a miss on the third target.

I expelled a breath and hiked a leg onto the fence rung. Eric and Jimbo had another four loops to ski and three bouts to shoot and I was going to have to tough it out with them.

In the distance came the wail of a siren.

I watched the Russian and the Finn jockeying for the lead, and then I watched Jimbo on his second lap coming down the track like friction didn't exist.

More sirens, close now, and the growl of heavy trucks.

Walter turned, eyebrows lifting.

The noise reached the parking lot, crescendoed, and then the sirens cut off and the truck engines idled down.

Heads turned. In the officials area Len Carow got to his feet, knocking over his chair. My brother, on the range in marksman's pose, paused with his rifle mid-air. On the track, a skier came up out of his tuck and collided with another skier.

Lindsay was on the loudspeaker, calmly telling the racers to continue.

The crowd was no longer watching the race. The people nearest the parking lot backpedalled. A path cleared and I could see vehicles massed at the edge of the lot—fire engines, police, sheriff, ambulance—and I thought someone must have had a heart attack. Then I saw the trucks, heavyweight gray-green beasts. A man in camouflage jumped out the back of a truck and others bailed after him and I could read National Guard on the helmets.

Uniforms—police, sheriff, fire, medics—poured into the crowd and widened the pathway and the Guard massed behind them at the mouth of the parking lot.

The loudspeaker crackled and then went dead.

Krom appeared in the pathway, carrying a bullhorn, and on his heels was Mike Kittleman in his volunteer firefighter gear.

I hadn't seen Mike since the meeting at the Inn, spiffy in his best suit sweeping the stairs, and I wasn't surprised to see him again doing Krom's bidding.

I figured I knew what that was.

I knew what was coming. I'd dreamed of this. I knew the

words even before Krom raised the bullhorn. I could have chimed in with Krom's amplified voice. *This is an evacuation.*

Blood pounded in my ears.

Krom's voice was unhurried, sure of itself. "You will all move," he told us—and Walter grasped my arm—"in an orderly manner under direction of the officers toward the parking lot, where you will start your cars and exit under the direction of the National Guard." Krom was grim, big shoulders slumped, bullhorn dropping to his side, but his face was flushed and his hair ruffled like he'd skied a race himself. He gave off a hot shock of energy.

I listened for the thunder and my toes curled in anticipation of the shaking.

I saw Lindsay elbowing through the crowd, her face white, and now Krom saw her as well, sending a nod her way, and then he raised the bullhorn and said, "Race_officials, disarm your shooters."

Stobie, the team armorer, moved to obey. Jimbo, the nearest shooter, moved to hand Stobie his rifle.

Now Lindsay and Krom were in a huddle. Abruptly, she knocked the bullhorn from his hand.

I gasped.

Stobie's hand froze on the rifle butt.

Krom bellowed, "*Disarm the shooters*," and bent to pick up the bullhorn.

Lindsay shouted, "*Wait*."

Stobie, at an impasse, shook his rump.

I wanted to scream at him stop kidding around, *this is an evacuation*, but Stobie would likely be shaking his rump in the midst of an ash fall in the hopes of cheering everyone up.

And then his kidding stopped.

Time stopped for me, then. Deep inside I'm yelling *wait* and no one hears. Not my brother, who decides to take back his rifle, and not Stobie, who is holding onto it in vacillation. Not Walter, who is moving for Lindsay. Not Lindsay, who is turning to look in surprise at Mike Kittleman.

Mike's sprinting onto the range.

Mike hasn't been on a biathlon range for years, ever since Georgia kicked him off the team. I'm wondering what Mike's doing out there now.

Jimbo keeps reaching for his rifle and Stobie keeps vacillating, until the hurtling blur that is Mike slams full-body into Stobie and the two of them stumble. They don't fall, because Jimbo gets into it, grabbing for Mike. Mike whips around and gut-punches Jimbo and my brother goes sprawling.

People are running. Lindsay is almost to Mike when Walter catches her. I see Eric coming, very cool, kicking out of his skis, and I scream hurry.

Mike grabs Stobie and they dance round and round in a bear hug. Mike in his fireman's gear is bulked-up as Stobie.

And now I understand what Mike's doing—Krom's bidding. Trying to disarm the shooter.

The Mammoth cops are moving in. They're shouting. They all know these guys.

Before the cops can reach the dancers Stobie throws off Mike. Except Mike's got hold of the rifle like a man on a cliff edge holds fast to a tree.

Stobie and Mike are both in possession of my brother's rifle when it goes off.

And then time jumps and neither of them wants the rifle—it's dropped, abandoned—and Mike stands alone looking down in horror at Stobie's rag doll form, the doll's head reddening the snow.

I no longer screamed. I moved to help, only I hadn't moved, I was paralyzed.

It was Adrian Krom who took over then, Krom who'd come

prepared for disaster. His cops herded people away from Stobie and his paramedics swarmed. His ambulance crew broke for the parking lot and rushed back with a gurney and medical kits. His fire crew hit the sirens. His paramedics bundled Stobie onto the gurney and then hustled through the stupefied crowd. His Guardsmen recovered the rifle and moved to disarm the shaken biathletes on the range. Krom kept it all moving at a brisk clip.

I was moving now, toward my brother.

But Lindsay was already there with her arms around Jimbo, and Walter was already speaking to Mike, who stood with his hands tucked into his armpits.

They all seemed to be a very long distance from me, and I seemed to be wading through chest-high snow. I kept moving, and my eye caught on Krom, who was closer, and I was moving so slowly I had an eternity to watch Krom.

Adrian Krom was now head-to-head with Len Carow. Carow appeared to argue with Krom. Krom passed a hand across the back of his neck and shook his head. Carow looked away, his glasses mirroring the sun, and his attention settled on Lindsay. Krom too broke away. His elbow cocked and released in a vicious backhand tennis stroke and the bullhorn cartwheeled across the snow. He headed for the parking lot, where a small army lounged against the trucks, and he returned with a heavy Guard escort.

"This is an evacuation," he bellowed—no reassurance, no bullhorn and none needed because a silence had taken the Lake Mary basin—"and you will all move in an orderly manner under the direction of the National Guard toward the parking lot."

And then he was coming my way and I looked at him, stricken, and he shot me a hard look and said in passing, "It's a drill, Cassie."

I stood dumb. It's a drill.

The crowd was moving fixedly toward the parking lot.

The taste of bile was in my mouth. Relief tastes like poison.

I took off after Krom. "You can't continue."

He kept walking. "Why not?"

"*Stobie*'s why not."

"Unfortunate as hell." The sure-of-itself voice. "But it's a better drill now."

In the evacuated parking lot, only three cars remained—my Subaru, Jimbo's Fiat, and Walter's Explorer, in which he had ferried Lindsay to the race. It was unclear if Krom meant to leave us behind or if it was an oversight, but Walter, Lindsay, Jimbo, and I stood listening to the fading sirens.

Finally, Walter stirred. He said, "Here's what we're going to do. Lindsay, you'll take Jimbo home in his car and fix the both of you something to eat. Cassie and I are going to remain to take a few soil samples. We'll keep the cell phone on and you'll call us if you get any news from the hospital—if we need to come. Otherwise, we'll meet you at the house within three hours."

And do what? I wondered. Make hot cider?

16

I WAS GOING up the stairwell from the parking garage to the hospital when I ran into Mike Kittleman, on his way down. The stairwell was lit like a sunrise with sodium bulbs and the concrete steps had a wet-dog smell.

Mike sidestepped to go around me.

"Hang on," I said.

His face was sickly in the yellowish light.

I said, "It was an accident. People know that."

"Yeah, right."

We stared at each other. The fundamental and unchangeable connection between us was enmity. I thought, Mike wouldn't take my hand if he were drowning. He wouldn't offer me his. If I were drowning alongside his cat, he'd save the cat and then think twice about me. It came back—as it always does with Mike and me—to the gondola station, loading mountain bikes. He was fifteen and I was fourteen, and he always bossed me around and I always took it. I could feel the heat of that summer day when Eric dropped by, when the gondola stalled. Smell the hot oil odor of the machinery Mike was fruitlessly trying to fix. Hear myself telling Mike to stop before he broke something. I could see myself sashaying over to Eric like a cat with her tail in the air, telling Mike, *you better let Eric fix it*. And Mike leapt, face grimed with oil and red with heat, and he got me by the hair and put a screwdriver to my neck, screaming *shut up, shut up, shut up* until Eric took him down. In the aftermath, it became Eric's and my problem.

I regarded Mike, now, and the man on the stairs called up the same image the kid had called up: that of a guy with a need to make the world like him better than it did. With a temper to reciprocate.

I said, "Everybody saw it was an accident." Everybody didn't see it that way, really. Plenty of people blamed Mike, although officially it was indeed declared an accident and no charges were being filed. Plenty of people, actually, blamed Krom for letting things get out of hand. A few people were even muttering about asking the Council to replace Krom. A few people were saying a surprise drill was just what we needed to keep us on our toes. Nobody seemed to notice that Krom had turned Lake Mary into a battleground, and that Lindsay had come out the loser.

Mike started down the stairs.

I said, "I know how you feel."

"You don't know anything."

Oh yes I do, I know how it feels to blame yourself for something that happens by accident. Doesn't matter that you didn't intend something awful to happen. Death by inattention. Doesn't hurt any less. I said, "You pull yourself to pieces."

He kept moving.

All right, I thought, you stubborn shit, don't take my hand. And I'll feel no qualms asking you the question I couldn't ask Jimbo. "Can you help me with something, Mike? How many kinds of biathlon powder are there?"

That stopped him.

It was the question heavy in my mind when Walter and I

dragged back to the house yesterday, but one look at Jimbo and I'd held my tongue. In the parking lot, after the race—after the drill—I'd thought Walter was wrong to keep us there. All I'd wanted to do was go somewhere and kick something. But he'd been right. Kicking through snow and digging like a dog had been right. And it worked, for awhile. And it paid off. We'd done a field test right there, sorting under the hand lens with a pocket knife. Dimples was there all right—no surprise—but there were also *four* other makes. And *none* of those four matched *any* of the mystery makes of gunpowder in the evidence, whose silver faces were burned into my memory. It made no sense. Just like it made no sense for Jimbo to lie about having a cartridge.

Mike turned. "What's this about?"

"Biathlon powder." I didn't add 'in the evidence' but he was smart enough to make that leap. I didn't want to risk adding that I was asking him because he used to be on the team. "Mike, is there more than one make?"

"Why do you need to know?"

"I can ask somebody else if you don't know."

"I know." His pale skin bloomed with sweat. "Fine, there's half a dozen makes. But only three I think perform when the temp gets down in the teens and I think Fiocchi and Lapua are the best of those and my personal choice was Fiocchi." He eyed me. "And your brother thinks so too, I happen to know."

Dimples.

My confusion deepened. So there are several makes of biathlon powder, and none but dimples matches my evidence. Therefore the unidentified gunpowder is not biathlon powder. Then what *is* that stuff and where did Georgia pick it up?

Mike was moving down the stairs.

"Wait a minute," I said. A knot like a fist sat under my breastbone. "How's Stobie?"

"Coma." The word echoed up the stairwell.

17

I SAID, “Tell me I don’t need to be worried.”

Lindsay and I were in the laser shed, a crude box on stilts hanging on the side of Lookout Mountain, which overlooks the northwest loop of the caldera. I’d managed to blurt it out while she was lining up a shot.

She gave me a cursory glance. “About?”

“A vendetta.”

She aimed the laser, squinting like a sharpshooter. A red beam zapped across the caldera to score a bullseye on the reflector site and zapped back to the instrument monument in our shed. Ten days ago Lindsay had shot the same circuit, and if the beam’s travel time has changed between then and now it means the skin of the earth has stretched.

My heart pounded. “Well?”

She read the monitor. “Oh-point-five parts per million.”

“I meant about the race. The drill.”

She shot me a look, an ice-blue beam: we’re doing volcanology here. “And I mean the change from the background strain rate.”

Strain rate is a relative measurement. The earth’s crust is

always straining, pulled this way and that by shifts in temperature, in weather, in tides. It can also be strained by rising magma. My own strain rate was rising fast. I said, "Are you worried?"

"I always worry about ground deformation, honey."

"That's not what I *mean*. You know what I'm saying. Adrian Krom is after you. First he sandbags you at the Inn meeting with his road alternative and then..."

"The Council voted to continue work on the Bypass," she said. Then added, "They also voted to study his suggestion. Typical political fence-straddling."

"And *then*," I continued, "he sandbagged you at the drill. He didn't just stick a pin in a map and choose the race for his drill, he chose it because of *you*."

"I'm not the victim," she said, thinly. "Stobie is."

I'd talked to Stobie for an hour, yesterday. Everybody's taking a turn, in case he can hear us. I'd talked to his blank face about the weather, how construction on the Bypass is going, what I had for breakfast, what I planned to have for lunch. I'd said beer was a lousy idea for Bill, and I expected him, Stobie, to recover before Bill's birthday with a better idea.

I said, "It's not just Stobie. Mike's a victim too. He was doing it for Adrian. You'd think Adrian would have tried to stop him—he's got to know about Mike's temper."

"Well well," she said. She tapped her fingers on the laser. Her heavy rings pinged its hull. "You appear to have joined the anti-Adrian camp."

"Is there a camp?"

She smiled her cat's smile and bent to the laser. She wore jeans and a long sweatshirt and from the back she looked like a young girl.

I felt a pang. When I was a young girl, I would never have questioned Lindsay's motives.

She straightened and gave me a level look. "And how is your case evolving?"

About as well as this talk. "It's not." Walter and I have been putting in the hours, and going nowhere fast. We've got gunpowder that says look where there's shooting but the Casa Diablo and Lake Mary soils say keep on looking. We'd built the profile on the evidence soil and it damn well didn't match the Casa and Mary soils. But, then, soil can be tricky. It can concentrate a rock's trace elements so that a parent rock having a minute percentage of, say, magnetite can yield a soil in which the magnetite concentration is hundreds of times stronger, but you go ahead anyway hunting for a site where there's magnetite-rich rocks because you just don't know. And even if you find the magnetite jackpot you can still screw it up because of where you choose to dig. Oh, soil can outfox you. It can show one face in one sample and a totally different face in the next, taken just a few meters away.

She said, "And Walter can spare you this afternoon?"

I suddenly flared. "I make that call. I came out here with you because I'm worried about you and Adrian. And because I'm goddamn worried about the volcano, too. And I've been putting in a boatload of overtime and so taking off a couple of hours isn't…" I stopped myself, before I threw a fit. I produced a thin smile. "And because I enjoy your company."

She winked. She read me too well. She shut down the laser and shuttered the windows. "Shall we move along? There's a little fellow I want to visit."

"Yes," I said, "let's move along."

She locked the shed and I followed her in silence through the snow. She and Krom, I suddenly thought, speak the same language. Little fellow. Unpredictable chum. The volcano's a *he*, someone they know personally, someone they're on intimate terms with. Maybe that's the way it is when you spend your life wondering if your work's going to blow up in your face. I don't do that. I don't call my soil by name, I don't give my evidence a gender. Maybe I should. Maybe if I give the bloody red hematite-stained cinders a name, they'll tell me where they came from.

We took Lindsay's Range Rover down the Lookout logging road and hit the smooth tarmac of Highway 395 just about where the Bypass is due to hook up. Lindsay headed south on 395 and ten minutes later, when she slowed to take the Hot Creek turnoff, my stomach turned over. She barreled along the rutted road. There was no barricade to slow her. There was, thankfully, no blue Blazer in the parking lot.

She shut off the engine and swiveled to retrieve her gear bag, a tight weave in bright colors. Guatemalan—the Atitlan caldera. Lindsay not only does field work in the large calderas of the world, she shops the towns. Her turquoise rings come from New Mexico—the Valles caldera.

I thought of the gear in Krom's pack, the monitor he'd brought in order to impress Len Carow, and wondered if Lindsay knew about Krom monitoring her volcano.

We started walking, bypassing the trail down to the creek, heading out along the tableland above the gorge.

I followed the Guatemalan bag into the calf-deep snow of the desert. A simple field trip, after all. I had been on so many field trips, like this, with Lindsay. I always followed, or we walked abreast. I never led. When I was eleven, not long after I'd begun hanging around Walter's lab, there had been a particularly nasty quake swarm. I had nightmares. Walter found out and that's when he introduced me to Lindsay. She took me on a field trip deep into the caldera. She paced in front of me cheerily explaining the difference between ordinary tectonic quakes and low-frequency quakes that mean fluid's on the move. Her teaching hadn't moved me—she heaped on too much too fast—but her cocksureness did. I wanted to ape her finesse, the way she coolly took the elemental forces in hand. But I could not take on a volcano. I could fear it, even learn its nature, but I could not stop it. I made no difference. And so Lindsay didn't lure me into volcanology as she'd expected. She's never understood my choice of Walter's lab. There, I have a fighting chance to put things right.

Lindsay pointed. "There's my little fellow."

Across a small ravine a finger of steam issued from the snow. Two pinyon pines were in its path and their needles were browned. "How's his breath?" I asked, using the lingo.

"Tolerable. But it's his age and location that interest me more. He's nearly six months old and he's up here all by himself."

So he'd been born around the time the volcano started acting up. I wetted my lips, gone dry in the cold air. "So we have activity outgrowing the creek."

"We have a single vent up here," she said, easy. "It's one more thing to consider." When the volcano does anything worth notice, she grows progressively cheerier but it's a focused sort of cheer like that of combat pilots in old war movies who joke their way into flak.

I said, uneasy, "Should this whole area be fenced off?" This is, after all, the heart of the south moat, a trough in the caldera where the unrest has been concentrated.

She swept a hand, encompassing the creek, the gorge, the tablelands. "How? You could block the road, of course, but anyone on foot can gain access." She gave me a level look. "I explained this to Adrian, when I told him about my little fellow. He's making an issue of it nonetheless."

I gave a glance to the gorge, although we were not close enough to see down to the creek. Nonetheless, I pictured Krom making an issue of it down there three days ago. And then I pictured Krom and his swim that night.

Lindsay nudged me and led the way across the ravine. We stopped just short of the fumarole. "Stop *worrying*," she said. "I can handle Adrian." She knelt and extracted a gas collector from the Guatemalan bag.

I squatted beside her and screwed the gas tube into the pump. I said, "There's something I should tell you."

"Oh yes?"

I took in a deep breath, a biathlete breath, and then told her about Krom's swim at Hot Creek. And the courtly bow. And the extended finger.

Very slowly, she pulled a gas filtration mask from the bag. She said, finally, "That was ill-considered. Following him."

"That's all you have to say?"

"Have you told Walter?"

"No."

"Good. Don't tell him. He thinks you have good sense."

I wanted to raise my arms in defense.

She eyed me. "And why are you telling *me* this? Now?"

"Because of the drill. Because I could just dismiss the swim as...eccentric...until the drill. It's not the drill itself that gets me —I know we need to drill, I *want* to drill, but... Adrian was willing to..."

"Sacrifice Stobie."

I had been going to say, he's willing to suffer casualties. After the fact. He hadn't cared. But that's not the same as sacrifice. Sacrifice implies intention. I shrugged.

"Very well," Lindsay said, "given Adrian's ill-considered actions, there's something I should now tell *you*. I've kept quiet about this because, number one, it was told to me in confidence and I respect confidences and, number two, because I recognize my dislike of the man and I didn't want that to influence my judgment." She paused, then said, "Adrian and Georgia were having an affair."

"*What*?" I dropped the pump.

"In regard to your case," Lindsay said, "you might want to consider a lovers quarrel."

"But they..."

"Sex, Cassie. I hardly think romance had any play in it."

"But how do you know?"

Lindsay picked up the pump and checked my fittings. "She bragged."

"But she had to be fifteen years older than Adrian."

Lindsay snapped, "That's why she was bragging, one old crone to another." She yanked the gas mask over her face. Her skin, where it showed, was a deep rose. She snatched up the gas collector and tramped over to the fumarole. She snaked the probe into the vent, shoving it here and there like she meant to ream the little fellow out of existence. She stalked back, dragging off the mask, speaking as soon as she was within earshot. "And don't think he wouldn't go after *you*."

I said, wary, "Me?"

"It's not just *mature* women like Georgia who've succumbed. The man's dishy. I saw that first time I met him at Rainier, although in my eyes he couldn't hold a candle to Walter. Still, I saw him cut a wake with the local ladies." Her eyes, quick and bright, held mine. "And he'll take a pass at you, too, if you have something he wants."

"Like what?"

"Like information about a case in which he has an interest."

"So it's not just my charming self he's after."

"I doubt it."

That stung. And rang real true. "Here's what he likes about me—the geology. He was impressed when I told him what I could do with it. He wanted to know how I was going to follow it to Georgia. I don't know what that proves. Doesn't prove he killed her."

"Honey, just this—he is not a trustworthy man."

"You tell Georgia that?"

She said, after a moment, "No. I didn't have a loving relationship with Georgia."

All the fight went out of me.

Lindsay turned her attention to the disassembly of the gas collector. "In any case," she said, "Georgia wouldn't have listened."

I picked up the Guatemalan bag and held it open while Lindsay stowed her gear.

"Now," she said, "in light of our lovers-quarrel scenario, I'm going to show you something."

Our scenario? I'd only just found out about Adrian and Georgia.

Lindsay shouldered the bag and set off. I moved to catch up. My thoughts skittered, from midnight swims to sex to sacrifice. I was churning by the time we reached the trail down to the creek. Lindsay, however, had abruptly grown cheery. She led the way down to the bottom. Instead of turning right, as I had with Krom and Carow, I turned left in Lindsay's wake. I followed her in silence along the creek bank. We rounded a couple of bends and came to a secluded pool, almost hidden behind a massive boulder. Lindsay turned to me. "As a matter of fact, Georgia came to me for advice in her quest to win Adrian's heart. She wanted to know where to find fossils."

"Why?"

"Adrian collects. She wanted to give him a gift. I suggested a crinoid and told her an easy place to find them." Lindsay hiked a shoulder at the boulder.

I moved it for a closer look. The boulder was limestone—unlike the rock of the surrounding cliffs. It was clearly an erratic, transported here ages ago by glacial action. The gray limestone was studded with white disks the size of eight-penny nail heads.

In one spot there were visible cuts where a couple of the Paleozoic sea lilies had been hacked out.

Lindsay said, "The gift was a success and she followed up by bringing Adrian here to show him her 'find.' And here," Lindsay waved a hand at the little pool, "is where they had their first romp."

I gaped. I said, repeating myself, "How do you know?"

"Because she was grateful. She brought me a crinoid as a thank-you gift. Appropriate, I thought—a fossil flower." Lindsay smiled. Not a mean smile; a real one. "And we ended up the first time in our association having a nice little chat about men and sex, us two fossils."

"Lindsay, I didn't mean..."

"Of course you did. You're young."

I reddened, and turned my face to the boulder. And it was then that I noticed how the limestone jutted out enough to shield a patch of ground from falling snow. I knelt and examined the soil there. My nose stung. The soil was studded with yellow crystals—hydrothermically deposited sulfur, now oxidizing.

I thought about the boot soil evidence, studded with calcite and sulfur.

Lindsay came over and studied the soil alongside me. She sniffed. She looked at me. "As I recall," she said, "there is sulfur in your evidence soil."

I nodded.

"If I were you, I'd be taking some samples here." Lindsay stood. She looked around. "In fact, I'd be wondering if Georgia and Adrian returned here at some point. And he, perhaps, showed his bizarre feelings for the creek. Or he talked about sacrifice. If I were Georgia, that would concern me. It might even alarm me."

I nodded. I saw where Lindsay was going with this.

"Perhaps Georgia decided she had put her town in the hands

of an unstable man. In which case, perhaps she told him—in her inimitable manner—that she'd be calling for his replacement."

"So he killed her to shut her up?"

Lindsay gave a graceful shrug.

"But what about the notes?" I asked. "When did she have time to write in her Weight Watchers notebook?"

"I couldn't say."

"That's kind of a hole in your theory."

She lifted her chin. "Other than the question of the notes, do you find the theory credible?"

"Not without evidence."

I borrowed a box of baggies from Lindsay and began to take my samples. Just eyeballing the soil, I was doubtful of a match. Another concern was the lack of a source for the gunpowder. But then, I supposed, Georgia and Adrian might have walked at the biathlon range and then gotten into his Blazer and driven here for another romp. Doubtful, but not out of the question.

As I worked, Lindsay produced a thermos of coffee and two plastic mugs from her Guatemalan bag. When I finished, she pressed a warm mug into my hands. "It's a Neapolitan blend."

Naples. The Campi Flegrei caldera.

She poured herself a mug and lifted it. "To our hometown."

I touched my mug to hers.

"And don't worry, honey, about vendettas."

She said it the same way she says don't worry about the volcano. Meaning, she'll let me know when it's time to worry. Meanwhile, she's taking care of things. I drank, but the coffee tasted bitter and I dumped the rest into the creek.

18

In the shower that night, after my afternoon in the field with Lindsay, I took her theory apart.

Some people sing in the shower. I deconstruct.

Of course the samples I'd taken would tell the story—and I'd get to that first thing in the morning—but the story Lindsay'd concocted had a major flaw in logic. Adrian Krom, who was single-mindedly rebuilding his reputation, would not risk killing the mayor at Hot Creek. He was bizarre, certainly, in his relationship with the volcano. Ruthless, absolutely, in his continuation of the drill, in his campaign to destroy Lindsay's reputation. But he wasn't stupid. The creek's a very public place. The creek's a very long way from the glacier, so how does he get the body there? If it's by horse, where does he get the horse and how does he go from creek to glacier unnoticed with a body across the saddle?

I'd have had the same questions about Casa Diablo as the site of death, had the soil there not ruled it out. The biathlon course at Lake Mary had been a better candidate, geographically, until the soil ruled it out.

As for Adrian Krom as a killer... I didn't like to consider it.

We needed to be able to rely on him. It was one thing to blame him for what happened to Stobie. But Georgia? That's an order of magnitude beyond.

My eyes suddenly stung. Shampoo leaked down from my hair and I had to stick my face into the hot water flow to flush the contaminants.

Tension drained along with the Pantene.

By the time I was toweling dry I had pretty much deconstructed the lovers quarrel.

I still liked the idea of a hot spring, though, as a source for the sulfur. Some other hydrothermically active area, someplace else. Some place where people had been discharging firearms.

I opened the bathroom door to release the steam and heard the doorbell ringing. Once, twice, three times, four.

I wrapped in my robe and went to answer.

Eric stood on the porch. He seemed surprised to see me. Or, maybe it was my robe, decorated with grinning trout. Old boyfriend; Fish and Game; didn't work out but this was one fine fleecy robe. Eric stared until I flinched.

I said, "Hey Eric."

He said, "Jimbo here?"

I thought, that's a little abrupt. How about, hey Cassie, good to see you—is your brother around? I regarded Eric Catlin—the guy who simply by standing there made me feel very naked in my trout robe, the guy I'd trust with my life if it ever came to that, the biathlete and cop who posts bullseye targets on his office wall—and I said, "You know that gunpowder in the evidence boot soil? Nearly half of it's Fiocchi."

Eric stiffened. It was the way he had recoiled, ever so briefly, when he missed the third shot in the 20K. He had recovered to ace the fourth shot and now he brought himself around as quickly. "No shit?"

"Jimbo says you guys shoot at Casa Diablo and Lake Mary. Anyplace else?"

"That's where we shoot," Eric said.

"Does Stobie shoot too? I mean, he's the armorer and..."

"He shoots too. In practice. At least, he did."

"Got any theories that explain where Georgia picked up all that gunpowder?"

"No theories." Eric's voice was rough. "When do you expect Jimbo back?"

I shook my head. "Should I give him a message?"

"Yeah. Tell him he's a real..." Eric considered. "Jerk."

Before I could ask, he thrust a folded newspaper at me then pushed down the steps and when he'd been fully consumed by the night he called back, "Didn't mean to take it out on you, Cass."

Mystified, I went inside and turned on the hall light. I read, standing against the doorjamb.

It was the local rag, the *Mammoth Times*. The headline grabbed me first, as headlines are meant to do. And then the photo—Hal had run a very large photo above the fold. I studied it with the same scrutiny I'd given the cliff face today, and when I'd fully absorbed it, a very cold hand took hold of my heart and squeezed.

I ran for the phone.

19

I SAT at a window table in the Ski Tip Cafe across from Jeanine Povorenko, who was the girl most envied by other girls from preschool all the way through high school. Jeanine does sports promos now on local cable, a gig originally arranged by Georgia in a fit of brilliant PR. Jeanine has a blond ponytail to the waist and broad Slavic curves and I hated her for a month when I hit adolescence.

Jeanine said, "Now *he* is a *hunk*."

I looked. The Ski Tip pulls in a young hungry crowd, skiers and boarders who've spent big bucks on lift tickets and are looking for a feed that is cheap and filling. Guys come back from the slopes like jungle cats with a burn in the muscles and a shine in the eyes, strutting. Almost any of them could have caught Jeanine's attention.

Any guy but Jack Altschul, my high school history teacher, by himself at the counter, or Bobby Panetta and the DeMartini twins in a back booth. Not so much because these guys didn't meet Jeanine's definition of hunk but because none of them—or the other dozen or so locals I spotted in the room—had anything resembling a shine in the eyes. Watchfulness was more like it. When they took their eyes off their plates it was to search the room for something, and not seem to find it. Lost hope, maybe. The story in the *Mammoth Times* must surely have shaken faith.

We were a crabbed bunch of worried locals watching the visitors like they're from another planet.

Jeanine reached across the booth, nudged my arm, and leveled her gaze two tables away. A dozen guys wearing National Guard fatigues shouldered around one of Bill Bone's huge family tables.

She slouched back and gave me a slow wink.

This, I supposed, was why it was Jeanine and not some other female who was in the newspaper photo: her knowing take on men, and theirs on her.

"Soooo...Caaasie." Jeanine ran her hand down her ponytail, working it like a pump handle, drawing up the words. Jeanine's the laid-back queen. "What's the deal?"

I searched her face for the pinch-eyed look we'd all taken on. I didn't find it. She was looking good. She had a high-altitude tan and her winter blond was whiter than last summer's, her ponytail embroidered into a French braid. She was framed by the curlicue cutouts of Bill's wooden booth, and if I hadn't known her I would have taken her for a Nordic biathlete. Well, no. The set of her face had the unfazed air of a snowboarder. American all the way.

In the booth behind us someone growled, low and long.

"Thanks for coming," I said.

She grinned. "Free food."

"Uh-uh, gotta sing for your supper." I smiled. We're not exactly friends; our lives just intersect a lot. She teaches Jazzercise where I pursue last year's fitness, she used to date my brother, I bought my used Subaru from her. We get along because she's always blunt and I'm always easy. I wasn't sure about tonight. I said, "I need to know what happened at Hot Creek."

She took a drink of her Coke. "Read the paper. Everybody else has."

"I did. I need the details."

"Jimbo won't tell you? He's been braggin his ass off."

Then Eric was right, my brother was in on it. I took a long drink of my own Coke. Knot by knot, my hometown was coming undone. "Jimbo's not home. You're the one in the paper so I'm asking you."

"Why do you wanna know?"

"It scared me."

"Yeah?" She hooked a thumb at Bobby Panetta and the DeMartinis—Jimbo's buddies—in the back booth. "Guys said it was cool."

Bill Bone appeared at our booth, red-faced and harried, and set out mammoth bowls of chili heaping above the rim with red onions. The food here is straightforward; Bill believes in an honest serving for your dollars. The ambiance is mountain-resort kitsch. The place used to be called Little Switzerland and it's painted blue and white and most exposed wood has been carved. When Bill bought the cafe he changed the name; every New Year's he resolves to redecorate. He unloaded a basket of breadsticks. "Chili's under-spiced," he said. "You'll be disappointed."

I tasted it. It was under-spiced. I didn't care.

Jeanine called after him, "Your chili's always hot, Bill." She turned her grin on me. "Hey, birthday idea—let's get him a certificate for Great Expectations. The dating service? They find your soul mate? You know?"

I didn't, clearly.

"So, Cass, what d'ya wanna know?"

"How you and Adrian Krom ended up in the creek."

"Started at the Bear Pen. He hangs there when he's not here."

He went to the breweries with the locals. He became their best friend. "And..."

"And I sit down. And he likes that. And we order drinks."

"He didn't wonder why you joined him?"

She hooted, a spoonful of chili halfway to her mouth. "What, he's gonna ask if I know what I'm doin?"

Somebody should have. "What did he have to say?"

"He told me how hot I was." She ate the spoonful. "Well, what he said was *beguiling*." She wiped her mouth. "Same thing."

He cut a wake with the Tacoma ladies. He beguiled Georgia. I wondered if Jeanine knew he'd beguiled Georgia into Hot Creek, but if she didn't know, I wasn't going to spread the gossip. I said, "What else?"

"Bar talk. You've been in a bar?"

"What's your hobby, that sort of thing?"

"Sure, Cass. That sort of thing."

"Well, then, what's his hobby?"

She selected a breadstick and bit off an end. As she chewed, she gazed overhead at the heavy beveled rafters where Bill had hung antique skis with cracked leather straps. Maybe the answer was up there, and if it was, I gave her the space to find it. She came back to me. "His hobby is mind-fuckin this town." Her eyes narrowed to slits. "Shock you, Cassie?"

It did, actually. Like the swim in the creek. "*How* is he mind-fucking this town?"

"That's what I'm trying to tell you. Okay, so we were slammin margaritas—only mine were virgins but he didn't know that—and we're talkin about getting crazy and I was working around to, let's...get...crazy and go down to Hot Creek."

"You mean it was your idea?"

"To start. She reached for her braid, then dropped her hand.

"So he tells me the creek's off-limits now. Road's gonna get fenced."

"By him?"

"Guess so." She shrugged. "Anyway, he gets really weird about it."

I sat forward. "How?"

"One minute I'm thinking I don't have to work very hard to convince him. You know?" She trailed a hand down her shirt, flicking the buttons between her breasts. "And then he kind of turns off. He's got those bedroom eyes but one minute he's looking at me all hot and the next he's, like, cold. He says that shit about it being off-limits and I'm like *so*? You're the man. And he doesn't get off on that, he just gives me this cold look and says it's dangerous down there. And I was getting a little nervous."

"But you went."

"He made me."

"He *forced* you?"

"No. He just...turned things around. *I'm* supposed to be the one getting *him* so wasted he'll go down to Hot Creek. Only he's not drunk. He's had three fuckin margaritas and he's stone sober. He's putting it to me. Creek's dangerous, gases, a bunch of volcano talk. And I'm like, that's okay, I know where it's safe. And he jumps on that. It *isn't* safe. And he wants to know if I fully understand that."

My head began to throb. "Did you?"

"Said I'd sign a release if he wanted so let's get on with it." She looked hard at me. "He says if we go down there he's responsible for my safety. Like he's my father? Then he says... 'he's unpredictable'. So I ask who he means. And Krom says—get this—the volcano. And so I say *whoa*, it talks? I'm trying to be funny, you know, lighten things up cuz the situation is getting a little creepy."

"Did he laugh?"

She widened her eyes, the whites stark against her tan. "Yeah. So we went."

At the Guardsmen's table, Bill was trying to place the correct plate in front of the right guy, and the Guardsmen were laughing and shooting plates across the table to one another as fast as Bill could put them down.

"We took his car. He drove and you couldn't even tell he'd been drinking. When we park and get out he asks me again if I'm sure about this. Like he's in charge? So I just went along with him since I had other plans."

"You and my brother."

"And Bobby Panetta."

I stole a glance at the back booth, where Bobby was pouring a beer for Matt DeMartini. Bobby caught me looking. His face showed nothing, beyond its mask of freckles. I had a deep affection for these guys—we'd grown up together—but I had to say they'd not grown much beyond high school. Neither, evidently, had my brother.

Jeanine said, "So we get out to the creek. It's about midnight. I lead him to a spot and we strip off. He's not bad, you know?" She gave me a half-lidded look.

I nodded. I'd seen.

"Except for the scar."

"Scar?"

"Yeah, big one on his arm. All white and raised, but he's got a cool tattoo over it. A spiral like one of those Indian swirly things? And then you see it's all made out of words."

So that's what I'd seen, my night at the creek. "What did it say?"

"Too dark to *read*. And I'm, like, a little busy? It's cold, I'm freezing my butt off. So's he, I guess, but he's too macho to show it. I'm trying to get him into the water—cuz the guys are waiting—and then he gets weird again. Gets all...courtly. I mean he holds out his hand like I'm too—what?—*scared* to go in first and he's gonna lead me. And he's looking at me the way he did in the Pen, that cold look, I mean it was dark but not so dark I couldn't feel it. And then he says—the way you say something you got memorized—" she lowered her voice, "*abandon all hope, you who enter here*. Well I heard that back in school." She gave a short laugh, a bark. "Sure as hell what I did when I went into class." She threw a glance at Jack Altschul at the counter. "*His* class, for sure. You remember it? The saying I mean."

"Dante," I said. Ye, who enter.

"Oh yeah." She held up her hand, took a bite of chili and a swallow of Coke.

I said, "And that didn't spook you, Adrian quoting that?"

"It weirded me out but then he smiled like he's joking, and anyway if he did anything I didn't like all I had to do was yell and the guys would be on him."

"Jimbo and Bobby."

"Yeah. Anyway, we only go in ass deep. The whole idea is to keep near shore, I mean the location was important. So I stop and give him the chance and for a minute there I'm thinkin the guy's wasted after all cuz he's just not takin the bait. But that's not it." She stopped.

"What is it then?"

"He wants us to swim."

The knot formed, behind my breastbone. "What'd you say?"

"I'm like, *no way*. It's *steaming*, where he wants to go."

"Where did he want to go?"

"The bench—that big slab of rock where everybody used to hang on, drink beer and grab ass. You know?"

I nodded.

"I say the fuckin volcano's made the water squirrelly out there. I say let's just stay right here, it's nice and warm, let's do it here. Know what the dude says? Says what do you think's making the water warm right here? Like I needed to hear that. Then he smiles. Says, how far will you go? Will you go out there?" She took on an almost thoughtful look. "It was like he was giving me the choice? Where you put someone on the spot and see what they're gonna do? And there's a good choice and a bad choice?"

I said, mouth dry, "What did you choose?"

She gave me a flat look. "He wasn't giving me the choice after all."

"Shit."

"He says *yes*, real soft, and he takes my hand and starts pulling me. We're going in. And he knows I'm freaked cuz he leans real close and says you think I'll let him win?"

We stared at each other. *Him*, again. The volcano.

Someone in the room began to sing *My Old Kentucky Home* and the Guardsmen picked it up. Jeanine suddenly grinned. She tapped her index finger on her chili spoon, keeping time, the grin fixed. Her eyes stayed on mine.

"And?" I said.

"I got him."

"You got him how?"

"The plan." Her finger stilled. "I mean, I'm *not* gonna go where he wants to go, so I just jumped him right where we were. Just wrapped myself around him and he's still trying to pull me out there—and he's got his hands all over me so the guys think this is it...and kapowie!" She sat forward, face alight. "Now we got him. The lights go on. Big spots, Jimbo'd snagged a couple of those emergency lanterns from the road crew and he's on one bank and Bobby's on the other. I mean the creek is *lit*, like we're on stage. God did the guys get pictures."

I said, "What did Adrian do?"

"Nothing. Just stands there watching me, and I'll tell you I got out of there fast."

"And then?"

"Then nothing. He does nothing. We *got* him. You saw the paper."

Oh, I saw it. In the photo, Jeanine has her back to the camera. We see her long ponytail wetted halfway, snaking down her spine, and the spreading of her hips, slick with creek water. We see Krom's big hand hovering, like it's heading for her behind but her behind is submerged and there's nothing patently obscene at the moment the shutter closed. We can see just a hint of Jeanine's left breast. Over her shoulder is Krom's naked torso, his groin obscured by Jeanine's round hip. This is what makes the shot so perfectly composed—it's printable, and we think we know what's going on. Krom's face is quite identifiable. The camera catches him at the moment of understanding. He's looking coldly toward the camera but he has yet to let her go. And then, lifting the photo beyond the realm of a grab-ass party in the creek, is the sign. We can see it at shoreline, a slab on a post just beyond the nudes in the foreground. It has replaced the old sign Lindsay had installed, warning that swimming is inadvisable. This new sign is blunter. *Extreme Danger!* it says. *Hot Creek Geological Site OFF-LIMITS*.

It's the sign Krom had installed, as the accompanying text points out.

I said, "Didn't it occur to you he might try to finish what you started?"

"You mean, like, rape? Nah."

"What about the guys?" I asked, tight.

She reached into her shirt front and pulled a lipstick from her bra. "What's he gonna do, beat 'em up? Land his ass in jail? He doesn't want any more bad press than he's got." She glossed her lips.

"One more thing."

"What's that?"

"Whose idea was it?"

She put a finger to her lips.

A secret? Her bare ass is on the cover of the hometown paper and my brother's bragging his ass off, so who's ass is she trying to cover for now? I said, "Tell me who fucking planned it, Jeanine."

She eyed me. "Your guru."

I didn't get it.

"Lindsay." She replaced her lipstick. "Lindsay who's-cooler-than-you-thought Nash."

I froze. I did not believe her. And then I did.

"See, your brother and some of the guys wanted to beat the shit out of him for the Stobe. I mean, if Mister Bigshot hadn't surprised us with his drill at the race then nobody would have got shot." She gave her braid a yank. "But this fixes him. Lindsay's sending the paper straight to FEMA. This is gonna get Krom's ass fired. This shows he doesn't give a shit about safety—I mean, he takes me to the creek, where *he's* putting it off-limits?" Her voice edged up. "Shows Mister Safety Dude doesn't take his job seriously."

When I unfroze, I raised my hands to my temples, which felt as though they were going to explode.

"So," she said, sliding the check across the table to me, "what do you think?"

I could not begin to say.

"Find out what you wanted?"

More.

She narrowed her eyes. But she was looking beyond me, and she took on that watchful look, that anxious hometown tic. Glance around, straining to catch what's in the offing. Then she snapped back. "It's cool, Cass. We're all cool. Krom's the one in deep shit." She swung her legs out of the booth. "See ya." She moved away, trailing past the Guardsmen's table, catching a round of whistles.

I watched her, numb. Her take on men, men's take on her. Maybe it would work. It sure made Krom look reckless enough. What it made Lindsay look was, to me, beyond reckless. It made her into someone I don't know.

I thought of Krom, in the creek, bowing, giving it the finger. And then with Jeanine. What was that? Playing at sacrifice? Like he's challenging the volcano.

Only, how do you win a duel with a volcano?

You don't. It's not an even match.

My headache erupted into nausea. There is, of course, one arena in which Krom and Lindsay are evenly matched.

Us. The town. We depend on them both. They each hold our future in their hands.

20

I WATCHED Walter lay aside the *Mammoth Times* and then square his face to begin the day, and I just couldn't tell him. Reading about Adrian Krom's night in the creek had disturbed him. Learning about Lindsay's role would stun him.

So I sat dense as rock and kept my mouth shut.

There was a jolt. I grabbed the test-tube ring on my workbench and secured the glassware. Mag four, if I had to guess, and it jolted me out of my stupor. I hoped it would jolt Lindsay, as well—to her senses. Sitting at her desk, no doubt, with the newspaper and a mug of coffee and her cat's smile. But of course a mag-four jolt would raise, at most, her eyebrow. What she's on the watch for are quakes you don't feel. Anonymous little buggers with a low-frequency motion, like a bell ringing, which means fluid's on the move. That's the kind of quake that rings Lindsay's bell. That's what she should be planning for—not sordid setups in the creek to take down her enemy.

"Mag four?" Walter hazarded. He'd been jolted out of his stupor, as well.

I said, "We don't have time for this." I went to his bench and took the newspaper and tossed it in the trash. I said, "I have a new lead."

He straightened. "Tell me."

I explained my theory that the calcite and sulfur in the evidence might indicate a hot spring.

"That's hardly a new lead. Hot springs are certainly one source, but there are other candidates."

"What if we knew that Georgia had an interest in hot springs?"

"Do we?"

I told him about Krom and Georgia and crinoids and Hot Creek.

His eyebrows lifted. No comment. Decorous Walter.

"So you didn't know. Well neither did I. Lindsay told me. Georgia confided in her."

He said, "And there is a reason Lindsay confided in you?"

"Yes. She has a theory."

"Which you are about to tell me."

I explained Lindsay's theory, the one I'd deconstructed in the shower yesterday evening. I explained that I'd come in early this morning and put the soil I'd gathered with Lindsay under the comparison scope, next to the evidence soil, and found no match.

He said, evenly, "So you've ruled out the site at Hot Creek."

"Yes."

"And the lovers-quarrel theory?"

I mulled that one over. I gave a glance to the newspaper in the trash can. No question Adrian Krom had some bizarre thing going with the creek. With women at the creek. But the jump from there to murder was a very large one. "Sure, could have happened somewhere else. But we have no evidence that it did."

"I must admit," Walter said, "I have trouble considering Adrian a cold-blooded killer."

"What about hot-blooded? In a fit of passionate anger?"

Walter shrugged. Shook his head.

"Despite the thing with Jeanine?"

"That was rash."

"And?"

"That does not make him a killer."

"So you think Lindsay's theory is a crock?"

Walter said, evenly, "Lindsay has distrusted Adrian for a very long time."

"You chalk up her theory to prejudice?"

"I'm not blind to her faults."

"I kind of thought you were."

Walter gave a thin smile, a crack in his seamed face.

I thought, Walter's greatest strength—and his greatest weakness—is loyalty. And that's why people value his good opinion so dearly—if he thinks you're a prince, you're set for life. Whatever you do, short of a capital crime, you're still a prince. And you want to live up to that. When I took psych in college I thought I had Walter figured. He'd told me about his own undergrad days; he'd gone through a rough spell, drinking, cutting classes. As misspent youth goes, his sounded tame, but he judged it harshly. Then in his early twenties he straightened out and found his calling. I'd asked what made him change and he said, "I got tired of being a bum." So when I got into Psych 101, I psyched Walter. My theory went: he's so fiercely loyal because he doesn't want others to judge him by his years as a bum. Now, I think my theory was a crock. Walter is loyal because it's his nature. And I think it's a good thing I escaped the murky waters of psych for the bedrock of geology.

The truth was, neither of us was a forensic genius when it came to reading people.

"Well then," Walter said, "shall we just do the geology?"

"Sure. If we had some geology to do."

"We have your new lead, Cassie."

"But...you don't buy that."

"I most certainly *do*. I buy the fact that we can now connect Georgia with a hot spring, at the creek. I certainly accept that we have sulfur and calcite in the evidence, which could have come from a hot spring, somewhere. Irrespective of why Georgia might have gone there."

"So you think it's worthwhile following the hot spring lead."

"I do." He slapped his thigh. "Let's do the acid test."

I put a pinch of evidence soil in a test tube and droppered in hydrochloric acid.

There were bubbles, and a nasty smell.

The acid test is a quick way to find out if your samples have certain minerals. In the presence of acid, calcite gives off carbon dioxide and the soil fizzes. Sulfur gives off the odor of hydrogen sulfide.

We already knew we had calcite and sulfur but the question was: in what concentration? High would suggest the sample came from a site near a volcanic source. Like a hot spring.

The sample fizzed madly. The air stank of rotten eggs.

And something else.

Walter grimaced.

I leapt. Snapped on the hood fan. Grabbed Walter's arm and yanked him off his stool and the two of us scrambled back, covering our faces. I could detect the unexpected smell of bitter almonds.

Shit.

Before either of us could recover our dignity, the smell dissipated. I took in an exploratory breath. The gas was gone.

Walter returned to his stool, throwing me a speculative look.

"You tell me," I said, when I could trust my voice, "what's cyanide doing in the soil?"

Walter was smiling now.

The liquid in the tube, I saw, had gone flat like old ginger ale. I knew what must have happened. When I added acid to the soil it found cyanide, lowered its pH, and drove it into its vapor phase. I just didn't know what that meant. "Walter," I said, "I'm not in the..."

"Mines." His eyes were blue as day.

Mines. I waited. His eyes always gleam when he's puttering around with the geology of ores. It's his one vice, in Lindsay's eyes, wasting time prowling old ruins. *Treasure-hunting* in her view, although he's in it primarily for the history—the treasure rarely being economically recoverable. We'd worked a case, once, following the geology of precious ore. I'm not inspired by old mining tales but I take a guilty pleasure in being the one Walter confides this passion to. Lindsay and I share a passion for shopping flea markets that totally excludes him. My shopping guru. I waited, stewing, for Walter to explain.

He did not disappoint. "Miners around here sometimes used a dilute solution of cyanide to leach the metals from slag ore."

The meaning fizzed up. We'd got another new lead—mines. The metallic minerals are often picked up by hot water circulating deep and precipitated out near the surface.

By hot springs.

21

THE DE-ICING SAND laid down on Minaret Road had mixed with slush and grit to form a startling brecciation along the sidewalk and I walked it with dread and care.

I had an appointment in half an hour with Adrian Krom.

On the way there, I planned to drop in on Lindsay.

My gut churned.

I said, "How could you?"

Lindsay lifted one fine eyebrow.

"*Hot Creek*," I said.

She swiveled her creamy leather chair around to the credenza below the window, and bent to open a drawer.

What was she after? I glared at the landscape of her desk, littered with the detritus of expeditions in the field and the shops. The brass pot-bellied fertility goddess. The tiny Japanese teapot. The bowl made from the skin of a dried orange. The pink tourmalines set like teeth in a bed of pegmatite. The delicate sea lily crinoid in a bed of gray limestone—Georgia's gift, I assumed. Why'd Lindsay display that? Some kind of memorial for the dead?

Lindsay swiveled to face me with a gun in her hand.

"Oh *shit*," I said, "that's a gun."

She laid the pistol beside the teapot. "Here's how."

I gaped.

"I was on the right bank, upstream of them."

I found my voice. "You were going to *shoot* him?"

She lifted her chin. "I was going to keep Jeanine safe. As far as the creek goes, I took measurements at the site before they arrived. Gases were stable. No temperature fluctuations."

"But you were going to *shoot*?"

"I would have winged him. If need be."

I shook my head. I hadn't known she knew how to shoot. I wondered if she'd shot targets out at Casa Diablo, to practice winging people.

"In any case, there was no need." She held my look. "And further, honey, he saw me there after they all left. I made certain he saw me."

"Waving a gun."

"No," she said, deadly calm. "Holding it steady."

"And that helped *how*?"

"It clarified where he should direct his wrath."

My chair hit the floor and I was moving with a sudden laser fury and I didn't know where to aim first, didn't know if it was directed at Jeanine and Jimbo and Bobby for being so dumbass stupid or at Lindsay for using them like that or at Krom for taking the bait.

She said, "I'm sorry you're caught up in this."

"You going to tell Walter?"

Her face roughened. "No."

Me neither, I'd cut out my tongue before I laid this on Walter. And then I wondered just whose secret I was keeping because it was, after all, me who had given her the ammo. I had, after all, told her about Krom's midnight swim.

It was after six when I left Lindsay's office.

I followed Minaret to Forest Trail and took a right and came to the Community Center.

Lights were ablaze. It's a huge octagonal building, half windows. Inside looking out, it's like you're in a clearing in the woods. Expensive to heat. Georgia got a variance on the building code when she was pushing plans for the center. She wanted a building that mirrored her vision for the town: hub of the known universe. She got it.

I stood outside until my jeans turned stiff from the cold, then checked my watch. Six-twenty. I was early.

I waited eight more minutes and then went in.

There was nobody to be seen in the vast central orb of the building. This is the heart of the Community Center, the Circle Room. A skating rink could fit in here. Radiating from this hub are corridors which lead to offices.

I didn't know which corridor led to Krom.

I gravitated to the room's centerpiece, a great pit within which seems to float a good deal of Mono County. I began to circumnavigate the relief map. I saw him then, some thirty degrees northeast, hunched on one of the split-log benches that face the pit. He motioned me forward. I came along, my boot soles squeaking like mice on the tile floor.

He rose. He had the *Mammoth Times* in hand.

I stared, like he'd just risen naked and steaming from the waters of Hot Creek.

But of course he was dressed. Tan parka, brown cords, brown cowboy boots. Brown hair wet-combed into submission. Tanned face smooth-shaven. His eyes, though, were reddened like he'd not been sleeping well.

He waited until I got close and then tossed the newspaper onto his bench. "Seen this?"

No chitchat, no attempt to explain, no bullshit about consenting adults. Still, I could not help reading the headline for the umpteenth time. CZAR TRADES SAFETY FOR SEX. It was worse, this time, because the subject of the headline was standing in front of me.

I found my voice. "I've read it."

"And?"

"That's not why I asked to see you. I want to talk to you about Hot Creek, yeah. But not..." I scrupulously avoided looking at the paper, "not about you and Jeanine. You and Georgia."

He didn't miss a beat. "That was a private matter."

"Not anymore. Lindsay told me."

"I hadn't taken Lindsay for a common gossip." He glanced at the newspaper. "I hadn't taken Lindsay for a blackmailer, either."

I almost didn't let that pass. "Lindsay told me about you and Georgia at the creek, because there's sulfur and calcite in the evidence." That was stretching the truth; she told me because she bears a grudge against him. "Meaning, the last place Georgia walked might have been near a hot spring."

"She die at Hot Creek?" he asked, bluntly.

"No. No match there. But I wondered if...after the creek... Georgia might have gone looking for another spring."

"That doesn't necessarily follow."

"I'm speculating." Wild-ass leaping, more like it. "Georgia had a romantic streak—I mean, going to the creek, to that chunk of limestone to dig out a crinoid for you. That's not how she normally shopped. But what a perfect gift. I know what that's like, wracking your brain to find the perfect gift for your boyfriend. When you're in love—or in lust, whatever—you go the extra mile, so to speak. You get a little black dress, a sexy number to wow your guy. So the crinoid was her sexy black dress. Metaphorically speaking. And it worked. Wowed you enough that you two ended up in the creek." I ran out of breath. I waited for him to say something.

He didn't.

I leapt onward. "If it were me, I'd want to, I don't know, repeat the encounter. If I were in love, or in lust or whatever."

"She didn't."

"She sure liked it. Enough to tell Lindsay."

"She liked the experience. But Hot Creek was too public for her."

"Then why'd she bring you there?"

"She didn't. I brought her. After she told me where she got the crinoid, I wanted to have a look. I collect. And there we were. I like the place." He looked hard at me. "As you well know."

I held his look. I thought, if a shrink got hold of him there was probably a diagnosable condition. The intense need to control. The over-compensating ego. The delusions of grandeur. The almost symbiotic relationship with the volcano and its offshoots.

I said, raising my question again, "Well then, if she liked the experience, I'm wondering if she went looking for another hot spring. Less public." A place, I thought, where the soil was rich in sulfur and calcite and pumice and cinders and granite. And gunpowder. And where in the Sierra was *that*?

Krom suddenly reached for me.

I flinched.

He grazed the small of my back and turned me to face the relief map. "Have a look. *You* tell *me* where she went."

I looked down at the map. It was eerily real. If you flew over over the actual landscape in a small plane, it would look a lot like this relief map. The flat oval of the caldera is ringed by mountain ranges, like a broad barrel. It always puts me in mind of that carnival ride where you're spun inside a barrel and the floor drops out, which is pretty much what happened when the old magma chamber vented and the valley floor dropped a mile. The mapmaker had pinched up the mountains into folds so that you can look down upon the topography and feel the climb in your legs. The lakes and streams are so blue they splash. Mammoth Mountain's broad summit and muscular slopes are sculpted to ski, and beneath, the town in tiny jewels clings to the brawny land.

But the mapmaker could not show change.

There was no indication of the rapid swelling in the caldera, where magma's forcing its way up. There was no depiction of the churning evolution at Hot Creek. Hot Creek was just a slash of pretty blue.

I turned back to Krom. "I don't see anything."

"You don't?" He pointed. "There's Casa Diablo, where you taught me how it's done."

It took all the will I possessed not to look down.

"And just to the south is Hot Creek. Where the safety of your town is being toyed with."

"That's a bit over-dramatic."

"Is it?" He pressed his hand again into my back, like a dance partner, turning me. "Let's go to my office. I want you to see what's at stake."

He escorted me to a corridor and we passed closed doors—Georgia's office, still unoccupied, Parks and Rec, Senior Volunteers, the men's room—and came to the office at the end of the hall. Door was open. I looked in. Prime real estate, double size, the back wall a window with a view of the woods.

He said, "Georgia set me up here."

We went in.

Busy office, big desk, phone bank, in-box stacked to the roof. Computer hutch. Storage cabinet. Maps on the wall, calendar filled in. Aerial photos; roads highlighted with black marker. Sketch of Pika Canyon, the new escape route he pitched at the Inn. On top of a bookshelf was a display of rocks—obsidian and lapilli and Pele's tears and all the other stone faces of volcanism. Tucked in amongst disaster was a fossil sea lily, the crinoid gift I assumed.

He turned me to the near wall.

Photographs. A mural of death. Aerial shot of three bodies in the bed of a pickup, composition in gray, landscape and truck and bodies fuzzed in ash. Mount Saint Helens; I'd seen that shot before. Other things I hadn't seen. Closeup of an arm, carbonized, the hand terminating in stubs. Another closeup, mummified face cooked to the color of sunset. Medium shot of a charred family—about to run?—frozen in motion. I'd heard of that, when volcanic fire burns so hot the muscles go spastic at the moment of death. More photos, closeup, long shot, group, color, black-and-white, which was hard to tell from ash gray. Melted flesh, arms, legs, feet in shoes, not one part connected to another. One lone head, open mouth plugged with ash.

He said, "A reminder."

He didn't have to turn me again. I moved as far from him as I could and came to the wall flanking his desk. Another mural, a wall of framed certificates. In grateful recognition of. For outstanding devotion to. In appreciation for. Service. Professional conduct. Excellence in Management. Courage. Courage was the award that held me. No gold seals, no Gothic font, no long-winded dedication. Just a plain paper that read in block letters *To Adrian Krom. For His Courage. From the people of Homer, Alaska.*

He said, "That's what I bring to your town."

I turned.

"And now my reputation is on the line." He stuck his hands into the pockets of his brown cords. "You see, Cassie, I got a phone call this morning, *early*, from Len Carow. You remember Len, the man who wants to achieve nothing more in his professional life than to take my scalp. He's back in D.C. Lindsay emailed him a copy of your newspaper and he's emailing it up and down the line. Doesn't matter I was set up by a small-town slut. My side of the story won't carry. Len's concerned, Cassie. Len fears I've made light of my own safety measures. *Made light.* And I've been getting calls from the Council as well. Instead of deciding escape routes, they're diverted by gossip. So your little town might just get what it's after. You know the saying—be careful what you ask for." His hands formed fists in the pockets, deforming the drape of his trousers. "So, Cassie, you see enough at the creek the night you followed me? Enough to tell your chum Lindsay?"

I flinched, yet again. "I'm not sure I understand what I saw."

"You saw a man who challenges his enemy."

"The volcano's your enemy?"

"Yours too."

"Okay," I said. "But my problem is, you see our volcanologist as the enemy too."

He laughed, mirthless. "And how would you describe her? The architect of that fiasco in the creek."

"I don't approve of that," I said. "And I don't approve of you trying to undermine her."

"Enough." He circled the desk and sat in his chair. "Let's repair the damage. Let's snatch victory from the jaws of defeat.

Another saying. Something you should know about me—I like sayings."

I knew. Abandon hope, ye who enter.

"Let's strike a bargain. You help me and I'll help you."

"Help you with what?"

"Find me what Georgia found. If that involves hunting a hot spring, go hunt your hot spring. But *find* it."

"I plan to. It's my job."

"Oh it's more than that, with you. I've watched you. I see you." He assessed me, the way I'd assessed his wall of merit. "You look again and again, you keep going, against all odds. I understand that about you. Never say die. Right?"

I nodded, stiffly. He got that right.

"I want you to keep me in the loop. Because Georgia found something that alarmed her. *No way out*. It's almost a saying, isn't it?"

"Could mean something personal." I sounded like a broken record.

"You're after a hot spring," he said. "What does that say? Aside from your little black dress. It says *volcanism*."

"You saying she *did* go looking? You thinking she found a new spring?" Hot springs live off the roots of past eruptions, or new dikes of magma, but one new spring wouldn't herald an eruption. Then again, it would certainly be of interest.

"Whatever she found, I want to know when you find it. But I want more than that. I want you to tell me where you're looking, where you're even *speculating* about looking, so that I can report to the Council, and to Len, that the mayor might have found something noteworthy and that I am being kept apprised of the progress of the search."

"You mean you want something to *spin*? To play *politics*?"

"That's exactly what I mean. So that I can get the focus back where it belongs. You give me the heads-up and I'll take it from there. All I need is the *spin*, because I'm fighting the *spin* your chum cooked up at Hot Creek."

I took that in. "And what's your end of the bargain? How do you help me?"

"I stay on the job. I save you. You and your town."

"And what if Georgia didn't find anything? What if it doesn't matter?"

"Then I need time to prepare."

"Prepare for what?"

"Foretelling the future."

I thought, in wonder, he *is* nuts.

He came out of his chair and leaned against the desk beside me. He unbuttoned the right cuff of his brown flannel shirt and folded the sleeve in neat packets to the elbow. He rolled his arm so that the inner forearm showed. It was a remarkably graceful gesture.

I stared at his forearm.

The scar was white and raised, as Jeanine had described, and covered with a swirling tattoo. I understood why she couldn't have read it in the dark at the creek. Hard enough with his office light ablaze to follow the trail of words snaking round and round in ever tighter circles. He held his arm still, rigid as the family on his wall burned into spasm. He gave me the time to read.

In the fourth gulf of the eighth circle of hell are those who presumed to foretell the future, their heads fixed face-backward on their necks.

"Dante," he said.

"I know."

Our eyes fixed on each other.

He said, "I've been in that circle of hell."

"At Rainier."

"Yes." He dropped his arm. "Know this, Cassie—I won't go there again."

I was in my own maze, trying to find the right path. Keep the emergency-ops man in the loop, so he can save his rep? I stared at the swirly tattoo. And save us in the process. I glanced at his wall of merit, at the sincere thanks from the folks of Homer, Alaska.

"By the way," he said, "you could take 'foretelling the future' as a metaphor. But it's damn close to my job description."

I thought, Lindsay's too. I said, "Anything I find that has to do with the volcano I'll report first to Lindsay."

"I wouldn't expect anything else."

I said, "I'll want to run this past Walter. He's doing field work too."

"Good idea." Krom stuck out his hand.

I took it. We shook.

I intended to keep my part of the bargain but with eyes wide open. In fact, I intended to undertake this hunt with my head fixed face-backward on my neck.

22

I ENTERED THE FOG.

At times it clung so low I could see no more than the red slick of my skis, and at times it peeled from canyon walls to reveal iron-oxidized cliffs. It was the fog that darkened the red stain of the cliffs and put me in mind of blood.

Of course it was hematite, not blood—soft earthy iron oxide that colors soil and rock red. Hematite, from the Greek for blood, loosely translated as bloodstone. I squinted at the cliff rock. A kind of purplish red color, really. Come to think of it, a color much like the livor mortis on Georgia's skin, where the blood pooled. She died on her back and lay there long enough for livor to fix.

Wherever *there* was.

I heard a sound and turned my face to look backward. Nothing to see. Could have been a whitetail jackrabbit, schussing through the snow.

Little jumpy? Nobody around but you and the bunny.

When I'd parked in the lot near Lake Mary, there were no other cars. As I'd looped the lake, there were no other skiers. When I'd left the lake and begun the climb up Coldwater

Canyon, I'd encountered the fog. Fog wrapped and hid me and then capriciously lifted to reveal me. Every time I turned, I saw shapes through gray veils. Tall thin-trunked shapes that could be nothing but lodgepole pines and the smaller shapes that were likely young hemlocks whose droopy tips put me in mind of hands.

No Jeffrey pines here—I was climbing above their range. At any rate, the Jeffrey-pumice mix I'd found in Georgia's mouth had tested negative for cyanide, which deepened my conviction that it was of a different origin from the rest of the evidence. A mystery, to be put aside and taken up later, like the gunpowder.

I headed up the canyon which glaciers had long ago bulldozed between Mammoth Crest and Red Mountain. Red Mountain, beneath its snowcap, is in places lava-patched granite.

Gold country.

Over the years I've picked up a few sayings of Walter's, regarding the metallic ores. He says, where two different kinds of rock meet, that's a clue that precious ore might be found. It was, here, a century ago. Tunnels were dug, ore was crushed, and for awhile some got rich.

I too was on a treasure hunt, only the treasure I was after was liquid and steaming.

My talk with Krom had bolstered my theory that Georgia went hunting for a hot spring, a good source for the sulfur and calcite in the boot soil. And the cyanide suggested that spring was in the neighborhood of a mine.

I halted and pulled out my compass and maps. Walter had downloaded a map of mine sites from the net, and we'd compared it with a geologic map of the region, and marked sites where mines intersected with deposits from hot springs. We'd split the sites, each of us canvassing a different neighborhood.

I checked the next mine on my half of the map, got my bearings, and pushed on.

The fog-hung canyon narrowed and I had to stop again and again to dig out snow clots that wedged between my boots and skis. As I knelt, I looked back. I could not help but leave tracks, which anyone with a pair of skis could follow. Even in fog.

I told myself once again to get a grip. There is no other skier. There is nobody, nothing, not even the rabbit. All was quiet.

The silence up here was palpable as the fog, giving this country a funereal feel.

I said, "I have nothing of interest to tell you."

Krom motioned me to join him on the split-log bench overseeing the relief map. "Where did you go?"

"Up Coldwater Canyon."

"What took you there?"

"Pumice. Sulfur. Calcite. Granite. Trachybasaltic cinders..."

"What's trachybasaltic?"

"Extrusive rock intermediate in composition between basalt and..."

"Never mind the geology lesson. What did you find?"

"Nothing of interest."

"No hot spring?"

"Nope."

"What about Walter? Where did he go?"

I told him where Walter went and what Walter found. Nothing of interest.

"Cassie. Give me *something*."

I said, "I really don't think this is working. It's not helping you and it's a waste of my time."

Krom raised his hands. "Then just tell me where you plan to go tomorrow."

I searched the relief map, my eyes coming to rest at Crater

Meadow, settling on the two small cinder symmetric as breasts. "Somewhere around Red Cones, most likely."

"Why there?"

"Calcite. Sulfur. Trachybasalt. Pumice."

He shook his head.

"I can give you a lesson in *forensic* geology if you like. We'll be here all night."

"Look." Krom hiked his big shoulders. "I need to be able to go out for a beer with John Amsterdam and talk about the case as if I know what the hell is happening. I need your chief of police to see that I'm closely following developments, that I'm ready to *respond* to whatever you find. Whatever Georgia found. I need John to tell his chums on the Council that I'm on top of things and that I'll spring for a round of beers. I need to repair the relationships. I need to know what the hell I'm talking about." His polished brown eyes held steady on mine. "I need your help. Let me be the judge of its worth."

I hesitated.

He gave a slight smile. "I'm an official with a valid interest."

"Okay, here's something new you can tell John. We found cyanide in the soil, which might have come from old mining tailings. And hot springs are associated with the precious ores. So that's a lead I'm following."

Krom considered. "So I can tell John you're looking for a mine."

"Yup. And maybe he'll spring for the beers."

I followed Laurel Creek, a good three miles east of Red Cones, as the crow flies.

Two more mine diggings were crossed off my map and a third was ahead. I had widened my sampling field, checking sites farther from the glacier, although the farther afield I went the harder it was to envision hauling the body from the scene of death to the scene of disposal.

I was going now more on hope than belief.

I came to a steep bluff, shorn of snow. The face was roughly striped. The layering tilted, striking to the northwest until it bent down and back upon itself in a recumbent fold. It looked like a large striped cat had tucked itself under the face and stretched recumbent upon the snow.

It brought me a vision of Lindsay. Her cat's smile when she told me not to worry about vendettas. Her face roughened when she told me not to tell Walter about her role in Hot Creek.

It brought me a vision of Georgia, writing furiously in her Weight Watchers notebook. No way out. No way out no way out no way out.

I shivered. *What did you find, Georgia*?

All was silence.

"What did you find at Red Cones?"

"East of Red Cones, actually." I sat on the ledge of the relief map, facing Krom on his split-log bench. "I found nothing of interest."

"Cassie."

I flipped a hand. "You don't find something, you move on."

"Move on *where*? I'm running out of time, Cassie. I'm getting phone calls, courtesy of Len Carow. And if you're thinking you don't give a damn about my fate, then think about your town's fate. Remind yourself that Georgia found something important *over two months ago* and then she was killed and tell me if you give a damn about *time*."

I said, softly, "I give a damn. I want to find it as much as you do. I'm just frustrated. I don't know where to look next. Walter and I have run out of likely mines."

He said, equally softly, "You disappoint me."

Surprisingly, that stung.

He stood, and hiked himself onto the ledge next to me. "Let me help you."

"How?"

"Tell me about your evidence. Tell me what you were looking for out at Casa Diablo that day. Besides calcite. Calcite's real common." His eyes shone beneath the heavy lids. "Your own phrasing. You said it that day with a dismissive tone. You wanted me to see calcite as a general example. But now we're working together."

I thought, all right. I said, "Gunpowder."

He frowned. "In the *evidence*?"

"Yes."

"But Casa Diablo..."

"There's a shooting range there. The targets are down for the winter."

"And that's why you stayed behind after the drill? To search the biathlon range for gunpowder."

"Yes."

He was frowning deeply now.

I thought, *he didn't know*. He didn't know there was shooting in the place Georgia died. I felt a sudden relief. He didn't know where Georgia died.

"And Red Cones?" he said. "And the other places you went to? Who shoots there?"

"I don't know."

"So where are you going tomorrow, Cassie?"

I was at a loss. I'd checked all the mines on the map that were anywhere near a hot spring. I could move on to mines without springs, which is what Walter wants to do. Put the hot spring aside. We don't *know* the calcite and sulfur came from a spring. We do know we've got cyanide. Follow the cyanide angle until we hit pay dirt, or until it stalls. The way we did with gunpowder.

"Cassie. What are you going after tomorrow?"

"The truth."

He laughed, softly. "I was right about you. You have belief. Not hope. Hope won't get you out the door." He slid a look at me. "Am I right? You still have belief? You'll find what Georgia found?"

I gripped the ledge. I didn't know.

His eyes sharpened. "Are all mines mapped?"

I went north, driving Highway 395 the sixty miles along the Sierra scarp to the county seat at Bridgeport. In the old clapboard Victorian, with the cupola sitting atop the second story like an old lady's hat, I spent half the day reading microfiche. Notices of location filed by the scavengers who'd picked over sites after the big mines played out. They located claims by landmark. One mile south of Deer Creek bridge and ninety feet northwest of the tunnel adit, and...

Claims so ephemeral they never made it onto a map.

Five claims were described as being near hot springs.

Three for me, I thought, and two for Walter.

Thank you, Adrian Krom.

23

I WAS up Coldwater Canyon again.

I skied past the turnoff I'd taken two days ago and paused to check behind me. No fog today, just sunshine. Nobody in sight, just me and my visions.

Ahead was a stand of lodgepoles with their trunks snapped off above snowline, unlucky enough to grow in an avalanche trough.

I kicked up my pace and didn't slow until I left the canyon trail behind. I was concealed now, in the hemlocks and silver pines. The climb steepened and my muscles burned. I topped a ridge and followed the map I'd made around an outcrop of granite, finding my way to the little fold in Red Mountain. Here was the nearly hidden draw that I'd read about at county records, that its claimant had expectantly named Gold Dust.

I skied in.

The draw backed into the mountainside, to a tunnel whose entrance showed a reddish cinder face. The adjoining rock wall showed another face, gray granodiorite.

It was a place where two different kinds of rock meet.

It looked like someone, sometime, found something here worth scavenging.

There was the stone foundation of a building, still timbered. A stream bisected the old camp, and frozen into the waterway was a rusted contraption of gears and teeth. Slightly uphill were snow-covered mounds that looked for all the world like sand dunes. That was likely the dump, boneyard of discarded ore. Below that was a circular depression—the cyanide pond where someone had leached the remaining gold from the tailings. I'd seen its like before, couple of days ago, at two other sites on Red Mountain. I didn't know precisely how much cyanide the leaching process left in the soil. Way too much for the good of the environment. Ironic, that it would bode well for my case.

But not here, because this cyanide pond did me no more good than the others, because the snow of this draw spread sparkling and unbroken. There was no hot spring.

Still, my eye fixed on the stream, where several bushy trees bent beneath the weight of snow. Mountain willow—dwarfish at this altitude.

Georgia had picked up a willow leaf somewhere.

I decided to sample the draw.

Because the soil would be bared in the tunnel, I began there. Exchanging skis for a flashlight, leaden with cold, I went in, stopping just inside. The tunnel was a skinny incursion into the mountain, high-ceilinged at the front end. At the far end, it closed down to a narrow throat. I played the flash over the rock face, half-expecting to see lusters of gold, but the only luster my flashlight caught was in the flattened cans of Mountain Dew that littered the floor. The floor was hard rock dusted with a thin soil, which not surprisingly looked cinder-red. Here and there it was studded with dark nodules. Upon closer examination of the nodules near the entrance, I identified them as animal scat. Alpine chipmunk or pika, I figured, at this altitude.

I took a soil sample near the entrance and went out into the light to see what I had.

I spread a tarp, laid out my tools, and put a hand lens to the dish of soil. Oxidized cinders, bits of pumice. A wink of mica, duller hornblende, milky quartz, pinkish feldspar—granite. I assumed the nearest source was the gray rockfall, chunks of which had weathered and crumbled, and that decomposed granite had fed into the soil.

My interest stirred.

Not lab conditions, but in the field under the hand lens this soil looked a close match to the evidence from Georgia's boots.

I sat back on my heels and thought it through. What was missing? Well, cyanide for starters, although there was the obvious source. I debated whether to dig a sample near the ore dump but the snow there was deep. I decided to put that off. As for the hot spring minerals, there was no visible source of sulfur and calcite.

And then the obvious hit me. I felt like a fool.

What if Georgia *had* found a spring here—the spring the prospector described in his claim—and it had subsequently died? She's been dead over two months now. In two months, a hot spring can die too. And then the snow comes and buries the corpse.

For my purposes, dead's just as good as alive.

I scanned the draw. A grid search of this place would take well over a day. If need be, I'd come back with Walter and do the work. For now, I was willing to stipulate that there was a spring here somewhere, dead and buried.

Okay then, move on to the next missing bit. Gunpowder.

I looked at the tunnel. Soil was bared there so it was worth another search. I went back in, pausing again at the mouth. This time, playing my flashlight over the soil, I was looking for boot-prints. There was some scuffing here and there but nothing identifiable. Might have been animals, might have been the Mountain-Dew drinkers, but the thin soil wasn't saying. I went farther inside the tunnel and did a thorough sampling.

Outside again, spreading my haul on the tarp, my eye was drawn to the mouth of the draw and I stared until every shape resolved itself into a tree.

I bent to work and was rewarded in the second dish. I stared, in disbelief. I took the twenty-power hand lens and looked again. And then, feverish, ransacked all the dishes. Strike after strike: the mother lode. Not dust of gold but disks of silver. Their faces burned into my memory. Including dimples, my old friend.

Gunpowder.

My hand was shaking. I set down my lens.

Somebody did a great deal of shooting in the tunnel—or in the draw and then somebody or a lot of somebodies tracked the powder around.

Somebody who used biathlon powder.

Shit.

What *happened* here? And why was Georgia involved?

And who was here with her?

I went very cold. Georgia, den mother to the biathlon team, indefatigable booster who brought the biathlon World Cup to Mammoth.

But I could not make the leap from the biathlon course up here to Gold Dust. I couldn't even venture an onageristic estimate on that.

Wait. Back up. There were still all those unidentified grains of powder, that were *not* biathlon powder.

I didn't get it. I was ninety percent convinced I'd found the place she last walked—I'd bump that up to one hundred percent in the lab—but I had no idea what she was doing here.

Okay, so back up again. How in hell did she come here in the first place? Did *she* go to county records and find the Gold Dust notice of location? And if she did, why? Well maybe she wasn't after a hot spring, after all, maybe she was looking for a mine and the spring was secondary. But *why*?

And what in the name of all that is logical did she find so compelling here? Enough to write *no way out*.

If indeed she wrote it here.

Well, there was the hot spring. The stipulated hot spring. Although a hot spring—one that was so ephemeral that it died—was hardly enough to set her heart racing. Was it?

I shrugged. Just go back to the lab and do the analysis.

As I was packing my field kit, I thought about the quirky mix of Jeffrey pine bark and pumice that was in her mouth. No Jeffrey pines here—it's too high for Jeffrey, too far from the nearest Jeffrey forest for an animal to ferry in enough bark to mix in any significant proportion with the soil here.

I thought back to Georgia's body on the tray in the medical examiner's lab. The bruising around her mouth had led to my assumption that someone had opened her mouth and dumped in the pumice-bark mix.

No wild-ass guesses necessary to conclude that whoever was here with Georgia brought that quirky mix.

I gritted my teeth, and I thought about Adrian Krom. I thought about Lindsay's theory, and I could concoct my own corollary—Georgia finds a new hot spring here, a new place for a romp—and brings her lover but he's not as impressed as she'd hoped. He says something in his brusque way, and she responds in kind. Or maybe he gets weird. Maybe he invites her for a dip and quotes Dante and even if she's lovestruck she's not stupid and she says what kind of nonsense is this? She fears we've put the town in the hands of a nutcase. She decides what must be done—get him fired. No fooling around like Lindsay with reputations, she's the goddamn mayor and she's got clout with everyone who counts, when push comes to shove. And it does, because Krom sees her react. She tries to cover but she's Georgia and she's lousy at evasions. She manages to steal a moment alone—maybe in the tunnel—to write her quick notes in the Weight Watcher's. But in the end, Krom finds her.

The sun dipped behind the rock wall and Gold Dust fell into gloom.

Suddenly in a hurry, I finished packing and geared up.

In the process, my corollary to Lindsay's theory fell apart. If Adrian Krom had killed Georgia here, why in the name of all that is logical was he trying to help me find this place? If it wasn't for Adrian Krom, I might not have thought to check county records.

I pushed off. I skied full-out to the mouth of the draw but when I skirted the granite outcrop, my skiing turned awkward. I was following the tracks I'd made on the way in and it took me two or three glides to figure out what was wrong.

I bent to the tracks.

Too many basket holes, too close together. When you ski cross country you don't break new trail if there is already a set of tracks going where you want to go. You take advantage of the first skier's labor. You'll set the tracks a little deeper. Hardly noticeable. But it's nearly impossible to ski and set your poles in someone else's basket holes. Judging the progress of the basket holes, I figured the skier had come just to the bend, just far enough to sight up the draw. He'd done a kick turn and headed downhill in the same tracks.

The tracks didn't say how long he'd stayed.

I got my field knife and opened the blade, listening to my own sharp breathing, and then because I couldn't ski with an open blade I put the knife away. I ran on my skis until the slope angled enough to take the downhill in a tuck.

Drops ran down my spine—not the sweat of exertion but the cold oily trickle of fear.

When I reached the Lake Mary parking lot I saw Mike Kittleman changing the tire of his Explorer.

I saw his skis racked on top, caked with snow.

Mike Kittleman was on the biathlon team as a kid, before Georgia kicked him off.

I watched him a moment, recalling that day in the gondola barn when the machinery broke and Eric came and I told Mike to let Eric fix it, and I recalled just how strong Mike had been when he grabbed me by the hair and put the screwdriver to my neck—and I wondered if I needed to be afraid now. But there were other cars in the lot, and there was a family unloading a sled and the dad was big and burly.

I took off my skis and approached Mike.

He saw me. He pretended not to, his head bent to the job.

I said, "Mike."

He looked up. Feigned surprise. Spoke, at last. "Yeah?"

"What are you doing here?"

I waited for him to say *what does it look like, I'm changing a tire.* Mike is unrelentingly literal. He said, instead, "Just came back from a ski."

I was blunt. "Did you follow me?"

He lifted the spare tire onto the wheel studs. He screwed each lug nut back on, slowly and meticulously, by hand. He said, finally, "No," like he was so unaffected by my question that he nearly forgot to answer.

"Then what were you doing? Where did you ski?"

He picked up the tire iron and tightened the first lug nut. He shot me a glance. Face set in naked hatred. "It's a free country."

"Yes it is," I said. "And I'm free to tell the chief of police my unfounded suspicion that you've been following me. And you're free to prove me wrong."

24

I WENT straight home after my trip to Gold Dust. No reporting in to Krom, no chats on the split-log bench.

I ate an apple and cheese for dinner and had little appetite even for that. I took a steaming hot shower. I went to bed early. I had a nightmare in which Krom followed me to the hidden draw and barged in and dug a hole in the snow and when the steam licked up, he forced me into the hot blue pool. I awoke sweating and went outside and stood for two minutes in the snow to cool off. Went back to bed, back to sleep, and had another nightmare, in which Mike followed me and confronted me while I was pondering the gunpowder under my hand lens, and he knocked me over and put a screwdriver to my throat.

That time when I awoke, I heard Georgia chiding me. *You're not the victim, I am.*

Early the next morning I went to the lab and laid out my findings for Walter.

Walter took his time, poking through specimen dishes,

plucking out items of special interest, comparing gunpowder grains under the comparison scope, scrutinizing minerals under the polarized lightscope.

I waited, watching. On the screen of the lightscope, minerals floated like fish in the sea.

Walter finished and turned to me. "We have a soil match."

"I agree."

"More than that. We have a gunpowder match. This is especially significant because the powders are so unusual."

"I agree."

"We need to hurry along the gunpowder lab. We need an ID of those mystery powders."

"I sent an email last night. I praised the chief examiner for a paper he presented at the last conference of the American Academy of Forensic Sciences, and asked if he could move things along."

"Was it a good paper?"

"I wouldn't know. I just googled it and grabbed the title."

Walter's eyebrows lifted, and then he smiled.

"So," I said, "what we need now are exemplars that contain the hot springs minerals, and cyanide. Means we have to dig."

Still, Walter smiled. "I'll take the cyanide pond."

"You and your mines. Okay, fair enough, you have fun with that and I'll start the grid search for the spring."

"Tomorrow morning?" Walter said.

"Early. Lot of digging to do."

"In the meantime," Walter said, "we have all of today to do a thorough analysis on the soils."

"I need to get caffeinated first." I poured us both a cup, and we took the time to nurse the brew in companionable silence. Enjoying the small moment of victory. A good-sized step in the direction of solving the case, finding out where Georgia died.

And, I had to admit with a small stab of guilt, just the simple pleasure at doing the geology.

Walter finished his coffee and turned back to the lightscope. He rotated the polarizer, turning a hexagonal crystal to its point of extinction, where all light is absorbed.

I took a moment to do scutwork, labeling the gunpowder samples. Unidentified powder number one. Number two. And so on. And, finally, the one powder from the tunnel that I could identify: dimples. Fiocchi, choice of many a biathlete—including Mike and Eric and Stobie and my brother Jimbo.

My gaze shifted to the Alice-in-Wonderland poster on the wall behind Walter's bench. Alice is tumbling down the rabbit hole. The message being, you follow the evidence wherever it takes you, down the rabbit hole if you must.

Even if you don't want to go there.

We worked until the dinner hour and my stomach growled and then Walter left to go get takeout.

Five minutes later, Krom knocked at the door, same time as he opened it.

I sucked in a long breath, and motioned him to take Walter's stool.

He scooted it over beside mine. He assessed the specimen dishes laid out on my bench. He took off his parka and laid it across his knees. His gaze came to rest on me. "I haven't heard from you for two days, Cassie."

"I've been too busy."

"Nothing of interest to report?"

I considered our bargain. I decided I'd better warn him. "I might have found the place Georgia died but I have to tell you, there's nothing there that impacts your job. Nothing to do with the volcano." I shrugged. "Nothing you can use to spin, over beers with John Amsterdam."

His hand slammed down on my workbench.

I jumped.

He took hold of my arm, as if to steady me.

I pulled away.

"*Listen to me.*"

I stiffened.

"Give me your hand," he said, softly. "Please."

I looked through the storefront window, at the crowds passing by, tired from the slopes and ready to find a place for dinner.

Krom caught my look. "Please, Cassie. Please."

I gave him my hand.

He shoved up his right sleeve and placed my hand on his forearm, on top of the tattooed scar, so that my palm cupped the raised flesh. "I want to share a vision with you. I want you to feel it."

His arm was hot. My hand was unaccountably cold.

"On the other side of the world," he said, "a volcano out of the blue starts erupting. There's a tribe living on its slopes and they blame the outsiders who've been drilling holes into their mountain. You see, these outsiders are after geothermal energy. But the tribe thinks the mountain is their mother and the drilling has made her so mad she's exploded. The tribe runs to escape her anger but two of them—a man and a woman—run *toward* the eruption, not away from it. The sacrifice satisfies their mother and she lets the rest of the tribe escape."

His flesh was beginning to warm my icy hand.

"The volcanologists come and have a look and decide the mountain is letting off steam. It's just getting started." His arm tensed, beneath my hand. "I was one of those outsiders drilling into the mountain. When things got bad, the scientists warned us. Our camp was evacuated. It was chaos."

I thought of the photos in his office.

"It was dark and raining stones. My truck got separated from the group. Driver went the wrong way, *toward* the eruption, not away from it. Truck stalled in the ash. Driver and I got out to check the engine. He got hit by a lava bomb. Killed him. I was shit-scared I was going to die. Then I got hit, in the arm. Pain like I've never known. I got back into the truck. My arm was a blessing, a sacrifice. I screamed in pain. Pain moved me beyond the fear."

He fell silent, waiting for me to speak.

I did not know what to say.

He resumed. "Later, I heard about the man and woman who offered themselves up to save their tribe. I decided that's what I'm going to do with my life."

He cupped his hand over mine and pressed. My fingers splayed, the tips coming to rest on the boundary of the scar, where its rubbery surface rose from the soft hairs of intact flesh.

"And I've already proved I can take the pain."

I asked, "So we're the tribe?"

25

LATE THAT NIGHT, I stood at the window of the cottage out back of my parents' house, waiting for Eric.

I'm bunking here now but this cottage used to be the hangout of my brother and his friends. The paneling is darkened cedar, hung with their old snapshots. It's one big room with a toilet and sink in the closet, and it's showing its age. The floor tilts. The wall heater wheezes. The window is crisscrossed by sash bars that have been painted so many times a knife will go in a quarter inch before hitting wood.

Outside, the yard slopes down to a stream gully. The stream borders the six houses on our side of the street neatly as a fence. Beyond the stream is a meadow. I've always liked that because it gives the illusion of wilderness in my backyard.

I'd picked off two layers of peeling paint when Eric at last appeared. I swung open the door.

"Evening, Cassie." He wore his Mammoth PD jacket and he refused my offer of a beer. I ducked into the closet, which stays cold as a refrigerator in winter, and got two Cranapples. When I emerged he was reading the names carved into the old table. All Jimbo's buds had immortalized themselves there. "This place."

He shook his head and hung his jacket over a chair. "It's a time warp."

A fitting place to dive into the mystery of old gunpowder.

He moved to examine the photos on the wall. He halted in front of the one where the boys, in their early teens, stand on top of some peak. They must have put the camera on a rock and set the timer because all of them are in the picture: Jimbo, Eric, Stobie, Mike, the de Martinis, Bobby Panetta, and Corey Steiner who's since moved away. I've seen enough shots of them with their tongues out, and worse, but in this one they're solemn kids on top of the world.

"Thanks for coming," I said. I gave him the juice.

He tipped the bottle to me. "Can't stay long. I'm going to see Stobie."

"Jimbo saw him this morning."

"Any change?"

"No. Jimbo would have said. He was rushing for work." Although the Council was still debating escape route options, work on the Bypass continued. "There's a change, Jimbo rushing for work." I took a drink. "Have you seen him lately?"

"Not after I caught up with him and told him what an idiotic stunt that was at the creek."

I tightened, waiting for Eric to mention Lindsay's name. And mine.

He didn't even look at me. He was staring out the window. "What a fuckup. All of it. You know, when we pulled Georgia off the mountain I thought, this is it. This is where the bad stuff happens *here*, not someplace like L.A. Lot goes down in L.A.—I saw that when I was at the academy. And I know we've led some goddamned sheltered lives up here, but our turn had to come sometime. I thought, with Georgia, we'd taken our hit. Some other place was up next. But no. It's not enough this volcano's all over us, we've got to fuck it up ourselves too."

"We had some help."

He turned. "Krom? Yeah, guy's a real cowboy. But he's got a job I wouldn't want."

"You still think he can do it?"

"You mean after the creek?" Eric studied his juice. "That took him down a notch or two in my book. Word is, they're talking about a replacement."

"Dicey time to replace him. Changing horses in midstream, and all that."

Eric slowly nodded. "So what can I do for you, Cass?"

I moved to the table. In a green box were the files I brought from my condo. Unpaid bills, journal articles to read, sales on silk long underwear—my hot file. I pulled the front folder and handed it to him.

He read. He closed the folder and said, neutrally, "Nice range of exotics."

"They were part of that powder John couriered to the gunpowder lab for us."

"Oh?"

Tonight, when I'd come home from the lab, I'd checked my email and found the report. I sent my thanks and promised to buy the chief examiner dinner sometime. And then I'd phoned Eric.

Eric returned the folder to me and lifted the Cranapple to drink.

I said, "The gunpowder was in the soil I traced to a mine claim called Gold Dust."

The bottle stalled at his lips.

"There's a tunnel, about forty meters before it narrows down, almost as long as a biathlon range. I've been thinking—wind wouldn't be a factor indoors. And it stays cold in there." I remembered the guys as boys talking endlessly about which ammo worked best in the cold. "The one powder in the evidence that I could ID was Fiocchi. Mike told me it was the best. So Fiocchi was the control, and you test-fired the others against it? Exotics, you call them? But none of them ever outperformed Fiocchi." The chief examiner at the gunpowder lab had identified the mystery makes as limited-production cold weather powders, off the market for over a decade.

"Heavy artillery," Eric said. "I'm impressed."

"I'm not interested in impressing you."

"Then what can I say?"

"Help me with the chain of events." I was able to come at it this way, evidence to be dissected. "The evidence—including those unique powders—places Georgia at Gold Dust. It says that's where she took her last steps."

He said, evenly, "Why ask me about it?"

"Because we just established you guys used to shoot there. Because Georgia used to sponsor you."

He drained his juice.

I said, "How did Georgia find out about the place?"

"Because we shot off our mouths and she overheard us." He shrugged. "Made us a deal—take her there so she could be sure it was safe and she'd keep our secret hangout secret."

"Did Lindsay know about it?"

"Never saw her there."

"Was there a hot spring at Gold Dust?"

Eric cocked his head. "Yeah. Great place to soak. Why?"

I mentally filed that; confirmation of the spring. "Remember the notes Georgia wrote? She found something."

"Damn straight I remember."

"Evidence says what she found could be a hot spring."

He frowned. "If she meant our spring, it's sure as hell nothing new."

"Maybe it was active enough that she thought it was a big deal."

He eyed me. "Is it?"

"It seems to have died. At least, I didn't see it. Where was it?"

He shook his head. "Long time ago. Best I recall, few yards from the tunnel."

"How many yards?"

"You want a guess? Ten. Fifteen. Twenty."

"Which direction?"

"Southeast, I'd say."

"Can you show me?"

"What, take you there? Sure. I've got Wednesday off. It's a date."

"Not till Wednesday?"

"I've got a job, Cassie. Protect the peace." He eyed me. "What's the hurry? If the spring's no big deal."

"The hurry is I'm going back up there and I'd like to know where to dig."

"Then wait until Wednesday and I'll go with you."

"I don't want to wait. I want to find out if there's anything to worry about. I want to solve this *case*--we owe it to Georgia."

He said, "Don't make it personal."

"How do I not make it personal when the vic is Georgia?"

"I'm not talking about Georgia. I'm talking about you carrying a load of guilt about your little brother and trying to make up for it with every case you work."

I said, tight, "This isn't about Henry."

"You can't always save the day, Cassie. If you save the day fifty percent of the time then you're doing damn good."

"You speaking from experience?"

"Yup." Eric moved for the chair where his police jacket hung. "Glad I could be of help."

I got there first and rested my hands on the nylon shoulders. *Focus*. It's about Georgia. I said, "I'm not done, Eric. Tell me what you know about Georgia and Gold Dust."

"What makes you think I know squat?"

"Because you were such a jerk on the retrieval. Because you were ready to send two able-bodied people—and Walter's still able-bodied, thank you—back down the mountain. And Stobie was on board with you. I think you suspected from the get-go it was murder. I think you knew Georgia was snooping around Gold Dust. I don't know if one of you guys saw her, or what. And then when she was found, I think you didn't want two forensic geologists up at the glacier finding that soil in her boots." I held up a hand. "I know you wouldn't diddle the evidence. I just think you wanted time to look it over and see if you were right, if she'd died in your secret place."

Eric flipped the empty bottle, caught it. "That's conjecture."

"All right then, explain *this*. I asked Jimbo for a cartridge to compare to my evidence and he said he didn't have one when he did. I asked where you guys used to shoot and he couldn't remember you tested in the mine tunnel."

"Ask Jimbo about his memory."

I hadn't had the heart, after the disaster at the race. "I figured I'd get a straighter answer from you."

"You got an answer."

"A non-answer. You owe Georgia. You owe a straight answer."

His eyes, which absorb everything and give nothing, remained on me. Georgia was there when he lost his left eye. She was there for every milestone. I'm eleven and he's twelve and there's a Fourth of July party in the meadow behind our house. The boys are trying to launch tuna cans with M-80s, which are illegal for good reason, but the explosives won't light. Everyone gives up but Eric, who finally gets one to ignite. It blows up in his face. And it's Georgia on the spot with the first aid kit. It's Georgia who drafts tough new regs about fireworks. It's Georgia who scolds Eric when he recovers, and then sets up a junior firefighter course. He grew up fast after that, faster than I'd realized at the time.

"All right," Eric said, "straight answer." He hiked himself onto the table. "Starts with Jimbo's Fiat. He and I were heading out to Casa Diablo to get in some shooting practice before the Cup—targets were still up. Jimbo's car died. Big surprise."

I nodded. Jimbo's never heard of car maintenance.

"Then Mike comes driving by, in that Kia of his. He's heading toward town. We try to wave him down, catch a ride, get to the Chevron and arrange a tow. He blows right past us, like a bat out of hell."

"Where was he coming from?"

"Hot Creek."

Hot Creek, I thought. Always Hot Creek.

"So we're about to find the number to phone the Chevron when another car comes hauling ass up the road. Georgia's." He paused, then said, grimly, "Like a damned car chase out of a movie."

"When was this?"

"Few days before she disappeared."

I sat on the bed.

"So we wave her down." He gave a brief smile. "Georgia being Georgia, of course she stops. She's really shook up. And, uh, her hair was wet, her clothes were wet, like she'd pulled them on in a hurry. We ask if she's okay. We don't ask if she's been to the creek because where else would she have been."

Yeah. I said, "Was she with someone? At the creek?"

"Adrian Krom."

Yeah. "She told you."

"Yup."

"And?"

He gave me a flat look. "Come on, Cass, you don't need me to spell it out."

No. I didn't. Lindsay had spelled it out for me. And Krom had spelled it out for me. I said, "Just spell out the part about Mike."

"The way she told it, Mike had gone to Krom's office on *business*," Eric made air quotes, "and saw Krom's car pulling out of the lot, with Georgia riding shotgun. And...I don't have to tell you how Mike felt about Georgia. So Mike jumps in his car and follows them. All the way to Hot Creek. Mike gives them enough time to get down to the creek, get where they're going, do what they came to do, and then he follows. Surprises them, like an *avenging demon*--Georgia's words. He starts his accusations, how he came to Krom on important business, saw them, followed them. He accuses Georgia of luring Krom away. Of pulling another gotcha like Jeanine did. Only Georgia is worse, Mike says, because she's the *mayor*. And she's trying to ruin our guardian. And get us all killed."

I stared. "You're not shitting me?"

"I am not shitting you."

"What happened next?"

"Mike left, charging up the hill. Georgia got out of the creek, got dressed, followed, thinking she's going to catch up with Mike, set him straight, kick his ass, I don't know. She was furious. Furious then, furious when she told Jimbo and me."

"And Krom?"

"He stayed in the creek. Georgia's take, he didn't want things to escalate."

"Your take?"

"Not impressed."

No. I stared at my off-kilter floor. Tired of Mike's asshattery. Tired of Krom's manipulative sex life. Tired, I hated to say, of Georgia's sad love life. Tired of fearing what's in store for us.

Eric said, "You okay, Cass?"

I looked up. "Yeah. What happened next?"

"Georgia drove us back to town so we could get that tow. We told her what happened at the creek was none of our business and we'd keep our damn mouths shut."

"Jimbo too?'

Eric gave a dry laugh. "Yeah, he can keep a secret. Believe it or not."

I found I could believe it.

Eric came off the table. "I'll take that beer now."

I got two. We drank halfway down.

Eric said, "Here's another straight answer for you—about me being a jerk on the retrieval. You're right about me wanting a first look at the evidence. I was a jerk, Cassie, because I wondered whether things had escalated between Mike and Georgia."

I went rigid. "You think Mike killed her?"

"I think Mike's basically a good guy only he's got a problem with his temper."

"He had a problem back in the gondola station when you pulled him off me."

Eric made a sound—inhaling, exhaling, the calm-before-you-shoot cadence.

"And then," I said, "you just let it go."

"I had a talk with him."

"Wasn't enough, Eric. If you'd gone to the cops or his dad—someone in charge—maybe he wouldn't have had the problem with Georgia."

Eric said, voice tight, "So you buy it? Mike and Georgia at Gold Dust?"

"How do the two of them end up there?"

"Don't know."

"Let's say you're right." I didn't want to say it. But shit. I said, "If Mike killed her at Gold Dust, why transport her all the way to the glacier?"

"If Mike killed her at Gold Dust, it'd be in a fit of temper, and he'd be in shock afterward. You *know* him. You get that?"

I nodded. I got that.

"So it would take him awhile to figure what the hell to do next."

I nodded. "So, a day. Long enough for livor to settle in her backside and rigor to come and go."

"Long enough to work out that he'd be a fool to bury her at Gold Dust, not knowing if anybody else knew she was going there. Long enough to consider alternatives—he's backpacked all over the place so I'd guess he knew the glacier. Long enough to figure he'd need a horse to transport her. And yeah, the lab results came back on that hair we found on her--it *is* horse hair." Eric drained his beer. "That's as far as the lab's gotten. There's still one hell of a lot we don't know about this case."

"You know enough to think it's Mike. Want to cover for him."

Eric set down the bottle. "Let's go back to the gondola station." The edge in his voice cut to the bone. He moved to my brick-and-board bookshelf and picked up a chunk of wormhole sandstone that I use as a bookend. My books slumped over. He anchored his fingers in the stone. "I've gone over this for fifteen years. How it could have turned out different. What one little thing I could have done to change things. Or you could have done."

I held his look.

"Yeah Cass, maybe I should have gone to the cops but I thought I had it covered. I thought I could guarantee Mike's behavior." He raised the rock and sighted through one of the wormholes. "It was like this for me—framed. The way things are framed when you're fifteen. Mike's a buddy, Mike's got a problem, Mike's listened to me in the past, he'll listen again. Real simple. And maybe it would have worked." He lowered the rock and gave me a hard look. "But what you did, Cassie, was hang me out to dry."

I said, "I was scared."

"You didn't trust me."

"You were a *kid*. It wasn't a kid's problem. And I got left with it."

He took a long time with that, then nodded. "Why'd you go to Georgia?"

"Because Georgia was the one you go to when you're scared."

Eric nodded. "Gotta admit, you went to the big kahuna. And you got results."

"All I did was ask her to straighten Mike out."

"So she kicks him off the team."

"She was trying to *help* him. Shock some sense into him."

"You have any idea how fucking big a deal it was for Mike to be on the team? He wasn't exactly anyone's first choice. And, no argument, he picked a couple of fights."

"A *couple*?"

"Kicking him off was the worst call she could have made."

I said, mulish, "It worked."

Eric's good eye widened. "Did it? I'd say it turned him into a time bomb."

"He was already a time bomb."

"And the kicker was, Mike never bought that I didn't sell him out."

The beer soured in my stomach.

Eric looked away, staring at the photos on the wall as if he were cataloging a crime scene. Mike with the others on the peak, back when he was one of the guys. Eric said, finally, "You blind-sided me, with Mike."

I fixed on the rock in Eric's hand. Was that the one little thing I could have done to change things? Tell Eric I was going to Georgia? Tell him I thought he'd hung *me* out to dry? And then it would have turned out differently. I said, finally, "I'm sorry."

"Yeah, me too."

"Is that why you're trying to protect Mike?"

"I felt responsible for him. I had it in my head I'd check out the evidence and if it looked bad I'd get him to confess. Maybe he'd get a lighter sentence."

"Why don't you just ask him?"

"I did. He denied it."

"But you're still covering for him."

He passed a hand across his eyes. "I guess I thought you and I and Mike started something back in the gondola station that ended up with a body in the ice."

A saying came to me, some biblical phrase—you reap what you sow.

Eric moved to the bookshelf and replaced the sandstone, refitting my books until they packed in tight as sediments compressed by the weight of the earth's crust.

I said, "Can we ever get past the past?" And then I honked an embarrassed laugh because that sounded so utterly idiotic.

Eric stood. Turned to face me. He came across the room in his cop stride—no smile, no laughs certainly. I started, at the last moment, to meet him but he reached me first, and so it was Eric who took the lead and kissed me.

And it was Eric who broke away first. "I don't know, Oldfield."

I took in a breath. "So what was that, Catlin?"

"Trial run?" Now he smiled, fleeting. But the scarred skin beneath his glass eye remained taut. "The past is biting us in the butt. This case is toxic. We're not done with the past yet."

26

NEXT MORNING at dawn Walter and I made the journey to Gold Dust.

On the way up, I told him the story of boys testing gunpowder. It was a hard ski and we didn't have the breath to say much more. When we got to the draw, Walter was agog at the hidden old mine site.

We agreed to postpone speculation until we did the geology.

We sat on our skis and ate breakfast—oranges and trail mix—cataloging the lay of the land.

I mentally paced it off, to the southeast of the tunnel. Ten yards, fifteen, twenty. Just snow and a wall of rock. On this visit, though—unlike my last visit—I knew with certainty there had been a spring. Dead and entombed now, but presumably alive back when Georgia came here. Presumably Georgia saw it. Then Georgia died, then the spring died. All I had to do was find it.

I carved an orange, studying the rock wall.

It was a fine example of exfoliation. Big hunks of granite, like this dome that borders Gold Dust, build up internal pressures and every so often shed their skin. It falls in slabs. At the base, the slabs crack into smaller chunks. Over the years—it looked to have been years—the rocks had nearly mortared themselves into a solid wall. There were chinks, where one hunk jutted askew of another, and presumably there were small bits of granite beneath the snow, decomposed by years of weather.

Walter got to his feet, hefted his field kit, and waded through the snow to the ore-tailing mounds. He settled happily in at the cyanide pond.

I sucked the juice from an orange section. Trying to decide where to dig. Ten, fifteen, twenty yards from the tunnel, Eric had said. Twenty yards put it inside the rockfall. I chose fifteen.

I stowed my orange peels, hefted my field kit, and went to work.

Half an hour in, I straightened and stretched and took a breather. Walter was still at work. I glanced, reflexively, at the mouth of the draw, checking for visitors.

I glanced, idly at the stream, which trickled beneath a thin ice roof. A water ouzel was playing there. I watched him. Funny little bird, the ouzel, gray and round as a tumbled stone. He bobbed up and down on a rock with a game eye on the water—insects for breakfast. Or not, for the ouzel suddenly took flight and shot over my head and disappeared into the rockfall.

That was odd.

The ouzel is a water bird. He nests above streams and waterfalls. Even his nickname, the dipper, comes from his habit of bobbing as if preparing to cannonball into the water. What was so attractive to a water bird in that pile of rock?

I went over for a look.

In the flat morning light, chinks and crevices threw no shadows so that I had to inch my way along the wall to find the ruptures. One drew me close: a vertical cleft that flared at the base, like a door opening. The door was sealed along most of its length but there were cracks through which the dipper might have fit. Lower down, the cracks widened. The door became a

Dutch door, with the bottom half ajar. A wedge of snow filled the space. I kicked it free. I got my flashlight, sank to my knees, and peered inside. One slab had come to rest against another, leaving a shallow cavity.

I'm not a spelunker. I like my enclosed spaces tall and wide, with a healthy structural integrity. I sat back on my heels. There was no reason in the world to go in. There was every reason not to.

Walter called out, "Success!"

I called, "High five!"

"What are you doing?"

I called, "Come on over."

He joined me, on his knees. I explained the dipper. He said, "Let's have a look."

We stuck our heads into the cavity and I shined my flashlight around. The soil was the red cinder of Gold Dust, with a flouring of decomposed granite. I would have backed out then, and gladly, but for the sound that caught my ear—running water. Soil was dry, yet I heard water.

As did Walter.

We looked at each other.

I said, "This is worth some speculation."

Walter lifted a hand to me.

"Suppose," I said, "way back when the guys came to Gold Dust to test their powder, this exfoliation hadn't yet occurred. Meaning, the rockfall didn't block access—suppose that's where their spring was. Back there, about twenty yards from the tunnel. About where Eric said the spring would be." I listened to the sound of water. Sounded like snowmelt over rock. "And we got lucky. Thanks to the ouzel."

"And Georgia?" Walter said.

She sure didn't get lucky. Not in the end. I said, "Turns out she'd already seen Gold Dust, with the guys. So she remembered the spring. Couldn't locate it this time. So let's say she poked around until she found this break in the rock wall."

"Which begs the question of why she came here looking for the old spring."

I swallowed, and told Walter what Eric had told me, about Mike finding Georgia and Krom at Hot Creek. Another damned Hot Creek fuckup.

I'll give Walter this--he didn't look shocked. He did shake his head.

"And," I said, "we have Georgia humiliated and pissed at Mike, and we'll say still looking to keep things going with Krom. And, let's say, get even with Mike in the process. And a fitting place to do that is bring Krom here, to the spring the guys used to soak in—that Mike used to soak in."

Walter just stared at me. Disbelief.

I gave him the rest--Eric thinking Mike's the killer, Eric covering for Mike.

Now, as the speculations settled in, Walter looked shocked. Pained. All he said was, "Adrian. Mike. As suspects?"

Or somebody else, somebody who I didn't grow up with, somebody who wasn't our safety czar. I shrugged. "Guess so. What do you think?"

"I think there is no good answer."

Neither of us speculated further.

I turned to the rock. "Let's go see what she found."

We went into the cavity, me first.

I had to go on hands and knees. It took me no more than half a minute to crawl the length, flashlight clamped in my teeth. At the far end, where I had thought the slabs joined in a seam, there was in fact another crack. The sound of water was quite definite, and another sound now mixed in: birdsong. I bellied around the corner, my heart in my ribs.

And finally there was light, and space, and I could stand.

Walter followed, and grunted to his feet.

Here, the exfoliated slabs had fallen like open leaves of a stiff old artichoke. We were in a small grotto, bounded by the outer leaves. Through the leaves I saw that the rockfall backed against the steep lava western slope of Gold Dust. The water we'd heard was indeed snowmelt, running down the slope. The dipper's song was just outside.

Something was melting a lot of snow.

We wove through the rock leaves and came out into a pocket of land wedged between the lava slope and the granite dome.

And we saw what Georgia must have found.

We saw the outcrop where the dipper played in snowmelt, and saw that the melt was indeed a consequence of steam lifting from a blue hot spring to the slope above. Water so hot I felt heat from where I stood shivering. The boys' spring, the plum Georgia sought, my long-sought holy grail, my nightmare.

Not dead after all.

Walter gasped.

But not at the spring. And surely it was not this spring that Georgia had written about in her notes because the spring in all its three-alarm heat was merely peripheral. What was central—what made it inconsequential, what was stopping my heart like it must have stopped hers—was the rip in the earth.

The little pocket of land was split nearly in two. Steam rose from the fissure and laid bare the reddish soil of the banks so that it looked like an open wound.

An old nightmare rose, in which I'm running through the caldera as the ground beneath me rots.

And now, up here in this hidden place on the outermost lip of the caldera, where the crazy dipper bathed in snowmelt and sang its happy demented song, the ground was, it seemed to me, rotting away.

Walter gripped my arm.

I could not move. I had the urge to run but, unlike in my nightmare, my feet were rooted. I told myself I should measure the fissure but I could not move.

If you made a list of the phenomena that raise a volcanologist's blood pressure, ground cracking is right up there along with quake swarms. When magma rises it forces rocks apart and deforms the ground and if the magma gets close enough to the surface the crust cracks open. And the question then becomes, is it an old crack wherein the magma subsided and there is only residual heat? Not too old—it wasn't here back when the boys were soaking in a hot spring. It's more recent. *How* recent? Is there seismicity? Because, then, we have a new worry. We have activity where there has not been activity detected before. All the activity that has been detected, that spooked us and brought Adrian Krom to town, has been in the caldera's south moat.

Georgia came in search of a hot spring but what she found was truly new.

"No way out?" Walter said.

"From *here*?" I said. "For *her*? For *us*?"

He shook his head.

Get Lindsay, I thought. Get her now. I said, "We need to get Lindsay."

And it was speaking her name—like cold water in my face—that got me moving. Got Walter moving.

We paced the fissure, keeping clear of the steaming mud, measuring the displacement across the crack. This thing was measurable in meters.

I wanted Lindsay. I wanted a temperature probe; I knew it was hot down there but was it volcanically feverish? I wanted a tape measure and a gas collector and a camera but most of all I wanted Lindsay.

The dipper gave a fluting cry and funneled back into the rockfall.

We followed, pausing just long enough to scoop handfuls of the soil near the spring and dump it in our pockets. Then we bolted. I was burrowing back through the rockfall in the dark when I had a moment of clammy fear that someone would be waiting when we crawled out.

We emerged to find ourselves alone in the sun-struck draw. We geared up and pushed off, filled with the imperative to get Lindsay.

27

We halted at the mouth of Gold Dust and Lindsay lifted her chin. "Where?"

Perhaps it was the surprise at this hidden gouge in the mountain, but there was surprise in her voice.

I said, "Then you've never been here?"

"Should I have?"

I kicked off. "This way." For the first time in the field with Lindsay, I took the lead. It was midday and Walter's and my earlier tracks had softened in the sun. Walter had bowed out of a second trip to Gold Dust in one day. Truth was, he was giving it to Lindsay and me, the volcanologist and her pupil.

The rockfall was once again seamless in the flat light. I led Lindsay to the door.

She whistled. "You have young eyes."

I told her about the dipper.

She bent to examine the Dutch door. She looked cold, the flush of exertion draining from her Dresden skin.

Urgency welled in me. I took off my skis and went first through the cavity and she passed me her knapsack and I shoved it around the corner. She followed me on her belly and when she reached the grotto she grunted in amazement. I did not give her time to read deeper into the geological record. I snatched up her pack and moved out through the granite leaves into the little pocket. The dipper had not returned.

She followed, and blanched.

I had not prepared her. I had told her only, there's activity. I had wanted her to come to it raw.

"Oh honey," she said, and her face just opened like a flower. I handed her the knapsack and got out of the way.

She went alone to the fissure's rim.

With Lindsay in the field, I've always hung back upon first examination of an object. I would wait for her to take it in, and when she'd processed it, to draw me close and explain. Even when I knew as well as she what the object signified, I would wait for her to speak. On a primitive level, no fumarole or stratum of ash was real to me until Lindsay said it was. If we had gazed into the face of Mount Pelee herself in eruption, I would have waited for confirmation from Lindsay. If Lindsay had said honey it's a mirage, I would doubtless have stood there admiring the volcanic hallucination until the hot cloud incinerated us both.

I joined her, finally. Heat from the fissure had returned the flush to her face, and steam had wetted her skin like dew on the flower.

She said again, "Oh honey." Now her face tightened.

The way I read her face, the flower opening and then closing, was that she was seeing here something every volcanologist both dreams of and dreads. She was seeing her volcano unloose its bonds.

28

IN TOWN we parted without ceremony, Lindsay to alert the Geological Survey and me to report to Krom.

We took facing chairs in his office. I sat sweating, still wearing my thermo-lined snow pants, and told him about the fissure up on Red Mountain. He showed amazement, like he was stumbling upon it along with me, following in wonder through the grotto and then halting to gape at the rockfall's secret. He sat silently, seeing it.

I gripped the arms of my chair. It was death to just sit here.

He spoke, finally. "Then she really did find something."

I nodded.

"What did Lindsay say when you showed her?"

"It's a big deal. Not in those words, but..."

"No way out?"

I glanced at Krom's wall of photos, at the frozen family who didn't escape. "Lindsay didn't say that."

"Tell me everything she did say."

"She didn't say a lot. She took measurements. She took photos."

"And what is she doing now?"

"Alerting USGS."

"Good."

I said, "What about you?"

"I'm going to contact *my* people."

"So you can spin it?"

His hand slammed down on the desk and I jumped.

He too looked poised to bolt. Both hands on the desk, forearms braced. White scar stood up from brown skin, Dante rising. He said, "So I can do my job."

"Glad to hear that." I stood. "That's why I came to tell you."

"Let's be clear," he said, "there's no more spin involved. I'm going to notify FEMA that the situation has altered, then I'm going to go have a look for myself and consult with USGS. Then I'm going to study the maps and reprogram the simulations and see where we go from here. Then I'm going to telephone everyone on the Council, then email my report to the home office, and copy it to Len Carow. And in the course of doing my job I'm going to reclaim my reputation." He looked at me squarely. "I win, we all win."

"I sure hope so." I headed for the door.

His voice followed me. "We're finished, you and I."

I turned. "Finished?"

"The bargain. You delivered. In fact, you might very well have saved us, finding that fissure. Congratulations." He looked down at the scar on his forearm, then back at me. "No sacrifice required."

I didn't feel much like a savior. "I just found what Georgia found. She's the one who deserves the credit."

He briefly bowed his head.

"One thing," I said, "that surprises me. You didn't ask about Georgia—what happened to her there."

"Do you know?"

"No. But I'm getting close to saying she died there--pending analysis of the evidence and exemplars. I'll copy you our report. I thought you'd want to know."

"What do you *think* happened?"

"I think she was murdered. I don't know if we'll get an ID on the killer." I shrugged. "I can't foretell the future."

29

It was impossible, now, to think of Gold Dust as hidden.

There were people everywhere—laden with instrumentation, in big parkas and gaiters and wool caps and you could tell the men from the women, more often than not, by the beards. They were in the mine tunnel with headlamps, they were taking the temperature of the dipper's stream, they were scouring the mountain for cracks in the snow and newly dead trees. There was a field camp in the shell of the cabin and it looked like the miners had returned to work the lode. There was a bearded man tending a radio and he was in contact with the USGS field station set up in Mammoth's fire department, and that in turn was in communication with Survey headquarters.

It looked like USGS had been here a week but it's been just thirty-six hours since Lindsay made her call and the Survey put its Western Region Event Response Team on a plane.

A path had been blasted through the rock wall. Nobody need negotiate the cavity behind the Dutch door.

The snow looked like it had been paved.

Amidst this buzz, Walter sat on a crate waiting for the okay to go back behind the rockfall and dig. He chafed his hands. He's not used to being a sideshow to other people's business. He wanted more samples from the hot spring because the soil we'd hurriedly scooped and stashed in our pockets had orange-peel particles from our gloves and had to be considered contaminated.

I paced, from the Dutch door to the mouth of the tunnel. From the tunnel to the cyanide pond.

"What are you doing?" Walter asked, as I passed his crate.

"Trying to figure what order Georgia picked up the stuff in her boots."

He strained for a glimpse of Lindsay. We'd seen her an hour ago, disappearing through the blasted corridor. She'd nodded in passing. Was already looking beyond us, seeing the fissure. She's consumed by it, she's stripped to raw energy, she's an exposed high-voltage wire and Walter's been trying to keep an eye on her.

"And what are your conclusions?" Walter asked, on my next pass.

I halted. "I figure Georgia picked up the leaf near the stream, and then tramped through the tailings area and acquired the cyanide. Looking around for the hot spring. Picking up bits of the native soil. Then she found the door in the rock wall, crawled through, found the spring, acquired the sulfur and calcite. Found the fissure. Freaked out." No wild-ass guess needed for that. "And maybe that's when she wrote what she wrote in her Weight Watchers notebook."

Walter nodded.

"And then she crawled back through the cavity. In a panic. Intending, I'd hope, to get Lindsay. And maybe that's when she encountered her killer. Or, alternatively, he caught her back at the fissure."

Walter nodded.

"I'm thinking that they ended up in the tunnel—because of

all the powder she'd acquired. So that's where I'd say she took her final steps. And then there was a struggle, and she took no more steps." And who was struggling? Georgia and Mike? Georgia and Krom? Georgia and someone else? Death by fury? Death by passion? Or was it death by cold calculation? And how did the killer end up at Gold Dust with her? The timing bugged me. "Anyway," I said, "that's one theory."

Walter gave a brief nod. He was looking at the fissure. "She's been back there for hours."

Lindsay, not Georgia. An hour at most.

He rose. "I believe they've forgotten us. I'm going to go collect that sample."

I snatched up my pack and followed him through the corridor.

This time, the hidden pocket was different. First time, when Walter and I came, and even the second time with Lindsay, this had seemed like a lost land whistled into existence by the dipper. Now, it was mapped and staked, concrete as a crime scene. Orange tape roped off the hot spring and fissure. People hovered over the great wound and the banks were draped in silver tarps upon which instruments had been laid out, like the fissure was due to undergo surgery.

Lindsay was at the fissure, head to head with Response Team leader Phil Dobie, who was unmistakable due to his beard—notable even among USGS beards for the quartz-white vein that diked through the black.

We took our samples at the hot spring then went to join Lindsay.

"Phil," Lindsay was saying, "we're *there*." She looked worse than she had earlier, eyes bloodshot, skin drawn, like she'd waved off sleep because there was no time to sleep.

I butted in. "We're where?"

She collared me, fingers like hot pokers. We were goddamn snuggled right up to the rim. "Cassie saw him."

Saw who? All I saw now was the fissure.

"You remember my little fumarole?" She didn't wait for my memory to kick in, she turned back to Phil. "He popped out six months ago and if you'd care to draw a line from here down to the caldera's south moat, my little fellow is sitting on that line."

Phil, who is about as low-key as white noise in the network, said, "It's not out of the question. Moat activity's at a depth of about ten kilometers so, sure, new surface phenomena could be offset by that much."

I stiffened. From Phil, this was worry. The fissure's certainly been worrying enough to spark an event response from the Survey but all on its own, it's not enough to do the trick. It's the location that's raising blood pressure, the idea of a dike reaching out from the caldera's magma chamber and thumbing up through the crust here, an area thought so placid that the Red Mountain geodimeter station is sampled only once a year. But it was sure being sampled now and I had to wonder if it had measured new deformation of the earth. I asked, "What's the strain rate now?"

"Up ten parts per million," Lindsay snapped.

Phil said, "We need the quakes..."

"We've *got* them."

"You've got low-frequency?" I swallowed. Magma's on the move.

"We do," Phil said, "but we need them at a little shallower depth."

"*We'll get them*," she said. "*I know this volcano*."

I looked at her in alarm. She was flying by the seat of her pants.

"Maybe," Phil said thoughtfully, "you're a little too close, Lindsay."

"Horseshit."

Walter cleared his throat. "We all get ahead of ourselves at times. I certainly have, in my work."

Not that I'd ever seen.

Lindsay shot a red-eyed look at Walter, decades of rivalry and devotion in that look: geology *is* volcanology, honey.

I felt a charge run from Lindsay to me, her fingers grounded in my neck, and the circuit ran from the fissure to Lindsay, and by chance of touch through me, and back to earth again. It did not loop through Phil or Survey headquarters. It was Lindsay and the volcano, a closed loop. We all leaned toward the fissure, like yearning toward water when standing on a bridge, Phil stroking the quartz in his beard, Lindsay drumming her fingers on my neck, Walter fairly itching to consult, and me, damned if I was going to come unglued.

"My volcano," Lindsay said, "has extended his reach."

30

THE MOOD WAS ugly at the intersection of Minaret Road and the Bypass.

The rolled-gravel escape route branched off Minaret and disappeared into a forest of Jeffrey pine. Somewhere in there, the trucks and dozers and cats sat idle. Work had stopped because the road crew was here along with the rest of the town.

It was a whipped crowd, sunk deep into parkas. Council members huddled in their own group, not looking any happier than the rest of us. They've got their own emergency meeting, so I've heard, in three hours.

I couldn't wait three hours. I had eyes now for only four people:

Phil Dobie, more haggard than he'd looked five hours ago up at the fissure.

Lindsay beside him, hot-eyed, still riding the fever.

Len Carow, babying a cigarette until it flamed.

Krom, on his cell phone, watching Carow.

It's been forty-eight hours since I sat in Krom's office and told him about the fissure. He's moved almost as fast as the Survey.

He got Carow into town yesterday and now, right here, he's got his own Event Response going.

It can't come too soon.

"*Man.*" My brother dug his elbow into my arm. "Man, it's cold."

Walter, on my other side, said, "Cassie, are you warm enough?"

I said "yes" and my breath condensed like a fumarole. Come on, I thought, before we all freeze, it's getting later by the minute.

Krom pocketed his cell phone, then tilted his head back. Others, noticing, tilted their heads as well. Carow's cigarette tipped skyward and Phil's beard rose and even Lindsay lifted her chin. The movement rippled through the crowd. Walter and Jimbo followed suit and I couldn't resist if I'd wanted.

We all looked up to a view we've seen a million times. The plateau on which the town sits rises to the broad Lakes Basin, which is bordered by a string of peaks.

Why look? Everybody knows what's up there.

There came the distant rumble of an engine and a big-bellied helicopter rose above the toothy skyline. I didn't get it. But I couldn't take my eyes off it.

The chopper came to hover above Red Mountain.

It looked like some kind of rescue attempt.

But it wasn't. The chopper dipped its nose and came our way, skimming treetops, laying down a smoke trail. As it barreled over our heads, I saw the National Guard insignia on its belly. I covered my ears and turned along with everybody else to follow its path as it shrank into the morning sky.

We were left with smoke in our eyes and the taste of sulfur on our tongues.

"What the shit was that?" said Jimbo.

"A simulation." My voice shook.

Lindsay obviously thought so too. Phil had to know. Carow surely got it. People lifted fingers, following the smoke trail, tracing the chopper's route. It began at Red Mountain and paralleled the Lake Mary Road down the three miles to town. It crossed Minaret and then followed the Bypass in its push northeast toward highway 395.

It was a simulation of an eruption from the site of the fissure. The smoke was meant to show the likely path of the avalanche of burning gas and rock known as a pyroclastic flow. A pyro is probably the deadliest thing Mother Nature can throw at you. The ground flow moves at around eighty miles an hour. It throws off a cloud of hot ash that goes at, say, a couple hundred miles an hour. You can't outrun it. You can't out-drive it. You can't out-fly it in a helicopter. Although, clearly, you can do a convincing simulation with a chopper trailing smoke. You can show the path the ground flow would take, seeking the clean funnel of the Lake Mary Road and then burning right through the Minaret intersection—where we all stood—and barreling along the Bypass.

Of course, a real flow wouldn't confine itself to this one path. It would send fingers into every inch of hospitable terrain of the Mammoth plateau.

But this display confined itself to the fact that the Bypass was in the pyroclastic flow path of an eruption from Red Mountain.

Krom had confined himself to the matter at hand.

I'd asked for this, hadn't I? Do something, I'd demanded.

And now he gave those who hadn't understood a lesson in topography. He didn't use a bullhorn, as he had at the race. He made us hold our breath to listen.

"We're now fighting a battle on *two fronts*. The caldera is the first front and that's been enough to command all our resources. But mark this, chums—we're sitting two thousand feet above the caldera." He put out his hands and raised one above the other. "An eruption down at the caldera—the most likely sort our friends in the Geological Survey will predict—would not destroy our town. Damage us, yes, but we could weather it. With a caldera eruption, topography is in our favor." He waggled the upper hand. "But a *second front* has been discovered up on Red Mountain. It is an offshoot, so I am informed, of activity centered around Hot Creek. When I insisted on fencing off Hot Creek, I didn't know of that connection, but I wish I'd pushed harder. Now, it's fenced."

That's totally out of line, I thought. Reminding us that Lindsay was the one who resisted the fence. Making himself the hero of Hot Creek, instead of the sex czar.

Krom smiled. "We mustn't blame our volcanologist friends for not finding this second front sooner. Resources, as I've said, are spread thin. We can only be grateful that *finally* it was found."

Thank Georgia, why don't you?

He did. "And that is one comfort we can take from the tragedy of our mayor. We don't know who killed her but we do know she died a hero. She just might have saved our bacon. She's the one who found the fissure and she knew enough from working on evac plans to realize what she'd found. In fact, she wrote it down."

A buzz went through the crowd.

"Officials kept that a secret for good reason. We didn't want to cause panic. And we didn't know what her notes meant. We do now."

He let the moment run, and then he continued:

"*No way out*, she wrote. And she was right—not if we leave things as is."

And then he drove it home:

"You've just seen how an eruption up there would reach us

down here. Us, and our emergency escape route. And, I might add, it would take out the only road that currently exits town. Highway 203."

Heads turned. Back and forth. We were at the intersection of the uncompleted Bypass and Minaret Road, which becomes Highway 203 on its way out of town. We were at the deadly intersection of two escape routes that the volcano could wipe out.

"Chums." Krom lifted his lower hand—his caldera hand—above his town hand. "Topography is no longer in our favor."

There was silence. If he'd shouted motherfucker in church he could not have shocked this crowd more. He'd shocked me, and I'd already had this vision, two nights in my dreams and about once per waking hour.

He said, almost gently, "You thought you were building a safe evac route. You're not. We're up the creek, as the saying goes, without a paddle."

The hush was broken by Mike. He called out, "So what do we *do*?"

That's a setup, I thought, that's Krom moving Mike's mouth but I didn't care, I just wanted the answer.

"If I had my druthers," Krom said, "we'd move everything we've got to extending the forest service road that cuts through Pika Canyon. Do what we should have done a month ago."

He paused, letting us do the math. A month ago, the meeting at the Inn.

"Still looks good, chums. Looked good back then because it got us out of town without passing the Inyo volcanoes. Looks even better now. Go home and study your maps. You'll see my route cuts southeast of the likely flow path from Red Mountain—it should be spared by intervening ridges." He gave a graceful shrug. "Of course, back when I hammered out that route I didn't know what was brewing up there. I can't foretell the future."

I gave a little jump.

"But I do take credit." He flashed a wise-up smile. "I thought back then the Pika route was a damn good one, good enough to take whatever our volcano throws at us." He hiked a shoulder south. "Should we decide to build it."

He paused, letting us recall the reason we didn't start a month ago, although he didn't look at her. He didn't have to, because nearly everyone else was looking.

"Hey Lindsay," Phil DeMartini yelled, "you picked the wrong way out."

"She didn't *know*, asshole," Jeanine yelled back.

I was rigid. Lindsay didn't know about the fissure but she should have known a whole lot better than to come here. Why'd she *come*? She could have skipped this setup and waited three hours for the Council meeting to pull the plug on the Bypass. Why'd she come here and let Krom humiliate her?

Walter started for her but she waved him off. She raised her chin. She ignored the crowd, the Council, Phil Dobie, Len Carow. She was looking at Krom and he was returning her look. Her brows lifted. She seemed to be asking Krom's permission. And he seemed to give it, with a smile of indulgence. His favorite, indulged dear lady. She spoke then. "Have you a schedule, Adrian?"

I understood now why she'd come. She was showing everyone with her presence that the volcanologist is, at last, in agreement with the emerg-ops guy. The battle is over. Lindsay capitulates, for the good of the town. Krom wins. He's the hero.

But it's Lindsay, in my eyes, who just did the stand-up thing.

Mercifully, Krom turned from her. "Let's ask the expert if there's time to build Pika." He motioned, and Jimmy Gutierrez came forward, patting down his white crown of hair. "How about it?" Krom asked Jimmy. "If we all pull together?"

Jimmy got out a calculator.

Carow angled for a look over Jimmy's shoulder, nodding.

Jefferson Liu and a few other Council members were edging in.

"*Yo Jimmy*," my brother called. "More overtime?"

A couple of people clapped, and then a few more, and by the time Jimmy's flushed face raised in assent there was a palpable sense of relief at the intersection of Minaret Road and the Bypass.

I caught Lindsay and Phil Dobie at his Survey truck. He had the door open and she was detaining him.

She said, "Are you going to call it or not, Phil?"

I butted in. "Call it?"

"Ask Phil."

I didn't want to ask Phil, I wanted to ask her, it's her volcano. I said, "Call it *how*, Lindsay?"

"Alert level WATCH," she said. "Are you going to call it or not, Phil?"

I took in a breath. There is alert level WATCH—intense unrest—which triggers an event response from the Survey. And then there is alert level WARNING—meaning eruption imminent, or underway—and that's when you pack your bags and go. If you're still around after that, it's largely too late.

Phil said, "Actually, Lindsay, we called it just before the meeting. I hunted for you but when I came down from the fissure, what with all this... And, uh, Len Carow was asking, and then I had a call into headquarters, and then I had to meet with..." He swallowed the rest into his beard.

"What?" I said.

"He said Adrian Krom." Her breath steamed. "He said I'm out of the loop."

"That's not precisely it, Lindsay. It's more that..."

I didn't hear what more it was. I heard only that Lindsay Nash is out of the loop, and we're under a volcano watch.

31

I'M at a crossroad and each direction is hung in fog and if I take the wrong road I'll step into oblivion. Krom comes. He's a giant brown bear. I ask him which way is safe but he won't tell me. He starts to leave and I grab his bare arm to stop him. Fur doesn't grow there. The scar's a live thing beneath my hand, and it's got a pulse. I let go. Krom leaves, taking the right-hand road. His head is fixed face-backward on his neck and he's smiling the wise-up smile.

I woke in a sweat and fought my way out of the covers. The cottage air chilled me fast. The nightmare shrank and one thought filled my head.

One thought. He lied at the demo last week—he *can* foretell the future.

We hurtled through a chute of ice, Walter's Explorer planing like a bobsled.

I held on tightly, thinking this is one hell of a tight place through which to move a town of fleeing vehicles.

Walter counter-steered and the car regained its grip on the road.

Pika is one of those classic eastern Sierra canyons, a skinny gash in the steep mountain flank, narrowed further by thirty-foot walls of snow thrown up by the plows. Nevertheless, it was all that Krom promised. We were above the caldera, out of the line of immediate fire from Red Mountain, and away from the Inyo system. We were tucked down deep. Not untouchable—nowhere around here is untouchable—but this would get us out.

Krom knew what he was doing.

He'd known, I thought, for a good long while.

I had one question, to test my nightmare hypothesis, and the man I needed to ask was up ahead.

We traveled more slowly through the gorge until we came to the place where the walls widened and the road pitched downhill and the orange cones sprouted, and I knew we'd reached the end of the line.

Walter shut off the engine.

I searched among the road workers in orange vests before finding the man with white hair thatching out from beneath his hard hat. Walter and I caught up with him and I asked, "Jimmy, how long did you tell Adrian this road was going to take?"

"Told him to give me three good weeks on her—and another thrown in for weather." Jimmy waved his clipboard at the frozen landscape, and grinned. "So the sonofabitch says do it in *two* and gives me the friggin army corps of engineers! We start on her today."

"When did you first give him the estimate?"

"Oh jeez, that'd be somewhere back around mid-December."

"Thanks," I said. I had my answer.

I gave a nod to Walter and we trudged back toward the Explorer.

He asked, "Are you ready to enlighten me?"

"Just go with me on this, okay?" I plunged in. "When we made the bargain with Adrian, I got it wrong. I thought he needed to be kept in the loop so he could recover his reputation. He was urging us to find the site, all right, but not because of that."

"I don't believe I'm following you."

I sympathized. I hadn't been following Krom, either. "When I stalled with the evidence, he said I was a believer—that if I thought something was there I'd never give up." I glanced at Walter, wondering if he knew me as well as he thought, if he knew how much I wanted to believe that. "It was tactics. Adrian was giving me a kick in the butt. And he kicked me in the right direction, to county records, to find the Gold Dust claim. But he already knew about Gold Dust. He already knew about the fissure and he needed me to find it."

"Why?" was all Walter said.

"To save himself from Lindsay."

Walter started walking again, silent but for the crunch of his boots on gravel-pocked snow.

I came along. "Think it through. He comes to town and finds the woman who trashed his reputation at Rainier. She goes after him again. And she's already doing *his* job, building an evac route. So he does what he does best. He digs in and courts the locals. Gets in tight with the mayor. And then the mayor goes looking for that hot spring at Gold Dust, and finds the fissure. And, being Georgia, she writes down her thoughts. And then, after she recovers herself, she goes and gets Adrian. She'd intended to take him to a hidden hot spring for another romp, but now she's got something much more important to show him."

"You have proof that she went to get him? That he accompanied her?"

"No. Just a wild-ass guess. Maybe not so wild, though. The timing works. Think about it—Georgia gave Krom the gift of a lifetime. A way to save his reputation and take down Lindsay in the process."

"The fissure," Walter said.

"Yeah. It makes Lindsay's Bypass a death trap. Here's the opportunity to make his mark. He'll champion another route, a safe route. And, he had to kill Georgia because she sure wouldn't keep her mouth shut about the fissure. He needed to keep that quiet until he could set up Lindsay. So he gets out his maps and walks the geography and finds an alternative that's out of range of anything Red Mountain throws. Pika Canyon. He consults Jimmy." As Jimmy just confirmed; the only solid piece of evidence I'd yet trotted out. "When all his ducks are lined up, he calls the meeting at the Inn and presents his route. Knowing Lindsay will oppose it. Knowing he will crucify Lindsay and her Bypass when the fissure is found."

Walter said, thinly, "This is enormous speculation, Cassie."

I didn't argue the point. "Look, he lied at the demo. Back when he was considering routes, he *did* know what was brewing on Red Mountain. That's why he picked Pika."

We both looked up the road. There was a car coming down the chute toward us.

"He knew he had the ammo to kill Lindsay's route. He just needed to hold on until he could use it. He couldn't have the fissure found too soon after publicly championing Pika—that would be too coincidental. But he couldn't wait too long, either. Len Carow was here, looking for any excuse to sack him. That's why Adrian made Hot Creek into a battleground—he's fighting Lindsay to fence it off. Mr. Safety." I watched the oncoming car. It was Krom's Blazer. "He was playing for time. That's all he needed."

"And what about the drill at the race? Another battlefield?"

"You tell me. Lindsay den-mothers the guys, and here's the World Cup on their home turf. She's sure not going to cancel that. And for Krom, that's opportunity knocking. He'll humiliate her on her own turf. The volcanologist is up there playing games and the safety czar interrupts with grownup business. On a ski course that we later find out is in the *path* of an eruption from Red Mountain." I shook my head. "And Stobie, well… That's fall-out. Adrian can play that game."

Walter was listening.

"What he couldn't play was the sucker game at the creek. Trading safety for sex."

"No," Walter said. "That was not grownup business."

I ached, for a moment, thinking about Lindsay's role in it. I still saw no reason to lay that on Walter. I said, "Well, the thing with Jeanine almost worked. A lot of bad press. It really looked like he was going to be replaced. And so at that point, time's *really* against him. He can't just wait any more for me to find the fissure. He needs to push. So he makes the bargain with me. With us."

Walter grunted.

We fixed our attention on the Blazer, which parked in front of Walter's Jeep. People piled out. Council big shots and the man himself, Adrian Krom.

"Is that all?" Walter finally asked.

I nodded. I had no more. Walter waited, perhaps for me to whip out the missing piece of evidence, the magic stone that would tie Krom to the fissure, to the scene of death, to the scenario I'd just spun. I didn't have it.

He cleared his throat. "There are holes."

I knew.

"Why does he transport Georgia's body to the glacier?"

"He needs it to be found. He needs the evidence on the body

to be traced to Gold Dust. Which it was. And we found the fissure. Which is what he needed."

"The body was found only by chance. By an ice climber."

I said, "The climber phoned in the report. Voice was garbled, staticky. Maybe the 'climber' was Adrian—when he's ready to set his plan in motion."

"There's still a difficulty. He needs to *know* that the evidence on the body will be traced to Gold Dust. That is a large assumption. He didn't know about the geology—according to what you told me—until that day at Casa Diablo when he learned how we could track the soil. And, further, he couldn't count on the fact that it would lead to the site of death, and the fissure."

I shrugged. "You're right. I haven't got it all worked out." Not that I hadn't twisted it a dozen ways. "Okay, let's say he had plan A to help the cops along. Whatever it was, he set it into motion with that meeting at the Inn. And then he found me and the geology at Casa Diablo and hatched a better plan. Plan B. And it worked. I found the fissure for him."

"No, the timing does *not* work. What if you took too long?"

"I don't know." The damnable timing. What if things heated up before I found the fissure, what if Krom didn't have time to build a new way out before we had to go? I watched him, now, herding the Council. He's a master manipulator but he can't time the volcano. Any more than Lindsay can.

Walter said, "Are you planning to present this theory to John?"

"Not until we have some proof."

"We have *no* proof," Walter said. "And there's simply too much we don't know."

"We know plan B worked. The only snag, for him, is if we can place him at the scene." My pulse gave a little leap. "Maybe he has a plan C, in case we can."

Walter looked at me in alarm.

"Don't worry," I said, "we seem to be failing at that."

There was a long silence and then Walter, bless him, laughed.

In that, we caught the attention of the person I'd hoped to avoid. Krom was walking the site with the Council in his gravitational field. Now he changed direction and intercepted us before we could reach the Explorer.

"You here for me?" he asked, and when I shook my head, he asked Walter, "What's funny?"

"Very little," Walter said. "A small release of tension."

Krom gave a sympathetic shrug. His attention pulled back to the Council. He smiled to himself and moved on.

32

I WAS in the shower when Jimbo banged on the bathroom door. I shut off the tap. "What?"

"Get on a towel," Jimbo said, "I'm coming in."

Despite the steam, I was abruptly chilled. Not since childhood has Jimbo entered the bathroom when I'm showering. I hastily wrapped up.

Jimbo came in, examined the tile floor, then took me in a hug so tight my head knocked his chin. My stomach turned hollow. "Mom and Dad?"

He muttered into my hair, "Lindsay. John Amsterdam called and said we've lost her."

"Lost?" I had a crazy vision of Lindsay fleeing across the caldera, playing my role in the nightmare, and then I thought, she's angry at being out of the loop and she's left town and the chief of police is going to retrieve her, but none of this made sense, and even if it had it would not have driven my brother into the bathroom with me. Lost? A thousand alarms went off and cutting through them was the rising wail of my own voice. Jimbo picked up the towel and wrapped it around me. I said, "Lost *how*?" Jimbo was watching the floor again, the blond wings of his hair shielding his face, and he said "dead, shit, she's dead" and he took away the world as I knew it.

My brother drove me downtown and ushered me through the congestion outside the scene at Lindsay's office building. He lifted the police tape for me and left me in the care of a uniformed officer we had both known since kindergarten, whose name I could not produce.

"John's in the office." The officer stared at my shoulder, her round face blanched by the cold. "He said to send you straight in. Cassie? Man, I'm sorry."

"Thank you," I said. "Margy."

I moved into the hallway and pressed against the cold plaster wall. Someone came around the corner. Slat-thin, angling head-first into his walk. Disappearing blond hair, buzz cut on a tanned field of scalp. Chief of Police John Amsterdam. Gossiped with him two weeks ago after hypothesizing with Walter up at Pika Canyon. Almost gave him my half-baked theory. Now, he looked past me at the wall, filling me with terror.

He said, "Such a loss."

Loss—that confusion again. If only she were lost. Then she could be found. John led the way, as if I couldn't find Lindsay's office all by myself.

At first I saw only backs, a roomful of people with their backs to the door. Someone was laying dust over the map cabinet, someone was draining a coffee cup into a vial, someone was taking photos. Everyone's back was to me. A back was bent low over the creamy woolen legs and calfskin ankle boots on the floor. I knew all the backs. Mammoth P.D. The officers doing the crime-scene ident were Bo Robinson and Lupe Cruz-Rios and Jim Breuss. The photog was Don May, Stobie's roommate. Eric was here. Randy Burrard from the ME's office was on the floor, attending the body.

There was an awful odor in the room, body waste and a stale coppery wash of blood that I could taste as well as smell.

I had to cover my mouth and turn away. Lindsay's lost, isn't she? That's not Lindsay. John caught me as I buckled and put me into a chair. A couple of the backs turned. I shut my eyes. Hideous hot tears burned my face.

Someone breathed on my cheek and whispered, "Here when you need me, Cass."

I looked at Eric through blurred eyes. "Where's Walter?"

Eric led me across the crowded office and I punctiliously skirted the open evidence collection kit, not out of crime-scene etiquette but out of horror. I caught a glimpse of the body, prone. It lay on Lindsay's periwinkle blue jute rug.

Walter was in her high-backed desk chair, turned to the window. He appeared to be taking in the view. His head lay against the leather cushion, his hands were folded in his lap, his legs sprawled like a rag doll's.

I knelt.

"Thank you for coming, Cassie."

I took his cold hand, gripping so hard the knuckles rolled.

"You take care of things for me, will you?"

I said, "I can't stand this."

"I know." He watched the Sherwins, worn old mountains, his face a mirror of the range. He withdrew his hand and patted my head. "Your hair is wet." His hand dropped back to his lap.

John approached and courteously asked for my help.

I stood. "What happened?"

"Sheesh, nobody's told you? The changes indicate that she... a time somewhere between ten and twelve last night. She was shot." He passed a hand across his buzz cut. "Cassie, she went right away."

I fixed on John's long kind face.

He said, "She'd been reporting threats, going back to the... that helicopter thing out at the Bypass. Well, you were there, you saw how it was." He made a helpless gesture. "We'll check it all out. You know, she'd actually gotten herself a pistol. We found it in her credenza. But she clearly wasn't able to..." He angled toward the desk. "Anyway, we got one lucky break—the janitor cleaned yesterday morning so any prints we find should be fresh."

Her desk was an expanse of white lacquer grained with fine black dusting powder and splotched where pressure-wound tape had lifted prints.

"Check them against Adrian's," I said.

"*Adrian*? Cassie, I can't see why he'd..."

Neither could I. He'd already destroyed her.

"Actually, he's not here. He's flying to Sacramento this morning. Supposed to go last night, but the snowstorm... We'll ask him to cooperate when he gets back. If he has any information to contribute."

Clearly, John didn't want to consider Adrian Krom. Who did? The volcano's ramping up, and Lindsay's lost. We need Krom, now more than ever.

"She has a lot of knickknacks," John said, escaping the subject. "We need to establish if anything is missing. You'd know, would you?"

I looked at her desk. So cluttered. So many pretty things. I could never work at such a cluttered desk.

"Is everything there?"

"I guess."

John glanced around. "Anything else you'd know about? What about her rock collection?" He indicated the tall cabinet.

I looked. These were the minerals not pretty enough for her desk, the business stuff. Obsidian and basalt and rhyolite and andesite and scoria—the evidence from old eruptions to help forecast the new. "I don't know." I was muddled, confusing her collection of volcanics with Krom's. "I think everything's okay."

John nodded. He said, "She was working at the time."

I could see that. It was warm in the office; although the first responders would have turned off the heat, the room had not yet cooled. Desk lamp was lit. Her computer was on, the Matisse screen-saver. "Go ahead," John said, and I tapped a key and the screen morphed to seismograms and I studied until it became clear this was a current picture of low-frequency quakes in the moat. I tapped another key and Red Mountain came up, with its two new fissures.

John said, "Evidently she kept up on the situation."

Jim Breuss, I saw, was taking measurements of Lindsay's apothecary cupboard and reading off numbers to Lupe, who was sketching. The cupboard is an antique, in which Lindsay stores her coffees. Eric and Carl knelt on the floor. Everyone was occupied—even Walter, with the view of the Sherwins. I could no longer smell the foul odor. The olfactory nerves go numb after a few minutes in such straits.

I began to sink and gripped the desk for support and John made a small noise and I saw what I'd done, I'd just smeared the dusting powder and added my own prints. "I'm sorry, I'm sorry," I said, "I know better." I wiped my gritty hands on my jeans, again and again as though I were a princess whose hands were not to be soiled, crazy just crazy because my hands are not lily white, my hands are stained by chemicals, calloused from hammers and cold chisels, and my nails are so at risk that polish is out of the question. Even Lindsay, who used sunscreens religiously, has the hands of a field geologist. And here I am—what? —cleaning up before approaching Lindsay, as if she would object to grit on my hands. She's immaculate but if she gets dirty she doesn't make a fuss, she just goes about her business and cleans up when she can. I fastened my hands and stopped the obsessive wiping.

I saw John and Eric conferring, glancing at me. "What?" I said.

"Ummm." John skimmed his hair. "Randy is ready. To go. But in her ring, there's some dirt and... we just need to make that collection and Eric said he'd do it."

Eric smiled at me, so gentle. "I got it covered."

"*Cassie does it.*"

Every head in the room snapped up.

Walter turned in Lindsay's chair. His face was angry. His color was not good. He looked from face to face, not seeing anyone, not seeing me, and then, not finding what he sought, he turned back to the window. He began to cough, dissolving into a helpless fit of coughing.

My head swelled again with tears. I didn't want to do the collection. I said, "I don't have a kit."

"What do you need?" Eric asked. "Tweezers, evidence bags. Anything else?"

I began to panic.

"Cassie, do you want me to..."

I strode to the body.

She was, for the first time since I had entered the room, alone. Someone had covered her with a metallic blanket, the kind you carry on backpack trips. This was disconcerting—the deceased covered by a survival blanket. But it had been done kindly, for my benefit, because the material covered every sprawling inch of her body except for the right hand.

I knelt. I was hollowed out, my sickened core removed, leaving this kneeling husk. I seemed to have gone elsewhere, like Lindsay.

I bent close enough to kiss her hand. The skin was waxy and translucent, the signs of age and fieldwork dimmed as if she'd found some miraculous beauty cream. Her hand was curled so that the fingertips pressed into the rug, and there at the tips, where blood had pooled and lividity was now fixed, her skin was purplish. It looked as though she'd stained her fingers picking berries. She wore rings on the pointer, ring finger, and pinkie. The ring on the pointer was a wide gold band with open scroll-work. I recognized this ring, which she'd bought in Argentina. The Cerro Galan caldera. I stared until the hand with its odd coloration and exotic rings became a composition, framed against the periwinkle blue of the jute rug. Like the folk art prints framed on her walls.

There were tweezers, I noticed, and a hand lens and plastic evidence bags on the rug beside me.

I took the lens and tweezers, reviewing the movements necessary to extract evidence. First you do A and then you do B. A finely calibrated robot could do it.

Her ring was crusted near the web between the pointer and index fingers. Under the lens, the crust resolved into mineral grains, and I should have been able to do an eyeball ID but the names and properties of even the most common minerals were lost to me. I was a robot, able to perform physical tasks but dead to thought. I plucked the grains from the filigree, the stuff that had caught someone's attention upon initial examination of the body, that had necessitated calling in forensic geologists. I bagged the evidence.

I tried to rotate the ring but it would not budge. And then her hand was in mine and I tried to pry it open, just enough to see if there was crust on the underside of the ring, but she was in advanced rigor and her hand was as rigid as if it had been fossilized. So for a moment I just held her hand, the warmth of my own flesh against her cold skin. Warmth leaking vigor into cold, basic wilderness survival technique.

I found myself looking at her wall, at a carved mask she'd

unearthed in Mexico, a hideous face with slitted eyes and a snarling mouth with its tongue sticking out. I'd hated it the first time I saw it, and I'd asked her why she bought such a thing. "Keeps me on my toes, honey," she'd said.

She deserved her money back.

33

"CAAASEEE." Jeanine came through the doorway, swinging a grocery bag like a large purse. "Luh-uunch."

I dropped the sieve. "You didn't have to do that."

She kicked the door shut, rattling the lab window. "No prob. I'm just the delivery girl." She held up the bag. "Turkey and cheese, and some other shit, and something mondo fattening for dessert. Where d'ya want this sucker?"

I showed her the fridge where I'd stored the Ski Tip lunches that Bill Bone had been delivering, unsolicited, for the past week.

"Bill says sorry he can't come himself." She set the bag on the counter. "Place is *jamming*. Rumor central."

The window rattled—a quake, this time. Once or twice a day now, something rattles or shimmies. Of course there are hundreds more every day that we can't feel. Classic quake swarm.

"Fucking quakes," Jeanine said. "They're talking about a WARNING alert, you know?"

Eruption likely within hours or days. "They're calling a WARNING?"

"Nah. Just talkin." She found her ponytail and began to twist it.

I glanced outside. Heavy traffic. Cars piled to the roof with stuff, more stuff lashed on top. Some people are leaving for an extended vacation, some for good. Some are staying put, because it's within the realm of possibility that the volcano will settle back down. Some are hedging their bets—ferrying stuff to storage down in Bishop, fifty miles south along the Sierra fault. Jimbo's already taken five loads down from the house. I spent all last week packing, when I wasn't at the lab. Anything to fill the hours. Outside, a big Lexus passed, fully loaded. Driver was Cindy Mathias, the fire chief's wife.

"Sooo, Caasss. You the honcho around here now?"

"Walter's at home," I said, level.

"So how long's he gonna stay home?"

I shrugged.

"You're pissed."

I took up the sieve and a dish of soil. "I'm too busy to be pissed."

"Jimbo says you're pissed. Jimbo says you don't talk to anybody."

I dropped the dish, peppering soil across my workbench. "Look, I've got a bureau in Los Angeles that wanted a report on this evidence last week. I got a call this morning from Costa Rica and they have a corpse with dirt down its throat and a diplomatic situation and they want Walter to come to the jungle before the deceased rots. I've got..."

"The Georgia stuff."

"Yeah." The pumice-Jeffrey mix—the puzzling soil from inside her mouth—sat in a box on the catch-all table, in limbo. If I listened I could hear its siren song, Georgia calling: Come have another look. Keep looking and I'll ID the killer for you. Georgia hanging in there, in limbo, never say die. Just like her.

"And the Lindsay case," Jeanine said.

Very carefully, I began to recover the spilled soil.

Jeanine's hands alighted on her hips. "You're not the only one who's bummed about Lindsay."

I flushed, not because I was taken down by her remark, although she was right enough, but because it was exactly what I wanted to say to Walter.

Jeanine scuffed to the door. "So if you decide to take a break and hang out, we'll be at the Tip awhile. Jimbo's there. DeMartinis. Out of work, you know?" She eyed me. "Pika's done. Krom's a real creep but he sure got the road done. So now what? We just kick back and wait, right? Dude says get out, we got a guaranteed way out now, so no sweat. But I'm thinkin nothin's gonna happen after all. So that's cool—we still got a new road. Shortcut to Bishop." Her eyes slitted. "You pray, Cass?"

I should have.

"I'm startin up again. Can't hurt." She opened the door. "So anyway, see ya." She reached under her sweater to yank down the back of her bra, hiking her front, and eased out the door.

"Thanks Jeanine," I called after her.

The L.A. soil sat waiting on my bench. I had not yet touched the L.Nash evidence. Bad procedure. So far, the cops had next to nothing—no DNA to sequence, no prints to compare against Krom's or anyone else's. They did have some fibers; Sears wool. John was waiting for the mineral evidence but he put no pressure on me. He was leaving the scene sealed, should I recover myself enough to go have another look. Eric's been dropping by, at least once a day. Gives me a smile when he leaves, scar tissue crackling under his eye, a living example that time heals all wounds. But he puts no pressure on me.

Nobody, really, expects me to pull myself together enough to sit upright at my workbench.

But grief isn't the problem. I've been waiting for Walter.

Walter's only directions, regarding Lindsay, have been to ask that I go through her mail and pay her bills. Even as executor, Walter is unable to cope.

And I'd pissed away the past week doing our bread-and-butter work that was critical to somebody and about which I cared nothing now, *nothing*.

I gathered the Los Angeles material and dumped the lot on Walter's workbench. I put the culture dish containing the L.Nash evidence on my bench. Time to do the initial examination. Goddamn well past time. I stuck a scalpel into the stuff in the dish, stuff that in some way had to have some link to the perp who left no other trace.

"The *color*, Walter."

He looked. "I'd attribute that to...silicon." He thought awhile. "Or aluminum."

"That's not what I meant."

"Chroma...slight departure from the neutral gray...I'd assign it a one, or..." He lifted his head. "Where's Munsell?"

"*Forget* the Munsell charts." I'd spoken heresy. Color's always the first thing we look at, and we calibrate it by the Munsell color charts. I had no quarrel with Munsell. I'd already ranked the evidence and I didn't need Walter to confirm it. I was getting at something else—only I wanted it to occur to him, independently, as it had occurred to me. Electrified me.

And here he sat, parked on his stool, waiting for me to tell him why he should forget the god Munsell. Eyes blue and mild as a baby's; I'd rank them hue of blue and value of eight and chroma of nine, virtually pure. All the acuity—the shadings of knowledge and intellect and wit—was gone from his eyes.

I was sick with impatience. "What is it we're *seeing*?"

"What is it? What is it?" He gazed beyond me. "Grains of limestone."

"Yes I *know* but I want you to look at the color."

He said, weary, "Chroma is a one and..."

I snapped, "You sound like a broken record." I thought his eyes darkened, impurities in the blue. Irritation with me. Whatever it takes. "I *need* you to think. That's why I asked—no, that's why I begged you to come in today."

He said, "I'm tired."

I got off my stool. "I'll make coffee."

"*No*."

"You're giving up coffee? That's going to help?"

He looked at me as if he didn't know me.

"Walter, there's two pounds of beans in the fridge. Are you going to just leave them there?"

"That's enough."

"That's enough coffee to last indefinitely, or that's enough Cassie and shut up?"

"That's enough, Cassie."

"I drank coffee made from her beans too." I glared but I didn't have Jeanine's gall, and as bummed as Jeanine may have been about Lindsay, I was a thousand times more bummed. And Walter. Bummed beyond endurance. Even coffee caused pain. In truth, I had not gone near the beans either. "Go on home," I told Walter. "I'll take care of it."

He said, contrarily, "I'll stay."

He'll stay because he's lonely at home, or he'll stay because he's decided to help?

He made a close study of the evidence.

Not what I asked. I needed him to leap. I couldn't stand the wait so I watched the laden cars passing on Minaret. Minaret and I are in different time zones—opposite sides of the date line.

It's yesterday on the street. It's tomorrow where I am. The world has flipped.

Walter said, "Use the spectrophotometer on it."

I almost screamed. Yes, I've done it, I've bingoed the element lamps and I know it was aluminum that painted our limestone gray. It was not gray from iron or silicon, which would have pointed me to other limestones, other places. It was aluminum and that pointed me to a very specific place. I said, "You've seen this stuff in the field. You know where it comes from."

"I'm sure I've... Somewhere."

"We talked about it. Right here. Day we vaporized the cyanide."

For the first time this morning, for the first time since we lost Lindsay, Walter's eyes met mine. Not just gazed in my direction, but settled there. "Hot Creek," he said.

"So you remember." My core was ice. "Lindsay told Georgia where to collect a crinoid for Adrian. A lover's gift. Georgia got one for Lindsay, too. A thank-you. And Lindsay must have been touched by the offering because she put it on her desk with all her treasures."

Walter gave me a hollow look.

"John asked me to look at her desk. The day that... See if anything was missing. I looked but my heart wasn't really in it. But I visualize it now and I don't think the crinoid was there. Did you see it? That day?"

The blue of his eyes shaded.

"Then I guess I better go look."

34

The yellow crime-scene tape was still in place. It seemed right that this place was sealed. It should remain sealed for eternity.

I unlocked the frosted glass door and ducked under the tape.

Her office had not been disturbed. Every surface that would hold prints was fuzzy with black powder, and there were wads of discarded tape on the floor. Actually, it made being here easier. I could not picture Lindsay at that grimed desk. She would not sit shivering in this cold. The room had finally cooled down. I kept my jacket on.

The irregular dark stain on the rug looked permanent.

I could not look at that. I looked, instead, at her desk. All the pretty cluttered things. And no pretty crinoid.

I took a seat in Lindsay's desk chair. Creamy soft leather. A dream of a chair. The thought came that Lindsay would want me to have it. I stiffened. I could never sit and work in such a chair.

But surely this is where she sat that night. Working. Monitoring the progress of the quakes. And then the perp barges in. Does he show the gun right away? Soon enough. And what about her gun? I pictured, vividly, sitting on the other side of this desk and asking her how she could have set up that thing at Hot Creek, and I saw, vividly, how she had to swivel her chair to retrieve her gun from the credenza, to show me how she had the situation covered. She can't do that now, with him. She swivels and he says freeze, or something. Whatever he says, whatever he wants, he gives her time enough to think up a plan. His gun tells her she may not come out of this alive. She can't reach her gun. She sees the crinoid on her desk—the symbol. At some point while he glances away—maybe she distracts him, says who's that in the hallway—she palms the rock. She drops her hand to her lap, hidden from him by the desk, and she sets to work.

She's scared, of course, but she's Lindsay and her wits never leave her. So here she sits, worrying grains from a telling stone into the matrix of her ring, knowing it won't escape the attention of two cop geologists, should it come to that. Knowing they'll get the message.

And what's the gunman doing? Just watching? What does he want? Why is he going to kill her? Why doesn't he shoot her right away? What does he *want*?

My head was spinning. I opened my eyes.

And once she works the grains into the ring, what does she do with the rock? He never sees it—if he saw it he would have known enough to see what she'd done. After all, he's fallen in love with forensic geology. He would have taken the rock and the ring. But he didn't. The encrusted ring stayed on her finger.

So where's the crinoid rock?

I'm Lindsay and I have to hide this rock and I can't make any obvious moves or he'll notice. I'm standing on the jute rug when he shoots me, so I had to have hidden the rock before I got there.

It had to be in the desk.

I reached to open the top right-hand drawer. No. He'll see my arm move.

And then the obvious hit me, as it must have hit her. There is a shallow center drawer, and all I have to do is raise my knee to slide it open. The modesty shield on his side of the desk will block his view.

I raised my knee and nudged the drawer open and it slid silently because her desk is the kind of quality craftsmanship that makes drawers slide smoothly. I looked inside. Keys. Hand lens. Flashlight and batteries, pens and pencils, paper clips. Tape measure. Clinometer. Rock hammer and cold chisel. A geologist's catch-all drawer. Not surprisingly, containing a rock. Bo or Lupe or Jim would not have found it odd upon checking the drawer to see a rock. Not worth mentioning—she had rocks on her desk, in the cabinet, on top of the apothecary cupboard. She used a rock as a doorstop.

I took out the chunk of gray limestone with the white disk standing in high relief. I used her lens. Under high-power, the limestone looked the same as the ring evidence I'd examined in the lab. Or darned similar to. I bagged the crinoid.

I felt nauseated.

There was a terrible odor in the room and it came from the apothecary cupboard. I hadn't noticed when I first entered because it was so familiar. Someone had left the cupboard doors ajar and the coffee bean oils were scenting the office. I covered my mouth but the odor was on my hands. It was in my clothes, in my hair.

Quite suddenly, I was furious with her. Indulging her eccentricities to the point that a simple cup of coffee became a ritual and Walter and I had to drink from her cup as solemnly as though we were meeting with the gods.

I waited until the urge to retch had passed, then restored the scene and locked the door behind me and ran through the hallway. Outside, in the cold, I took in a long breath of fresh air but it was some time before I left behind the scent of coffee.

Aged Sumatra. The Toba caldera.

35

It's very strange now.

Everything's gone quiet. Quakes, which built into a swarm in the past week, have all but ceased. Gas emissions in Hot Creek and on Red Mountain have subsided. Strain rate's dropped. And in the absence of activity there is a vacuum, a stifling feeling like the sky is falling, only very very slowly.

Lindsay described this kind of thing to me once. It's called premonitory quiescence—a brief interruption in the unrest that often leads to an eruption.

We're still at alert level WATCH. Volcano watch.

Phil Dobie phoned this morning. Without Lindsay I don't have a backdoor into USGS anymore and so I've been calling Phil and getting non-information. As Lindsay put it, Phil has to weigh all the variables before he'll decide whether to order the burger or the chicken nuggets. This morning he decided on the chicken nuggets. *He* called *me*. He said something about owing it to me and to Lindsay's—and then he muttered something I think was *memory*—to call and give me a heads-up. The Survey is considering declaring alert level WARNING. I swallowed and asked Phil if he thought we were going all the way. He said without a pause to weigh the variables "it's not out of the question."

Phil must have phoned Krom as well because Krom has issued his own decree, closing the town to nonresidents, clearing the backcountry of snow campers.

We're left in town with only ourselves for company.

Meanwhile I'm on watch, in sync with the volcano.

I sit at my bench and stare at the specimen dish of pumice and bark, and I still can't say how it got into Georgia's mouth and I still can't connect it with Adrian Krom. I can't place him at the scene of her murder. I stare at the specimen dish of gray limestone, which does not place him at the scene of Lindsay's murder. I know he killed them, but I can only watch the dust gather on my specimen dishes. My evidence exists in a vacuum.

Today, I could stand it no longer and so I fled to Hot Creek. The gate was unlocked. There were two Survey trucks parked in the lot. I parked and got out. I needed to walk. The gorge was swarming with Survey people. I headed out into the tableland above the creek, intending to pay a visit to Lindsay's fumarole, her little fellow.

The snow was soft and my boots made no noise and in this vacuum I became invisible. This is how he came back from the airport, I thought. Invisibly. Snowstorm postponed his flight and maybe he took that as a sign. Tonight's the night. Tonight he has to kill her. There must be a reason, of course—nobody kills without a reason. Nobody's on the street in this storm, nobody sees him. It's late, her building's nearly deserted. He wears gloves so he will leave no prints. He wears a cap so he will shed no hairs. He sheds Sears wool but that's not going to nail him. He brings clean shoes and changes in the hallway so he will leave no soil trace, or maybe he ties plastic bags over his boots. That alarms her, although not as much as the gun in his hand. Maybe he just intends to scare her, some final humiliation, and things get out of hand. She says something, indicates she will not be cowed. Scared of course but even in fear, we are who we are. Maybe it's just a look from her that does it. The lift of her chin, and he shoots. Then he goes home, gets some shuteye, and rises early to catch the flight out.

I could not breathe well. This thick air. I once went snorkeling in Hawaii and all I could hear underwater was my own labored breathing. This was like snorkeling, just me and an ocean of snow and the faraway horizon where the caldera lip rises. And that crazy sky, blue as the ocean, sitting down on top of me. I walked faster, underwater breathing, and I wanted to scream to break the silence but the feeling of pressure was so great that I was afraid to open my mouth—it would be like opening my mouth underwater.

Her little fellow was steaming.

I turned and ran for my car through the crazy thick air, breathing ragged, heartbeats like gunshots.

36

HARMONIC TREMORS IN THE MOAT, new ground cracking on Red Mountain, and the fissure is belching acid gases.

The premonitory quiescence has broken, like a fever.

Walter and I were at the open door. The storefront window, cracked by quakes and secured with duct tape, rattled until its protest was drowned by the roar of oncoming trucks. I moved out for a better look and all along Minaret Road others were stepping out of doorways, the lot of us like prairie dogs popping from our burrows in alarm.

There was a line of trucks from here to the horizon, and although it's seven in the morning they came into town with their headlights switched on as though dark had already fallen in Mammoth.

The noise grew insufferable and we retreated inside.

It's as if burglars have been at work in here. The lab's stripped bare, most everything moved to Bishop. What's left is now boxed and waiting by the door—the bare-bones equipment we've been using the past few days, and current cases. Los Angeles, Costa Rica, a new one from Tucson, and of course Georgia and Lindsay. The small lab television plays with the sound off. It's tuned to King Videocable, which keeps playing the same tape with a crawl updating the evacuation schedule. I've been watching for two hours. I switched the TV on at home at five A.M. when the civil defense alarm went off and shocked me awake. Jimbo and I knew the drill and we'd moved in sync packing last-minute stuff, and then Walter phoned and we agreed to meet at the lab to pack our skeletal equipment. We were packed and ready to go by six-thirty but Minaret was closed in anticipation of the National Guard convoy. When it passes and officials open the road again, we can bring around our cars, load up, and head home.

Plan is, we evacuate by home address. My street's in the second-to-last group and Walter's is in the last. So far, everything is going stopwatch perfect. It's a perfect day, clear and no storm forecast. There are no visitors in town to burden us, to clog the exit. Plan is, last I heard, to evacuate out highway 203—with Pika Canyon as backup in the case of flat tires or engine trouble or fender benders or anything else to slow 203—but either way we should all be out within four hours.

We sat waiting. The workbenches and catchall table and metal shelves were too heavy to be worth moving—moving twice should we return. The stools on which we sat were too cheap to bother with.

I thought of Lindsay's leather chair. A real waste. We'd packed nothing from her office, although it was no longer sealed, no longer a worked crime scene. We'd packed nothing from her house. We leave her things alone, Walter said. I asked about her personal stuff—didn't he care about that?

He said, never love anything that can't love you back.

So all we have of Lindsay is what's in the box. A gold filigree ring and some grains of limestone. She would be pissed, I thought. She was a shopper, she valued things. What a waste.

I stared at her carton. She's in limbo, like Georgia. The two not-so-old crones boxed up, one on top of the other. Village elders sitting in judgment. Both royally pissed with me. I could have gone into volcanology but I'm a failed forensics chick who can't nail one guy for two murders in my own backyard. Stop whining, Georgia snaps. Lindsay just raises one fine eyebrow. Honey, what a waste.

I spun on my stool and said to Walter, "It just royally *stinks*. We know he did it."

Walter said, dully, "There is no evidence."

"There's the crinoid she put into her ring. Why'd she *do* that if not to tell us it was him?"

Walter didn't reply. There was no reply, and we both knew it, and we were both royally sick of this dead-end talk, and so he just sat quietly waiting, his shirt untucked, two fingers bandaged from paper cuts. Beaten. Lost.

He got up and walked over to the TV and flipped up the sound.

We'd seen the tape three times already.

Jeanine, our local TV star, wearing a prim sweater dress, is standing at a lectern. Jeanine, of all people, has been tapped to read the USGS hazard alert, the WARNING declared this morning. A mouthful for anyone and for Jeanine the laid-back queen it's the challenge of a lifetime. But it was somehow comforting to have Jeanine on the tube with the official word.

"...indicates that a volume of maaagma," she read, "is being injected into the shallow crust with a *strong* possibility..."

I knew it by heart.

"...still possible that the maaagma may yet stop short..."

I knew at precisely which point Jeanine's hand was going to wander to her hair. I knew how her hand was going to stop short and that—given the gravity of the situation—she would stifle the need to tug on her ponytail.

"...and an assessment of its *im*plications for possible... volcanic...hazards." She looked directly into the camera, her eyes slitting.

I knew Jeanine had acquired a new war story, a companion piece to her battle with Krom in Hot Creek.

I knew I should be fixing my attention on details at hand—I help Walter load the Explorer and keep room in my Subaru because Jimbo called and said there's more boxes waiting at home—but I could not help wondering what Krom was thinking. He's won. He's built his road, he's vanquished his human foe, and his nonhuman foe—that nasty-tempered unpredictable chum—is about to be vanquished as well because by noon Krom will have whisked us all beyond its reach.

On TV the tape rolled and Jeanine began again.

And then there was a blast and then another and another, one blast rolling into the next and the window crack widened and the door sucked open and my ears buzzed and Walter and I hit the floor and rolled beneath our workbenches and I began to pray.

37

THIS IS IT, I thought, already through the door.

The road was clogged with people. The convoy was stopped, the gray-green line broken as trucks had veered to avoid rear-ending each other. Drivers hung out windows, people ran out their doors, and we all gaped east, down Minaret Road, in the direction of the caldera.

It's what we all expected, what I'd dreamed of, a dark cloud rising.

A neon-yellow fire truck came screaming down Minaret, the driver blasting the horn in fury but the convoy could not get out of the way because there was no room in the road. The fire truck came halfway up onto the sidewalk, screaming a warning, and people scattered as it passed.

"I'm going to see," I told Walter, and set off at a run before he could stop me.

I ran down Minaret to the intersection with Highway 203 and followed others who made the turn onto the road out of town. Down 203, I could see flames rising above the Jeffrey pines.

This was wrong.

A horn blasted and I threw myself out of the way to let the

ambulance scream by.

I ran until my muscles seized then slowed to a limp and finally stopped and crouched over my cramping thighs. It's too far. I'd made it as far as the ranger station on the edge of town. Close enough to smell the acrid smoke and hear the snap of flames but not close enough to see the damage. Others caught up, gasping. The foolhardy. We were a small panting crowd, the kind that races toward the scene of an accident only none of us had the wherewithal to make it. Bo Robinson was in my face, yelling "where do we *go*?" and I shook my head. I didn't know where to go.

Screams. Fire trucks. Ambulances. Police.

I started back to the lab, no longer wanting to witness this accident.

At the intersection of 203 and Minaret, I ran into Krom. His blue Blazer was stopped at right angles to the stalled Guard convoy, its uniformed crew looking ready to stampede. The driver's door of the Blazer was open and Krom stood in the road with a cell phone to his ear. "Calm it down," he was saying to someone. He held his big frame straight and wore the heavy parka and thick corded pants like a pelt. Calm, sure of himself.

I listened to the sirens scream.

He lowered the phone and told me to go home.

"What *happened*?"

"It's under control. Go home and be ready to evac."

The yellow fire truck careened by and then an ambulance and I glimpsed inside something blackened, and I turned to watch, I'd become an accident junkie, and then from another direction an amplified voice rose over the sirens. *Remain calm, proceed to your homes in an orderly fashion, tune in to KMMT for further instructions.*

Krom got in his Blazer and peeled off.

I ran.

38

"WHERE YOU *BEEN*?" Jimbo swung the door wide and pulled me inside.

He was white. His eyes, which like Mom's are the color of lichen that grows on the north-facing shank of tree bark, were showing the whites. He wore his portable radio with the earphones around his neck and I could hear its tinny voice.

"Traffic's a mess," I said. "There was an explosion."

He nodded.

I felt the hairs rise on my forearms. I stared at the radio. "It's on the news?" The radio in my car doesn't work. Hasn't for a year. Should have gotten it fixed. "What happened?"

"You don't know?"

"I don't know."

My brother said, "Somebody blew up 203."

I could no longer hear the radio's tinny whisper because blood was pounding in my ears. I'd thought it was an accident. Guard truck carrying explosives. Something like that.

"You know the bridge? Over the culvert? It's *gone*. Whole thing went." He bounced a fist against his thigh. "You know what that means? Means we're not getting out that way."

I could only nod.

"But it's gonna be okay." His eyes pinned me. "Pika's okay. Explosives there didn't go off."

"There?"

"Yeah, there too."

"There too?"

He grinned, a ghastly pleading grin. "But they said it's gonna be okay. On the radio. Said it was all ready to blow only it was, like, wired wrong. Said they're going over it with dogs to be sure it's okay."

I couldn't speak. I couldn't take this in.

"We still got a way out. So it takes a little longer."

A little longer? How about three times as long—it's a one-lane road. I said, "Who did it?"

"They're not saying." He raked back his hair. "What do you think?

I couldn't think.

He said, "I think it was Mike."

"*Mike*?"

"Hey, he's been a real case ever since Stobie. He thinks we all blame him. He thinks everybody's against him. He's sure had access to explosives on the road crew, I mean, we all have, but shit nobody but Mike's crazy enough to do something like this." Jimbo stared at me. "You think it could be Mike?"

Yes. And then I was thinking of Krom, the way I think of him every time we plunge deeper into shit. But it couldn't be Krom, Krom's drilled this evac into us for weeks—*it's his plan*—and if we don't get out in time his rep's gone. And the man I saw in the street half an hour ago was scrambling to hold it together. Calm it down. I felt a surge, the drill-reflex kicking in. It's okay, we can do it. Would have been better to have two evacuation routes, sure. But we don't *need* 203—in fact, ever since Krom's simulation of a pyroclastic flow taking out that highway I'd considered

Krom's route, Pika, as the safer way out. We've drilled on Pika and even though we've never gone all the way and emptied the town, we've gone far enough that we know what to do. It works. The drill works. Just follow the arrows, just do what you're told. Do it in your sleep. We can get out Pika. Hasn't snowed for a week. Nothing's erupting. Krom can do it. I'm on his side today.

Jimbo said, "Cass?"

I focused on my brother. "You do a good job on Pika, Jimbo?"

He nodded.

"Then it's going to be okay. What time do we go?"

He searched my face. "Radio said keep listening for revised times." He clapped the phones back to his ears. Half-on, half-off, a jet jockey dividing his attention.

I headed for the stairs.

He was on my heels. "Where you going?"

"See if we missed anything important." Keep moving. Focus. Be ready.

"We *got* it. Stuff to go's in the garage so let's get down there. You said you got room? My heap's full."

I took the stairs, snapped on the hallway light, wove in and out of rooms. We're not taking everything. We've prioritized. Mom and Dad are trusting us to take care of things. They've picked up a cartooning gig in Scotland and they can't afford to fly home and then return. And what if they fly home and nothing happens? We've e-mailed packing lists back and forth. Dad wanted us to take it all but Mom prioritized. Take the good china, leave the Sears set. The good china's in Bishop now.

I dropped to my knees and looked under my parents' bed. The safe was gone.

"I got it." Jimbo checked his watch. "Come *on*."

"All right let's go." I moved along the hallway, whose walls were now bare of photos, thinking this is what this room looks like and this is what that room looks like, thinking I might forget. I passed the laundry room that used to be Henry's room, where I was babysitting my little brother and staring out the window, and that was one room I would not miss. I snapped off the hall light and followed Jimbo down the stairs and through the family room and into the garage.

The garage runs half again the length of our house. Three cars can park in here, with room left over for Dad's workshop. There are walls of shelves and a loft jury-rigged from the rafters. The unshelved wall is planked with pegboard and hung with hoses, lawn furniture, flashlights, power cords in orange braids. Half the space is devoted to old sports gear: skis, snowboards, bikes, camping stuff, ropes, pitons, and at least a dozen helmets that look like giant shellacked insect heads. A lot of it is junk. Mom had e-mailed if it's worth over five hundred, take it. Leave the rest. She's expecting to return.

Jimbo's Fiat, as promised, was full. Seven cartons sat in front of his car.

"My Soob's in the driveway." I hit the garage door opener. "I can fit these boxes." The Lindsay and Georgia evidence boxes, which I'd packed in my Subaru instead of Walter's Explorer, didn't use much room.

And then there was a shudder like logs rolling beneath the concrete, and the stuff hanging from the walls set up a racket and a box shimmied off the loft and split open on the floor, spilling old baby quilts. I held my ground.

"Shake and bake," Jimbo said, grinning. White.

Across the street, Richard Precourt gave us the thumbs-up then went back to securing a tarpaulin over the mountain of stuff in the back of his pickup.

Richard's hanging in there, I saw. Okay, we can do it.

Jimbo and I carried the cartons to the driveway and loaded my Subaru. It looked like I was embarking on a truly bizarre trip: roof racked with skis, tail hung with mountain bike, interior filled with field gear and boxes. In my passenger seat was a porcelain doll in a glass case that Lindsay brought me from Argentina. The Cerro Galan caldera.

I got a lawn chair from the pegboard and Dad's workshop radio and took a seat on the driveway, returning the waves of my neighbors.

It was unreal.

Like a block party, only instead of Buddy Precourt's garage band there were packed cars and radios blasting KMMT. I focused on my street. Looked exposed, hanging on the edge of the bluff. Houses looked unstable, piled three and four stories like cake tiers. I've had a meal in every house on the street, I've gathered cones for the fireplace from every pine, I remember what the Maser's place looked like before the propane tank explosion. I know everybody on the street, I remember everybody who moved away, and I can guess who would and who would not return to rebuild.

Jimbo said, "You think it's gonna blow?" He was behind me, hands on my chair, which vibrated from his incessant jiggling.

I shrugged. People evacuated the towns around Rainier and it didn't blow.

Jimbo came around to face me. "You don't act scared."

"I'm scared. I've been scared so long it's second nature. You're used to seeing me this way." I scuffed my boot, peeling a layer of snow. "It's been a nightmare so long I have a hard time accepting it's real. In the dream the ground's rotting but it never gets to the eruption. I wake up first. You don't die in dreams, do you?"

"Shit, I don't know." He went into the garage and got a chair and sat beside me. "So. You never said if you think it's Mike."

"I don't know."

"He holds a grudge, you know?"

"I know, but... Grudge enough to sabotage the *evac*?"

"Look what Mike did to Georgia."

It took me a moment, to make the leap to Gold Dust. I said, slowly, "You saying Mike killed Georgia?"

"I'm just saying *maybe* he did. You know?"

"I *don't* know."

"Well didn't Eric ...?"

Very slowly, I came alert. "Didn't Eric what?"

"Aw shit," my brother said. "Shit."

"Tell me," I said, "what you know. What Eric knows. Tell me, Jimbo."

"Okay, but only because I'm through covering for Mike. If Mike did 203..." Jimbo gripped the arms of his chair. "Look, I know you know all about Georgia and Krom, getting caught by Mike, and all that. Eric told me he told you. Guess he left me out of it. That's Eric, the go-to guy, taking it all on himself. You know?"

I nodded. That I knew.

"So after Georgia disappeared, Eric and I were talking about Hot Creek. And we thought maybe that might have set Mike and Georgia off, against each other. And Eric said to keep it between us, that he'd bird-dog it. He'd take care of things. And then after you guys found her in the glacier—only you figured that's not where she died—I mean, Eric told me that. Anyway, so when you found out there was gunpowder in the evidence and, uh, you wanted a cartridge from me..." He expelled a biathlete breath.

"You suspected the evidence powder was biathlon powder?"

"Shit yeah. And I thought Gold Dust, right away. Sorry Cass but I didn't want you finding it. I mean, not until Eric had the chance to get up there and check it out and find out if anything there nailed Mike."

I took that in. "Eric went to Gold Dust?"

"Yeah, couple days after the race. And he didn't find anything that pointed to Mike. So we kind of breathed easier."

"*Easier*? Shit, Jimbo, we're talking murder and you were content that Mike wouldn't be *nailed*?"

"No Cass, we *hoped* we were wrong about Mike."

I recalled Eric in the cottage, trying to talk me into his version of Mike—misunderstood, mistreated. I thought about Eric, bearing the burden of Mike, going up to Gold Dust to find out if his fears were justified. And then I suddenly stiffened. "*Wait* a minute. I asked Eric about the hot spring at Gold Dust, where it was, and he stonewalled me. But now you tell me he'd already *been* there, so he must have seen the spring was gone. He must have seen the rockfall that blocked it. And the fissure..."

"*No* Cass, come on, he didn't find that thing. And the rockfall was nothing new—we saw that way back when we used to hang there. The spring was right in front of it. So when Eric didn't see the spring this time, he figured it was dead, under the snow."

"You're saying he didn't notice there'd been new exfoliation, which would explain why the spring that used to be in *front* of the rockfall was now *behind* it?"

"Why would he? You're the geologist. He's not."

I relaxed. Jimbo was right. Eric wouldn't have noticed. If he'd noticed, he would have gone straight to Lindsay or Krom. Just as I had, when I found the fissure.

Jimbo said, "So we clear now?"

"Partly. I think I get what took Georgia to Gold Dust. Georgia's pissed at Mike, wanting to keep things going with Krom, so she goes to check out the spring she remembers. But I still don't know the how and the when of it. Since you think Mike killed her, care to explain that?"

"Um." Jimbo popped his fist on the chair arm. "Eric and I kicked around a few ideas."

I waited.

"Okay, so she goes up there to find the spring, like you said.

And I think when she found it—and it turns out to be more than a spring—she's really hyped and she comes back to report it to Krom. I mean, cops found her car in the Community Center lot. But she runs into Mike inside. And she can't help it, she puts it to him. Or maybe he puts two and two together and figures where she's been. And he wonders why she's so cranked about it. And he says he's gonna go check it out. And she takes charge, you know, like she does, and says Mike's not going without *her*. Gets her gear from her car, and they drive up to Lake Mary, and from there..."

There was a rumbling, a throat clearing, shivering our chairs.

Jimbo said, white, "So what do you think?"

I said, slowly, "Why do you think it was Mike she ran into? Instead of Adrian?"

"It was a Sunday."

"So?"

"She *disappeared* on a Sunday. Didn't you look it up?" Jimbo shook his head. "You make a lousy cop."

"What's so special about Sunday?"

"Mike mans the office for Krom on Sundays. Krom takes the day off. You didn't know?"

I stared at my brother. "I didn't know."

"Hey, no sweat. And you're not such a lousy cop. I mean, *man*, when you started in that night about powder in the evidence... Wish I gave you that cartridge. Wish you'd figured out about Mike and Georgia—then he'd be in jail and we could evac out both roads."

"Wish you'd told me about Gold Dust."

"That was Eric's call. Anyway, I figured you'd figure it out eventually." Jimbo slumped in his chair until his butt was on the edge and his legs bridged out over the snow.

I glanced at my brother. Let somebody else do the damn

dishes. Our world's about to come undone, but Jimbo's still Jimbo. It was, oddly, comforting.

It wasn't until three twenty-five that we heard a sound like garbage trucks waking the neighborhood. Jimbo snaked up from his chair and shouted across the street to the Precourts, who were already piling into their pickup, "Gentlemen start your engines!"

My legs were rubber.

Jimbo hooted. A police Jeep was turning the corner, followed by a Guard truck and then a line of cars I recognized from the next street over. The Jeep slowed and Eric rolled down the window and yelled, "Let's *go*, Oldfields."

Jimbo was already in his Fiat and it peeled out of the garage and backed into the driveway beside my Subaru. Somehow, I was in my car with the engine on. Somehow, I was backing down the drive. My arm was hooked on the windowsill. I saw the minute hand on my watch leap from three twenty-nine to three thirty.

Two hours left of daylight.

39

I WAS CHOKING. That's what made it real.

This was no dream, no drill, this was the real thing and I knew it because our fleeing neighborhood—and the neighborhood that fled before us and the neighborhood coming behind us—filled the air with exhaust that seeped in through the vents, in through the nose and mouth and eyes and burned the message into the tissues. It's real.

Jimbo's Fiat was in front of me and the Precourts' pickup was behind me and the high Pika walls flanked me. That was the immediate neighborhood.

We crawled. Twenty-five miles per hour. Safe and sane.

My second hand leaped to four o'clock.

Jimbo's radio fed me a steady whisper of advice. Stay calm. Keep moving. Leave two car-lengths between your vehicle and the vehicle in front. I wore the phones, like Jimbo, half-on and half-off my ears so I would not miss the onset of an eruption.

Up ahead, someone honked.

Another honk, and then another.

Jimbo slowed and I gained on him and then I slowed too, and I watched the rearview to be sure Rich Precourt was going to slow. We were doing fifteen, and holding our two-car-lengths-pace beautifully, when Jimbo's brake lights went on and his Fiat squirreled into the right-hand snowbank. I slammed on my brakes and the Subaru's nose slid left, and up ahead I heard nonstop honking and in the earphones *stay calm leave two car-lengths* and then all I heard was the screeching of brakes up and down the line and somewhere far behind the Precourts, like distant thunder, a crumpling of metal on metal, time after time.

Jimbo was already out when I got out, both of us choking on the haze of exhaust. And then mercifully people began to shut off their engines.

I killed the Soob.

Now, there were screams. I braced for an explosion. No explosion came—just nonstop screaming. It came from up ahead.

The Precourts were crowding behind me, and behind them the Robinsons and the Wargos and the Ruiz's, the whole damn block. They swept me up and we engulfed Jimbo and in front of him the Werneckes, and like the accident junkies we'd all become, we surged forward toward the screams.

Some twenty vehicles up the line the crowd stopped and swelled like an aneurysm and I was squeezed against a little sedan. I'd lost Jimbo. I wormed along the sedan and then suddenly I got a clear view and saw why we had stopped our flight.

Between our crowd and another crowd plugging the canyon up ahead was an unpopulated stretch of road. Vehicles were stopped at odd angles, doors open. Roaming this no-man's-land was a bear. Big as a truck, within a paw's swipe of someone's Taurus. It reared as if trying to see over the crowd, and the screamers who had not once let up screamed even harder. The bear froze. Ears went flat. The ground gave a little jolt, and nobody in the crowd noticed or cared about one more shake, but the bear did. It launched itself backward, landing on its belly, then lumbered up with a howl of anguish like the snow's on fire. It shook itself and snow crystals popped off the cinnamon fur.

Dragged out of its winter sleep, I guessed, by the same rude shakeup that sent us all scrambling for a way out.

Something jammed into my back. I turned. It was Jimbo's elbow. He held his biathlon rifle, pointed skyward, but I could see the clip was in firing position.

"You can't stop a bear with a twenty-two," I hissed.

My brother hissed back, "Got a better idea?"

Of all times to decide not to duck out, Jimbo chooses this.

In my earphones a voice was advising calm and I didn't know if that was the standard evac spiel or if emergency communications had caught up with the bear.

The bear wasn't calm. It was trapped and snarling and it lowered its anvil head and began to come our way.

I was deafened by screams. I lost Jimbo again and then I saw him worming his way out front of the crowd, rifle held high. He yelled "back up, back up" and the crowd did its best, heaving backward but there were just too many of us squeezed in at this block party, and the people farther back could not hear, over the screaming, my brother's cries.

The bear heard. I saw the silhouette of teeth, and then the big cinnamon started forward again, all its anguish homed on Jimbo.

Jimbo shifted into marksman's stance and like he has done a thousand times before he brought the rifle to his cheek and sighted and squeezed off a round.

There was a bellow from the cinnamon that stopped my heart.

Someone nearby yelled *Jimbo you idiot.*

But it looked for a moment as though Jimbo had done the

right thing, for the bear froze and twisted, focusing its rage on the pinprick in its shoulder.

"Okay," I said, heart beating again.

At both ends of no-man's-land the crowds had shut up.

There was gunfire upcanyon.

Jimbo raised his rifle again and I elbowed him because across the gulf, Eric had appeared. He had both hands wrapped around his service weapon, leveling it at the bear.

And now the bear and I had two marksmen to worry about. A shooter with a glass eye and the knowledge that accuracy is not his trademark, but he's got a whole lot more firepower than the other shooter, who's armed with a weapon meant to knock down mechanical targets.

Eric sidled along the road. The bear turned, nose into the air, and zeroed on Eric. They were no more than a couple of truck-lengths apart. Eric eased forward, waiting, it seemed, for the bear to lift its chin and present its best target.

I wanted to scream.

There was gunfire, again, upcanyon. The bear reared up.

And now the crowd behind Eric convulsed, and five Guardsmen trotted into the clearing, one behind the other like a line of geese. They carried heavy artillery and the cinnamon hardly had time to shift its focus to this new threat before they'd wheeled into a firing squad. The bear seemed to flinch, and then the sound of automatic weapons swamped all else, even its roar of surprise. The shooters fired for what seemed minutes, shredding the bear until the wall of snow behind it was splashed red and cratered with plugs of fur.

Jimbo fumbled to eject his clip. "Let's *go*."

He was shoving me, everyone was shoving again, back the way we'd come, back toward the cars. I didn't need shoving, I had plenty of adrenaline pumping me along. And then someone said "bears" and Jimbo caught it—bears, plural—and my dumbshit brother turned with his rifle under his arm and fought his way back toward Eric. By the time I caught up Eric was saying, "Bears are all down, bears aren't the problem."

I said, sick on adrenaline, "What *is* the problem?"

"Pileup." Eric pointed back toward town, the way we'd come. "Back in that throat where the canyon starts."

I looked. Vehicles to the horizon. No access.

"How big?" Jimbo asked.

"Big."

I said, "How big is big?"

Eric met my look. "It's all clear up ahead. Be ready to move in fifteen minutes."

I was looking back, toward the throat of the canyon. I said, my own throat constricted, "No way out."

"We'll get them out," Eric said.

"Walter's back there."

"I'll check," Eric said.

"No, I will." I started off. Vehicles to the horizon, and way back there, beyond the throat—beyond the pileup—vehicles waiting to get out. Walter was in the group behind ours. How many neighborhoods to a group, how many vehicles to a neighborhood, how many miles back in the canyon was Walter's Explorer? Beyond the throat? I started to run.

Eric caught my arm. "I'll find out where he is, Cass. I'll see him on his way. If he's behind the pileup, we'll get him out. We got a lot of people stuck back there and you can be damn sure we're not going to leave any of them behind. I give you my personal guarantee."

I shook my head. "I'm going to check."

"Aw *shit*, man," Jimbo said, "you want a sister?"

Eric said, "No."

I tried to move.

Eric tightened his grip and said, weary, "You see those guys?"

There were Guardsmen moving our way, monitoring the flow of the crowd. They moved like they were under fire. I saw one guy look up the canyon walls. He was skinny—all helmet and uniform. He planted his hands on his wide fatigue belt and scanned the cliffs far above. He looked like he was expecting a bomb to fall. His head snapped down. He spat. He didn't want to be here. He looked like he wasn't going to be patient with anyone who slowed him down.

"There isn't an option," Eric said.

Death by traffic jam.

With a sense as strong as I have ever had of making the wrong choice, I let Jimbo tug me back toward our cars.

40

ALONE, in a cute little motel room in Bishop. Chintz pillow shams, wildflower walls, street view through white ruffles. There was the sound of TV coming through the thin wall from Jimbo's room next door. When he'd left my room he'd said he was going to get some sleep. Not likely. I heard the tattoo of his fingers drumming a table. I felt the thump-thump-thump of his feet bouncing the floor.

Unlike me—I was glued to the television and I didn't move a muscle.

I watched King Videocable's live action team on the spot at the intersection of highway 203 and the chasm blasted across it where the bridge had been. Highway 203 had been severed about halfway between town and highway 395.

On the Mammoth side of that wound there was an endless line of parked vehicles—the vehicles not caught in the pileup, the vehicles blocked by the pileup and forced to reverse direction on Pika and head back into town. They'd fled as far as they could, from town out highway 203 until they were stopped by the chasm. I searched for Walter's red Explorer but the line of vehicles stretched too far for the camera to capture.

Refugees swarmed past parked vehicles. Refugees on foot, on skis, on snowmobiles, every one of them laden with bundles and casting ghostly shadows under the intense white of the big CalTrans lights. Refugees pausing to look at the ground when a quake hit, and then moving a little faster. And when the live action team zoomed in for a closeup, the refugees squinted into the cameras and groped for a sound bite. I recognized most of them. Knew them well, or casually, or enough to greet in passing. I didn't care. Didn't care that my old high school teacher Jack Altschul was leaving Mammoth with nothing but the pack on his back.

I waited for Walter.

On the other side of the chasm, the refugees were hustled into vans and trucks and buses and ferried down 203 to 395, and then the forty miles south to Bishop. If I shifted my view from the TV to the street outside I'd see them rumble through town.

My eyes stayed on the tube. The next refugee fixed in the lights would be Walter.

The camera cut to an aerial view of Pika Canyon, the live action team's eye in the sky floodlighting the pileup of vehicles that choked the narrow throat. Vehicles entangled with vehicles, vehicles on top of vehicles, vehicles looking like they'd tried to crawl up the canyon walls. There was a patch of burnt-out vehicles, where quakes had shaken the unstable edifice and the friction of metal on metal had sparked leaking gas tanks. The smoking skeletons were dusted with Forest Service fire retardant.

I searched for Walter's Explorer in the mess.

The camera cut to an aerial of highway 395. The evacuees had overflowed Bishop and were now on the way to the next towns south, Big Pine and Independence.

The camera cut to Adrian Krom, as it's been doing every half-hour or so through the night. He was framed in front of the burnt husk of a truck on its side. He wore the same clothes I'd seen on him twenty hours ago at the intersection of 203 and Minaret. Now he seemed to sag within the big parka. Now the pelt hung loose. His face was washed quartz-halogen pale, his eyes squinty. He looked like he'd had a rough twenty hours. He looked beat.

He looked beaten. The interviewer, some ingratiating Bishop news anchor, was saying, "You couldn't have foreseen the bears," and Krom seemed to shrink. He said no but he took responsibility nevertheless. I sat forward on the nubby chenille bedspread and if I could have reached through the screen I would have taken him by the neck and screamed you *lost*, you were supposed to get all of us out and you didn't. But I didn't have to throttle him. He knew. He looked beaten.

There was a big quake, and the camera jimmied.

I heard a *shit* through the wall.

When the camera steadied again on Krom, he'd changed. Maybe the anchor didn't catch it, but I did. Krom was rallying. He leaned into the microphone and answered a question the anchor hadn't asked. "We'll have them out by dawn," he said, voice nearly burnt out.

Then he made a movement, which I'm sure the anchor didn't catch. But I did. Krom inclined his head, the slightest move—he made a little bow.

I'd seen that bow eons ago, midnight at Hot Creek, as he bowed to his enemy and gave it the finger.

41

DAWN, and I did not see Walter.

I spent an hour trying to reach Eric, routed from one command center to another, one official to another. When Eric finally called back I blurted "where is he?"

"He's gotta be out. His car was parked with everybody else's, along 203. But I gotta tell you I did not personally see him leave. I blew that. I owe you, Cassie. Hang in there, okay? There's nobody left in town."

"Thanks," I said. "You sound beat."

"Beyond."

"Please take care of yourself."

"You better believe it."

I called Walter's cell phone. Then I dialed, for the fifteenth time since midnight, the motel down the street where Walter was booked. The desk clerk was beginning to worry.

I went out to the Soob and unloaded the Lindsay and Georgia boxes and parked them in my room. I wrote a note to Jimbo. *Antsy. Driving down to Big Pine & Independence. Check motels. Maybe got signals crossed with W. Got my cell on.* I left the note on my dresser then locked the door. Jimbo has a spare key.

I didn't turn southbound on highway 395, as my note promised. The worried Bishop desk clerk had already phoned every motel and B&B in Big Pine and Independence for me. She promised to keep trying. She promised to call on my cell if she located Walter. I promised her a fancy dinner for her efforts, when this was all over.

I promised, in my heart, to apologize to Jimbo for my lie, when this was all over.

I turned northbound on 395, heading home. There was no traffic, just me following the long Sierra scarp. And then in the distance, just spilling over the lip of the caldera, which sits on the Long Valley plateau above Bishop like a hanging lake, came a National Guard truck down the highway grade. The last of the evacuators were now evacuating.

And above and beyond that was the unchanged bulk of Mammoth Mountain. The old mountain looks me in the eye: coming back?

The Guard truck and I passed each other and I craned to look. The back end was half open and the guys in camouflage were slumped.

I hadn't really thought he'd be in there anyway.

At the top of the grade there was a barricade. Nobody in sight. I went around it on the median. Just past the Hot Creek turnoff, I reached another barricade. This one was manned.

I pulled over and checked in with my motel clerk. Nothing new.

If a call came on my cell and caller ID said it was the clerk, or Walter, or Eric, I would answer. If a call came from any other number, I would not answer. I counted on Jimbo to sleep until noon. If he woke earlier, I counted on him to try calling a few times and conclude I was in a no-service zone, and then decide to try later. I counted on him to be Jimbo and go hook up with Bobby or the deMartinis. I counted on him not to alert someone that I'd gone missing, because I intended to be back before he put two and two together. I did not intend to have someone come after me and stop me. And if I encountered a problem, I did not intend to have someone come share the risk.

I hadn't really expected the guys at the barricade to let me through. Didn't matter. I had a Plan B. I headed southbound, as if going back to Bishop. Around a curve, out of anyone's sight, I took the unmarked turnoff. I knew this Forest Service road—I'd taken it in summer, on field trips, and I knew where it accessed another lateral that would put me in the neighborhood of the Lakes Basin. I wondered, briefly, if Krom had walked that lateral in his quest for an alternate route. If he had, he would have rejected it because it would put evacuating traffic in the neighborhood of Red Mountain. I didn't reject it. There was no other choice. Two miles uphill I turned onto the lateral, just wide enough for a snowplow. I crept along, fingers crossed, but within a few hundred yards the road ended. Hadn't been plowed. Every available snowplow, I guessed, had been diverted to Krom.

That much farther to ski. So I'd better get going.

As I was stepping into my bindings I gave a glance to Lindsay's doll. She has porcelain skin like Lindsay's and a proud chin, and she brought me Lindsay's voice, which I had lost in the crime-scene horror of her office. She says, sharply, don't do anything foolish, honey.

I promised to be wise.

I followed the unplowed road, which banded the mountainside, and then began a gentle descent. The snow was slow but once the slope steepened I kicked into a smoother stride and picked up speed.

Within two hours I'd reached the Lakes Basin. I came downcanyon in a tuck, trying not to think about the lay of the land, about the rift up on Red Mountain. There was no other way in. It was just that simple. Just ski. Don't fall, don't break an ankle. I tried not to think about Walter lying off the road someplace with a broken ankle. I tried not to think at all.

The cell phone in my pocket was silent. Jimbo was sleeping, or he'd gone straight to breakfast without checking my room. I didn't blame him.

I focused on my stomach. It was hollow. Nothing to eat since last night in Bishop, and that was toast forced down me by Jimbo. Now, I was hungry. I fantasized swinging by the house and grabbing something. It's on the way. Jimbo cleaned out the fridge but what about the freezer? Last time I looked there was a sweet potato pie, microwaveable. I wanted that pie. So creamy, like a sweet cloud in your mouth.

The canyon road dipped below a ridge and the slope fell into shadow. I hit deeper snow, and had to work. My stomach growled.

Jimbo ate the pie. I just knew it. Didn't matter. I wasn't going to the house because Walter was not there waiting for pie.

There was something. I stopped. A rumbling, deep within the mountain. I waited, but detected no movement. The sound trailed off as the earth settled itself. Okay, another quake. So what's new?

There was thunder and I looked up to the clear sky, and then to the ridge above me. Even as the thunder died another sound came—a thick sucking. In utter amazement I watched an entire section of snow detach from the bowl beneath the ridge and slide in a great slab downhill toward the road. The leading edge wrinkled over a cluster of boulders and loosened and slurried ahead of the main body of the avalanche.

In slow motion, taking forever, I bent to release my bindings.

Wind hit me, roared past me. The snow in front of my skis humped up and I felt the ground below me move. Snow exploded up and the crust under my skis crumpled. I was ripped off my feet. I gasped, inhaling needles of snow.

Swim.

But the snow's got its own agenda and it's tumbling me along like I'm a load of wash and I can't see and can't breathe and all I want in the world is to get my head above the snow. Then without knowing how I do it I'm swimming all right, fighting for the surface. Something hard bangs into my leg. My ski. A rock. I'm swimming, dog-paddling to beat all hell but I don't know which way is up.

And then the snow and I slow and finally come to rest and the snow, which only seconds ago had been liquid, turns to cement.

I lay pinned. I could see nothing but my mind was free to roam and it dived down into the crevassed glacier, blue walls closing around me. I screamed.

There was snow in my mouth. I spat but it was already dissolving on my tongue, creamy as sweet potato pie. I stuck out my tongue, tasting cold air. Free air. There was a hole in the snow around my face. Hope surged.

My muscles convulsed, futile, but then my hand moved and I realized that my entire left arm and shoulder were free, encircling my face. I located the rest of my body. Right arm pinned across chest, legs bent at knees, toes wiggling in boots. Intact. With my free hand I probed the cavity. Walls were solid, cement. I pushed, panicking, then willed myself to stop and clamped my mouth shut. Don't waste air. Slow small breaths. Get the cadence.

So dark. I'd never seen such darkness with my eyes open.

I clawed at the snow, digging until my fingers stung.

Oh you fool, which way is up?

Well flip a coin. Just dig, what else can you do? I clawed one side of the cavity, fingers on fire, then clawed the other. I put my fingers in my mouth and tasted blood. And a thought came, a gift. I dug out a chunk of snow and put it in my mouth and mashed it, melting it, then opened my mouth and let it out. Snowmelt ran down my right cheek. *I'm lying right-side down*. Up is to my left.

I dug. For minutes—hours? although it couldn't have been hours because there wasn't enough air to survive hours—I dug, and the cavity filled with loose snow and I compacted it into the downhill wall. Trying not to breath too much, trying not to think. And then came a time when I was digging mechanically, hope long since gone, just digging because it was something to do. Finally it hurt too much to continue.

Fear got me around the throat and I cursed myself for that note to Jimbo—such a clever note making sure he wouldn't worry—and if he could have heard my scream right now I'd scream my head off.

I did not have the air to scream.

So cold. So dark. There was a part of me that was already so cold and tired I thought I was approaching an accommodation to death.

You fool, you reap what you sow.

Fear seized me again, and I began yanking my right arm, which was pinned to my ribs. The arm moved, snow scraping the back of my right hand. It moved, millimeters at best, but that was something and I yanked and yanked and my arm moved back and forth. Skin stung. I yanked, and torqued my body just enough to give the arm clearance. I moved it up my breastbone and felt my heart pounding on the other side of that hard wall. Arm was coming free.

Two hands free. One was on fire and the other was numb.

Shifting my shoulders, I placed both palms against the snow roof and shoved. Pounded. Nothing moved. I screamed, clawing and digging, calling myself every name in the book and *foolish* was the kindest of the lot.

There was a rumbling and my icy bed was ever so gently rocked.

Quake. I froze. What's the effect of a quake on snow? Loosen it, right? I began to pound again, digging now with my knuckles.

Snow avalanched onto my face.

The roof had cracked and there was light. I cried out and reached up to widen the crack and more snow came loose and I was laughing and crying and, now that there was light, finding it very funny that I had drooled my way to digging in the right direction.

Cold dry powder drifted in. Snowing outside. How long had I been buried? I enlarged the fist hole that had let in light and snowfall. Indeed it was snowing and the flakes landing on my raw hands tickled uncomfortably. The light was dawn gray. How *long*? I tore at the remaining snow roof and pushed up onto my right elbow, trying to see above ground.

And then I screamed for Lindsay.

42

Ash peppered into my mouth.

In a thin and silky rain, ash was falling, ash so finely scattered that it appeared to have been sieved, and it seemed that this sieving could never cover the ground, but it had, for the ground and snow and trees and rocks were all the uniform pearl gray of that desiccated rain.

There was noise, the fitful roar of a faraway crowd. Ash congealed in my mouth like paste.

Dreams do come true.

There's blood everywhere and I'm tearing at the ground and fighting the snow. My hands are finished but I'm out, and I get to my knees and then to my feet. My legs are mush but I can stand on the rigidity of terror.

This looks like a dream world in which the sun is in eclipse and trees and rocks have familiar shapes but no definition, as though they are in danger of dissolving and disappearing from sight altogether.

I couldn't find a horizon.

My parka was gone. My cell phone was gone. My watch was gone. My yellow sweatshirt was wet and gray, growing woolly with ash. My hands were gray and ash clumped where the flesh was torn and it looked as though I'd grown thick gray scars.

An observation formed itself like a cloud at the top of my head: this is a very light ash fall. This ash is the consistency of dust. This ash is cold, light gray. There is no yellow tinge of sulfur. What do I do now, Lindsay?

She says the obvious: Find shelter, honey.

I took a few steps upcanyon but upcanyon was veiled in falling ash. Can't walk through this to the car. Too far. Ash veils everywhere. Where's it coming from? *Red Mountain.* I stood stunned, in the helicopter's flight path, waiting for the worst.

But the ash above Red Mountain was the same as the ash everywhere else.

What's erupting?

She won't say.

I decided to go find Walter.

There was no trace of skis or poles, nothing but an annular depression in the snow where I had lain. I set off on foot downcanyon. The ash was shallow; I've skied deeper powder than this. Ash kept falling and I couldn't keep it out of my mouth. I turtled inside my sweatshirt, setting my hands on fire, and got my bra free and tied it like a surgical mask around my face. I descended through the dream world and when the ground shook I braced for another avalanche, but here the canyon had broadened and its walls held their cover. There was just the incessant feathering of ash, blurring the topography, turning hemlocks into people. There was no reason Walter would have come this way, so far from Pika Canyon. Nevertheless, I scrutinized each hemlock as I passed. The forest thickened, and in time I came to a great round empty field. Lake Mary: site of the 20K biathlon race, site of Krom's evacuation drill. What foresight. I didn't need a drill. I knew the way. Three miles to home. I hugged the lake's shore, coming around the east side until I hit the wide gray ribbon that was the Lake Mary Road. As I have done a thousand times, I headed down the road toward town.

The road edged the eastern slope of Mammoth Mountain, which humped its ash-softened shoulder at me: still here?

The faraway roar lowered in pitch.

Ahead, I could make out chairlifts in the sky. Beginner runs there. Watertank, Christmas Tree, Lupin. Skied them almost before I could walk. The road ahead tucked into a tunnel that cut beneath the ski runs. There is a viewpoint just before the tunnel, from which one can see all the way down into Long Valley, into the caldera. I turned, thinking maybe the ash fall will be thick enough to block the view.

It wasn't.

I had known, of course, that the ash fall originated somewhere but I couldn't believe in the eruption—not fully—until I saw. You can't believe there is a snake in the sleeping bag with you until the hissing starts, and even then you aren't willing to believe but finally you have to look and you find in raw shock the very thing you knew all along was there.

Through the screen of ash, I saw. Boiling clouds of black and white, black metamorphosing into white, black lobes splitting open like mouths and breathing white puffs. The white clouds climbed and the black fell.

I saw the core, a black column that anchored earth to sky. It swelled, contracted, swelled, and pulsed. The snake. Not creeping on the ground but risen to strike.

I saw how the thing was put together, snake cloaked in clouds. The vertical black jet threw off black clouds and as they rose and split, dark rock debris fell back to earth and the white water vapor rose higher. Steam white.

The noise, which pulsed with the column, was the roar of a giant.

Nothing for me to worry about. Not yet. It's down there, I'm up here. The larger heavier stuff was falling in the south moat, and downwind the clouds strung out and appeared to be dragging a curtain of ash over the caldera. All I was getting up here was drift from the winds.

I watched the eruption, growing giddy at the sight. I know just what this is. Heard about it from Lindsay, saw the evidence laid down by ancient beasts just like this one. Phreatic, a steam-blast explosion. That hot tongue of magma in the south moat had pushed all the way to the surface where it met ground water, flashing the water into steam. And now the steam is pulverizing old rock, grinding it to pebbles and ash, and shotgunning the lot into the sky. I know this is probably a prelude. I know what happened here hundreds of thousands of years ago and what can happen again tomorrow, or a week from now, or today even, but I can't seem to make myself move. I can't stop looking. This is astonishing. This isn't like my dreams. The ground isn't rotting, and right now I'm more dazzled than scared. I know I should be getting out of here but this is incredible. This is like watching fireworks in the meadow behind my house when I was little enough that fireworks took my breath away.

Lindsay you should be here to see this. The Survey alert level WARNING does not do this justice. They need another level. HOLY SHIT.

Even for this, she would not come.

And it was her silence that brought me out of my slack-jawed gawking. I started downhill, looking constantly over my shoulder to see if the sight was still there. I took shelter briefly in the tunnel to clean ash off my face, out of my ears, from the folds of my lingerie mask.

Hightailing it down the Lake Mary Road, I kept replaying the image of that snake. I went over every detail, turning that eruption column around in my head wondering, is this big?

Small? How is this going to progress? I wanted to go back and look again and at the same time I wanted to get as far away as possible. I was buzzed. I was scared again, but looking that thing in the eye had kicked me into a kind of thrill-ride fear. I wanted to scream and close my eyes and then look and see it all again. You're nuts, I told myself, you're crazier than the guy who challenges the volcano but I had come to this weird space where I felt that because I'd looked it dead on, that I was free. I was above it. I had come out of an avalanche and seen this and here I was free to go on my way. I was alive.

I was a cat with nine lives.

I came to the outskirts of town and cut off the Lake Mary Road, toward Walter's neighborhood. The streets, the houses, were gray. Everybody gone but me. Me and the houses with their coatings of ash like sheet-draped furniture in unused rooms.

Walter's house was dark. I pounded on the door. He didn't answer so I got the key he hides behind the rain gutter. Dim inside. I flipped a light switch. No power. Okay; ash had shorted out the transformers. I yelled for him. Silence. I ran through his house, tracking his carpet with ash, knocking into his captain's chair—and why hadn't he moved *that* to storage, one more good chair left behind. He wasn't home. Okay. I knew now where he was. At her office.

Outside, the ash fall had thickened.

I hesitated. I'd promised her not to do anything foolish. I decided to go home first and gear up.

Stuff's getting deep, I thought as I walked it. Get skis.

My street was like the others, my house like Walter's. Dark. I broke into a run, cutting up the empty driveway past the lawn chairs. Keys were in my purse; purse was in the pack. Gone. I got the snow shovel that Jimbo left last time he cleared the path to the woodpile, and smashed the kitchen-sink window. Nothing stops me. I climbed onto the sill then stepped into the sink. Glass crunched. I leaped to the floor, crunched across the kitchen, and grabbed the flashlight from the catch-all drawer.

I shone the light. Cabinet doors stood open. The floor was a sea of broken glass and crockery and dented cans and supine boxes.

I ran to the living room and found the phone table tipped over. Phone was dead.

It's okay. Just gear up and go.

I ran upstairs to the bathroom and rooted through the stuff spilled out of the medicine cabinet and found bandages and tape and Neosporin. I turned on the faucet and was glad to find that quakes hadn't ruptured the water pipes. Water sluiced gray mud from my hands and it hurt like hell. My right hand was raw, my left fingertips chewed. The wounds were clotted with dark stuff; ash, blood, I couldn't tell. I looked in horror. I wanted Lindsay here to bandage my hands. No, I wanted someone alive. Walter.

There was a small earthquake. I bandaged myself, making a mess of the job.

I went into my parents' room and ransacked Mom's drawers and fumbled out of my wet clothes and put on hers. Too big; I added layers. Cold as shit in here and getting darker outside.

I moved downstairs. Walk, don't run. Don't fall and break an ankle.

Down in the garage, everything was on the floor. I waded in, striking gold again and again. Folding snow shovel. Rope. Pitons —take them, who knew? Water bottles, backpacking stove, very good. A compass—yes, yes, good, great. Flashlights. I chose three. Batteries in the kitchen drawer. I shone my light over the helmets and found Jimbo's old spelunking hard hat with the caver's headlamp. Pure gold. I reached for skis, then reconsidered. Snowshoes more versatile, take those. What else, from my father's emporium? I moved to his workshop and selected knife, duct tape, two screwdrivers, flat and Phillips head—who knew? A new appreciation for my father's skills flooded me. Walter can't change a water filter. Walter wouldn't know where the water filter is. I hunted for my father's dust masks. Couldn't find them. Come on, he's got a million of those things. Buried somewhere. Shit.

The garage shook.

And then like a gift I knew what to do, mind leaping ahead. Nothing stops me.

Back into the kitchen, crunching glass and kicking cans. Ash coming in through the broken window. What a mess. I dropped my gear and went to the catch-all drawer. Batteries, matches, safety pins. I took them all. An old windup watch; I took it. I dug around. Ahhh, rubber bands. I moved to the counter and found the nesting coffee filters, beautiful just beautiful. I put together two coffee-filter-rubber-band dust masks and packed the materials for more. I filled the water bottles.

I ran upstairs and took the first-aid supplies and carried the stuff back down.

Done?

Breathing hard, I swept the flashlight around the kitchen. Must be something else. I hefted the pack. Weighed a ton. I wanted more.

Food.

Nearly blew that. Cans, packages, bags on the counters, on the floor. I started to grab. Wait, prioritize. I emptied a box of granola bars into my pack. Dried apricots, there's a prize. A package of Oreos. My mouth watered. I spun to the freezer and there was the sweet potato pie. Hard luck, Jimbo. Then my heart sank. No power to nuke it.

I opened the fridge. Empty as Siberia. Bottle of catsup on its side and a sponge. My stomach growled. Back to the cupboard and I found an open sack of pretzels and crammed them into my mouth. Stale. Salty. Wonderful. I drank long and deep from the kitchen faucet, eschewing a glass. I'm alive, I'm surviving, I have no time for such niceties as a drinking glass, should one be left intact.

Now *go*.

I got Jimbo's caving helmet and, thank you very much, found batteries to fit. I strapped on the helmet, put on goggles, fitted the dust mask—a success—and put on heavy work gloves. That hurt. Pain didn't stop me. I got into the pack. Lord in heaven, *heavy*. I grabbed the snowshoes and went out the door. Didn't lock it, didn't look back. I'm outta here.

And I walked into night.

Three in the afternoon and the street was gone. Jimbo's headlamp caught ash like infinitesimal insects, and beyond that, nothing. Blackness. How am I going to find Minaret and Lindsay's office if I can't find my own driveway?

You fool, I thought, you fool with a coffee filter on your face and everything but the kitchen sink on your back.

I went back inside and slammed the door.

My pack weighed a ton. My legs weighed twice as much. I got out of my gear and would have curled up on the floor but for the breccia of glass and ash. I took a water bottle and the bag of pretzels and headed into the living room. I dropped into the big corduroy armchair by the fireplace. From here I could see out the front window, should light return. I considered shutting off Jimbo's headlamp, to save batteries, but I didn't want to sit in the dark.

I thought about Walter, unable to change a water filter.

I let my head drop to the arm of the chair and cradle there, knocking Jimbo's light askew. I thought about the pie defrosting in the kitchen.

43

It's morning in the High Sierra, Lindsay, but this place looks like Los Angeles on a bad smog day.

You hear what I'm saying? The air is ash dirty. Everything's coated. You know the term *ghost town*? When I was a kid Dad took the family over to Bodie to see a ghost town and I was disappointed—just a bunch of old mining buildings, no ghosts. Guess what? This, here, is a ghost town. Buildings are here but the people are gone. It's silent. Far as I can tell, the south moat's not in eruption anymore so there's simply no sound. It's gray. No color, Lindsay, you'd hate that, although gray I realize is one of your colors. This gray is nobody's color. This is the color of ghosts.

I just came out of the lab, Lindsay. Had to break the storefront window to get in. Walter's not inside. It's so spectral in there I sensed him, though.

There's more ash on the ground today so I'm assuming the eruption continued last night. I can't say for sure—I was asleep. You hear that? I curled up in that corduroy armchair of Dad's, the chair you once called too ugly for Goodwill, and I slept through part of your eruption. I'm assuming this beast is still in its phreatic phase, judging from the type of ash. Don't know when, or if, it will progress to the next stage, erupting fresh magma.

If you were here you'd no doubt get yourself down to the moat while nothing's going on and whack off a fresh sample close to the vent.

I don't really care to do that.

When I say nothing's happening, I mean visibly. There are still quakes. Low-mag, little bumps. Not doing any damage. Here, anyway, I suppose they're tearing up rock somewhere, magma trying to clear itself a path. You hear what I'm saying, Lindsay? These quakes of yours are getting on my nerves.

No, you don't hear me. You've just packed your ghost bags and gone where the real ghosts go. So I'll be on my way.

I trudged up the road. I'll go talk to Walter.

I passed the Ski Tip then came to the building that houses Lindsay's office. I dropped my gear, tried the heavy glass main doors, and they were unlocked. I went inside, switching on my light. The crime-scene tape was gone from her door. I prepared to knock, then paused. Door was just off-plumb. I angled my light; latch bolts jammed open. Adrenaline shot through me. He *is* here. And he didn't have a key so he broke in. "*Walter*," I yelled, pushing inside.

Fallen bookcases. Books, binders, artwork, knickknacks on the floor. Map cabinet skidded halfway across the room. The apothecary cabinet still stood in place, its doors open.

"Walter?"

"Huh?"

I went rigid. He really is here.

There was another soft sound, an exhale.

"Walter?" I looked around, my headlamp sweeping the room. On the floor between the desk and a supine white bookcase was a body. I choked back a scream. My headlamp caught a face. And then relief hit me. The body was Adrian Krom.

His arm came up to shield his eyes from the glare of my light.

"Where's Walter?" I said.

His arm went limp.

I was on my knees, cupping his chin, comparing his pupils, feeling the rise and fall of his chest, running my hand down his leg to where it disappeared beneath the bookcase, and he flinched, and I was surprised to find myself glad to suddenly have some company. It could have been the devil himself and I'd be glad.

His eyes were open and tracking. I had to suppress the urge to tug on the leg; if it could be pulled free, I guessed he would have freed it.

"What are you doing here?" I whispered.

"Evac sweep." Hardly words. More like croaks. "Water?"

I pushed up. "It's outside."

I ran, leaving him in the dark. As I picked up my pack, the thought came: I could just go. Continue my search for Walter as though I'd never stumbled across Adrian Krom. If he remembers me at all, he'll call it a hallucination.

I felt, suddenly, every ache. The memory of yesterday's crazy high astonished me. The more calculated confidence with which I'd set out from the house this morning, full on sweet potato pie, just evaporated. I gripped the snowshoes, seeing clearly. Get going, find Walter, get out while you both can. You want revenge? Here it is. Leave Krom. You think he'd hang around this ghost town if you were in there pinned on Lindsay's rug? You can't prove he killed Georgia. You can't prove he killed Lindsay. But you've got him. Walk away and he's nailed.

Only, he might know about Walter. I turned and went back inside.

Krom was up on one elbow. I opened the water bottle and gave it to him. He sipped with surprising restraint. I realized, he's been there before, trapped in his truck screaming with a burned arm as the tribe's volcano rained fire on him. He's learned to survive. Ration supplies, don't be greedy. He drank for a long while, pausing finally like he was going to speak but he was unable to take his eyes from the bottle and he drank again, draining it. In the end, greedy after all.

"Have you seen Walter?"

He took so long to answer I thought he hadn't heard. Then he shook his head.

My heart turned over. I stood and headed for the door, and it was his stone cold silence that stopped me. Even now, pinned beneath Lindsay's bookcase, he seemed able to reel me in. I turned. He simply watched me, eyes flat in my light, waiting to see if I'd really go. I felt pity, astonishing myself. Evidently, I'm capable of anything. I asked, "Are you hurt?"

"Leg."

I came back and got on my stomach and shined Jimbo's light into the space beneath the bookcase. Leg looked intact. There were books under here, and they had probably cushioned his leg. I pushed on the bookcase. Like pushing a wall. I worked my tender hands under the edges. "If I can lift this, can you pull free?"

He nodded. I wondered. It didn't matter anyway, because I could not budge the case. My mind raced. Car jack? No, no room to slide it underneath. Some kind of pulley? Maybe, if I knew how to rig a pulley and what parts I'd need, I could break into the hardware store, assuming there was any hardware left. First, though, I'd need to break into the library and find a book that explained pulleys. Or was it a block and tackle I wanted? Shit. I was helpless as Walter. Not my father's daughter after all.

I had to fight off the sudden impression that the walls of

Lindsay's office, beyond the gloom, were made of compacted snow.

He coughed. "What..." He swallowed, and gestured at the window.

I said, "What's going on? That what you're asking?"

He nodded.

I thought hard about that one. Didn't need him to panic. Had he panicked during his stay in that truck? I said, flat, "Phreatic eruption in the moat. Stopped, for now."

He nodded. Not the type to panic.

I dug in my pack and set up an emergency supply kit beside him: water bottle, flashlight, granola bars, Tylenol. I said, "I'm going to look for Walter."

"I'm cold." He jerked his chin, toward the chair. "Parka." He added, "Please."

How about pretty please, you shit? But I went over to Lindsay's chair and picked up his big heavy parka and dropped it on him, then walked out the door before he could demand something more.

I left the building and headed down the road. Nothing was happening, no black column in the sky, just fine ash hanging in the air until it lost wing and idled down.

I walked the town. The Ski Tip. Community center. Hardware store, Von's, Grumpy's, hospital, Center Snowmobiles. No snowmobiles to be had. I walked home, got skis, tried Walter's house again. I skied out of town, along 203, passing that long line of cars—abandoned vehicles of the refugees. I looked; no keys. I found his Explorer, just where Eric said it was. Locked. No keys. Cartons of casework and equipment inside. Wouldn't he have taken that? He hadn't. He hadn't got out. I moved on, all the way to the chasm and in the ashy daylight it looked more savage than it had on TV. Guard trucks parked here. No keys.

How simple, on my skis, to detour the chasm and keep going. Get out.

I worked my way back to town, zigzagging across 203, checking every ditch, every hollow. He was nowhere.

Finally I made my way back to Lindsay's office. Krom lay flat, arms folded beneath his head. The water bottle was half-empty, the food gone.

He spoke. "Help's on the way."

"Help?" I stood dumb. And then I saw Krom's little emergency radio lying beside him. And I realized why he'd wanted his parka, and why the parka was so heavy—because his radio was in one of the deep pockets. I said, faintly, "Who's coming?"

"Search and Rescue," he said. "From Bridgeport, where I set up the emergency ops center. It will be hours. Once they hit the ash zone, they'll have to go slow. They're worried about ash clogging air filters."

"Do you realize what you just did?"

"They're volunteers, Cassie. And once they get here and free me, I will get *all* of us out safely."

"*You* will? Your leg..."

"Does not affect my training or my skills."

"What about sacrifice, Adrian? What about the tribal elders who sacrificed themselves so the others could live? I thought that's what you wanted to do but now that it's real, you don't want to. You're willing to have other people do the sacrifice and come into a goddamn *eruption* zone."

He regarded me coldly. "No sacrifice will be necessary."

I returned his icy look. I wondered if that's what he was thinking when he lay here pinned, alone. Hearing the eruption. I'd bet he was pissed. The volcano's winning, and he's lying here in his enemy's office, on the rug stained with her blood. I bet he sure in hell thought about the sacrificial irony in that. The volcano wins, she gets her revenge.

But then of course I came, and everything changed. I looked at his radio.

He clamped a hand on it. "You can't call it off, Cassie. You have no authority."

I knew. I knew exactly how Search and Rescue worked, how volunteers got charged up on adrenaline and bravery and then went with open eyes into whatever lay ahead. If I could get the radio away from Krom, I could go outside and call Bridgeport and tell them he'd died and I was going to ski out on my own, self-rescuing.

But Krom held the radio to his heart.

I shivered. Cold. And, suddenly, afraid. A new species of fear —unlike the fear of the eruption, of another avalanche, which were fears that had made themselves at home. My fear of Krom was specific, at a point I could fix in my solar plexus as accurately as I could plot a coordinate on a map. I was afraid of this man under a bookcase, who likely didn't have the strength to walk two steps should he be set free to walk. But he still had two good strong hands with which to take me by the neck, should I get too close. He still had the power.

"Of course," he said, "you're free to leave right now."

"No I'm not. Why do you think I came back in the first place? Walter didn't get out. *That's* why I'm staying."

His eyes closed. The earth shook, hard. He seemed not to notice.

"Call Bridgeport, Adrian. Ask if anyone has located Walter."

He opened his eyes. "If you like."

He radioed and a half hour later Bridgeport radioed back. Walter was not in Bridgeport. Nor in Bishop, nor in any other little Sierra town, as far as the emergency operations center could ascertain.

So he had to be in Mammoth.

I went out and looked again. Roamed the town, went up the

Bypass until stumbles interrupted my stride, then gave in and went back to Lindsay's office to wait for rescue.

Krom was asleep. I made myself a place in the corner and curled up. The room was a tomb, dim and cold with stale air that tasted of ash. I'd brought the smell in on my clothes, in my hair, or perhaps it had just seeped in. The pervasive smell of ash. Almost masked the coffee scent coming from the apothecary cupboard. I lacked the strength to go close it. I drank. Ate. Granola bar tasted of ash. I glanced up at the desk. The little Japanese teapot was near the edge; one more quake should send it over. I thought about rescuing it but didn't. Never love anything that can't love you back. I aimed my headlamp at the empty wall where the Mexican mask had hung. I played the light around the floor and found the thing amidst the debris, its hideous tongue sticking out at the ceiling.

There were two sharp quakes and the teapot went. Krom's eyes opened.

I said, "Why are you here?"

He rolled his head to look my way. "Doing my job. I saw the lights on, through the window."

"Really?"

"I don't leave until everybody's out."

"Who was it?"

"Nobody here when I came in."

"How'd you get in?"

"Forced the lock."

"Why'd you take off your parka? It's cold in here."

"It's cold everywhere. I decided to put on a thermal undershirt. I'd just got my sweater on over that when the quake hit and the bookcase fell."

I looked at his pack, lying beside her desk.

"Gloves in there. Gaiters. Wool hat. Help yourself."

I looked back to him. "How did you get to town?"

"Took a Guard jeep."

"How'd you get the key?"

"From the *driver*. And then I had him evac with someone else."

"Where's the jeep?"

"In the parking garage around back."

"Why didn't you just park on Minaret?"

He turned back to the ceiling and studied it. "Habit," he said. "I always park in the garage."

"How long were you in here?"

"Cassie," he said, "I'm in your debt. For the water. The food. But I won't put up with this much longer." He coughed, and cleared his throat. "You want to know why I'm here? Because I waited until everybody was gone and then I came back to town and drove every street to be certain. I almost lost these people, with your damned bears, but I turned it around. And I got them out. And then I came back to be sure. And when I was driving down Minaret I saw the reflection. So I checked. I wasn't going to leave somebody behind."

"Like Walter."

"Walter is out. *Everybody* is out. There is nobody here but you and me."

And Lindsay's ghost. The smell of coffee oils suddenly hit me. I got up and went to shut the doors to the apothecary cabinet, where she stores her beans and paraphernalia. I froze. The shelf was swung aside. The shelf wall was a false wall. Behind that, in the real wall, there was a hole. Rectangular, deep. I scoured it with my light. It was a safe.

She had a safe. She'd never told me that.

I gazed into the empty hole, wondering what she'd kept there. And then I came to. Never mind what she kept there—who took it? Who opened the safe?

Krom lay quietly watching me.

It couldn't have been Krom. How would he know? And if he'd terrified her into telling him, if what she had in the safe was what he'd come for the night he shot her, he would have opened it back then and taken it. Why was the safe open now? Well, how about Walter? Walter knew about it and he changed his mind. He did want something of hers. Something that could love him back. Love letters, I thought. Love letters guarded in her safe behind her coffee. *When did Walter come*? It could have been days ago. Weeks ago. Or it could have been yesterday.

Maybe it was Walter who left the lights on.

And maybe Krom came in and found Walter at the safe.

Maybe it was more than love letters. Maybe there was a letter that incriminated Krom. And so Krom killed Walter and took the letter and hid it in his pocket. I stared at him, at his tan parka draped over his trunk, his brown sweater, his brown cords, pelt draped loosely on his frame. I stared at his arms, which could wrap around me quick as a snake strike, and I kept my distance.

If he killed Walter, I would have found Walter.

I shut the apothecary doors and returned to my corner. The quakes were picking up, two and three per minute. I listened to the rattling of loose stuff—background noise. I listened for the sound of rescuers from Bridgeport. I thought about topography. We're not in a bad place, here. About fifteen hundred feet higher than the moat. Wind's away from us. And if the moat progresses to a magmatic eruption, if it's the main event? Hard to say. I seemed to have acquired the rectitude of the Geological Survey's calmest of the calm, Phil Dobie.

The earth shook, hard, and Krom's hand lifted a moment, then dropped. If he had been a stranger, someone inexplicably trapped here, I would have gone over and taken the hand. I would have held the devil's own hand, waiting in this miserable place, but in the end I did not care to take Krom's.

I closed my eyes.

It was some time before I noticed that the quakes had slowed. Maybe one per minute now. I said nothing to Krom. His eyes were closed again. I may have dozed off myself. Sooner or later, I'd learned, you go to sleep unless the roof's falling in on you at the moment. I got up and went to the window. Same old, same old. Dark ashy sky. Was there any other kind of sky, anywhere in the world?

I took my empty water bottle and went to fill it next door at the bathroom sink. By my headlamp in the mirror, I caught a look at myself. Halloween night. I turned on the tap then realized there was no way to wash my face without soaking my bandages. *And washing matters*? I started to laugh, and I was still there hooting when the bathroom door opened and someone shined a fat beam of light in my face and said "Cass?"

Eric filled the doorway in a huge pack and hard hat and slick yellow suit that shone even in the dark, and even when I'd got my own beam focused it took me a moment to recognize him with his blackened face and the goggles and dust mask around his neck, but I sure did know his voice. It made my heart drop. Why did it have to be Eric who came, why not some other adrenaline-charged rescuer? And then against all my fears, my heart lifted and I ran to him.

A second yellow-suited figure crowded into the bathroom. "Where is he?" Mike said, "where's Mr. Krom?"

"We've got a problem," Eric said.

We moved out into the hallway, leaving Mike to finish splinting Krom's leg.

I said, "What kind of problem?"

Eric assessed me as if he were lining up a shot. "How you doing, Oldfield?"

"I'm okay." I'm dying. I'm doing beautifully now that you're here, except that I'm doing hideously because it's you who came. I shrugged. "Always problems, Catlin. What's the problem?"

"Have you been outside?"

"Sure. Not for awhile though. I fell asleep. You believe that? What's outside?"

He put his arm around me and led me out. I saw ash. Always ash. I heard a faint hissing, far away, like sprinklers turning on. I went into the middle of the street and peered down toward the caldera.

"Not that," Eric said.

I went numb. Understood the problem. Didn't want to see it. I stood frozen.

Eric nudged me forward until we passed the office building and then he turned me ninety degrees. "Look up."

I looked up.

"You didn't know?"

I shook my head. I had a fine view, a line of sight that shot straight up the two thousand or so feet of elevation gain that separated us from this new eruption on Red Mountain. I was transfixed, although as spectacle it wasn't much. A plume of ash, like chimney smoke. Rising above the murky silhouette of trees, it could have been a small forest fire. Phreatic, judging from the look of it.

Activity was no longer confined to the caldera. The volcano had opened its second front.

Topography was no longer in our favor.

44

"*WHERE*, CASSIE?" Eric checked his watch.

We were packed and ready, and the three of us—Eric and Mike and I—stood around the open tailgate of the National Guard jeep. Krom sat in back, propped against packs, his splinted leg straight. A sled and snowshoes were racked on the roof. The jeep was parked inside the police department garage, where Eric had cannibalized a vehicle left behind in the mechanic's pit. Only when we had a dozen spare parts was Eric satisfied. Soon, *real* soon, we were going to have to expose the jeep to the elements. The only question was, which way to go?

"Where haven't you looked, Cass?"

I met Eric's eyes. "Nowhere."

"What's *that* mean?" Mike said. "Does that mean she's looked everywhere, because if she has then I don't see how she can ask us to look there *again*. And if she means she hasn't looked anywhere then why should *we* be the ones running around looking where she should have *already* looked?"

I felt the pulse in my throat. "Give me an hour."

Eric said, "It's already three-fifteen."

I wanted to burrow into his yellow-slick chest and plead.

Instead, I studied his face. Grimed, eyes red-veined. Like Mike's. They'd risked their lives coming into town—it didn't matter that Mike hadn't risked his for me, that he'd come for Krom—they'd volunteered to come get us out and now I was asking them to stick around and hunt for someone I couldn't prove was here. In truth, I couldn't answer Eric's question. Where to look?

I said, "I won't hold us up."

"Good call," Eric said.

We were pressed around a lantern on the garage floor, like it was a campfire. Wherever Walter was, I hoped he was warm.

"All right people, Bridgeport says we assess the situation, make the decision on site, and report in." Eric nodded at the squat field radio that sat on the tailgate. "It's our ass, so let's look at the options. The Bypass is out for obvious reasons."

Part of me, a mulish grieving part, wanted to protest. That's Lindsay's route. That's her option. Inyo hasn't erupted, and if her road *had* been finished and we'd gone out that way, everybody would have made it. But now, of course, Red Mountain is venting. And she, of course, had given up on the Bypass the moment she realized what the fissure meant—she'd publicly capitulated the day Krom called in the chopper to show the path of a pyroclastic flow from Red Mountain.

"That leaves two options," Eric said. "Pika, and 203. Let's look at option one, Pika. I was up there night before last. Canyon's choked with vehicles—wall to wall. It's impassable. We didn't even consider trying to clear it. Take days."

Mike said, "We can climb over the obstructions."

Eric shook his head. "Goes for damn near a mile."

"We can carry Mr. Krom."

"He's got a double fracture of the tibia. He barely withstood being carried here."

We glanced at Krom. Even recessed in the back of the jeep,

he drew attention. His face was worn from pain. He'd refused the morphine.

"We'll go slow," Mike said. "We'll be careful."

Eric said, evenly, "There've already been explosions. And everybody had a full tank of gas. We gonna go on tiptoe? It's fucking unstable, man."

Mike's mouth opened, then closed.

"Let's look at option two. Mike and I came in that way. Truck died on 395 before we got to the deep ash zone. We snowmobiled it from there, almost to 203. That's where the snowmobile died. From there, it took us over three hours to walk to town. Assuming this jeep gets us as far as the crater in 203, we walk from there until we get far enough out of the deep ash that another truck can reach us. Gonna take a good five-six hours. Maybe seven." Eric gestured at the sled. "Depending on how this thing pulls loaded through deep ash, and how fast a ride Mr. Krom can withstand."

We glanced, again, at Krom.

"Long haul," Eric continued. "Time's my biggest concern. That, and the likelihood that the moat will start up again. In fact, we thought about that on the way in."

I bet they had. I bet when they saw Red Mountain starting to vent, they'd thought real hard about it. The moat was quiet when they came in but it had vented intermittently last night, so they said. I hadn't known. Tucked into Dad's corduroy chair at home by the fireplace, I'd slept through it all.

We listened a moment. Listening for the thunder, for the reawakening of the moat.

Krom spoke, then. "How deep is the ash? At its worst."

Mike answered. "Above the knees, sir." He pointed to the spot.

"And you pulled the sled through that?"

"Oh yah."

"I weigh two hundred and seventeen pounds." Krom stared at Mike's wiry frame.

"We can pull you," Mike said.

"Eric," Krom said, "how deep is the ash on Pika?"

"Don't know. My guess is it's gonna be shallower. It's farther from the vent."

"That's right," Krom said. "Pika was built with that in mind."

I felt the change. It was swift as water hitting rock and diverting its course. Eric had adjusted his stance to directly face Krom. Mike already faced him. Command shifted. It was just that easy.

Krom said, "We go with option one. Pika."

There was silence around the campfire. Eric appeared uncertain. Mike wore a tight little smile.

I saw Krom's point. Ash'll be shallower. Pika was built with a whole lot in mind, hunkered down deep, safe as anything around here *can* be safe from lava bombs and pyroclastic flows. But it wasn't built with spooked bears in mind. As Lindsay pointed out at the Inn, it's a bobsled run. No room for accidents. He hadn't foreseen that. But he surely saw it now. We've got a problem there. Ash'll be shallower there, sure, only it's not ash that's the problem. It's the wall of tangled steel, the leaking gas tanks. It's a man-made problem. But it's *his* route.

I spoke. "How about option three?"

They turned. Eric said, "What's that, Cassie?"

"We go up the mountain."

Mike gasped.

Krom shook his head. "That doesn't get us out."

I said, "Let's look at it. I've skied Minaret as far as the Bypass turnoff. Ash is pretty shallow. Assume we can drive Minaret all the way up to the lifts. We hole up there if need be. At the Inn." Back to where we started, over two months ago, debating how to get out. "We'll be well out of reach of the moat. Mammoth

Mountain will be between us and the Red Mountain vent. From there, if we can, we continue over Minaret Summit."

Mike said, "Oh yah, and maybe you forgot the road over the summit is *closed* for winter? It's not plowed."

"I didn't forget. We walk it, ski it, snowmobile it if we can."

Eric was nodding. "Gets us out, all right. Gets us down to the backcountry, and then we've got the whole Sierra crest between us and the eruption. Only thing is, Cass, that's a long way, real tough haul. And it gets us into a wilderness camping situation." Eric regarded Krom.

Krom eyed me. "You're forgetting something else, Cassie. Mammoth Mountain is a volcano, too."

"I didn't forget that."

"And you want to risk it?"

"Yeah, it's risky." My mouth was dry. "But so far the activity's elsewhere. Shall we weigh risks? Let's start with option two—203 to 395. What happens if we're in the middle of that seven-hour journey and the moat starts up? How about if it's a magmatic eruption and it goes pyro? How about a race with a hot cloud going six hundred miles an hour?"

"I agree," Krom said. "Option two is out."

"So," I said, "option one. Pika. Let's say we can climb the pileup. Let's say it doesn't collapse and explode on us. Let's say we're carrying your two hundred seventeen pounds plus the sled plus our packs plus our skis and making, oh, three or four yards an hour? Let's add quakes. Let's add rockslides. And avalanches. And just for the hell of it, let's add a *little* fallout from a pyroclastic flow. Just a *smidge* of burning ash, carried by the wind. I'm sure your computer sims factored that in. You didn't factor the bears or a fifty-car pileup—who could know? But there we are. There's option one."

Krom said, softly, "Tell me, Cassie, does your plan hinge on the fact that you don't want to leave the area? You planning on doing a search for Walter on the way up the mountain? Because if that's what you plan, you'd better make it clear exactly what kind of sacrifice you're asking of us."

I stared at Eric and Mike. They stared back. Is that what I planned?

Krom said, "Option three is out. We go with option one."

Eric leaned against the tailgate. "I'd like to hear if Cassie has anything more to say."

"Hey, man," Mike said to Eric, "she's not authorized. Mr. Krom's authorized, and you are, and I think we should..."

"Can it, Mike."

Mike went silent and tucked his hand into his armpit.

Eric smiled at me. "So, Cass, why do you want to go up?"

I found my voice. "Going up puts us above the moat. Going up puts Mammoth Mountain between us and the Red Mountain eruption. Plus, wind's in our favor if we go up."

"That it?"

"Yes."

"You planning on taking off to look for Walter? Because if you do, I'll have to go after you, sacrifice or no sacrifice."

"No," I said. "I'm not planning on running off."

"So you believe this is the best choice?" He wore the comradely grin. Old times. The two of us needling each other over the merits of the burgers at Grumpy's or the chili at the Tip. A chick flick or a car-chase movie. New times, in the cottage, the merits of a kiss. He grinned but the scarred skin beneath his glass eye was taut.

I inhaled, exhaled. Used his biathlete's trick. "Let's go up."

Eric switched on the radio, clapping Mike on the shoulder, and Mike's pale face turned even paler but he ducked his head and tunneled a pissed look at me.

"*Detective.*" Krom straightened, bracing himself. He withdrew his own radio from his parka pocket. "The decision rests with me."

"I'm afraid not, sir—you're the victim. You're in our charge." Eric held out his hand. "And it's best I take charge of all comm equipment. Keep the lines of authority straight."

Krom blinked. He shifted his weight, cautiously, as though testing the hold of the splints, the way an animal might try to extricate itself from a trap. Even now—leg mummified, corduroy pants ripped from cuff to pocket, parka stained red with my blood, ash graying the brown of his hair—even now he seemed as though he might snap his fingers and bring Eric to heel.

But Eric kept his hand out and Krom finally relinquished his radio and then Eric called Bridgeport on the field radio to report our plan of action.

Krom went still.

His eyes, though, were alive on me. It was surely my over-taxed imagination but I thought he inclined his head and made me a little bow.

45

WE HEADED in silence out of town.

Eric drove. Mike rode shotgun. I sat in the back seat. Krom remained in the rear, in the baggage area, braced by our gear. He was, after all, cargo.

I watched out the left window toward Red Mountain as Eric nursed the jeep along Minaret. Still not much in terms of pyrotechnics but it was a mighty consistent eruption. I swiveled to look behind, toward the caldera. No fresh plume from the moat. No discernible quakes. Winds continued in their normal direction, to the northeast. We got drifted ash.

I watched the back of Krom's head a moment, that thick brown pelt. No whimper of pain from him. I turned back to Red Mountain.

We inched along, murderously slow. Even at this speed, the jeep stirred up clouds of ash. I had ample opportunity to brood on the topography of Minaret Road as we turtled along. Going up, just barely. The Red Mountain plume was visible above treetops. Don't do anything yet, I prayed.

No ghosts appeared, waving down the jeep. Nobody left in town, of that I was convinced. Nobody alive, anyway.

I thought I'd feel at least a twinge of regret, leaving town. Thought I'd feel something but it's not my town any more. Did feel something. Urgency. Floor it, Eric. Screw the ash. We've got spare parts.

We passed the intersection of Minaret and the Lake Mary Road and got a dead-on view of the Lakes Basin peaks and the plume dirtying the dirty sky. Maybe it was our change in position but I could hear the eruption now. Boom boom boom, like a small war being fought on the ridge. Please don't progress to the next stage. Please don't go pyro now.

We came, in moments, to the Bypass turnoff. Eric slowed, unnecessarily. Heads turned right. In the back, Krom made a sound, an exhalation. Far as I could see, it still looked navigable. Scuffed in ash, like Minaret. No volcanic bombs raining down, no sign that Inyo had awakened. Looked inviting, this Bypass, but for the fact that it dead-ended a good four miles short of 395, but for the Red Mountain plume, up and to our left. I felt a little dizzy. My ears buzzed, like a helicopter had just flown overhead.

I scanned the Bypass for Walter. It was her route, after all.

Minaret wound lazily toward the mountain. Still Jeffrey pine forest. Bad luck, Jeffrey, you're too low—downhill from the Red Mountain plume—you're never in the right place anymore, are you? And right now I wanted lodgepole, red fir, hemlock. I wanted elevation.

Eric stopped the jeep.

I sat forward. "What are you doing?"

"Checking the filters, Cass. Just take a sec."

I died, as Eric got out and went under the hood. We all die as the Red Mountain vent goes pyro and sends hot rock at us but the incandescent cloud races ahead of the flow and we're stopped in the road. I did not look back at Krom, Krom whose truck had stalled in ash, who had gotten out to check his engine and seen his driver killed, who'd been hit by a lava bomb, who'd returned to his truck for shelter, where he screamed in pain and forgot fear.

Eric climbed back in and I breathed again. We accelerated to our snail's pace, but our filters were clean and we were going up.

Lodgepole pine. Red fir.

We climbed. I kept an eye on the Red Mountain plume until the solid hip of Mammoth Mountain came between us and the eruption. Finally, topography was beginning to be in our favor.

The road steepened. I peered down gullies for a wrecked snowmobile. For a body. For a waving ghost.

No ghosts. Skeleton trees, though. No more than last time. Okay, then.

Minaret snaked, and climbed, and at last leveled and delivered us onto the broad flat shoulder of Mammoth Mountain. Eric stopped in the roundabout beside the statue of the woolly mammoth, woolled in ash.

We all peered up at the Tyrolean Lodge, the gabled gondola stations, the venerable Inn. It wasn't the ash that so transformed the place, for ash had become the benchmark. Sky's blue, grass is green, snow's white? Not anymore. What made this place so eerie, so wrong, was the emptiness. On the lousiest ski day of winter, on the most blistering day of summer, there are people here. This is Mammoth Mountain. There's always somebody here to ski it or board it or bike it or hike it or sit by the fireplace at the Inn and admire it. Not now. Not a car in the lot. Nor a snowmobile. Nor even a pair of skis staked in the snow.

We're here.

"Gives me the creeps," Mike said.

Eric shut off the engine. "End of the line." At the far end of the lot was a wall of snow, beneath which Minaret Road continued unplowed. Too late to go any farther because the dark sky was already grading into night.

Well, I thought, you won. You picked the movie. Now sit through it.

Krom said, "I could use a john."

Mike snapped out of his seat belt. "We'll get you right into the Lodge, sir."

"No," I said, "the Inn."

"But there's emergency keys to the Lodge in the box around back of the gondola station, or at least there used to be and I don't see why anybody would have put them in a different place since I was working here."

"The Inn's safer," I said.

"Why is it safer, I don't see..." Mike, despite himself, leaned on the dash to get a look up the mountain, up the two thousand feet of vertical world-class drop. The Lodge snuggled at its base. The Inn was across the parking lot, that much farther from an avalanche of Mammoth's fabled snow. "Oh," Mike said. "Oh, the Inn. Only how do we get inside?"

"Break a window," I said.

Mike's face bloomed in wonder.

Eric and Mike took Krom in a four-handed carry and I found a window. Inside, I followed my flashlight beam through the murk, skirting a fallen housekeeping cart and toppled tables, and let them in the big main doors. As they bore Krom across the colonnaded great room toward the public restrooms I recalled that meeting, that night, when the only question was how we get out. Not whether.

I went back outside and crossed the roundabout to the gondola station and got the keys—Mike was right. I toured the ski barns and the Lodge and then returned to the Inn. They were coming out of the Men's; I raised a hand in passing, and Eric gave a weary nod. I wandered up and down hallways, keeping an eye out for other lights, listening, shouting now and again.

When I returned they were assembled around the cold mouth of the fireplace, Mike standing before it, Krom laid out on a chaise, Eric straddling a chair with his arms crossed over the back and his forehead on his hands. I collapsed onto an ottoman.

Mike shifted from foot to foot. "It's cold. Shouldn't we go find blankets? What about lanterns? Won't they have propane lanterns around for power outages? I'm referring to regular outages. I'll do blankets and lanterns. What about food? They could have left food. Cassie should go find some food, shouldn't she? We should bring our packs in, anyway, since we've got rations. Oh man, shouldn't we contact Bridgeport?"

"Yeah," Eric said. His forehead remained on his hands.

What, I thought, the female gets the food? I didn't want to go find food. We sat, beat. I didn't want to leave this ottoman. I gazed past Mike into the fireplace, conjuring a merry blaze. The eruption still sounded, muffled, but it could have been the cannonade of avalanche-clearing guns after a heavy snowfall. There were no quakes. There was damage done from earlier quakes, lamps and such knocked over. Worse done at a party. It was dark but cozy-dark, like when the power goes out in a storm. Candlelight dinners, huddling for warmth, romance. Mike had returned a fallen wooden candelabra to its stone shelf on the fireplace flank. He lit the fat beeswax candles. They cast a buttery glow upon us all. I didn't want to get up off this cushy ottoman. I didn't want to go on another futile hunt for Walter. I didn't want to ever leave this hospitable place.

"Yeah, all right." Eric got up. "I'll go get the radio." Eric clapped Mike on the shoulder, thumped my boot with his, and headed for the door.

I pushed myself up. "For your dining pleasure, we have the Yodler Restaurant and Bar, the Mountainside Grille, and a wine cellar I'd bet. No room service."

Mike said, "You shouldn't be making jokes."

You are such a pain, I thought, you're such a world-class judgmental pain and you're a bigger pain now than when you used to boss me around the gondola station. You're going to get your ego pierced somehow in this mess and you're going to lose your temper, like you did that day in the station. Like you did at the drill, when Stobie wouldn't listen. Like you did with Georgia? Did you?

I glanced at Krom. He watched me. He tugged the little knot of fear in me.

"Sorry," I said to Mike. Sorry it was you who volunteered to come back. Sorry for us all. I took my flashlight and set off in search of the kitchen.

Mike and I were wildly successful. We brought blankets, goose down coverlets, cushions, feather pillows, hurricane lamps, canned salmon, canned mandarin oranges, Greek olives, dried pears and cranberries, cracked pepper water biscuits, anisette biscotti, and a wheel of parmesan cheese that had hidden in the dark pantry recesses. We brought out china plates and the good silverware and carafes of water and glasses. Eric carried in wood but none of us expressed any enthusiasm for a fire. We were warm enough wrapped in wool and goose down. In truth, I was afraid that a big quake would come while we slept and knock flaming boughs from the fireplace to set us all ablaze.

We slept, in fits and starts. Exercise hard—slog through snow and ash. Lie in pain from a broken leg. Raise the heart rate with intermittent bouts of terror. Wears a body out. We all slept. Never slept so hard as the times I slept through Lindsay's eruptions.

Sometime in the night, somebody screamed. It wasn't me. I froze. There were quakes again. Hard little jolts. Rattled the dishes and lamps and knocked the candelabra off its shelf. Beeswax burned on the hardwood floor.

"People all right?" Eric moved to put out the candle.

Krom said, "Alive."

Voice right in my ear. I jerked around. He was right beside me. He'd been on the chaise when we went to sleep, a good yard from me. Had he been the one who screamed? When he maneuvered off the chaise and dragged himself along the floor, had fractured bone scraped bone, more than even he could bear? I saw into his eyes, pools of pain. Or maybe it was just the squirrelly shadows cast by the hurricane lamps, which warped us all.

We lay close as lovers. Krom's big hands could caress my face, my neck, only he was holding one of the Inn's fine goose down pillows.

"Cass?" Eric said. "Mike?"

"I'm fine," Mike said, his voice a whisper.

I unfroze and shoved up and took my blanket and lay down beside Eric.

Tell Eric, I thought. Only not in front of Mike. Mike belongs to Krom. Wait until Mike drops off again and then tell Eric. Doesn't matter if Krom sees. He knows I'll tell. And he knows I can prove nothing, other than that in the terror of the night he craved the closeness of another human being enough to endure the pain of dragging himself and his pillow to lay by me.

I had no doubt he could have endured the pain of being carried on a sled, or Mike's back, through the minefield of Pika. All he'd cared for was to get us out on his road. At least one of us. I couldn't prove that, though. And I couldn't prove there was something he hadn't wanted me to see in Lindsay's office. But I felt it. And I felt he'd shut me up, just in case, if he got the chance.

Funny the way things work out. I'm like Lindsay. I keep getting in his way.

I scanned the room for Eric's pack. I wondered if he had

handcuffs in there. I wondered if he had his gun. After all, he was on duty.

My hand brushed Eric's hand. We locked fingers.

We all lay still, listening to the dishes rattle. Every few minutes I peered at Mike, waiting for his eyes to shut. Like some kind of weird slumber party. I kept an eye on Krom. He lay still, eyes open, examining the timbered ceiling. His face was stony brown petrified wood.

There was a scraping sound and then a tattoo of thuds and Mike yelped and we all sat up and Krom exhaled sharply in pain. I gasped.

Out of the inky recesses of the great room, into our halo of light, came Walter.

46

WE BUILT A FIRE.

I gripped Walter's cold hand, grinning.

He would tell us nothing until we explained. Eric told him how he and Mike had come to be here, and Krom told his part, and through all that Walter sat stoically hearing them out, but when I had to explain what brought me back to town, Walter appeared to age before my eyes, a sight I'd never wish to see again.

We pressed cheese and olives and dried fruit and water on him but he refused it all. He said, "I've already eaten. I have my own supply."

"*Where*? Walter, I searched the whole Inn."

"You didn't search my room."

"I was shouting. In every hall."

"I found that the only way I can sleep, Cassie, is with earplugs. Did you know the Inn supplies earplugs along with the toiletries?"

"Then what woke you?"

"Earthquakes," he said. "I can't seem to get used to them."

Mike said, "Oh yah."

Walter cracked a smile, then, squeezing my hand, harder than I'd been squeezing his. He leaned across me to shake Eric's hand, then Mike's. His gaze shifted to Krom. Krom was out of reach, handshake-wise. A hard look passed between them. Or maybe it was just the shadows cast on their faces by firelight. Walter said, "You're fortunate Cassie found you, Adrian."

Krom said, "Blessed."

"What about you, Walter?" Eric said. "How did you come to be here?"

He cleared his throat. "I was trapped in town, along with a good many others. I was waiting my turn to go out. Perhaps the wait was too long. It gave me time to think, and I was at a very low point, and the two made a persuasive combination. I simply felt that—now that I was trapped—I should stay. I don't mean to sound melodramatic but I decided to do as she would. I came up here to wait and watch. To see what the volcano was going to do."

I let out a sound.

"I had no intention of dying, Cassie. I still don't. That's why I came all the way up here. This provides the safest vantage point. And all the comforts of the Inn." He forced another smile.

"How did you get here, sir?" Eric asked.

"I appropriated Bill Bone's station wagon. He'd been evacuated. He had no further use for it."

"How'd you start it?" I asked. "Every car I saw on 203 was locked and the keys were gone."

"I broke the window and hot-wired it. Something I learned in my undergraduate days. Then I drove up here and settled in. I parked the wagon in the garage by the gondola, where they keep the snowmobiles. Keeps the ash off it. It is, after all, Bill's property, and I intend to replace the window."

I gaped. Nothing stops him. He'd survived on vandalism, like me. "How'd you get in here? Break a window?"

"No, I used a credit card to let myself in the service entrance around back—the same way I opened the garage lock." He squeezed my hand. "A trick Lindsay taught me, the time she locked herself out of her office." He cocked his head. "By the way, Cassie, I had a thought on my drive up here. Bill could use a nice CD player for the wagon."

"*What*?"

"The gift," Walter said. "For Bill's birthday."

I was afraid Walter might crack open.

He lifted his eyebrows. "As I've told you all, I don't intend to die. Thoughts do creep in. Large and small. About this and that. Like Bill's gift."

Eric said, finally, "Sure, I'm in. Mike too—right, man?"

Mike said, "I already paid."

Walter turned a cold look on Krom. "Adrian? Are you in?"

Krom returned the look. "You bet your life."

The fire popped. Silence fell.

Walter broke it. "And so, my friends, here I am. Yesterday I hiked partway up the mountain and found myself a view. Stupendous."

And here he was. Here, not in a ditch or her office or the lab or mired in the muck of her half-finished escape route. Now Eric didn't have to worry about my running off. Now Mike didn't have to whine. Now Krom had one less thing to use against me. I tensed. No. I'd got that wrong. Now Krom had one more thing to hold over me. He had Walter. Because there was clearly something between them. Something had happened. Maybe something down at the 203 crater during the evac. Maybe something in her office. I considered the open safe. The love letters. I thought over Walter's story, trying to read it coldly—without the intense rush of relief and worry and anger and pity—and something was off. There was something he wasn't telling us.

I said, probing his story, "Why'd you have to take Bill's wagon? Why didn't you take your Explorer? I saw it out on 203."

Walter met my look. "I left my car in the expectation that people would assume I had evacuated. I left it hoping to avoid the very thing that occurred. You coming in here after me, Cassie."

47

HAD THERE BEEN the slightest indication that the sky was clearing, had the quakes stopped, we would have been content to sit tight at the Inn and wait for choppers.

But it was a grim dawn. Standing on the porch, stamping my cold feet and stirring up ash, I stared up the mountain. Bridgeport reported that USGS remote sensing indicated intermittent eruptions from Red Mountain and the moat, which had reawakened sometime in the night. Still phreatic eruptions. I could not see either eruption—I'd have to climb up to Walter's viewpoint for that. Mammoth Mountain, which protected us, also blinded us.

Quakes talked, though, loud and clear. Magma's on the move.

Eric and Mike came out carrying Krom. Walter followed. Walter was no longer in the mood to wait and watch. He wanted out, badly as I did. Walter's priorities shifted, with me on his hands.

Whatever it takes.

We all wore yellow survival suits. Eric's pack had carried three extras; he'd known he was coming after two survivors when Krom called; he'd also known Walter was missing, so he'd come prepared. His pack held suits, rations, flashlights, ropes—nearly as much stuff as I'd brought—but he'd come equipped for rescue, not arrest. I'd watched him repack his gear. He had no handcuffs, no gun.

We clumped down the front steps to the snowmobiles Eric and Mike had brought around from the garage. Krom, wrapped in one of the Inn's fine quilts, was lashed onto the sled; the sled was attached to Eric's snowmobile with ropes. We lashed packs and skis to the vehicles, Walter waving off attempts to help him load his bulging pack.

Eric said "one last check" and went machine to machine.

These were sturdy machines, used by crews to crawl all over this mountain, but I had limited faith in them. They have box filters meant to keep birds from being sucked into the engine but they have no defense against ash. I waited until Eric was squatting to check the front runners of his machine and then I squatted beside him. I leaned in close as I could, bulky suit to bulky suit, and in a whisper told him about Krom. He slid a glance back at the sled then continued fiddling with the drive-chain. He said, to the chassis, "You certain?"

"No proof."

"But you believe it?"

I nodded.

He rose, passing so close to my ear that I felt his breath same time I heard his words. "Count on me this time."

By the time I'd got to my feet Eric had his goggles and mask on. I pulled on mine, veiling my face, gamely pretending I did not want to hide in his arms.

The others finished suiting. We all mounted. We were bright tropical creatures with goggle eyes and plastic beaks and neon yellow plumage astride squat metal beasts. We were absurd, but against all logic my hopes rose.

Engines started smoothly. Headlights shone. We passed our lone Guard jeep in the parking lot and took the chute up to the unplowed continuation of Minaret Road. Eric broke trail, slow. We followed in line, at a distance, spacing ourselves so as not to eat each other's ash.

The road wound through mountain hemlock, burred in ash, the drooping tips like fingers trying to shake themselves clean.

Plan is, we round the north slope for about a mile and then reach Minaret Summit, the low point in the Sierra crest. From there, another five miles as the road drops down into the deep canyon of the San Joaquin River and heads north to the campground of Agnew Meadows. Primitive facilities, but space for a rescue chopper to land when the air clears.

Could be days. Could be weeks.

We crawled. Ash was shallow but Eric's runners kicked up twin plumes that flanked the sled. There was no apparent movement in there. Krom could have been dead and frozen as Georgia on her litter ride down from the glacier.

Walter followed, as he'd followed Georgia's sled over two months ago.

I followed Walter, eyeing his pack. Last night, when the two of us went to his room to collect his supplies, I'd asked about the open safe, the love letters. He'd shown surprise; he'd said he didn't realize I'd known about the letters. He'd agreed that the letters were what drew him to her office, that he'd collected them on the way up the mountain. Her office was empty, he'd said. There was nothing between him and Krom, he'd said. I eyed the bulging pack lashed to his snowmobile and thought, that's a whole lot of love letters.

We rounded the corner, and Eric and Krom up ahead rounded the next.

Ash worked under the edges of my dust mask and burrowed into my skin. Already, ash was scratching and frosting my goggles. My snowmobile sucked in ash and the particles were surely incising their way through the engine.

I began to worry about avalanches. Not so much here, but over the summit—once we started our descent we'd be at risk. I came around the bend and saw Walter's and Eric's snowmobiles and it was a moment before I realized what was wrong. They were not spouting ash. Eric was twisted on his saddle gesturing at Walter. Krom was sitting bolt upright.

Avalanche? I neared them, getting a better view. There were boulders in the road. Maybe a rock avalanche, from quakes. Please be that.

I drew up behind them, and Mike behind me. We left our engines running. Eric and Walter and I left Mike to tend to Krom, and we set out on foot.

The road was strewn with rocks—boulders, stones, chips, gravel, like a mad quarry crew had been at work. I examined the mountain. Where there should have been a scar, some indication of the source of this rockslide, there was nothing. I felt sick.

We picked our way through the field of rocks until the road turned the next bend.

There was devastation, far as we could see. Bigger boulders here, some large as snowmobiles, and the pulverized remains of others, and where the ground showed through it was no longer the familiar coating of ash but a congealed mud, and everywhere there were branches and limbs and stumps of trees, and those trees that had escaped dismembering were dead anyway, killed a decade ago by carbon dioxide, for this was one of the old tree-kills. Slightly upslope was a crater with fresh rock showing, like a tooth that had lost a filling. Steam issued from the hole.

I fought to get my glove off my bandaged hand and bent to touch rock, mud, splinters of trees. Cold. Walter scooped a handful of rock chips. We looked, heads together. "Old stuff," I said. He nodded. Quartz latite, basement rock. I eyed the crater, a few tens of meters across. It had spat out old stuff.

We moved around the next bend and it was the same, rock and steam.

"Let's get the hell out of here," Eric said and we all three broke into a run.

Mike was shouting "what, what?" as we hauled up.

Eric pulled down his mask, fighting for air. "Some kind of eruption," he got out.

"Phreatic," I gasped.

Walter was bent double.

"*What*?" Mike's voice rose.

"Steam blast," Krom said. He alone breathed easy.

Eric said, "What now, Cassie?"

I shoved aside my mask and wiped my face. I tried to think. What's setting off steam blasts up here? Compared to the eruptions in the caldera and on Red Mountain, this was a little guy, like someone had set off a charge of dynamite. But you wouldn't want to get closer than a football field to something like that. Is this puppy going to vent again? Are there others? What's the alignment? I looked at Walter. He shook his head. Years of Lindsay pouring this stuff in his ear, years of Lindsay drilling it into my head, and she hadn't made a volcanologist of either one of us. "Let's go back," I said, already moving, because we surely could not go forward.

Krom gave a nod. Both of us, momentarily, in alignment.

We retreated two abreast, in double line. I kept looking back, although if that thing vented again we'd feel it before we'd see it. My snowmobile died. I moved my gear to Eric's machine and doubled up with Mike. Walter's machine died not an eighth of a mile later. He put on skis and saddled up his pack. We paced Walter, creeping, and then Mike's machine crapped out and then Eric's. We all saddled up with gear. We had to abandon one pack. Eric dragged the sled and Mike and I took turns pushing from behind. We ran on adrenaline but that crapped out too. We took forever and a day to cover the last quarter mile.

When the lifts showed above the hemlocks, I let out a sob. We'd made it. And then I sank to the snow. Where to now?

Georgia whispered in my mind. *No way out.*

48

We dragged into the roundabout. We didn't have the strength to unload Krom and climb the steps to the Inn, so we took shelter beneath the porch overhang and sat in ash. We pulled off goggles and masks. At last, Mike got out a water bottle and passed it around.

The earth shook.

Mike said, "Now what?" He was looking at me.

"Call Bridgeport," I said.

Eric was already unpacking the field radio. He got a lot of static but he got through. No, they had not been aware of the blast on the north slope. Static. Still activity at the moat and Red Mountain. Bridgeport told us to maintain position while they investigated further.

Eric said, "Okay, people, we need to get indoors and..."

"It's not okay," Mike said. His head was bent. He was digging at his thumbnail. "We should go down and take Pika."

Eric said, "We just got the official word to stay put."

"I don't want to."

We stared at Mike. Whatever happened to his allegiance to the official word? He was caked in ash, he had a two-day stubble, and he humped over his knees and worked furiously at his thumbnail.

Eric said, evenly, "We asked for advice."

"Then who's in charge?"

"Whoever's in position to call it."

Mike squared his frame. "You want her." It was not a question. "If it weren't for her, we'd be out of here already." He turned on me and put his hand on my arm, second time he'd ever touched me. "You'll tell us not to go down, won't you?"

I hesitated. Waiting, I guessed, for Walter to jump in. Walter clutched his pack, and gave me a nod. You're doing fine.

"*Won't you*?" Mike said.

I licked ash off my lips, and nodded.

"Because? Tell them why."

"Because the moat's in eruption. Because Red Mountain might progress. Because nobody survives a pyroclastic flow."

"What about *Pika?*" He shot a look at Krom, a plea.

Krom smiled at Mike. You're doing fine.

"What about it?" I said. "You want to take Adrian by yourself? You can't handle the sled alone."

"I *know* that," Mike said, "that's why we *all* go."

I said, "Pika's a trap. Maybe a deathtrap."

Mike turned to the others. He still gripped my arm: got her, exhibit A. "You all heard that, and that's just what she said yesterday. Don't go out Pika, she said, because it's too slow. We might get stuck. Something terrible might happen." He lifted my arm, extending it; my jacket sleeve jerked back and exposed my watch. "Ask her how many hours ago that was. Ask her where we'd already be if we'd gone out Pika yesterday when *Mr. Krom*, who knows about what's safe, wanted to go. Ask her if we had enough time we could have crawled out on our bellies and still made it. Ask her if she can tell time."

Eric said, "It was *my* call on Pika too."

"Yeah but *she* made us go up here." Mike's voice rose. "To find Walter."

I fixed on Mike's hand, on the red angry skin around his thumbnail. Only a real shit would sit here and say I risked us all to come up here after Walter. I hadn't. I was surprised as anyone when he appeared. But it was clear enough that if we'd gone out Pika we would not have found him. Everybody had to be thinking it. Nobody said it. I said, tight, "I stand by my call."

"After what happened up the *road*?"

Eric said, "Shut up, Mike."

The words hung in the air. Walter broke the silence. "Cassie couldn't have predicted that."

I was rigid. Lindsay might have. I was racking my brain for the old lessons.

Mike muttered, "We should've gone out Pika."

Eric snapped, "*Shut up*, man."

Krom snapped, "We're wasting time." He undid the strap across his hips. He reached for the other straps—across his knees and ankles—but they were out of reach. He was grimed as the rest of us, worn in pain, and above and beyond that he'd endured his exile up the mountain. He regarded his bindings a moment, then folded his arms and took us in. "Let's get it under control, chums. Mike, you're out of line. Eric, calm down. Cassie, you're overwrought. Listen to what he said, not how he said it."

Krom was right. I was overwrought. Quite suddenly, I found an icy calm. I said, "Stop hiding behind Mike."

Krom's pain-glossed eyes went flat.

"Everything Mike knows about evac he knows from you. Everything you tell him he believes. You tell him we can spread our wings and fly out of here and he'll start flapping. Why don't you tell him the truth, for once? Tell him who's responsible for the mess we're in. You're the man. You're it."

"You're overwrought."

"You're the only one with a reason to blow up the 203 evac route."

There was a gasp—Mike. Eric shot a look at Krom. Walter's eyes never left me.

I said, "That night I followed you, Adrian? You stopped on 203. Right at the bridge. Like you were checking it out. That when you decided where to plant the explosives?"

Krom laughed. "That's right," he said, "I sabotaged my own evacuation."

I didn't laugh. "Yeah, that's absurd. Except that only 203 got sabotaged. Explosives on Pika were wired wrong. So all of a sudden Pika's the only way out. You're going to get us out, all right, but it's going to be on your road. You fought Lindsay for it. You beat her. And now you have to finish the fight. Your road, against her volcano." I stared at his slick yellow arm, where the scar hid. "I get the sacrifice thing now. The elders who offered themselves up to save the tribe—it's a symbol for you. You won't take it as far as they did, you don't want to die, but you have to personally intercede with the volcano on behalf of the tribe. That's why you built your road. That's why you blew up 203. You had to have the tribe in *your* hands. If they escaped on 203, *you* didn't save them, you didn't win. It could have been done without you—all the planning and drills could have been done by computer sims. Any good manager could have run that show. But that's not what happened with the tribe. That was personal. And you know what? I think you're *still* in a mano-a-mano with the volcano. And the only way you can win is to get us out on your road. And maybe you're even ready to risk the ultimate sacrifice, if it comes to that." My hands, I found, were closed into fists. I wanted to hurt him. I wanted to show he couldn't take the pain. "We all go out your way or we die trying."

Mike said, "What's she *talking* about?"

"Cass?" Eric said. His look shifted to Krom then back to me. "You certain?"

Krom said, "She's overwrought."

"No, Adrian," Walter said, "I don't believe she is."

Krom turned to Eric. "We're wasting time."

In the silence that followed, Eric called Bridgeport, who advised us again to stay put. Eric shut off the radio. He rubbed his forehead. "Let's just...figure out where the hell to go. Cassie? You real sure you don't want to go back down?"

Could I say yes? Could I say I knew one hundred percent we could not safely get out 203? Or Pika? Would I be saying the same about Pika if Krom had been a bloodless bureaucrat who went solely on computer sims and data streams? Could I be one hundred percent sure about my call? Because Eric's made his position clear. He goes with my call. As long as I'm sure. And I'm going on second-hand volcanology and gut instinct and fear of a man who doesn't count his wins the way I do. I wished I knew more about the volcanic plumbing. If I knew more, I could say with less fear that I'm sure. I was numb with cold and fear.

Krom said, to Mike, "Get these straps off me."

Mike sprang to undo the bonds. "We'll move you right now."

"Where?" Walter asked it of Eric.

There was a pause, during which time Mike unbuckled a strap and Krom shifted and Eric and Walter got to their feet. A vacuum, and if I didn't act now someone else was going to fill it. "I'm sure," I said.

Eric told Walter, "We stay put."

"Uh, no," I said. "Look, we know the activity started in the moat." I drew an oval in the ash, representing the caldera, and an ellipse within the oval representing the moat. "And then it diked up to Red Mountain." I drew a line from the ellipse to the southwest loop of the oval. "So maybe it's also traveled along the caldera's ring fracture to where it intersects Mammoth Mountain." I extended the line northward along the oval, and drew a triangle. "Here."

They studied my drawing. My heart pounded. I thought of Lindsay's drawing at the Inn, on top of Krom's. All the circles and stars and lines and crosshatches. All the volcanic plumbing. What a mess.

Krom said, "You're not a volcanologist."

I met his look. "Nobody here is a volcanologist."

Eric said, "What are you saying, Cass? The whole mountain could blow?"

"I'm not saying that." Any number of things *could* happen. "All I'm saying is there's complicated plumbing around here. All I'm saying is there have been phreatics on the mountain before —last time Inyo blew there were steam blasts up here. Lindsay showed me the old craters."

Mike's face darkened. "You *knew*?"

I'd known the challenge would come from Mike. "The last phreatics came with the Inyo system—five hundred years ago. Inyo's quiet, Mike. I *didn't* know there was a phreatic up here. Maybe Red Mountain's stirring things up this time. Maybe Inyo will still go. I don't know. I *didn't* know. But here we are."

Eric said, "You expect more like we saw up the road?"

"Could be."

"Could it be more than that?"

"Could be." I was dizzy, damp with sweat. "Not likely. Phil was monitoring up here—there's been no discharge of magmatic gases, no shallow quakes. My guess is anything more will be the same stuff, coming around the old craters where the trees have been dying."

"That your guess, Cass?"

I sought Walter's counsel. He looked as I've rarely seen him in the lab, casting about for the answer. This damned strange mineral. He's seen it before but what's it tell him now? He doesn't have the luxury of time so he'll have to make an educated guess. How Lindsay would have loved this, the two of us mulling this over. Finally we capitulate—geology *is* volcanology, honey. At least for now. I said what Lindsay always said, "With a volcano, the past is a pretty decent guide to the future."

Walter decided. "I agree. I would expect more of the same. Steam blasts in the old craters, perhaps, but not a fresh magmatic eruption on the mountain."

"Cassie," Eric said, "what do you want us to *do*?"

"Go up."

They didn't get it. Even Walter. Maybe they thought I was trying to ease the tension, with a joke. Then Eric got it. Eric, who knows when I'm joking and when I'm not. He stepped away from the porch overhang and tipped his head to look up the two thousand feet to the summit of Mammoth Mountain. "You'd better think again," he said.

Mike scooted out to stand beside Eric.

"We'd be well above the old craters," I said. "The likelihood of a new blast coming near the summit is less than one coming lower down." Could I be one hundred percent sure about that? Nothing's sure. The world is in eruption. I said, "It's the safest place we can be, right now."

Eric came back. "That's a bitch of a climb." He indicated Krom.

"I wasn't thinking of climbing. I was thinking of taking the gondola to the top."

Eric's mouth dropped open.

But Mike began to grin, like he'd just learned the secret of life. "You're right."

Mike thinks I'm right? Wrong becomes right, down becomes up, the world flips.

"She's *right*." Mike windmilled around us. "Oh yah, the machinery is housed inside the gondola stations and we'll have to see if there's any ash inside but I don't think so because it's solid workmanship from top to bottom. I didn't just operate the gondola, you know, I also lent a hand with repairs and I've seen all the schematics." He turned to Krom. "It's gonna work, Mr. Krom. The gondola cars are made in Switzerland and you all know the Swiss reputation for excellence. And the cables are straightforward, simple mechanics, and I doubt if ash has clogged the cable housings but if it has, just running the machinery should be enough to free the cables. We'll see. I have a lot of faith but I know we'll have to see." He halted, grinning at us all. "You realize we have a big generator? The power outage doesn't affect us. We're self-sufficient there. I know where all the keys are. I can get us in. I can get things working and then I think I can guarantee us an event-free ride to the top. You'll see, Mr. Krom. You've helped me and I know I owe you—so you just leave it to me."

Krom said, "*Mike...*" but Mike was already on his way—too wired, too ready to flap his wings and go—to heed Krom.

I watched my surprising new ally loping toward the gondola, wondering if having Mike on my side should make me reconsider.

Eric said, "If you're sure."

Walter said, "We're sure."

Okay Lindsay, I thought, we're going up. In the gondola. You believe that? Krom believes, Krom knows when he's whipped. Walter's signed on. I don't think Eric quite buys it but we *are* going up. Last time. Once we get to the top, you know, there's no place else to go.

49

AND NOW IT became Mike's show.

He cranked the generator and to everyone's surprise but his own the gondola motor came promptly to life. He ran the lift and stopped it, ran and stopped it, ran and stopped it with the brio of a conductor running an orchestra through its paces.

Satisfied that the gondola ran, he supervised the loading of items into the cars, checking weights and distribution and balance. There was a lot of stuff; he'd finally gotten into the ransacking spirit. He bossed us until one car was filled with gear, and the rental ski equipment he'd appropriated was stowed on the carrier. He placed us in the car behind, Krom reclining on one bench, Eric and Walter and me crushed together on the other, packs on the floor. He handed the operating manual to me, his onetime assistant. He lashed Krom's sled to the outside carrier, taking his sweet time.

Krom watched with a half-interested frown and I wondered if, against all evidence, he had accepted the need of going up.

I didn't worry long about Krom. I worried about the volcano, the unpredictable chum. I could hear the distant cannonade and feel the quakes that ran from the ground up through the cable machinery and down to our car. Forget the pre-flight check, I wanted to tell Mike. You're going to busybody us into oblivion. But Mike perversely fussed with the sled until it clung like a baby to the gondola's back. In truth, I was afraid to interfere with Mike's zeal and Swiss excellence.

Finally, his face beamed at the window. "I'm going to start her up. Cassie, you hold that door wide open. Eric, you be ready to take my hand when I say *now*." Mike bustled over to the switch.

I held the door. I had a horror, in the dark and suddenly noisy gondola station, of Mike missing the car, running after us, screaming for us to wait, but he just loped easily across the floor and paced the car as it scuttled around the track. And then, slick as though he'd practiced the move on lunch breaks, he caught Eric's hand and leapt inside and folded himself onto the floor amid the packs. Seconds later, the car gained lift and sailed out of the station into the ashy sky.

"Shut the door, Cassie," Mike snapped.

We swung skyward. Mike went over the operating manual, patiently paging. Krom closed his eyes. Walter and Eric looked out the windows. I followed suit.

Always an incomparable view from the gondola. Lodge and Inn and gondola station fast dropping away below. Jagged peaks of the Minarets to the west, stubby domes of the Inyo chain to the north, caldera to the east just coming into sight. This is how I remembered the view: the most faraway features incised. Didn't look that way now. In the perpetual twilight, landmarks were uncertain, distance was lost. The eye telescoped to the near view, to the gondola window where particles of ash already clung, themselves incised as snowflakes.

The thunder was louder but in motion we could no longer feel the quakes.

I looked east, down toward the caldera. The south moat did

not appear to be currently in eruption. The caldera walls were identifiable but the floor lay in murk. If the ground down there were rotting it would look like this. Liquefaction. Soup.

No one spoke. It seemed we were going to rise stoically to the summit.

I scanned the mountain below as it dropped away. No fresh explosion pits, no evidence of activity. It was as it had always been, but for the ash. I knew these runs: St. Moritz, Bowling Alley. Skied them. In snow, not ash. Wouldn't enjoy skiing this. Snowboarders the only ones crazy enough to ride this. Ash? Awesome, dude. I suddenly giggled.

Incredulous silence in the car.

We swooped toward the mid-station and as we passed through the dark lift building I wondered what degree of shelter this might afford.

We rose, and rose.

"There it is," I said.

Mike came up on his knees, Krom braced to a sit, Eric and Walter turned. To the southeast, the folds of the mountains embracing the Lakes Basin came into view. Red Mountain was venting, a fat smokestack of ash. Boom boom. Boom.

Just like in my dreams.

"There's town," Mike said, and we turned our attention downward.

The higher we rose, the more the town came into view. Same ghost town we'd abandoned yesterday. Eons ago. Events now seemed to unfold in geologic time.

Although if the Red Mountain eruption went pyro now, events would unfold in a flash. A hot burning flash rolling down to envelop the town.

I craned to look for the summit of Mammoth Mountain. Eleven thousand feet and some change. Gain some altitude above the moat, above Red Mountain. Good. We were going up and there was the illusion we would climb right out of the ash, rise to the clean blue sky that must exist up there somewhere.

"What's that?" Walter said.

There was a bump like we were passing through a cable tower, and then another bump and the car gently seesawed.

We stopped.

We stared up at the cable, waiting, and then I peered out the window and estimated the fall to the slope below. Probably not survivable.

Mike got to his knees to look. "We just need to wait until it starts again."

Krom said, "Wait? You've got the manual."

"I can't fix it from *here*. That's for when we get to the *top*, for maintaining the machinery so we're not stranded. Mr. Krom, you have to realize...." Mike stopped.

Of course Krom did not realize because none of us had thought it useful to advise him of contingencies.

Eric opened his pack.

Mike said, "Let's give it time to start."

"How long?"

Mike agonized. "Fifteen minutes?"

Eric looked to me. I scanned the terrain, getting my bearings. We were suspended over East Bowl, two-thirds of the way to the summit. To my left, I could just make out the Red Mountain vent. We were stopped cold. No hum of machinery. I thought, this is Mike's show. Mike does know his stuff, he's devoured the manual, he did lend a hand with repairs when he used to work the gondola, and if I hadn't interfered with his repair that long-ago day in the station he may well have fixed that problem. I said, "Let's wait and see if it starts."

"No." Eric dug in his pack.

"Ten minutes?" Mike said. "How about that, man?"

Eric said, "We go now."

I opened my mouth to protest, but really I didn't know if it was better to stay or to go, and so I let the moment pass. Walter was helping Eric with his pack. Mike tucked his hand into his armpit and kept his mouth shut.

"Go where?" Krom asked.

"Up," I said, "still up," and I crawled over Mike to sit on the sliver of bench beside Krom, to allow Mike and Eric access to the door.

Krom began to laugh.

Eric had the gear out and he helped Mike into the harness and roped him and tied the rope to the crossbar inside, and Mike went out the door and with a thump spread-eagled over the roof. Through the window we saw him reach down to unlash the sled. Eric hauled Mike inside and the sled came after him, screeching across the roof. With ropes and carabiners they secured the sled outside the door. Mike put his weight on it and raised a thumb. There it held, a step into nowhere.

"No," Krom said.

"It's fine." Mike went over the side. I stretched to the window and watched him rappel down.

Eric turned to Krom. "Now you. Just try not to stiffen and don't go limp."

For a dark moment I wondered if Eric would just toss Krom over and let him free-fall, if I asked. I moved to Krom's legs. Walter prepared to get him around the middle. Eric had the head. Krom watched us in surprise, as though we had not heard him decline the invitation. Contrary to instructions, he stiffened.

I said, "Ease up. We're wasting time."

"Wrong way," he said. He gritted his teeth as we moved him, biting off the pain. We worked him out the door and Eric strapped him in.

"Ready below?" Eric yelled.

Mike shouted.

We slipped the carabiners and began to let the sled down. Krom's eyes locked on me, and he slipped me back to that day in the lab when he'd told me where the wrong way led, where the driver who made the wrong call during the eruption took them. And then the sled descended out of my sight. Nothing for him to do now but descend to the mercy of the volcano, take the pain, and survive.

Below, Mike caught the sled.

Eric hauled up the ropes and harness. He helped Walter strap in and belayed Walter as he worked himself into position. I watched Walter rappel down, holding my breath for an eternity, thinking Walter's getting too old for this.

Eric hauled up the gear. "Cassie." He checked the hardware and webbing and then held the harness open for me, like an evening coat. I buckled in.

Eric shouldered into the radio pack. "I'll toss the other packs when you're down but I'm going to carry this baby mys..."

There was a bump, and we looked at each other in instant knowledge. Eric cursed. He spun to the door and then back to me and for a moment I thought he was going to toss me over anyway since I was already roped.

"*Throw them packs*," I screamed.

We lunged, grabbing packs, taking time only to aim wide, and Eric shouted, "*Wait there*!" and Mike was waving his arms and shouting too but we couldn't make it out because the gondola car yanked us forward out of earshot.

Ash consumed their faces, their shapes, and then there was just the yellow tinge of their survival suits and then ash assimilated that, as well.

Eric swung the door shut.

We rose, helpless.

I got out of the climbing harness, watching through pitted glass for explosion craters or crevassing, and when at last we topped the final hump of cable track and funneled into the gloom of the summit station, Eric shoved open the door and we jumped. I hit the floor hard and scrambled for the switch. It had been fifteen years but the simple skills of my first paid job were intact. I shut down the gondola.

Eric sprinted to the other car and unstrapped a pair of skis. I was on his heels. I reached for a second pair.

"Whoa," he said. "Not you."

"It's steep. We've got to haul that sled up."

"Three can do it. Stupid to risk a fourth. I'm bigger and stronger. I go." He put on ski boots.

The concrete bumped beneath our feet, like heartbeats. Quakes picking up.

I said, "Walter's down there. I'm going."

"The hell you are. This one's mine. My responsibility. *My* fucking fault. Mike thought it would start and I pushed us to go."

I grabbed a pair of skis.

Eric yanked them from me. "We don't have *time* for this, Cass. You're not going. You try to go, I'll have to stop you. You follow me, I'll have to tie you up and drag you back up here—and you damn well know I will."

"You are so royally *stubborn*, Eric—Walter's not young and yeah Mike's strong enough but they're both crapped out by now and the sled weighs a ton and you're saying you can't use a *fourth*? Yes you can. You need me."

We looked at each other, staring each other down. There were a thousand things to say. We'd only got started that night in the cottage. There were a thousand things to say but what Eric said now was, "I need you to stay up here."

I began to panic.

He said, "We need a fourth up here with the radio who can tell Bridgeport where we are if something goes wrong down there."

My heart turned over.

He tossed my skis. They hit the concrete, hard. "*Cassie*?"

I said, "Don't do anything foolish."

"Come up the knoll." He opened the big door and we tramped outside and up the knoll to the vista point above the gondola station. He pointed. "Here's the route. They're down in East Bowl. From there we're gonna traverse to Saddle Bowl and loop over the saddle and switchback up Dave's Run past Huevos Grande and then around up to here. Got your watch? It's twelve-ten. Three hours go by and you don't see us, notify Bridgeport. We get close enough you do see us, come down and lend a hand. Otherwise, I don't want to see you." He stepped into his skis and set his goggles and poles. He hesitated, then raised his dust mask and brushed me a kiss. His mouth was ice cold.

I met him, held him. We tasted of ash.

Eric broke away first. "Sizzling sendoff, Oldfield."

"Dynamite, Catlin."

He set the mask. "Adios."

50

I WATCHED ERIC PUSH OFF, double-poling, and then he lunged into a skate like he was starting a sprint. He caught speed and paralleled his skis and dropped into a tuck. His skis cut a long lovely track down the ash of Dave's Run.

I wiped my eyes and lifted my gaze, scanning from the mountaintop along the Sierra Crest to the Lakes Basin, and met the sight of the eruptive column on Red Mountain.

I turned and headed back to the station. I had no stomach for the view.

For a moment I thought of setting up our shelter in the interpretive center that sits atop the mountain with a roundabout view, but it's mostly glass-walled and I had no faith in glass walls right now. The gondola station is built to withstand blizzard conditions and protect what's inside. A whole lot safer than down in East Bowl.

I contacted Bridgeport. They had no advice.

Fifteen minutes gone by. I got to work, unloading the gondola and setting up house. Always the female who gets stuck. I laid out the Inn's quilts and beside those beds made a kitchen of the backpack stove and cook pot. I lit the propane lantern. I put out matches and spare fuel canisters. I organized the food. I created a first aid station and inventoried supplies. I piled beside the door skis, boots, poles, snowshoes, and climbing equipment.

My hands stung. I sat and dwelt on that awhile. Whether to reapply ointment and re-bandage, whether there was permanent damage. Hurts enough. Unlike Krom, I did not find that pain got rid of fear.

Forty-five minutes. Eric should be with them now. They should be climbing up.

Quakes. Magma on the move somewhere.

Where were they? A zillion things could have gone wrong. Eric fell and broke his leg. Eric couldn't find them. They'd been caught in an avalanche. The sled broke a runner. Eric decided it was easier to get them down to the mid-station.

I spent half an hour going through the manual. If they'd gone down to the mid, was it insane to bring them back up on the gondola?

Were they having a picnic down there?

I put on jacket, helmet, goggles, mask and hurried outside and up to the vista point. Eric's ski tracks were still visible. No sign of any living creature. No color but gray.

I sat in the ash and hugged my legs. The world at my feet. A dozen ways to look, even in ash, and what I chose to look at was the snake in the sleeping bag. I'd moved well beyond the stage of hearing the hissing and fearing what I'd find. I knew what I'd find and yet, perversely, I opened the bag and looked. Maybe the thing was asleep.

It wasn't. The eruptive column grown into a larger and fatter snake.

I gave myself up to it and watched in grudging awe.

I should be taking notes. Recording the progression of events. Lindsay would. Unparalleled observation point up here. I had no field book so I made mental notes. Estimated height of the eruptive column, estimated diameter. Color. Wind direction. Estimated speed at which the column climbed. Estimated composition of the ash.

I caught ash on my glove, like snowflakes, and studied it. Fluffy. This was not phreatic ash—ash pulverized from old rock. This was new stuff. This was ash from juvenile magma. It made my heart turn over. Not that the phreatic eruptions weren't nasty enough beasts in and of themselves, but this new phase, this magmatic phase, was the stuff of my nightmares.

I stared down Dave's Run. No sign of them below. Nothing to note. No estimated speed of climb.

Twenty minutes. I went back for my gear.

I dumped my pack and started fresh. Focus. Essentials. No kitchen sink this time. I couldn't find my pocket knife. I wanted my knife. My eye fell on Walter's pack, one of the packs Eric hadn't thrown overboard. The pack bulged—it held whatever Walter had taken from the Explorer when he'd abandoned the evac and headed for town. Maybe a knife in there.

Or maybe I just needed the excuse.

I found his knife but I didn't stop there. I looked for the love letters, not really believing in the love letters, and indeed did not find them but I did find something that was surely of value to Walter, because it was heavy and yet he had hauled it into exile —wrapped in a sweater for protection.

It was an oblong box, and for just a tick I thought it must have been hers, because its purpose was to monitor the heartbeat of the volcano. Then I remembered. The image formed—Krom with this device at Hot Creek, measuring the stinging gas. Clever little thing, his design. I'd been impressed. And Walter must have been impressed as well, when he'd come across it, or he wouldn't have stowed it in his pack.

Another image—Walter at her safe. Is Krom there? I couldn't see.

I couldn't see what it meant. Why did Lindsay have Krom's monitor in her safe? And why did Walter take it?

I fiddled with the switches. It was dead. I opened the battery door. Power supply, but no juice. It was dead and silent and told me nothing.

But it sure must have spoken to Walter. And to Krom. Walter and Krom, trading hard looks. Walter waving off all help loading his gear.

I'd bet Krom down there on the mountain knew that Walter had found Krom's monitor in Lindsay's safe—and why it mattered.

I returned the monitor to Walter's pack, but I pocketed his knife. I radioed Bridgeport and reported landmarks and routes. Bridgeport had maps; they could do the coordinates. I put on ski boots, shouldered my pack, grabbed skis and poles, and went. I clumped up the knoll, fastened into my skis, and started to push off. Which way? Would they still be down in East Bowl, or had they already passed the saddle? Because it made a difference. I had a choice of runs. I stared through ash. Nobody. Nothing. Which way?

There was a sound, or rather an absence of sound, that turned my head.

I took a look at the eruption rising from Red Mountain.

The snake was still there, fatter than ever. Lazy, like it had ingested a meal and was stretching to let its belly out.

I hung on the lip of the summit.

The air turned strange, a soundless stifling feeling like the sky was going to fall. There was no up, no down, only ash. And the snake. And then there came a moment of utter calm as though the vent had sucked in its breath, and the column of ash seemed to freeze in place, neither climbing nor expanding but just existing, suspended from the roof of the sky.

A shiver took me and I slipped my skis backward.

A low-pitched rumble came, from every direction, and it came with such a vibration that the sound waves rolled through the air like scattering boulders and I ducked.

With dread certainty I turned to look down at the caldera and saw the moat going, glimpses through the murk of fiery vents flinging superheated gas and ash into the sky—like the caldera had spat—and then I spun toward the snake but it was holding back, deferring to the display of its parent, and when I looked back to the moat I saw that the eruption there had fractured at the top and was spreading into the branching lobes of a mushroom cloud in full nuclear fury. It fluffed and sent arcs of lightning from one hemisphere to the other.

My legs buckled and I went down, hitting my knees hard on my skis, and on my knees I turned to face Red Mountain. The snake bobbed, and when it had commanded my full attention, it struck.

The column slumped and collapsed back down upon itself, and now it became a different beast. Its surface billowed and it glowed dull red from within, superheated to incandescence. An impossible beast, a dense dry mass of gas and ash and pumice that began to flow like fluid. A horrifying beast, this pyroclastic flow, a hot venomous thing.

With a hiss it spilled over the tree line and surged out of the Lakes Basin, downward, sending glowing tongues to probe every topographic depression in its path.

The beast flashed snow into steam and white plumes lifted in its wake.

Hardly had this avalanche begun when it threw off particles of lighter material and this cloud rose from the flow like steam from hot coffee. It boiled upward and outward, piggy-backing the flow, bulging into great gray and black blooms which swelled and burst and multiplied and spawned more. And then the cloud took the lead in the race downhill.

It was like Krom's helicopter spewing smoke.

It was worse.

The flow spilled wide at the plateau on which the town sat, one lobe shooting northward as though following the Bypass on its channel through the Jeffrey pines. The main mass continued downhill from town, down along highway 203, and then the advancing wall of gas and rock met the eruptive column in the caldera moat and then there were no longer any points of reference. The entire ground below, from the Lakes Basin down through the plateau of the town, well north beyond the Bypass, and down well into the valley of the caldera was a uniform sea of mineral foam.

I was on my hands and knees, dumb with disbelief.

Lightning coruscated the sky and winds eddied madly around me as the eruption engendered its own weather system.

And as the flow finally lost momentum, its attendant cloud untethered itself and, borne by the winds, came back across the valley and up over the town's bones. If Pika Canyon had been spared by the downflow it was surely caught on the way back up, for nothing was going to be spared because the cloud now rose to the very base of Mammoth Mountain and slowly began to boil up its flanks.

I knew it must rise to bury the Inn and Lodge and lifts and then scale the final heights of the mountain to overtop this summit.

As they died below, I would die right here on my knees.

But the cloud remained simmering far below. The onslaught came from another direction. Red Mountain had not yet finished its work. It spouted a new column, and the violent winds skimmed off tephra and swept it westward, toward my summit. Ash began to fall on me like powdery snow, thick and suffocating, and then I was pelted with a rain of pumice stones, and within the space of time it took me to come alive and struggle to my feet a gloom had fallen so dense that I could not see the gondola station. I switched on my headlamp and bent, curling away from the downpour, and started down the knoll. Something cold and wet hit my neck. I put out my hand and caught ash and it was no longer dry and powdery but falling wet like a thin stream of oatmeal. Water in the air—condensing steam.

I fell. I snapped out of my skis and continued on foot. The ground was rotting beneath me and the rain of thin cement poured in a curtain off the rim of my helmet. The gloom had become so thick, so Stygian, that it was hopeless.

I could not find my way back. I could not help them down below. I could do no good.

Wandering, aimless, I smacked into concrete.

It made no difference to me, but my gut led me inside. I closed the door and sat in a circle of light made by Jimbo's headlamp. My mind dulled. I had no more terror, no thoughts really, save one. I can do no good.

The noise outside was formless, sounds of wind and explosions and pelting ash fall merged to a monochromatic din.

Sometime later, I thought to call Bridgeport. I could raise nothing but static. I cracked the door and peered out. It was lighter outside than inside. I changed from ski boots to hiking boots, shouldered my pack, and trudged outside.

The sky, in every direction, was a damp gray-white fog. It seemed the output of ash had lessened, or the capricious winds had driven the bulk of it elsewhere. I heard no roaring, saw nothing but fog.

Once again, I climbed the knoll. The footing was tricky—everywhere a crust of ash, ice, cinders, and mud, and in places I could tread upon it and in places my boots punched through to a slurry like setting cement. I reached the vista point and started down Dave's Run, which disappeared below in fog, but as the angle steepened the stuff beneath my boots began to slide. I scrambled backward, sinking into it now. Couldn't get free. Here was the old nightmare, only I couldn't run and I didn't scream because I no longer felt any need to escape. I dropped to my hands and knees and crawled back up and anchored there at the summit.

I'd wait. In time, the stuff would congeal enough for me to go down and search. I had nothing better to do than wait.

Sometime later, the mountain tried to shake me off.

There was a screech, another class of roar in my growing catalog of beastly sounds, and I thought, here it comes. But the mountain did not explode. The sounds grew and the ground shivered and I *knew*, regaining enough of my senses to recognize the quirks of this latest of beasts.

The flanks of the mountain seemed to heave. Far down as I could see, the entire pack of muck was in motion, fluidized, slopping downhill and disappearing into the fog, and what was left behind was ground stripped raw. This beast was named *lahar*—a landslide of volcanic debris made fluid by steam-wetted ash and melted snow. What this debris flow did farther downslope as it picked up boulders and trees and chairlift pilings and speed was beyond my sight and desire to know.

Within the gray avalanche below, for a moment, I thought I saw a flash of neon yellow plumage, but the color disappeared so quickly I knew it must have been a hallucination.

I knew only that they were dead down there.

51

I WAITED until the rumbling abated, then started down.

Where the downslope side of the knoll steepened, its crust had crevassed and sheared off, and so I waded out of the mucky stuff onto a hardened mud cap. I descended slowly, automatically scanning for loose rocks and cornices but I saw nothing left capable of avalanching. I looked up; the gondola towers just outside the station stood. Downhill, they were gone.

It was primeval and I wandered lost down the landscape.

As I walked I chafed the skin of cement which coated every exposed inch of flesh. It came off in chips and left my face burning.

I came to a rise and far down the flank of the mountain I saw shapes. Towers? No, stumps. I tried to pierce the ashy fog. I looked up, saw how far I'd come, and calculated that the stumps must be the remains of the mid-station.

Then something was left standing. A brick or two. Not enough, though, to shelter four fragile packages of flesh and bone. Too far down, anyway. Even had they struck out for shelter at the first sight and sound of the cataclysm, they surely could not have reached the mid-station.

But I had nowhere else to go.

I got all the way down to the mid, and I would have kept going except the lumpy remains reminded me of something I'd read in the manual—Mike's bible. I'd been reading about the mechanics of the gondola, wondering if we dared risk riding it again, but there was more to the pages, including a maintenance map of the mountain. I closed my eyes and saw the page, saw the green square near the top of Ricochet run. Just at the patrolled boundary, a green square indicated a maintenance shed. I thought this over. Mike had devoured the manual; Mike would know about the shed. If they had come far enough up Dave's Run when Red Mountain went pyro, they might have struck out for the shed and reached it before the lahar hit.

I angled back up the mountain.

Once, I raised my eyes from the strange pitted asphalt-clad ground to look beyond, eastward. There was no horizon, no caldera, nothing below the mountain but bands and layers and eddies of ash. There was no town down there, certainly. But the scalped mountain was real enough.

I began to cry, plodding uphill, the caustic ash in the goggles washing into my eyes.

In time, through the fog, something took shape. Should be the shed. I traversed the fall line, and as I drew nearer the shape resolved into walls and a bit of roof. The shed's high enough on the mountain, I saw dully, that the lahar had not yet gathered enough force to obliterate. It had merely torn the building in half, and one half was gone.

No door to enter so I clambered over mud-caked bricks. Inside looked like outside. Rubble and muck. A twisted I-beam. In the corner where the two standing walls met, where there remained a semblance of structural integrity, there was a body.

I stood rooted. Please, not Walter. Not Eric. I let out a sound and the head slowly turned. He's *alive*, and everything changed and I scrambled forward yelling but as I knelt and struck my knee on hard metal I recognized this body—body and sled united. Adrian Krom. I tore around the rest of the room, finding nothing that could be human. They were gone, then. Krom, in the corner, groaned. He's survived, on pain. I will be forever stumbling across his body.

I came over. "Where are they?"

"Get it off." The voice was muffled, nearly unrecognizable.

He lay supine on the sled, wedged into the debris as if the sled had burrowed to escape the lahar. But his body was clear; nothing on top of him, save the same muck that coated everything. I bent closer, angling my headlamp. Cement covered his head like a hood. He wore a mask. There were the crude contours of a face but it was masked in cement. No hair, no ears, no eyes. There were the slopes of cheeks and the rise of a nose, and on the underside was a hole where something, perhaps a sneeze before the stuff was set, had cleared a nostril. Below the nose was a break in the mask where the cement had been clawed away to free a mouth. The skin that showed was black, and it was only when I looked still closer that I saw it was dried blood.

I removed a glove and touched the mask. It was a hard seamless casing; crack it and it would come apart like the halves of a mold. I stared at the scabbed skin around his mouth. No, the stuff was glued to him.

He lay so still, his arms in line with his body, that at first I thought the cement had glued him to the sled, but then I looked more closely, running my fingers along one runner, and I found a cement worm that bunched and crawled across his midsection to bunch at the opposite runner.

I shoved back. "*Who tied you*?"

His head turned.

Eric did. Had to be Eric. I stared at the worm; Eric had done it before the lahar. He didn't have cuffs but he had rope. I went cold. "What did you *do*? Why are you tied?"

Shallow breathing through crusted mouth.

"*Who got the stuff off your mouth*?"

He whispered, "don't know."

They did. *After* the lahar. They're alive. They cleared his mouth and then went to get first aid supplies. Their packs were swept away so they had to go to the summit. Should be back by now. But no. They didn't find me at the summit so they kept going. Search and rescue; it's what they do. It's a big mountain. All of them had to search. Even Walter. Especially Walter; he wouldn't be left behind.

I scrambled up.

He heard me. "Get it off."

"You can breathe."

I stumbled through the fog, yelling, and then I moved downhill because that's where they would be searching for me, thinking I'd been swept downhill. I took a different route this time, descending until I reached a drop-off. I thought I knew that drop-off. I peered over the cliff but could see nothing below. I began to traverse, searching for another way down, because if I remembered right there was a ridge below the drop-off, angling off to the south, and if the ridge was high enough to channel the lahar north then someone could have survived to the south. But the fog had lowered and the ash had thickened and the puny beam of my headlamp was not enough to lead me down. I kept going, searching for a way down. After a time, I knew I was lost. I headed back uphill, thinking I'd go all the way up to the station for lanterns, but I seemed to climb forever without reaching the summit. Didn't care, really. I wandered until at last I came upon the shed. Whole mountain's lost in black fog and here I come, back to Krom, like he's put out a beacon.

It had darkened so much since I'd left that I could not make out details. I moved inside cautiously, navigating the wreckage, sweeping my beam to the corner where Krom lay. No sound came from him and I thought he'd lost consciousness. No demands to get it off. Perhaps he'd died. And then there was a sound, a cough, but it did not come from Krom. I spun and my light fell on a body slumped against the I-beam.

I let out a cry.

His eyes opened. He squinted against my light. He hunched his shoulders as though to rise, then abandoned the effort. I didn't move. I was afraid I had assembled him here out of hope. I wanted so badly to believe in Walter that I just held my breath. Finally, I was assured of the existence of this cherished man with his face chipped raw and a blackened dent in his skull. "Are you all right?" I asked. "Yes," he said, then with an effort asked, "are you all right?" I nodded. We let that sink in. He said, "I had lost hope." I nodded.

He told me his head hurt. I rushed to him, unslinging my pack.

Rudimentary first aid. I cursed myself for not learning more. All our trips into the field, where anything can happen, and I never learned more than to treat hypothermia and snakebite and splint a broken bone. In horror and ignorance, I applied antibiotics and bandaged his head. Ashy scabs; no fresh blood. He was not convulsing, or vomiting, or seeing double, or talking nonsense about birthdays. But he sagged beneath my hands, he had no rebound. I gave him water and when he had drunk his fill I checked his vital signs. "Eric?" I said, finger on Walter's pulse. "Mike?"

His pulse skipped.

"*Neither*?"

"We went to find you." His voice was thin. "Eric and I. Couldn't see."

I knew. The Stygian dark. I could not breathe.

"We came back. Mike was gone. Adrian said Mike went to hunt for you. We didn't believe him."

"Then Eric was still with you."

Walter nodded at the ropes binding Krom. "Eric did that. Said he promised you."

I whispered, "What did he do then?

"He went in search for Mike."

My eyes stung with acid tears.

"I remained behind." Walter made that coughing sound. "I was spent. I was of no use." He took another drink. "After the lahar hit, after I regained myself, I found Adrian like this. I cleared his mouth. Then I went out in search."

I whispered, "You were hurt. You said you were spent."

"It no longer mattered."

I said, tightly, "It's a big mountain."

"Yes it is."

I stood and shouldered my pack. "I'm going to look."

"It's too dark."

I moved outside and outside was dark as inside, I needn't have moved at all to know that but I had to go look. I could see ahead a couple of yards along the beam of my headlamp but beyond that stunted reach it was pitchy black. I was a near-sighted creature, and beyond the very near I was blind. Blind as Krom beneath his hood. I swiveled, sweeping my lamp, carving a tight circle of light. "Maybe lanterns," I said, although I didn't know how many more visible feet lanterns would buy me, "there's lanterns in the station, Walter, it's not far," although I wasn't sure if I could find my way.

"You leave, he kills me."

I froze. It was Krom's voice. I simply clamped down my muscles, some animal instinct. Freeze and listen. Walter, I saw, had stiffened as well. He had come up onto his hands and knees and he was looking at Krom. My beam caught Walter in sharp profile and cast a long wolfish shadow upon the rutted ground. Had I missed something in my rush to nurse him? I'd been watching so keenly for the trauma signs—vomiting, convulsions—when I should have searched for something more fundamental. I watched now for a signal. Some predatory tic. What sign would Walter give if he intended to commit murder? I didn't know. That wasn't in my world view. "Walter?"

Walter said, "I didn't know he was still alive."

I moved back to Krom and pitched to my knees. "You didn't check him, Walter? When you came back from your search?" No. I knew how it felt to end up at the shed, used up, ready to drop and die here if that's what's in store. No thought to Krom. Nearly comatose himself. So what's changed? I watched Walter get to his feet and come settle down opposite me, a new lithe purpose in him. What's changed, I realized, is water. Rehydration. He's regained himself, and all that is inside him.

He touched the mask.

I pushed his hand away. "I'll do it." I tried to find an edge of the mask, a fracture where the mouth hole had been made, but the stuff was thick and set and of a single piece from jaw to scalp. I got Walter's knife from my pack and probed the jawline. "I'll try not to cut you, Adrian."

He whispered, "Water."

I got another bottle from my pack and touched it to his encrusted lips.

His head jerked. "*Use* water."

Of course. You ungrateful bastard out of hell. I poured a trickle onto the cement around his mouth. Rivulets skittered across the hard surface.

"Use the knife," Walter said.

I froze.

"Abrade it."

Of course. I put the blade to the mask and scraped, then

drizzled water over the abraded cement. "Needs to soak in." I sat back. "We'll be needing more water, sooner or later. And supplies from the station. But first I'm going to search." I thought, I'll pick up where I left off, down below the drop-off. South of the ridge. If *I* could remember the ridge, I was damn well sure that Eric and Mike could remember it. "Soon as it's light enough," I said, "I'm going to search." I watched Walter. "What will you do when I leave?"

He held my look. "Don't worry."

"Tell me why I shouldn't."

He waved a hand.

"Okay, while I wait for it to get light, we'll talk about what you know. I found the volcano monitor in your pack. Tell me what that means, Walter."

"Leave it alone."

"You took it with you to the Inn, you were going to haul it over Minaret Summit, what's it *mean*?"

Stony silence.

"Okay, I'll tell you what I think I know. Night of the evac you went to her office and found it in her safe. I assume it's not what you expected to find. What were you looking for? Not love letters."

"Something of hers," he said. "Something I might want."

"Well you found *something*. You took it. What's it tell you?"

"Leave it alone."

"I can't." I peered at Walter. He was in there somewhere, inside his own stony mask. What does he know? Enough to prove Krom killed Lindsay?

I bent to Krom. "You better help me, Adrian. You better tell me what he knows."

Nothing, from beneath the mask.

I put the blade to the mask and began to scrape, at the jawline. Water had done its work. The mask was pliable, some kind of thick gray skin. Rhinoceros skin. "Okay, let's start with what we all know. The monitor was in Lindsay's safe." I peeled a length of rhinoceros hide. "She was pissed at you Adrian, wasn't she? You're monitoring her volcano, you publicly humiliate her, and she somehow gets hold of your monitor. The two of you, humiliating each other. Some kind of playground *game*?" I moved the blade back to Krom's throat where the mask met raw skin, and probed for a new edge. "So you went to her office and demanded she return it and she wouldn't. That's why you killed her?"

Krom breathed audibly.

"But you didn't find it, did you? Because if you had, it wouldn't have still been in her safe for Walter to find." The knife slipped in my muddy hand. A bead of blood showed at Krom's throat. He sucked in his breath and brought his head down. I put the knife aside.

Walter eyed it.

"What brought you to her office, Adrian? *This* time." I could not finesse this job; I dug with my fingers. "You saw Walter at the window? And you surprised him and he had the safe open and there was the monitor. But no. If you killed Lindsay for the monitor, you would have killed Walter." I sat back. The mask bore long grooves, like an animal had clawed at it. "And I still don't understand—what's so important about it? Was there something special about the Hot Creek footage?"

Nothing from beneath the mask, not even a plea to get it off.

I looked up. "Walter?"

Walter's face was savage, not his own.

"You think it's proof, Walter? You must, because otherwise you wouldn't have taken it."

Walter did not deny it.

"What's it mean?"

"This is not the time."

"*Yes it is*. I want to know if you're looking for revenge."

Walter's face was stone cold.

I went down into the pit where I've been living lately, wandering in the muck of pain and rage and fear.

Krom brought me out. "Get it off, Cassie."

"I am." Damn you, I am. He lay helpless, a broken hooded thing. At my mercy. My great unplumbed depths of mercy. Only it wasn't mercy that moved me. It was fear. If I don't act, Walter will take up the knife and use it. I began again, at the jawline. I worked the way I work a dig, carefully removing the layers so as not to disturb what's underneath. And now there was something new, a new texture just showing through. I had to be careful. Never dig blindly through one horizon of soil to the next. Assess it first. Understand what it is. It was flesh. The new horizon, on close inspection, was pebbly flesh embedded with pumice. Yes, I had nearly reached bottom. I got the bottle and poured more water.

He screamed. Sound like an animal.

I jerked back, spilling water.

His shoulders convulsed, nearly lifting, but his blackened lips pulled back and he bit off the scream.

"Okay," I said, "no more water." Without water, the cement was going to harden again. "Let me think." I took the knife and moved to the door. Where the door must have been. My headlamp lighted a slice of foggy bald landscape. This was a world lost in time and space. We didn't exist in the real world anymore. We were in purgatory, in limbo. I stared into the ashy fog so hard my eyes ached. Where were they? This was like being back in Lindsay's office, waiting for the rescuers, hour after hour. But they finally came. There was a good reason it took them so long. If they were down below the drop-off, beyond the ridge, there was a good reason they were still there. Mike was hurt, Eric couldn't leave him. Eric was probably hurt too. I understood that.

"Give him an injection," Walter said.

I spun. Walter was fumbling in my first aid kit. I came over and took the vial from him and examined it. Demerol. I read the label. Morphine-like effect. Yes, that's what I wanted.

I knelt beside Krom. More excavation. I used the knife to slice the arm of the yellow suit at the seam, and skinned it down. I pushed the sweater and shirt up above the bicep and exposed flesh. It was shocking—the sight of his clean naked arm, brown and strong. Tattoo didn't bother me, though, nor did the waxy hill of scar. Old friends. Circles of hell. Round and round, going down. Sacrifice and survive.

Krom watched me through cemented eyes. Not even a face. He watched me with his head fixed face-backward upon his neck.

I leaned close. "Did *you* send Mike back out to search?"

Silence.

"Was he scared?"

Krom exhaled, barely a breath. "Are you?"

There was something hard in my chest. A small hard spot, cold and unyielding. This is why we're here, isn't it? Stripped raw like the mountain. Lindsay did this, blew her volcano the hell up, taking us to hell and back. Poetic justice. Leaving us here in limbo with Krom. Isn't it enough for her that he's lost? The volcano won. Her baby triumphs. All his grand battle plans for naught. He failed. He offered himself up for the tribe and he failed. His goal now shrunk to the merely tactical—survive. Survive and do battle another day, another place. He can't touch us anymore, Lindsay. Look at him. Adrian Krom cloaked in gray. Muck all over; must have seeped through his pores to coat him inside. Sleepy-eyed Adrian Krom who strikes with animal grace, lying here cemented and lashed to a litter. Roguish Adrian Krom who cuts a wake with the locals, his charms masked and his face good as gone. Hero Adrian Krom carted up the mountain with his tail between his legs. What more can he do? He can do nothing.

He whispered again.

"What?" I bent closer, ear to his mouth.

"Walter's not afraid."

I recoiled, turning to Walter to see if he'd heard. Walter was needling the Demerol vial. He grimaced in concentration. He could have been in the lab pipetting chemicals from one tube to another. I said, "*Walter*? He weighs two hundred seventeen pounds. What's the dosage?"

Walter came over and knelt. He held the syringe inverted, fully loaded.

"Did you do the math?"

He wiped Krom's arm with an alcohol swab. "Yes."

I held out my hand. "I'll do the injection."

"No, Cassie. Your bandages make you clumsy."

I let my hand come to rest on the bare arm. Walter cocked his head. We regarded one another. Two colleagues with a difference of opinion over lab procedure, neither willing to allow the other to blunder ahead. We both knew I was strong enough to stop him. We both knew I could break every remaining vial in the first aid kit. We both knew there were other ways, that Demerol was simply the kindest. We both knew I could not stay awake forever.

I turned to Krom. "Help me, Adrian."

He was silent.

"You have to say you're sorry."

He made a sound. It may have been a laugh.

"Tell him, Adrian. Isn't there some part of you that's sorry about Lindsay? Even if it's only you're sorry it came to that."

Walter said, "Don't, Cassie."

"It'll matter," I told Krom. "Walter might not believe you but he'll have to give it consideration. It's in his bones."

"Stop," Walter said.

"You want a sacrifice, Adrian? He believes life's inviolate. That's his home base. He kills you, he kills himself."

Nothing from beneath the mask. Nothing, now, from Walter.

A quake rocked us gently.

"*Damn it Adrian give me something that will help.*"

Whatever hell lay beneath that mask finally boiled out. "*Sorry.*"

It hit me hard, although I'd asked for it, but it did not alter Walter's set face. I said, urgently, "Make him believe."

"I am sorry."

The world did not shift. The sun did not come out. Walter did not relinquish the syringe. I did not let go of Krom's arm. The skin had gone nearly white where I clutched it.

"Sorry," Krom said. "Sorry."

I could stand it no longer. I snatched the syringe from Walter and fled to the doorway. Krom heard me. His voice flew after me: sorry, sorry, sorry, a raven of remorse. Sorrow filling the void. And then, abruptly, there was another voice—thunder in the distance. Eruptions again. I saw Walter straighten, listening. I watched ash in my headlamp beam, particles trapped like insects. I prayed through ash. *Scare* him, Lindsay. Save him.

Walter paid no heed.

I came back across the shed, grabbing an alcohol swab from the first aid kit on my way. I knelt beside Krom. Anchoring the syringe with two fingers, I worked open the swab. Clumsy work; Walter was right. I swabbed Krom's arm.

He flinched.

It took me so long to upend the syringe and squirt out a drop, to clear the liquid of air bubbles, that Walter had time to take this in, to calculate that at best I'd released a tiny fraction of the Demerol, to recall that I had not read the recommended dosages and so had not done the math myself, to understand that I was going on his calculations. He'd done the math and loaded the syringe and now I was ready to administer the injection he had prepared.

I laid the needle to Krom's skin and pushed. Needle found home.

Krom flinched, again. And still, I feared him. Masked, hobbled, cuffed—it did not matter. He threatened to pull in the both of us, this black hole called Adrian Krom. And Walter wasn't scared. I'd thought, ever since Walter had appeared like a ghost at the Inn, that I had to save Walter from Krom's wrath. No longer. I had to save Walter from his own wrath.

Walter watched me stonily and I returned his look.

Two can play this game, Walter. Don't forget you've trained me since I was a kid. I've aped your every move in the lab and ransacked your brain. I'm yours. More even than I was Lindsay's. I'm yours in a way she wanted, but I couldn't give her. I signed up with you at the get-go and I've never wavered. I'm with you, against the enemy. You're my home base. And you know me. You know that whatever you have in you, whatever accommodation you come to with justice, I'm capable of that too. I'll go as far as you will. You know that about me, don't you? Or at least you have to give it consideration. You have to fear I'm not bluffing.

I said, "We're a team, Walter."

He watched my fingers hook under the flanges, my thumb weight the plunger.

I hesitated.

He said, "Trust me."

I depressed the plunger, releasing the full load of Demerol into Adrian Krom.

52

"CASSIE?"

I fought through layers of fog, swam through ash, surfaced. My eyes were glued shut. Glue of ash and saline lachrymal fluid. Glue of grief. I rubbed my lashes apart and looked around. In the shed, home.

"Do you hear that, Cassie?"

We listened, trying to fathom this growling sound. What new category of beast was this? There was no point trying to escape because there was nowhere to go. There was no time. The sound was growing louder—a phreatic, perhaps. Sounded like it came from lower on the mountain, just where I predicted it would come. We lay still, watching the sky. No terror. Way beyond that, in another realm entirely. Limbo. We no longer drifted in and out of limbo; we'd taken up permanent residence.

Krom slept, at peace. He had a face again, of sorts.

"The color's different," Walter said.

"Of what?"

"The sky."

"Must be dawn."

The growling magnified, clarified. Oh, so familiar. I know this beast. I sat up.

Krom's eyes opened.

Walter got to his knees and began to hunt around, scattering our supplies. I pushed past him—I knew just where everything was if he didn't jumble it up first—and I found the radio and switched it on.

Static. Batteries had juice.

I lifted my face again to the sky and saw what Walter meant —the color's different. Day's breaking and the sky is white like a dawn that promises an overcast day, a day innocent of ash.

Voices crackled out of the radio. Voices and static. Logistics.

The growl from the beast was closer. It was plain enough, quite identifiable. Whup-whup-whup-whup, beating the air, whacking us out of limbo.

Static receded, words clarified. "How many survivors?"

I gazed across the shed and met Krom's eyes—which suck dry every look I give him—but this time was different, this time he had no further need of me. This time he broke our contact first and gazed up at the new dawn. I did not care, really.

I pressed the transmit button. "Three."

53

TWO WEEKS after escaping the hospital, I was back. Visiting, this time. Stobie boomed out a greeting, sounding too healthy to be here.

I said, "Hey Stobie."

"Cool 'do, Kiddo."

My haircut. Real short, real curly. There'd been so many cemented tangles the nurses nearly scalped me. Stobie'd lost some hair as well, on top, along with some pounds, giving him the piebald look of an overworked pack horse. We chatted, lurching from the weather to hospital food to Jeanine's new gig videotaping snorkelers in Maui, and then I told him Mike had been torn up about what happened at the race.

Stobie frowned, gathering the events. His short-term memory is patchy.

"Afterward, Mike visited you. We all did. I don't know if you heard us."

"Sure," Stobie said. But he clearly hadn't.

"I'm not trying to excuse Mike but I want you to know he was really torn up."

"Hey Cassie? You don't have to excuse him. Mike could be a

real butthead but aside from that he was okay. I don't hold blame, about this." He cocked a finger like a gun at his head, then grinned. "I'm gonna miss the butthead."

I had to laugh, and so did he, and for a sweet moment we went with that, but then I caught the pain in his eyes—or maybe he'd caught it in mine first—and I didn't want to risk slipping from Mike to Eric because I didn't want to start Stobie crying—not the Stobe. I didn't think I was going to cry. Not now. Tonight I'll cry, alone, like last night. I have a routine.

Stobie and I lapsed into silence.

Finally he said, "So what's new with you, Kiddo?"

I flinched. It sounded so normal. What's new, what's up. I reached. "My parents bought a place, here in Bishop." Few blocks from my scummy new condo. They drew me a housewarming cartoon—me on top of a stratovolcano with my thumb in its vent. I'm sure I'll come to love it. The way I came to love their cartoon showing Henry snug in his coffin, with Dad's caption, and Jimbo's, and then mine. Humor as therapy. I refocused on Stobie. "They've got a huge yard, so…Fourth of July, mark your calendar."

"Tradition." He reached for a smile. "What about you? You back to work?"

"Yeah." Just let me close it all out. "Actually I, ah, came with an ulterior motive. I hoped you could help me clear something up."

He settled against his pillows. "Tell Uncle Stobie all about it."

"Remember the horse hair we found on Georgia?"

"Sure."

"It was finally matched—to a horse at Sierra Ranch Stables. Where you work."

He took that in. He did not show surprise. He said, finally, "You think I know who took the horse?"

"Do you?"

"I can guess."

I said, gently, "Is Mike your guess?"

Stobie worked on that.

I said, "Eric told me he suspected Mike. Explained why he was covering. Explained why he was such a jerk on the retrieval —trying to send me and Walter back. He didn't rat you out, Stobie, but I can guess why you backed him up. Why you reacted so strongly when he found the horse hair on Georgia. You suspected Mike, too. And—just like my brother—you let Eric handle the problem."

Stobie didn't flinch. He said, "It was a hell of a messed-up thing."

I couldn't argue with that. "Any particular reason *you* suspected Mike?"

"You fishing, Kiddo?"

"I'm fishing."

"Then let's reel it in." Stobie eyed me steadily. "On the way up to the glacier, Eric told me he wanted to send you back. Told me why. And then...the horse hair...*that's* when I got my own suspicion."

"Why?"

"Because I knew Mike. I could believe Eric's theory. And the horse hair fit with Mike." Stobie shrugged. "Mike worked at the stable once."

I showed my surprise.

"For about three *days*. Horse shit grossed him out, and he quit. But he'd know where the keys to the barn were kept."

I nodded. Just like he had recalled where the gondola keys were kept. That's Mike, I thought, never forgets a detail. So it was not a leap to assume that Mike would know, years later, how to borrow a horse on the sly. "Thanks," I said.

"Sure." Stobie suddenly chuckled. "Mr. Clean and the horse shit. Hadn't thought about that in years."

"Mr. Clean?"

Stobie's face relaxed, going back in time. "Mike's nickname, at the stable. First day there, he decides the place stinks. So he comes up with this thing—mixes sagebrush in with the drystall. You know how sage smells real sharp? It worked, but man did he get raked. Mr. Clean." Stobie thought. "Maybe that's why he quit. All the teasing."

I said, "What's drystall?"

"Bedding, Kiddo. Soaks up the horse pee. Mashed pumice, basically."

It took me several days to make the leap from horse to cat.

Under the scope—in the cramped lab space I'd secured on a back street in Bishop—the drystall grains I'd got from a Bishop stable did not match my evidence. It was mashed pumice, all right, but only a second cousin to the pumice I'd taken from Georgia's mouth.

But it pointed me in the right direction.

Through Bobby Panetta I found Ali al-Amin, with whom Mike had planned to room, to whom Mike had evacuated his cat. I knelt beside the litter box in Ali's tidy laundry room, as Mike's high-strung Manx paced nervously. The room smelled—cat shit overlain by another, familiar odor. I pulled on my winter wool glove, making Ali as suspicious as the cat, and shoved my hand into the bin of clean litter. Ali warned me not to spill because it was Mike's special mix and Ali dreaded weaning the Manx to a new brand. I didn't spill. I withdrew my hand and inspected my glove. It was coated. I brushed it off. Litter still clung to the wool fibers. I brushed again. Not clean yet. Litter had even worked in under the cuff.

I got out my hand lens and squinted at the grains on my glove. Crushed pumice and Jeffrey pine bark. My glove smelled faintly of root beer. Pumice and Jeffrey pine, drystall and sagebrush—Mr. Clean had clearly taken an inventive pride in his work.

Mr. Clean was equally fastidious about his cat's litter box. I knew because I'd been to Mike's place once to pick up Jimbo when his car died and the two of them were in the garage looking for jumper cables, and the litter box was next to the workbench. On a cold November day, I thought, Mike might wear gloves in the chilly garage to prepare his special litter mix, and if he subsequently wore those gloves in another context, at an old mine site handling a body, bits of that special litter mix could fall out.

I pictured it, Mike and Georgia arguing, and then a shove, and then maybe Georgia falls and hits her head on a rock. I couldn't see Mike wielding the rock, hitting her. Perhaps he had done, but I couldn't picture it. Perhaps I'd become more forgiving of Mike but I could not credit him with cold-blooded murder. I was calling it an accident. In my report I'd lay out the scenario, of Mike's horror when Georgia was knocked out, of his futile attempt to revive her. I'd mention the bruising around her mouth, where Mike had grasped her, thumb and fingers spread just so, opening her mouth to give her CPR. Only she's not responding and in his panic he jerks his hand and the cuff on his glove rolls and the soil falls in her mouth.

And when CPR fails, he closes her mouth to end her silent scream.

54

THE DAY after he got out of the hospital, Walter accepted my invitation to breakfast at Bill Bone's new donut shop in Bishop. While Walter was giving his customary attention to dissecting the coils of a cinnamon roll, I placed an envelope on the table.

"Georgia," I said.

As he read I gazed out the window. Where the Mammoth refugees had snarled traffic a month ago, there was again a jam, this one caused by a parade of geese. A car with skis on the roof honked. Bishop, with the Sierra scarp at its back, is not so unlike Mammoth, which is both good and bad. Walter has no opinion on the subject. I worried about his disinterest. I worried about his mental faculties, although brain scans and clinical tests showed no damage. I worried about every fault line on his face.

He laid the report beside his plate like a napkin. "Your work is flawless."

"Thank you."

He drank his tea. "What brought you to it?"

"Stobie."

"Stobie's doing well?"

I nodded. Better than you. "So, we have Mike causing Georgia's death at Gold Dust, probably by accident in a fit of temper. Can't prove what got them up there together but I'd say jealousy. Krom's her lover. Krom's Mike's idol. She shows up at Krom's office, hyped, Mike's there and she lets slip where she's been. He goes to find out what she found. She follows. Or maybe they even go together. Anyway, it ends badly. Mike tries CPR, that doesn't work, and then he panics. But eventually he pulls it together and gets a horse and takes her to the glacier." I reminded him of Eric's scenario.

Walter nodded.

I saw Bill emerge from the kitchen carrying a tray of crullers. Limited menu here; limited seating capacity. Still, chatter was thick, more faces were familiar than not, and Bill was back in business. Good for him. I turned back to Walter. "You up for tying some loose ends?"

Walter shrugged. He was circling his tea cup, round and round.

"Question is, who found the body? Some random climber? *Possible*, but real coincidental. So try this on for size: after Georgia disappears, the town's in an uproar and Mike starts worrying someone will connect him with Georgia and Gold Dust, that he'll get nailed. He worries himself sick. Decides it's better if she's found in the bergschrund—it'll look like an accident. So he goes up there and scrapes the new snow off the body, so it will be believable someone could find her. Then he calls in the anonymous report."

Walter nodded.

"But weather's iffy so there's a delay before we go up there for the recovery. That's where Krom comes into it."

Walter eyed me. "Is this speculation, now?"

"Partly. John told me he told Krom about the climber's report as soon as it came in. Krom would surely wonder if the body was Georgia. And he'd surely think of Mike, how jealous Mike was of Georgia. And so he confronts Mike, and Mike caves and confesses. Can't you just see it? *Help me, Mr. Krom, I'll do whatever you say*. And yeah, I'm into speculation now."

"Continue," was all that Walter said.

"Once Mike's confessed to Adrian, he's surely going to have to reveal the fissure at Gold Dust. Maybe, Mike himself had been worrying about the fissure and *that's* what made him confess. Either way, Krom will sure want to see that fissure. So Mike takes him, shows him, and Krom reacts. Holy shit." I recalled that feeling myself. "But Krom also sees an opportunity. Remember, he's been battling with Lindsay about escape routes ever since he came to town. He can't abide using hers. He wants to build his own. And here, with the fissure, he finds a solid reason to kill her road."

Walter flinched.

"Now all he has to do is publicly champion Pika as *his* route, and then get the fissure 'discovered' to discredit *her* route, and he's the hero." I paused, to be sure Walter was with me. I wasn't speculating this time. I was extrapolating, from hard evidence. From the monitor I'd found in Walter's pack—the monitor he had taken from Lindsay's safe. This case had hurt so long I wanted Walter with me.

Walter cocked his head.

I said, "Mike being the killer—however accidental—explains the timing, something that never quite fit. I'd suspected that Georgia showed Krom the fissure and he killed her to keep her quiet—give him time to set his plan in motion. But why wait a month? Why not champion Pika right away? Now it makes sense. He *did* go public right away—Mike confesses to Krom, shows him the fissure, Krom makes his plan and then calls the meeting at the Inn."

Walter frowned. "Why didn't he kill Mike? Given your supposition that he would have killed Georgia."

"Plan A. Remember, there had to have been an original plan, before he came upon me and the geology. So plan A, I'd say, was to force Mike to confess when the time was right, which would reveal the fissure—and keep Krom's part in it quiet. I'm sure he promised to stand by Mike, get him a good lawyer, call him a hero. Do we have any doubts Mike would do whatever Adrian Krom asked of him?"

Walter expressed no doubts.

"It didn't come to that, of course, because plan B worked. I found the fissure. Mike didn't have to confess. And Krom found other uses for him. And—caveat—I'm speculating again but it's not particularly wild-ass. Krom needs to keep track of me while I'm hunting for the site of death, just in case I don't keep him in the loop. He needs to know if and when I find it. So he sends Mike." Poor loyal Mike. "It's possible he found another use for Mike—blowing up 203—but I don't think so. I don't think Krom would have risked that. I think he planted the explosives himself. I don't think Mike would have done it."

Walter said, "I agree."

"In the end, Mike became a liability. Krom couldn't have him making peace with his conscience in front of you. Or Eric." I took a drink of milk and it coated my mouth. What I wanted was coffee. I wanted the bitter scalding heat. "And so Krom asked Mike to step out into the eruption and Mike went."

Walter took a long time with this. He seemed to watch Bill, with a moment's freedom behind the counter playing online poker on his new laptop. Eight hundred birthday bucks well spent. Walter came back to me, finally. "Is that it?"

"No. There's still a loose end. Regarding the other case."

"Let's confine ourselves to the case at hand."

"Can't. The one leads to the other."

He worried his cup.

I said, "Jimbo took charge of our packs and things, from the mountain, when we were in the hospital. When I got out he dumped it all on me."

"I don't see..."

"Your pack. The volcano monitor."

He took a moment. "I see."

"Yup. I recharged the battery and ran it all, data and video. Whole nine yards. Sure explains why Krom wanted it back."

China scraped wood, Walter's cup circling and circling.

"My guess is, Len Carow told Lindsay that Krom was monitoring the volcano. And that pissed her off. So she decided to take it. Krom was supposed to fly to Sacramento, so there's her chance. I figure she used that credit card trick she showed you to force the lock of his office. She took the monitor back to her office. Played the recordings. And she must have been shocked, like I was. It was truly damning stuff. So she put it in her safe. Planning to go to John Amsterdam in the morning, I would hope. But Krom got snowed in and came back. Stopped by his office, found the door unlocked, or the storage cabinet open. He found *something* amiss, because he telephoned her, about an hour before she died. I had John pull his phone records." I paused. I could see it. Krom phones her, really pissed, and she tells him to take a hike. Or maybe she invites him over so she can crucify him in person. Not considering, in her arrogance, his response.

Walter anchored the cup.

"So, Walter," I said, "the loose end. *When* were you in her office? *When* did you find the monitor in the safe? Was Krom there? On the floor, under the bookcase?"

"That's some loose end."

"Did you leave him there, to the mercy of her volcano?"

Walter gave me a hollow blue stare. "Do *you* think I did?"

I took a very long time to answer. "No."

"Let me ease your mind, anyway." He gave a thin smile. "I

spent the night of the evacuation in her office. I was not in a good state. In the morning, before leaving, I wanted a keepsake. I thought she might have kept my letters in her safe. The two of us wrote one another, when we were off on assignments."

My heart twisted. "So you *were* looking for love letters?"

He nodded. "They weren't there. Most likely she kept them at home. What *was* there was the monitor. I had no idea of its significance. I was not in an analytic frame of mind. But she'd valued it enough to put in the safe, and so I took it with me when I went up to the Inn. *Before* the eruption."

Relief ran through me. "So you didn't know Krom was in town?"

"No."

"So he must have gone to her office after you'd left. But why?"

"I believe I left the lights on."

I gaped. "That's what he said."

Walter shrugged. "He spoke the truth, when he had no need to lie."

"Shit," I said. "Then it was just chance."

"Indeed. Chance I forgot to turn out the lights, chance I left the safe open. I suspect when he came into the office and saw that, it gave him cause to worry. He believed she had his monitor, he'd not found it the night he killed her, and now he saw where she'd kept it. He must have had a difficult few moments, wondering who took it."

I had to smile. "I doubt he wondered long. Who else would know about her safe, but you?"

Walter smiled then.

I said, "So he's in her office, freaking out, and then the quake hits. And the bookcase falls."

Walter said, evenly, "I'd offered more than once to anchor that bookcase for her."

"When did you figure out what the monitor meant? What it could prove—the motive for Krom to kill her."

"At the Inn. Battery was dead so I used the AC adapter. I played the video."

"Why didn't you tell me?"

All at once, Walter sagged. His chamois shirt appeared too broad in the shoulders, too loose, the weight he'd lost in the hospital suddenly apparent. He said, softly, "I was afraid of what you would do with the knowledge."

I flinched. Like he'd slapped me. And my thoughts spiraled down into the pit. If I'd ended up alone on the mountain with Adrian Krom—if Walter hadn't been there for me to worry over—what would I have done? Knowing Krom killed Lindsay, knowing he sent Mike out to his death, knowing he might as well have sent Eric—what would I have done? Knowing we might die there anyway. I said, finally, "I would have done what you did. Give him the correct dose. Put him to sleep."

"Thank you," Walter said. "You've eased my mind."

Just as he'd eased mine. Neither of us willing to take that final irreversible step. But we'd each thought about it, and we'd each wondered if the other was capable of it. I shifted my gaze outside, to the snowy peak of Mount Tom—a new skyline to get used to, although all high Sierra peaks will forever remind me of my home base, of Mammoth. But home was gone. Along with a few illusions about the people I loved. About myself.

Walter said, "Is that it?"

I came back. "Yeah, that ties it up. If you agree, we'll close out Georgia. Geology nailed it, all the way." The reality is, it's DNA or prints more often than the geology that places the perp at the scene. Not this time; we did well by Georgia. "And we may as well close out the Nash case. I've done the report. I didn't mention the monitor—as John told me last week, it may be motive for murder but there's no hard evidence to tie Krom to the scene." No fluids, no fibers, no prints. Crinoid's speculative. "So—bottom line, case-wise—we're batting fifty-fifty."

"You could look at it that way."

"I've tried. But the fifty percent on the failure side of the column is just too painful." I placed the second envelope on the table.

He opened it and read for a full minute, long enough to have committed my resignation to memory.

No other way out.

55

WE RETURNED to Mammoth as we had left, in convoy. This time it went without a hitch. Long line of vehicles herding home, four months and six days after we all hightailed it out of town, the mountain in our rearview mirrors.

Now the mountain looms before us: long time no see.

Jimbo and I, in Jimbo's heap, followed Walter in his new Explorer. Fire-engine red, like the one he'd lost. Walter had already put the mileage on it, wandering hither and yon for weeks at a time. He'd send postcards. I'd write letters. Other than that, I slept, ate, socialized when pressed, read, watched more videos than I needed. Boxed up lab equipment, put it in storage.

It took Resident Visitors Day, and its prospects, to rouse me from my torpor.

The Army Corps of Engineers had plowed a road across the ash-and-pumice tuff, following highway 203, and the cars raised a haze of ash. Erupted ash and pumice had filled in the gash across 203, the handiwork that had rerouted our evacuation. We passed a forest of gray tree stumps, stripped of bark, splintered. The intervening ground was wormy with charcoal. Just ahead was the hilly plateau on which the town had stood, and above that naked shelf was the mountain.

Landforms laid bare, a geologist's dream.

"*Man*," Jimbo said.

I glanced at Jimbo, barely visible behind the wings of his hair. First I've spent time alone with him since the hospital. He'd visited faithfully while I was laid up, jiving with the nurses, but we hadn't found much to say to each other. Eric was always there, and behind him, Mike. Ghosts aren't white, they're tropical neon yellow. Except for Lindsay, who is a winter and whose best color was always gray.

The road leveled and we came to that juncture where we'd always gained the first glimpse of town through the screen of Jeffrey pines. No screen now. In my dreams, nothing has survived, not a single shard to indicate that anything but ash ever existed on this plateau. In my memory, it's a mountain ski town in deep forest. But in reality the town looked like a beach, with mile after mile of sand castles eroded by the poundings of high tide.

Jimbo's head snapped right. "That the ranger station?"

I looked. Rubble, unidentifiable but for the fact that the ranger station is the first building on the right as you come into town. Didn't matter which way I looked. All buildings were the same, reduced to trace evidence. All tree stumps were the same, as though only one kind of tree had ever grown here, a barkless gray splintery species.

We drove on and I saw in the distance the ash trails of two Geological Survey vehicles heading for the Lakes Basin.

Halfway up Minaret Road a flagman directed us into a bulldozed parking lot.

It was a warm summer day and doors slammed and neighbors sieved among the cars. It was like countless occasions—concerts, races, barbecues, parades—which invariably began with greetings in the parking lot. We were a silent bunch today, going in the direction we were flagged.

Walter set off at a brisk pace ahead of everyone.

"What's up with you two?" Jimbo asked.

I strapped on my belt bag. "He's giving us some time together." Who knows when we'll hang out next? From here, Jimbo's off again on the summer roller-ski biathlon circuit.

My brother and I walked Minaret, arm's-length apart, like probers crossing an avalanche field. We came to the boxy perimeter of a foundation and Jimbo speculated that we had stumbled upon the Ski Tip. Hard to say. I found myself looking for curlicues of wood, for the kitschy soul of Bill's establishment, but of course that had not survived. Jimbo traipsed into the rubble to poke around.

I waited, resting my hands on the pouch at my waist.

Jimbo turned and the sun caught him full on, and I felt a shock. He'd aged. In my memory his face is still a boy's face—soft curves to the cheeks, the brush of thick blond lashes. In reality, his lips were thinner than I recalled, his forehead faintly lined. He stood fixed, solitary customer of the Tip today. He looked like he didn't have even ghosts for company.

I did, although their company brought me an unbearable ache.

I came over to Jimbo and punched his arm. "Let's go."

He looked down at his arm, as if I had left a mark. The shock of it. His dweeb sister trying for cool. Cool, the state he desperately needed to return to. "Hey," he said. He hooked his arm through mine. "Hey, you sure left the place a mess."

We abandoned the Tip and followed the crowd. Resident Visitors were making too much noise, stirring up too much ash, and the gray bones of the town seemed to shrink from us.

Not ours anyway. The Town of Mammoth Lakes is now home to scientists, engineers, and government agents and it's become a boomtown of trailers and behemoth vehicles. We came to the new town hall—seven motor homes parked in a U around stepped rows of metal picnic tables. A blue plastic canopy tented the area. There was a table with thermoses and platters of sandwiches and fruit, a table stacked with FEMA bulletins, a huge cork board of photographs, and three wheeled carts with video displays.

Jimbo said, "There's the Stobe," and headed for the food table where Stobie was hovering as his mom, Lila Winder, unwrapped a tray of cookies.

Always the female who does the food.

"Cassie!" An arm enveloped me and a tall form bent. Hal Orenstein raised a camera. "For the *Mammoth Times*? I'm putting out an issue." I smiled and he shot. He whispered, "The biggies are here today," and nodded at a plump woman shouldering a minicam with the CNN logo.

Good, I thought. I unzipped the belt bag. Very good.

I passed into the throng, which under the blue canopy took on an underwater feel. The displaced citizenry seemed not sure what to do, where to look—at the videotapes of faintly familiar steaming landmarks, at the densely captioned photo montage of their volcano's evolution, or at the real-time mess it had made. Many simply made for the food table. The place had an unreal air, a mix of science fair and refugee camp.

I wormed deeper, on the hunt.

Phil Dobie found me and we huddled. He wore his USGS jacket with the *Volcanic Event Response Team* logo. Very visible, very smart. He leaned in and his beard tickled my ear as he whispered, "You ready?"

"I need Walter."

"Why?"

"We're a team."

Phil and I jostled on until we bumped into Walter, who had

been hunting through the throng for me. I said, "Now?" and Walter nodded so I took the package from my pouch and passed it to Walter to give to Phil. A little team ceremony.

Phil set off.

"Over there," Walter said.

I looked, and caught sight of Len Carow's sharp profile and FEMA jacket, and beyond him the rest of the biggies—Council members and agency reps and reporters—and there of course was Adrian Krom.

Impossibly, Krom is smiling. He's bald, that glossy brown animal pelt gone, but it gives him a drop-dead cool air like some massive shaved-head athlete. The skin of his face is marred, and he's in shirtsleeves and the scar on his arm magnifies the effect, as if he's undergone ritual scarification for admission to some secret tribe. He moves haltingly, his right leg apparently braced beneath his slacks, but you get the impression he could cover the distance in a lunge should the need arise.

He smiles as if he's untouchable. He's been untouchable since the chopper evacuated him to the hospital, untouchable through the months of rehab. In a *Huffington Post* piece titled Road Back From Hell, he swears the real heroes were Eric and Mike, but the gist of the article is that he got caught in the eruption because he'd stayed behind to be sure everyone was safely evacuated. And he did indeed succeed. The only ones to die were those who came in after the evac: some crazy sightseers who'd come by dog sled, three Japanese volcanologists and their chopper pilot—and the two volunteers, the heroes. Walter and I get a mention, as well: I nursed Krom like an angel; Walter stood fast. The upbeat ending: Krom survived, and now he's ready to return to duty, to challenge another volcano and save the day anew.

He did not notice me or Walter in the milling crowd.

Phil's voice suddenly carried over the noise, "...and if you would direct your attention over here, we have some footage that..." and I didn't catch the rest, undoubtedly lost in Phil's beard, but it was all right because the crowd began to shift toward the video displays.

Walter and I buffeted our way through to the show.

There were two displays, and on each screen a different disaster movie. Here was a Mammoth Mountain montage—from treeless slopes to bald summit. Here was the fissure on Red Mountain, belching up steam.

People did a double-take.

It took them a moment to realize that while the Mammoth Mountain video was post-eruption, the Red Mountain fissure footage was pre-eruption.

Compared to the aerial views and tracking shots on the other screens, this fissure video was dull stuff. Single fixed camera angle. The only thing that changed was the buildup of snow—and, at the top of the screen, the date. And, for those science wonks in the crowd, the data crawl at the bottom showed daily fluctuations in mag field, strain rate, gas emission. Phil had started the video a couple of minutes ago, so we'd come in partway through.

"I don't get it," Lila Winder said.

Walter said to Lila, and to everyone within earshot—which was a good number of Resident Visitors and biggies—"Ask Adrian. It's his video."

Andy DeMartini bellowed, "*Yo, Mr. Krom.*"

I watched the display start again at the beginning, January ninth, and run to its end, February thirteenth. From the day after the Inn meeting to the day I found Gold Dust.

The day after the Inn meeting, Krom had taken me and Len Carow down to Hot Creek to see the activity, and Krom had showed off his specially-designed monitor. And then I'd left in a huff, and Len Carow had left to join Lindsay, and Krom had taken a ski up to

Gold Dust to install the device so that it could monitor the fissure. And there it remained until Mike followed me to Gold Dust. He saw I'd found the place, he retreated to the parking lot, and after our confrontation, after I'd gone home, he'd skied back up to Gold Dust to retrieve the monitor. And then Krom stored it in his office. And then Lindsay came and took it. And then Walter found it in her safe. And then, at last, it came into my possession. After we were rescued, I'd opened Walter's pack and learned what all the fuss was about.

I'd become something of a video junkie in the time after that, and this was one I watched again and again. Admiring the cleverness of the little microprocessor-controlled videocam he'd built into his monitor. Admiring the quality of the picture. It's like you're there. You can almost smell the sulfur. I could admire his solution to his timing problem. How easy. The monitor was his personal record of the fissure's progression. It told him he had time—time to champion his evac route, time for me to find the fissure. He didn't have to ski up there every day, he had the scene *telemetered* to his computer. How fucking easy.

I expect Krom admired it, as well, enough anyway to keep the data and video and not erase it. He couldn't frame it and hang it on his wall of merit, but I expect he had liked to replay it now and then. Lift a margarita, make a toast. His triumph over Lindsay. Private celebration. Certainly, he never expected her to break in and steal it. Certainly, he never expected Walter to find it in her safe. Certainly, he never intended it to go public.

And here he came, disbelief on his scarred face.

For just a tick, I felt fear—fear that he would find a way to survive this—but Lila caught him. She got right into his face, and she's big enough to do it, and she said, "You *knew*." She'd evidently gotten it now, she'd seen on the video how Krom had been able to foretell the future on Red Mountain. "You knew," she said, "you shabby excuse for a man."

Len Carow, still glued to the tube, grew a thin smile.

And now curious members of the town Council were crowding in.

Something new showed on Krom's face, the thick look of a cornered animal, and then the CNN minicam nosed out of the crowd and Krom panicked. He lumbered to the video cart and killed the picture. The fissure expired. The minicam swung for a head shot of Krom. He put up a hand, blocking the lens. Carow whistled and hooked a finger and the plump reporter altered course. Attention shifted Carow's way, leaving Krom for the moment free.

I moved in, close enough to smell his sweat. I said, "Are you scared?"

He had hold of the brushed-steel handle of the video cart. He made no answer, did not acknowledge he'd even heard, as though the blood was pounding so hard in his ears he'd gone deaf to all but his racing heart.

I waited with my own heart pounding, greedy for something more.

Walter was beside me. "Shall we?"

I waited until Krom finally swung his head my way, until his depthless brown eyes hooked on mine, and I tried to read in there his future—where he's pilloried for Mammoth—and then I turned and broke free of him and walked with Walter out from beneath the blue canopy into the open.

"Are you satisfied?" Walter asked, and I didn't know how to answer. The rush had passed, as adrenaline will, leaving me hollowed. I asked, "Are you?" He took so long to answer that we'd started walking, and when he finally said "It's a rough sort of justice," I didn't press any further. I wasn't sure how to quantify rough justice. On the one hand, Adrian Krom had committed murder and he was free. On the other hand, he wouldn't be playing hero in anybody else's town, playing challenge with anybody else's volcano. Was that enough?

Walter and I headed up Minaret, boots crunching paved pumice.

Minaret Road had grown noisy: chatter, shouts, somebody crying, the crash of rubble thrown on top of rubble. People stood out in bold relief, dwarfing the remains of buildings. Even in the distance, mile after unobstructed mile, tall figures could be seen tramping over the corrugated landscape.

We came upon what we judged to be the lab. We went inside and settled onto low seats of pitted concrete. I rubbed the ridged scar on my right hand, then pressed my hands between my knees. Maybe it's a female thing, trying to hide scars.

"Well." Walter braced his hands on his thighs. "What are you going to do?"

"Maybe go see if I can find the house." I suddenly wanted to go see it all—the house, Walter's place, Lindsay's. Eric's. I didn't want to leave a stone unturned. I wanted to see everything, burn it into my memory.

"What are you going to do for a *living*?" Walter said.

"Oh."

"You must give it some thought."

I had, actually. "Maybe go into geotech reconnaissance." Soil stability studies, make sure houses are built on solid ground.

Walter snorted.

Nobody gets killed. "What about you?"

"I'm too old to begin anything else."

I thought, he doesn't look too old. I've been treating him like old porcelain, but he looks crisp in his tan field jacket with the epaulettes and flap pockets. He looks jaunty with *his* scar, as though he's fought a duel and won. He looks as though he's finished aging, having reached an accommodation with the elements, his face settled into its high-relief topography.

He said, "I've been thinking about the name."

"What name?"

"Of our *business*. Sierra Geoforensics. I think we might personalize it."

Before he spoke again I understood what was coming.

"Shaws and Oldfield, Geoforensics." He looked at me. "I am proposing a full partnership."

"You're serious?"

"I do think my name should come first."

"I'm *serious*, Walter."

"So am I." His eyes, on me, were sharp again, astringent blue.

"You wanted more than you got, just like I did."

"Very well then, what do you expect? Batting rate of fifty-fifty? I say we can do better. Or you can go crawl around building sites and expect zero percent and achieve what you expect."

I flinched. "Do we need to do this now?"

"We need to do this here."

I got up, and paced the lab. Not much had survived. Concrete survived, blasted and tossed here and there. Steel survived, I-beams in tangles like ropes. The storefront window survived, shattered and melted and blackened. The lab was gone but its footprint remained. I felt the sudden sharp pain of loss. I knew it would last a very long time. A lifetime. And I knew, at last, there was but one way to bear it. Try again.

I turned to Walter. "I think we should stick with Sierra Geoforensics. After all, it is an established brand."

EPILOGUE

SIERRA GEOFORENSICS
TOWN OF BISHOP
INYO COUNTY, CALIFORNIA

WE'RE BUSIER than water on rock, and after work today I'll fill a thermos with coffee and catch the shuttle to L.A. to catch a red-eye to Taiwan to examine soil particles caught in a batch of black-market microchips. It promises to be an interesting case—one that will not raise my blood pressure.

Statistically, though, somewhere down the line a case is bound to come along that will grab me, again, in the heart. That's the one my ghosts will be watching.

That's the one I both dream of and dread.

THE END

I hope you'll join Cassie and Walter on their next adventure. For a preview, please turn the page.

PREVIEW OF BOOK 4: SKELETON SEA

CHAPTER 1:

When the detective phoned to enlist our services he characterized the case as a mystery at sea.

Thirty-eight hours later we got our first look at the ghost boat.

It had been found adrift and deserted. It looked ghostly enough right now, docked in the fog at the end of the pier.

Fog eclipsed the horizon. Best I could tell, the pier jutted into a channel near the mouth of a harbor. I strained to see farther but I could not find the ocean beyond. Best I could do was taste its salt and smell its kelp and hear its waves.

Walter and I stepped onto the ramp that led down to the pier where a man in a Morro Bay Police Department parka awaited us. He was tall and lean with graphite-gray hair worn in a spiky pompadour. He looked to be in his forties or fifties—younger than Walter's sixties-ish, as Walter liked to phrase it, older than my straight-up thirty—in any case, experienced.

The detective greeted us first. "I'm Doug Tolliver, and if I'm not mistaken you'll be Cassie Oldfield and Walter Shaws of Sierra Geoforensics."

I smiled. "You're not mistaken."

Walter said, "We're pleased to meet you."

"*I'm* pleased you two agreed to come on such short notice."

"You were in luck," Walter said, "we just wrapped up a case."

"Let's hope that luck holds." Tolliver gave us a probing look. "Because this one's damn strange."

Walter's eyebrows lifted and then he smiled, face seaming like a layered seabed.

I shivered.

Wished I'd worn a warm scarf.

Or perhaps it was a shiver of anticipation. I had to admit that the detective had hooked me, too. I felt curiosity kindling, the imperative to find out what happened to that boat, out there at sea.

Tolliver directed us down the pier. "Welcome to my patch of ocean."

Early this morning we'd left our home base in the California mountain town of Bishop, embarking on the four-hundred-mile drive to the California central coast town of Morro Bay. Bananas and donuts and thermos of coffee on the road for breakfast, In-N-Out burgers for lunch, vowing to eat vegetarian for dinner. We took turns driving and reading aloud—Walter, *The Rime of the Ancient Mariner*; me, *Boats for Dummies*. We arrived here at the edge of the sea in the early afternoon.

Tired, buzzed on caffeine, happy to stretch our legs, ready to collect the evidence.

As we moved down the pier the fog shifted and the boat gained definition. It was about twenty-five feet long, stacked with a wheelhouse and a mast and antennae and wires and lines that I had not yet learned about. The wheelhouse was at the front and on the open deck behind there was a big drum wrapped in netting.

The name painted on the white hull in red block letters was *Outcast*.

We halted beside the boat.

Tolliver asked, "You want the whole nine yards before we talk evidence?"

Walter nodded. "On the phone, you said the fisherman disappeared."

"Uh-huh." Tolliver folded his arms. "Here's everything we know. It's not a helluva lot. The *Outcast* turns up adrift, yesterday morning, not far outside the harbor. Nobody aboard. Had her running lights on, for night fishing. She belongs to an anchovy fisherman named Robbie Donie. No sign of Donie, or his body —the Coast Guard did a tide-currents-wind grid check. We assume he went out fishing the night before, Saturday—it's usually a nighttime job. Nobody saw him leave the harbor on that trip. Donie runs a small-scale operation. The fellow who crews for him is visiting family back in Pennsylvania, and he has an alibi. Nobody home at Donie's place. He lives alone, divorced. There's an aunt in Bakersfield who never sees him and doesn't much care. Not many friends. Nobody reported him missing. Hell, just see what he named his boat. *Outcast*."

"Are you thinking homicide?" Walter asked.

"I'm looking into it—the logbook's missing and the GPS is broken. That raises the question. But if we go the homicide route, we need a better motive than somebody thought Donie was disagreeable. I thought so myself."

"Any prints?"

"Donie's of course, and half a dozen unidentified sets. One set will be from Jim Horowitz, he's the crew. We also collected hairs and fibers. Old stuff, new stuff, we'll have to see." Tolliver glanced toward the sea. "Other side of the coin is, could be an accident. Fishing is a damn dangerous operation. And if that's what it was, that's sorrowful enough, but it happens."

"Cassie and I will shed some light."

Tolliver slowly nodded.

I said, "Endeavor to."

"Endeavor. Please. I've got three things I want you to shed light on. First is this damage on the stern rub rail."

The boat was angled so that the *Outcast*'s stern butted up to the pier. I'd read the relevant section in *Boats for Dummies* so I immediately ID'd the rub rail here: a vinyl strip protected the seam where the hull met the deck. There was room for only one of us so I took my hand lens from the field kit and moved in. A long scrape marred the rub rail and it was encrusted with tiny mineral grains. I put my lens to a large-ish grain. It came into twenty-power magnification. Size, somewhere around seventy microns. Shape, angular. Color, reddish. I used tweezers to pluck out the grain. Walter passed me a specimen dish.

Tolliver hovered. "What do you think?"

I said, "An oxide of iron." I passed the dish to Walter and he grunted in agreement.

Tolliver said, "I thought maybe the boat collided with something, maybe a rusting buoy. Or it got scraped by some kind of debris, tossed up there by turbulence. But it sure doesn't look like an impact gouge."

"Is the seafloor around here heavy in iron?"

"Despite claims to the contrary from boaters who've run aground, the seafloor doesn't just jump up and hit a boat."

I smiled. "I was thinking more along the lines of a...sand bar or something."

Walter said, "You did mention sand evidence, Detective."

"Make it Doug. Yeah, I did. There was sand in a duffel pack lying on the deck near the drum roller. The drawstring top was wide open. Looked like somebody ransacked the thing. Found what he was after, or it wasn't there to begin with. All we found was a bit of sand." Tolliver took a zippered baggie from his pocket and held it up.

We peered. Not much sand in there. A pinch.

Enough.

I said, "And the third thing?"

"Over here." Tolliver led us to a plastic bin, and opened it.

Smelled like brine. Smelled like the sea.

Inside was a rubbery stalk of brownish kelp with leafy fronds and fat bulbs, attached to a tangled root ball.

"We found that entangled in the anchor chain," Tolliver said. "It's giant kelp, grows in coastal waters. I'm looking at the idea that Donie anchored in a kelp bed night before last. And then pulled up anchor. And then went overboard. And then the boat went adrift."

Walter said, "Mightn't he have caught that kelp on a previous trip?"

"Not likely. No experienced fisherman is gonna leave kelp tangled in his anchor chain."

I said, "And our evidence?"

"In there." Tolliver indicated the thick tangle of reddish roots at the base of the stalk. "That's the holdfast—a chunk of it, anyway. It anchors the kelp on rocky surfaces. All kinds of critters live in holdfasts—anemones, sponges, crabs, what have you—but you'll be interested in the pebble caught inside. The holdfast has been to the lab and the techs got what they wanted. Thought you'd want to extract the pebble yourselves."

We both nodded. Grateful for a cop who recognized rocks as

evidence, who treated them with the same respect given to fingerprints or cigarette butts or bloodstains or what have you.

"I'll have you sign off on the chain of evidence and you can take this stuff with you. Oh, and, we'll be moving the *Outcast* to our storage dock so if you need another look, let me know." Tolliver ran a hand through his hair, spiking it even more. "I'm real eager to know what happened to her out there."

I peered through the fog, which had thinned enough to reveal the general lay of the land. Of the water. Tolliver's pier stuck out into a narrow channel, which extended southward into the mist. The pier was at the northern end of the channel, which bent westward and opened up into a harbor. At the harbor's mouth was a mammoth rock, a fog-hung ghost whose shape and height I could not clearly discern. Big. I looked past the ghost rock, out to open sea, just visible now as a gray rolling field beyond the mouth of the harbor. The sea was an inhospitable-looking place. Had been inhospitable, certainly, to the *Outcast*.

I turned back to Tolliver. "Are you sure Donie was aboard? Could the tie line have come undone and the boat went adrift? Or someone cut the line?"

"Let me show you something that says the *Outcast* didn't just goddamn wander off."

He moved to the ladder that was braced on the pier, rising to the railing at the stern. He looked back at us. "Come on, it's aboard."

We joined him.

He started up the ladder, adding, "Here's where it gets even stranger."

At first, as I stepped over the railing, I thought *blood has been spilled*. And then I saw I was wrong. There were stains sprayed across the deck in thick teardrops like projectile blood spatters. But blood dries brown. These stains were blue-black.

"Feel free," Tolliver said. "My techs have already sampled."

Walter approached the nearest stain. Squatted. Took out his hand lens.

Tolliver said, "You need a magnifying glass to tell you that's ink?"

Walter stood. "I'm not a mariner—much as I might have wished it. I see black viscous stains on a boat and the first thing I think is engine oil."

"Ink from *what*?" I asked. "Octopus? All this?"

"Squid," Tolliver said.

"You said Donie fished for anchovies."

"That's right. But he was also doing a little moonlighting, taking sport fishers out. My town's got two businesses—a working fishing port, and tourists. We get a lot of sport fishers, real hotshots. About a month ago, we got an invasion of squid."

"Invasion?"

"I'm not talking market squid, the kind on your plate. I'm talking jumbo." Tolliver lifted his right arm above his head, as if holding up a trophy catch. "Man-size."

I thought, holy shit.

"Invasion from where?" Walter asked.

"From southern waters, coming up from the Humboldt Current. They're called Humboldt squid."

"Why are they coming?"

"Hunting—the fish they eat are moving north, something to do with warmer sea waters moving north." Tolliver shrugged. "Supposedly."

I looked again at the deck, at the length and breadth of the spray, the sheer quantity of black teardrops. "You think..."

"I think hunting Humboldts is a whole new ballgame."

Tolliver pointed out a big smear of ink near the stern rail. There was a heel print in the ink. "Rubber boot. Slippery deck."

"I see why you think he went overboard."

"It happens."

"And the sport fisher?"

"We're checking missing persons reports. Still, if Donie *was* out squid jigging by himself... Risky business."

Walter cast a glance at the thick net wrapped around the drum roller.

"That's how you take anchovies," Tolliver said. "Here's how you take Humboldts."

Tolliver led us to an open fiberglass gear locker. We looked inside. Reels of heavy-duty fishing line. Foot-long tubes that looked like glowsticks, ringed by multi-spiked hooks.

"Humboldts hunt in packs, like a damn gang. They often come up at night—and light attracts them. Attach that jig to your line, bait the hooks, put the jig in the water. If they're around, they hit it."

Walter gestured to the ink. "And get caught."

"There were no squid in the hold," Tolliver said. "So I assume the one that got caught was used as chum. Humboldts are cannibalistic."

I said, "It sounds a little dangerous."

"Like starting a bar-room brawl."

— end preview of Skeleton Sea —

FROM THE AUTHOR

Thank you for reading—I hope you enjoyed the story. You might also like other books in the series, all standalone novels that can be read in any order. See a complete list with descriptions on my **website:** tonidwiggins.com

NEW RELEASES

If you would like to be notified of new releases, you can sign up for my mailing list: https://eepurl.com/GtdZn

JOIN ME ON FACEBOOK

facebook.com/ToniDwigginsBooks

LEAVE A REVIEW

Reader word-of-mouth is pivotal to the life of a book. If you enjoyed reading this story, please consider leaving a review. It would be much appreciated.

ACKNOWLEDGMENTS

"Writing is easy. All you have to do is cross out the wrong words."
— Mark Twain

I had some help identifying the wrong words.

I want to thank the following experts in their fields for information, reading the book, and giving me terrific suggestions: Roy Bailey, David Hill, G. Nelson Eby, Raymond C. Murray, John Thornton.

If there are factual or technical errors in Volcano Watch, they are mine alone.

To Chuck Williams, for support, patience, and wisdom—thank you. Seven houses full.

No book is complete without a cover.

I'm fortunate to work with a talented cover designer—Shayne Rutherford at Wicked Good Book Covers. She has created extraordinarily wicked good covers for my books.

Many thanks, Shayne. I look forward to working with you on the cover for the next book in the series.